Restoration and Ruin

LEGENDS OF CORALIA

Restoration and Ruin

KATE JENKINS & MORGAN MOREAU

4 Horsemen
Publications, Inc.

Published By: 4 Horsemen Publications, Inc.

4 Horsemen Publications, Inc.
PO Box 417
Sylva, NC 28779
4horsemenpublications.com
info@4horsemenpublications.com

Cover & Typesetting by Autumn Skye
Edited by Jen Paquette

Library of Congress Control Number: 2025939703

Paperback ISBN-13: 979-8-8232-0928-1
Hardcover ISBN-13: 979-8-8232-0929-8
Audiobook ISBN-13: 979-8-8232-0931-1
Ebook ISBN-13: 979-8-8232-0930-4

Dedication

For David, who brings me chocolate without being
asked when I'm having a bad day.
For my Co-author Morgan, who puts up
with so, so much from me.
For Kala and Nom for just being such huge
supports as we write this series.

~~ Kate

For Gavin, Avery, David, and Finley.
Katie, how do we keep thinking we can
condense plans into one book?
Thank you to Emily and Alane, who didn't
leave me at the Mexican restaurant.
For Grey and Tracy, who have spent a lot of time listening
to my persistent complaints about rheumatoid arthritis.
To the cast of "Interview with a Vampire"…
'cause how come you're so good? Still looking
at you, "Our Flag Means Death" cast.

~~ Morgan

Table of Contents

Cast of Characters

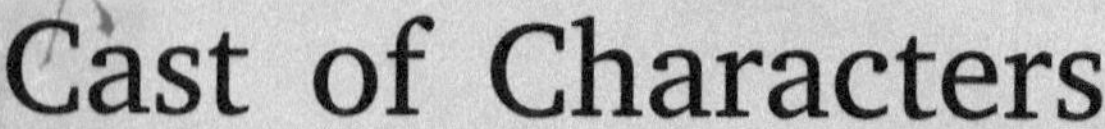

Agnes Aballe: Human. Queen's Maid.

Alba: Elf. Palace Servant.

Aphros: Nereid. King of the Nereid people.

Rhoslyn Almeida: Human. Sister of the Earl Veitel.

Wrenn Almeida: Human. Earl Veitel.

Aurae: Nereid. High Priestess.

Borin: Human. Guard.

Cadan: Riken's Army Commander

Carac: Human. Guard.

Ceto: A Nereid advisor to Aphros.

Garibald Crobán: Lord.

Tolan Dethenal: Half-human, Half-Elf. Palace cook and for-pay arena fighter.

Jayden Drake: Nereid. Duke and Ambassador.

Alaoin Bialaor Eiero: Human. High King of Fythias.

Xavier Eisenhart: Human. Head of Riken's Guard.

Lady Cecelia Elrick: Human. Wife of Lord Elrick.

Lord Elrick: Human. New Captain of the Guard, Minor Lord.

Farner: Young soldier in Riken's army.

Faron: Elf. Member of the Fythias Court.

Thomas Fletcher: Human with magic. Arrow maker and political activist.

Collette Venora Josselyn Gaillane: Human with magic. Queen of Coralia.

Gaillard: Human. Works for Ian.

Gisela: Elf. Palace Servant.

Gwane: Human. Child worker in Wildrun.

Cremisius "Crem" Hawke: Human. Commander of the Queen's Guard.

Diana Hawke: Human. Palace cook.

Heilo: Nereid. Steward to King Aphros.

Mallan Hialti: Regent of the Azmarin Empire.

Howle: A veteran of the King's Guard.

Ian: Human. Tavern owner in Galel.

Barris Ilthane: Human. Baron of Pontus Bay.

Indir: Elf. Survivor of the Urhadell massacre.

Jarin: Human. Guard.

Kenrick: A young guard.

Alexander "Pops" Leassitor: Shifter. Retired Mercenary.

Larent Leassitor: Shifter. Mercenary.

Nora Leassitor: Shifter. Retired Mercenary.

Lynessea: Nereid. Wife of Lord Barris.

Morrley: Human. Works for Ian.

Nieven: Elf. Survivor of the Urhadell massacre.

Nawalya: Elf. Mercenary.

Rowan: Human. Guard.

Rulf: Human. Guard.

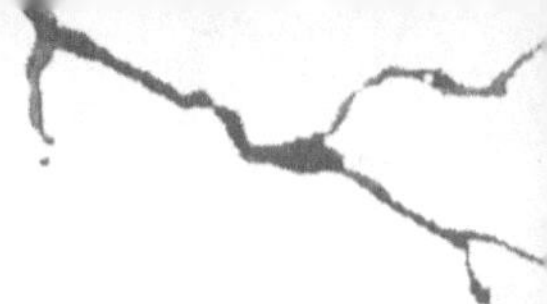

Sadon: Human. Guard.

Sara Whyldon: Human with magic.

Sargarus: Human. Former King of Coralia.

Riken Saullet: Human. Baron of Wildrun.

Arian Tal'Dela: Elf. Mercenary.

Brath Thancred: King of Azmarin.

Rion Thorax: Human. Furrier.

Amélie Vassetre: Half-Elf: Daughter of Sabine and Faron.

Elyna Vassetre: Half-Elf: Daughter of Sabine and Faron.

Éric Vassetre: Half-Elf. Secretary to Alaoin. Son of Sabine and Faron.

Sabine Vassetre: Human: High Minister of the Fythias court.

Zephraim Villot: Human. Earl of Norbrick. Brother to the Queen.

John Whyldon: Human. Captain of the Queen's Guard.

Azmarin Empire
Quenall
Barcomb M
Myrefall
Coralia

Other Locations

Catillatio: The Capitol of the Azmarin Empire
Gulf of Galel: Gulf bordering Galel and the Azmarin Empire
Sherrose Caverns: A cave system in Quenall

L'orilan

Fyithas

Galel

Pontus Bay

Nereid Kingdom

Veitel

A'lierdeen

Wildrun

Farner

Branlin

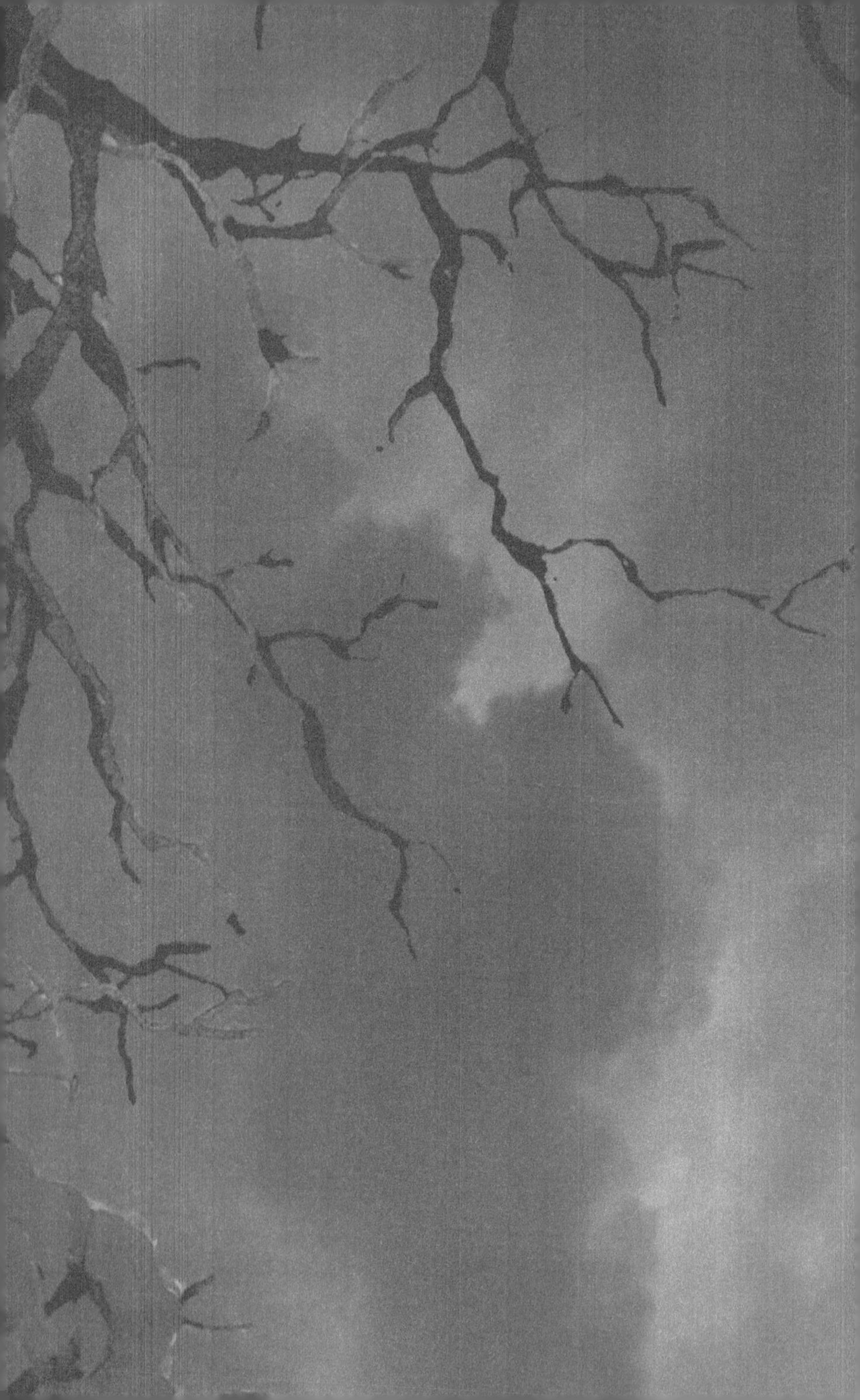

Chapter One

To Nora and Alexander,

I wish I could say I was writing to you with anything other than the worst news I can image, but I cannot. We won the battle against Coralia, but Larent was lost. He was taken from us by an arrow coated in Veinfire. None of us are taking it well, especially Collette, who we have come to find out wed Larent just hours prior to the battle. We will be sailing to Pontus Bay within the next several days. Collette has a plan I am not comfortable putting into writing yet. I am so sorry to have to deliver this news to you, and I hope to possibly have better news in the future.

Love,
Nawalya

"I'm going to Quenall," Collette announced, her position near Larent's body unchanging over the last hour. She couldn't move from that spot even if she'd wanted to, and Collette couldn't conceive of ever wanting to move any farther from Larent, unreachable though he was. Moving meant acknowledging and accepting that he was gone. Larent's body lay on a cot, hands resting by his sides, eyes closed, russet hair smoothed back from his face. Someone had washed the dirt and blood of battle from his face and neck. With Aphros's stasis spell, his body remained as warm and limber as if he were still alive and simply sleeping.

All of the members of her travel party, the friends and allies they'd gained from the Nereids and the Fythians, had joined her to sit vigil in the tent. A muted alarm rose, though Collette paid little attention to the words. Instead, her fingers carefully focused on plaiting the ribbons of Larent's bracelet around the gold bangle belonging to her mother. She had no idea where her own now lay, but she would not lose his.

She didn't look up as careful steps approached her or pull away from the rough hand now on her shoulder. A smaller hand than she expected, but calloused and firm. Surprisingly, when the person spoke, Thomas's voice was closest to her.

"I know losing Larent is hard," he said gently.

Collette knew he wanted her to speak, and a couple of times, she opened her mouth to try, only to close it again. Her eyes stung far too much, so she focused on her ribbon braiding, pausing occasionally to brush away the silent tears falling down her face.

Thomas took her silence as an invitation to continue. "I know you've already suffered your fair share of broken hearts these past months. It's appalling how much you've suffered, how much you keep bottled up."

"I'm going to Quenall, so it doesn't matter," she replied, knowing her voice didn't sound like her own.

"You're not going to Quenall, Joss," Rion said, rubbing at his gingery beard. He sat in a far corner of the tent, legs stretched out in front of him. He'd shed his armor, though the pile of metal remained within reach. "They'd kill you before you set foot in the city."

Collette looked over at her former lover, her expression void of humor or sarcasm. "Either I am your queen, in which case I shall do what I want, or I am not your queen, and you cannot stop me anyway. I am going to Quenall, and I do not need permission."

Whyldon stood, his blue eyes concerned, and he approached Collette as though to reason with her. "Why Quenall?" he asked. "To go after Riken? There are better plans to draw him out."

"I don't give two shits about Riken," Collette replied. "Not right now, anyway."

"Then you don't need to go to Quenall," Rion argued.

"I'm going to Quenall so I can bring him back," she said simply. Silence followed her explanation. She knew the others in the tent probably thought she'd finally lost her mind, but she didn't care.

Thomas gave her a look: sympathy, cynicism, and pity rolled into one. "No one can bring a person back from the dead. Not truly."

"I can," she replied.

"How?" Thomas asked. He rubbed the back of his head, blond hair briefly poking out in strange directions before settling.

"Sargarus was in possession of a spell, one that could be used for just this purpose," she replied as her fingers continued working. "I found it after he died. It would be difficult and very dangerous, but I think it would work."

"Collette, I've never heard of such a spell, and I grew up around women who were very well educated in all kinds of healing magic." Thomas looked over to Arian, seated near Larent's feet, looking quiet and withdrawn, pale beneath blood and soot, his eyes still red. "Have you?"

"Bringing Larent back would not fall under the category of healing magic. She wants to use death magic. Necromancy." Arian drew in a shallow breath, and he looked up at Collette. "I'll come with you."

"Arian—" Thomas began, but Aphros, who had taken vigil with them in the opposite corner Rion had occupied, cut him off.

"Necromancy and what she proposes to be a real spell are not the same. Not really." He looked to Collette, the Nereid king's golden cat-like eyes filled with deep pity. "I assume you believe the spell would bring him back fully, reunifying spirit, mind, and body?"

"I do," Collette replied, though she focused on Arian, the only person in the tent who had given her any support since her announcement.

Arian rolled his eyes at Aphros's correction, but he nodded slowly to Collette. He was with her, no matter what.

"Let's say you do go," Rion said, up and pacing now. "What is a trip to Quenall for a theoretical spell going to cost you? We won't address the sheer amount of danger a trip to Quenall alone would be. Heavy, dark magic like a resurrection spell always takes from the caster. I know you're aware."

Collette shrugged and finished braiding the ribbons onto her bracelet. Having finished it, she put the whole thing back on her wrist.

"That's not an answer, Joss," Rion said accusingly, "and your refusal to speak up tells me you know it will go badly. You can't be so reckless. You don't have the right."

Arian stood and brushed himself off, his shoulders straightening as he moved to Collette's side. "Your queen has told you what she plans to do. I do not understand why you are questioning her when her mind has been made up. She is going to Quenall. Either show your support and volunteer to come with us, or shut up."

Rion opened his mouth to argue, and though Whyldon did not hold him back, he did step between Arian and the much taller man. "We are not fighting amongst ourselves. Not today, not when we have just lost one of our own," Whyldon lectured.

"She's not in her right mind," Rion objected. "She's going to get herself killed. Are we supposed to sit by while she gets herself killed?"

Arian raised an eyebrow. "Who is fighting? I was stating the facts. If Rion is unhappy with the decision, it is not our issue."

Collette knew immediately that Arian was lying, and a small part of her wondered when she'd learned to read him so well. But she knew for certain, just by the set of his shoulders and the press of his lips, that had Whyldon not stepped in between them, Arian would have pulled one of his daggers on Rion just for daring to speak to her in such a way. Had she been more present, had the grief not consumed her fully, she would have been touched by this. Instead, she just felt numb.

"If Collette is intent on going to Quenall, perhaps we are better served in forming plans," Thomas suggested. He moved to stand closer to Arian, perhaps knowing his presence annoyed Collette. "Plans to continue providing aid here and getting Collette safely into Quenall."

"Not just Quenall," Collette replied. "Gadleigh Palace."

Nawalya sighed, mouth pinched in total disagreement. Like Arian, she'd positioned herself close to Larent's body, and Collette assumed she'd gone through many of the efforts to clean him up while Collette had been too out of it to do anything. "Most of us know the layout of the castle, but I have no idea how we'll get Collette close enough to get inside."

"Crem might have ideas," Whyldon said. "We could talk to him once we're there. Get a solid plan in place."

"Are you coming along, then?" Collette asked. She took a breath and rubbed at her tired eyes.

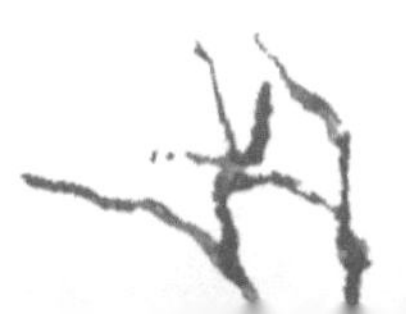

"I follow you, Collette. If you want to return to Quenall, then I will do everything in my power to help keep you safe and ensure you are successful," Whyldon promised.

Collette gave him the weakest of smiles and nodded. "Thank you."

Aphros cleared his throat. "I'd be happy to follow as well, and I would bring my army with me. We could stay ready outside of Quenall while you work, and I am certain you could count on Lynessea, Ceto, and Jayden to follow you into the city for the more covert part of your plan."

He stood and approached Collette. "I know now is not the time to plan an invasion, but when you are ready, we can discuss the details. I am certain Alaoin would follow."

"Then let us agree to take our fight to Coralia," Collette replied. "We can discuss more in the following days. Make plans for driving Rhoslyn's forces back to Coralia and organize who is going. For now, though, I am going to sit with my husband."

"Of course," Aphros replied. He stood from his chair, a simple wooden construction appropriate for their proximity to the battlefield. "Let me, or one from my court, know if you need anything." He nodded and left the tent.

Collette's attention returned to Larent, and she put her hand on top of his, wishing he was still there with her.

Chapter Two

After Collette's announcement and the ensuing chaotic argument, Tolan had decided he needed some time to get his own conflicting emotions sorted out. Being around Collette, Rion, and a deceased Larent would not help. And he wanted to help. He wanted to be able to soothe away all of Collette's pain, to assure her things would get better, even if he doubted she would ever really be okay again.

He left the tent, heading out onto the battlefield to see what he could help with. Earlier, they'd spent time combing the grounds, looking for those still living. He thought the task fruitless, but it gave him purpose. They hadn't paid much attention to the colors the dying wore. Nereid healers would attend to any who still lived, though the ones who fought against Collette would be detained and questioned. Years of experience told him that many of the Coralian soldiers would be there without choice. How those were treated would, and should, differ from the Azmarin soldiers and willing Coralians.

Throughout his search—a period he couldn't begin to account for—Tolan found two additional people, one from Fythias and another from Coralia, but it had been completely by chance when he had almost tripped over them. He certainly wasn't paying nearly as much attention as he should be.

As much as Tolan hated it, he couldn't shake the fog of Larent's death or the rippling effects throughout their immediate group. No matter the strained relationship between himself and Larent, they shared a history. Of fucking and fighting. Of protecting someone they loved. Of pushing her back toward a throne Tolan knew she didn't want.

How would Collette ever take her rightful place now? To say Collette was in bad shape was an understatement, so much so he'd been tempted to suggest a consistent watch be placed on her in case she decided to join Larent in death. Even with her declaration of going to Quenall, he was still worried. If she was determined enough to keep going in pursuit of reviving Larent, would she put this insane request ahead of her own health and well-being? Of regaining her throne? Tolan thought he knew the answer well.

He wondered if he should talk to Rion about how he'd reacted. Maybe Tolan was just being too sensitive, but he felt Rion's response to Collette was dismissive of her pain. Telling Collette she couldn't do something was not the right answer. All it would do was make her dig her heels in more. Rion, who had loved and had been with Collette, should have known that. No, right now Collette needed sympathy, understanding, and maybe a calm voice to talk her off her path, though Tolan had a gut feeling that the last part was going to be impossible.

Given the unlikely scenario in which she accepted Larent's death and carried on, Tolan knew he would need to step up and help where he could. She would need support, and though Arian clearly understood her pain, he alone could not give it. If needed, Tolan would serve as a buffer between Collette and Rion. He would make sure she knew her decisions were valid

and respected. He would follow her to Quenall, knowing the danger that existed there.

Glancing around the battlefield, Tolan let out a deep breath and turned back to the tent where Larent's body lay. He wanted to check on Collette. Slowly, he trudged back to the tent, only to discover Whyldon, Nawalya, and Jayden standing outside talking quietly.

"Anything I should know?" he asked, an eyebrow raised.

Whyldon looked over at him and shook his head. The shadows beneath his bright blue eyes showed his weariness and worry, all of which remained emphasized by the grime of battle, which none of them had the chance to wash away. "She's where she's been for hours," he shared. "I'm starting to wonder if she ever intends to leave his side."

Tolan knew the answer immediately, though he ran his hand through his near-black hair in frustration. "She won't leave him. Someone is going to have to persuade her. Gently. She needs rest, even if she probably won't sleep. And food, though getting her to eat will also be a challenge."

"One thing at a time," Whyldon said. "I can try to coax her away, though I'm doubting any success."

"I think we could convince Arian to help." Nawalya spoke up. "He seems to be the person she'd be most likely to listen to right now. We just have to impress upon him the need for her to rest." Her arms were wrapped around her body protectively, but otherwise, she maintained a level of control over her grief most of the others hadn't maintained.

"Is he in a right enough mind to listen?" Whyldon asked. "He's nearly as upset as Collette is."

Tolan's gaze met Nawalya's as he waited for her to consider her answer, though he had a feeling he knew what it would be.

"Yes. Despite his current state, Arian likes taking care of people he considers his. It will also be a good distraction for him," Nawalya replied.

"Getting both of them away from his body will help," Jayden added, casting his golden eyes back to the tent. Of the small group, the Nereid appeared the most calm, though Tolan doubted Jayden was any happier than the rest.

Whyldon nodded. "I suppose Nawalya should try to talk to Arian, then. If Arian can't convince Collette to leave, we'll come up with something else."

"I shall be back. With luck, Arian and Collette will follow." Nawalya turned on her heel and went back into the tent.

"She's right about Arian. He will put her needs above his own. I'll have to let Thomas know." Tolan glanced around. Not seeing the fletcher, he assumed Thomas was still inside the tent.

"Thomas remained with Arian," Whyldon explained. "I think he is aware of the major struggles facing them."

Tolan nodded. It made sense for Thomas to have stayed with Arian considering the elf's reaction to Larent's death. "Okay, what are our next steps after we get Collette to rest? Planning on how to get her in and out of Quenall safely, or just securing transport at the moment?"

"We have to give Coralia time to retreat," Whyldon said, his tone becoming more businesslike. It was something they could speak about factually. Something they could control. "We don't want to look like we are making chase. Once they are gone, we will need to make plans for traveling to Coralia again and how we want things to go. Alaoin and Aphros have pledged to follow, so we have support."

Jayden spoke up. "A few of our people are discreetly following the retreating ships to make sure they don't do something stupid, like turn around and try to approach the island from another direction. None of us assume they will do that," he reassured everyone. "This will allow us to know when we can leave for Coralia."

Tolan's mind blanked for a second at the idea that the retreating army could try again after such a loss, but he could see the strategy behind it. "So, the best thing we can do now is help with the clean-up effort, eat, sleep, and watch over Collette?"

"I fear if you try to watch over her as though she is a child, you will find you do not like the response," Whyldon said with an exhausted sigh. "Collette is still Collette, grieving or not."

Tolan conceded the point with a nod before saying, "I'm concerned about her health and that if she runs into too much resistance to her plan, she may go without help."

"She would, and hovering over her won't help. You should know this."

"I do," Tolan said, his shoulders slumping. He wanted to ask what they should do now, when Nawalya stepped from the tent.

"Arian has agreed and is talking to Collette as we speak. With any luck, they should exit the tent in a moment. He was talking about taking her to her room to lie down." Her words, soft and quick, would hopefully not be overheard by Collette.

"Good," Whyldon said. "She's been in a daze for hours."

"I doubt the shock will wear off anytime soon, but we will all need to be prepared for when it does," Nawalya said, her head snapping to the side as Arian, Thomas, and Collette emerged from the tent.

Arian and Collette didn't acknowledge the group, their heads bowed together as Arian said something to Collette that was too low for Tolan's elvish hearing to pick up. Instead, the two just keep walking back to the main building and hopefully their rooms.

"I'm going to see what I can help with," Tolan said as he motioned to the beach and the dead bodies strewn about. He

wanted to follow Collette and Arian, to check on both of them, but he felt his presence wouldn't be welcome at the moment.

"Didn't you just leave that area?" Whyldon asked him.

"Yes," Tolan admitted. "But if I go back toward the palace, I'm just going to want to check on Collette, and I shouldn't right now." What he wanted, what he wished he could offer her, was no longer his right and hadn't been since he'd left her in Azmarin. "Besides, before I was looking for survivors. Now I'll see if they need help cleaning up the bodies."

Whyldon disagreed with this choice. Tolan could see it in the frown lines bracketing his mouth, but thankfully, the older captain said nothing against his plan. "You've had a long day as well. Find your way to your bed in the next few hours."

"I will," Tolan said before adding, "thank you." He moved to step away, only to have Nawalya join him.

"I'll come with you."

He wanted to tell her no, to go back and rest as he took in the dark circles under her eyes, but he knew better. She wouldn't sleep anyway. Instead, he just nodded, and the two started back down the beach to where people were already handling the bodies.

Chapter Three

The lock clicked, and Collette abandoned the door, wandering aimlessly back into her suite. The emptiness of the space vibrated in her bones even though some part of her waited for Larent to speak, to hear his affectionate use of "Freckles" rather than her given name. She knew it would not come. Larent rested beyond her reach, at peace and without pain. He did not know what had been left behind, completely unaware of the ruin and devastation.

She ended up in the bedroom, the space pristine despite the day's events. Even at war, the palace staff had made the bed, organized the evidence of people occupying the space, and otherwise removed the lasting remnants of the last morning ritual Collette had shared with her husband. His travel bag, mostly emptied since they didn't know when they'd be leaving the island, hung from a peg near the wardrobe. Collette took a step toward it, though she paused as she caught her reflection in the dressing table mirror. She scowled, seeing the dirt and sweat and, along her side, the dark stain of dried blood.

Right. She'd been grazed by a sword.

She began removing her armor, letting metal and leather hit the ground with thumps and clangs she paid no attention to. The process went slowly, more than it normally would have, since every move she made felt distant, numb even. Her arming doublet, stained again with dried blood, fell to the ground without ceremony. She looked down at the scattered items, her brow furrowing when she spotted a small, carved figure, the one of the Lady which Larent had handed her just before the battle.

Collette knelt long enough to pick it up, then stepped away from her shed armor toward the bathroom. It was placed on a counter before she began filling the tub with water so hot she could see the steam rising toward the ceiling. Removing the last of her clothes, she stepped into the water, hissing a little at the temperature as she slowly sank into its depths.

The grime of the battlefield seeped into the water without the effort of scrubbing. Though she would need to empty the tub and refill it, Collette leaned her head back against the rim and closed her eyes, letting the water soothe tired, aching muscles. The silence of the bathroom, coupled with the occasional ripple of water, allowed her to drift in grief and planning without distraction or interruption.

The spell, which she'd hidden in her private office nearly four years ago, should still be safely tucked away behind the loose panel of a bookshelf on the uppermost floor of Gadleigh Palace. An old series of leather-bound books occupied the shelf, books which even the stupidest of people — of which Zephraim and Rhoslyn were included — would not bother with. Collette had no doubt she would find the spell once she was back in the castle.

Getting back into the castle would be the more difficult part. Oh, Collette was relatively certain she could waltz into Quenall without receiving so much as a raised eyebrow. People traveled in and out of the city on a daily basis, and with the length of time she'd been on the run, any careful observation of visitors would have ended. She could see herself strolling through the streets, through the marketplace, and even up to the gates surrounding Gadleigh Palace before anyone would take note. Of course, she couldn't just walk up and demand to be let in. She would need a plan for crossing over the bridge leading from the market to the palace and, from there, a plan to get inside. There was time, though. She would come up with something. She opened her eyes and took note of the water, now swirling with sediment left from the battle. She sat up so she could drain it and refill the tub.

She emerged from the bathroom half an hour later, scrubbed clean from head to toe. Though her hair was wet, she dried her body and redressed in something clean and comfortable before taking up residence in a chair closest to the fire. Physically, her body longed to curl up under the heavy blankets on her bed. To close her eyes and be engulfed by the dark silence of sleep.

Yet, she knew that would not greet her. Sleep would evade her, and if by some miracle she could slip into unconsciousness, her thoughts would be occupied by those last terrible moments of Larent choking on his own blood, of Arian wailing in the background. Collette could think of very little which could be worse, so she resigned herself to remaining awake as long as humanly possible. She looked at her wrist, where her mother's gold bracelet, wrapped in Larent's ribbons, still sat, though it looked drenched from her bath. No mind. It would dry.

When someone knocked at her door a little later, she had no idea how much time had passed, though a glance toward the window showed the once inky black was now tinged with the faintest pink. Morning would soon come. She reached up, covering a yawn with her hand, then finger-combed her mostly dry hair before pushing herself out of the chair. She crossed the floor, her bare feet making no sound.

She saw Whyldon when she unlocked and opened the door. Like her, he'd bathed and redressed at some point during the last several hours. He'd also gotten no sleep. "Yes?" she asked, not liking how flat her tone sounded in her ears.

She noticed he carried a small, covered tray in one hand, and she realized why he must be there. She stepped aside so Whyldon could enter, closing the door behind him once he was inside.

"How are you?" Whyldon asked her as he set the tray on the table near the chair she'd abandoned.

"Tired," she said after taking a moment to consider her feelings. "Numb." She blinked in surprise, as though she had been unaware of the lack of feeling, before crossing her arms. "I'm not … certain what I should be doing right now."

"I don't believe there is any expectation," Whyldon said quietly. He titled his head, watching her closely. More closely than she liked.

She went back to her chair and took a seat before looking at the tray of food with confusion. Why would she eat? She wasn't hungry. In fact, the idea of food repulsed her. "What did you do?" she asked, turning her gaze back to Whyldon. He'd seemingly lost so much more in his life. His wife. His first child. Collette's mother.

Whyldon seemed to have not expected the question. He took a seat in the empty chair close to Collette and leaned back. "Well, as you know, the first losses led me to enlisting in the King's Guard. The second… Well, I had you to look after. A distraction."

She nodded and let her head rest against the chairback. "I have no such distraction."

"You have a kingdom waiting for your aid, though I know that hardly feels like a worthy cause right now."

Chapter Three

Collette rolled her eyes. "I know what is expected of me. I won't let bringing back the other part of my soul interfere."

Whyldon sighed and leaned forward, taking her hand. "Screw the kingdom, Collette. You've never wanted it, and I know whatever part of you that felt obligated doesn't care anymore. Seeking it can be a distraction if you want it to be, but if you only have space to think about Larent, then that is what you should dedicate your energy to."

Collette stared at him, the surprise of his words penetrating the fog she'd been in for hours now. "What?" she asked, her tone no longer flat. "I can't just—"

"You absolutely can. You owe no one any more than what you've already given. You deserve to be happy and to seek whatever that means. I know, for you, happiness is tied to Larent."

Now Collette blinked, unsure of what to say. Whyldon had never pressured her regarding the throne, but his preferences had always been clear. She'd also known he hadn't been fond of Larent, though he'd now given his approval for her to focus on bringing him back.

The first of her tears had spilled down her cheeks before she'd realized her eyes were stinging. The sobbing arrived almost as quickly. Collette leaned forward, hugging her knees as she cried hot, angry, desperate tears. She vaguely recognized Whyldon rising from his seat and wrapping his arms around her, and even then, several minutes passed before she pressed her face against his shirt and just allowed herself to be held.

Whyldon rubbed her back, quiet and gentle, just letting her control the moment. Eventually, she pulled away, straightening in her seat as she wiped tears from her face. She felt stuffy and swollen now, which only exacerbated how awful things truly were.

"Will you do something for me?" he asked her gently. "Just for tonight. I will not ask you again."

"What?" she asked, her voice a little nasally now thanks to her crying spell.

Whyldon nodded to the tray. "I brought you something to eat, and with it, a vial of a sleeping draught Aphros provided. He said it will help you rest, and that rest should be dreamless."

Collette looked down, giving a weak shrug. "I'm afraid to sleep. Even if I don't dream."

"Why?"

"Because I'll wake up and he'll still be gone," she admitted, more silent tears falling down her face again.

"I know," Whyldon replied. "But you will be rested, more clearheaded, and better able to tolerate it. I promise."

Collette wanted to refuse, but she was tired and emotionally spent. She rubbed at her cheek again, then reached for a thick slice of bread since Whyldon asked her to eat before taking the potion. Although the bread came from a sweet, deep brown loaf, she barely registered the taste, nor the taste of the handful of citrus fruit that followed. With something now in her stomach, she took the corked vial from the tray and examined the deep blue liquid. Without further discussion, she removed the top and drank the liquid as she might have a shot of whiskey. The vial gave a tiny *clink* as she returned it to the tray.

"I suppose I should go to bed," she said after a few seconds. Already, she felt the effects of the draught, and she didn't think falling asleep in the chair would be particularly comfortable. She lifted herself from the chair, which prompted Whyldon to do the same. He followed her back in the suite, toward the bedroom, and after tossing back the covers, she crawled in.

Collette hadn't even fully settled before she sat up. "I need the figure."

"What?" Whyldon asked.

"The figure he gave me this morning. Of the Lady." She gestured toward the bathroom, and Whyldon went to retrieve it, returning moments later.

She took it in hand, studying it as though making sure it was alright, before setting it on her bedside table. Only then did Collette settle back against the bedding.

"Good night," Whyldon said. "When you're up for it, we will plan on getting you back inside Gadleigh Palace."

"Good night," Collette returned, closing her eyes again, letting darkness engulf her.

Chapter Four

Thomas pulled the curtains shut, thankful they shielded the room from the slowly rising sun. Sleep would not come easily for Arian, but he preferred that any obstacle he had control over to be dealt with. With the promise of a dark room, Thomas turned back to the rest of their room.

On a table near the fireplace sat two small trays of food and a vial of blue potion Aphros had dropped off while Arian bathed. Arian would, undoubtedly, be against the use of the sleeping draught, but Thomas thought it would be beneficial, at least for this evening. He wasn't planning on even giving his lover an option. Arian needed food and rest, and not just because he seemed to be handling Larent's death about as well as Collette was.

When Arian emerged from the bathing chamber, he hadn't made much effort to dry off. Water dripped from his blond hair onto his fair shoulders, though he paid it no mind. He had, at least, bothered to wrap the towel around his waist so the bed didn't get as wet as it could have.

Once Arian sat on the bed, Thomas noted he didn't do anything. He just sat there, hands clasped in front of him, staring blankly at the wall. Nothing about him suggested regal or peaceful, stereotypes humans often associated with elves. No. Arian was nearly as broken as Collette had been.

There wasn't much he could do for Arian. At least, not much he could do about Larent's death. He could take care of him in other ways, though. Thomas walked back to the bathing chamber, collected a towel, and brought it back to Arian. Knowing his lover would not make the effort right now, Thomas carefully finished drying his arms, chest, and shoulders. Only then did he use it on Arian's long blond hair.

Arian let out a deep sigh and the set of his shoulders relaxed as Thomas continued to dry his hair. "I need to inquire about Collette's climbing abilities. It is possible we can try and enter the castle through one of the many windows after nightfall. With luck, we can enter and leave without anyone knowing." The words were spoken softly, almost more to himself than Thomas.

"We have some time before we can leave for Coralia," Thomas replied. "You can talk to her in the next day or so about what she can do." Even if Arian was in a state to do actual planning, Thomas knew Collette was not, and until such a time where she was in a frame of mind to think through plans, there was no point in focusing energies there.

Arian looked like he was about to argue, the lines of his body tensing up once more, but just as suddenly, the tension dissipated and he buried his head in his hands. "You are right. Hopefully she is asleep by now. She is going to need it for the days and weeks ahead," he said, his voice slightly muffled by his hands.

Thomas tossed the towel back toward the bathing chamber and took a seat beside Arian. "Whyldon was going to take her something to eat, and Aphros provided a sleeping draught for her so she could rest without dreams," he explained. "The same was brought for you."

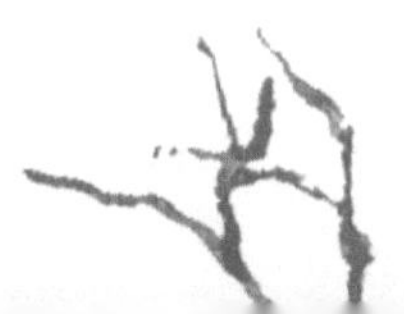

"If I say I am neither hungry nor tired?" Arian asked as he looked up from his hands, his eyes red and puffy.

"Then I am going to request you trust my observations for what your immediate needs are."

Arian let out a low chuckle, though it didn't sound humorous. "I assume from your observations you would like for me to eat, drink the elixir, and try to sleep?"

Thomas nodded. "Those are all things I think you should try to do." He rose from his seat and went to grab the tray and potion, returning to Arian's side in a few short strides.

Arian looked at the tray in disinterest. It was a light fare of fruits and breads, something that should sit easy on his stomach. He let out another breath and picked at the fruits, seemingly uninterested. It also seemed like he would decline for a moment, before his eyes met Thomas's and he picked up a small piece of fruit and popped it in his mouth. He grimaced as he ate it and picked up a different fruit next time he reached for the plate. "Are you going to eat as well?" he asked Thomas between bites.

"I ate while you bathed," Thomas shared. He also wasn't firmly entrenched in shock, but that hardly mattered right now. "So eat as much as you want. You need something in your stomach."

Arian nodded and slowly picked through more of the fruits and bread. He ate a few more bites before pulling away. "I do not think I can eat any more," he said as his eyes slid to the sleeping potion with even more disdain than he had for the food. "You truly wish for me to sleep that much? Could my time not be better spent planning for our trip? I already have several ideas that should make Collette's plan go much easier, and with little to no loss of life on our side."

"And those ideas should hold well enough until everyone involved has the opportunity to rest and regroup," Thomas said gently. He picked up the vial, removed the cork, and handed it to Arian.

Arian's eyes met Thomas's before they moved to his bag on the other side of the room, and then to the writing supplies Thomas had. He opened his mouth to ask a question before his eyes moved back to Thomas's. "Fine," he said, but there was no bite to his words. He downed the potion, the grimace becoming more pronounced. "I need to speak to whomever made that. It is disgusting."

"You can let Aphros know come morning," Thomas said. Honestly, given the Nereid king's very prominent role in the battle, his stasis spell on Larent's body, and his willingness to make a sleeping potion for those who needed it, a bad taste probably wasn't very concerning.

Arian shrugged and moved back on the bed so he was resting against the headboard. He looked back down at his hands. "I cannot believe he is dead." His breath hitched on the last word.

"I know," Thomas said quietly. He removed the tray and empty vial from the bed, setting them on the table before coming to sit beside Arian. He reached over and took one of his lover's hands, lacing their fingers together. "No one expected this sort of loss."

"I kept expecting him to sit up. As if it had never happened. I would say it is not right that he was taken from us, from Collette, but that would mean wishing this death on another, and I cannot do that either."

"Wishing he'd been spared from death does not mean you wish the grief on someone else," Thomas said gently. He brushed his thumb along the top of Arian's hand in slow, soft movements. "Of the people on the field today, he was one of the people who least deserved what happened to him."

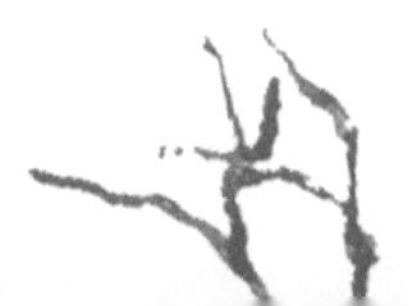

"He did not," Arian said and brought the hand up that Thomas wasn't rubbing to wipe at his eyes. "I am going to help Collette."

Thomas nodded. "I got that impression earlier in the tent." He leaned forward, contemplating the possible outcomes of such a crazy feat. He'd never try to stop any of them, but he did wonder how successful they could truly be. He also thought Rion's point about cost had been valid, even if the rest of his behavior had been questionable. She would likely die in her efforts to bring Larent back, and none of them could stop Collette. "Do you think she can be successful?"

"At getting in and out of Quenall? Yes." Arian tilted his head, thinking over his next words. "As for the ritual, I do not know. I am hopeful the answer is yes, but one never knows when using magic as powerful as this spell should be."

Thomas took a breath. "I know nothing is going to stop her from taking this path, but I seriously doubt Larent will appreciate her trading her life for his, if it comes to it."

"He will not. Hopefully it will not come to that. Hope is all we have right now. Collette has reached her breaking point. If the ritual does not work, I do not believe she will live long past its failure."

"She will not," Thomas agreed, which meant they would all have to do what they could do to make sure she survived. He gave Arian a soft smile. "Come on. Let's get you dressed and into bed before the potion has you sleeping upright."

Arian nodded and rose from the bed to go collect his clothes. "Thank you," he said to Thomas. "For being supportive of this."

"I don't know if it's the right decision," Thomas admitted after pausing for a long moment. "For her, or for anyone else, but I recognize it is what is needed right now, so we are going to do everything we can."

"And I appreciate that more than I can ever say. I am sure Collette will be as well."

"I think she will find very little to appreciate until she brings Larent back," Thomas said. "Now get dressed."

Arian gave a half-hearted chuckle at Thomas's tone and moved to do as he was told.

While Arian pulled on night clothes, Thomas pulled the bedding back for him and fluffed the pillows in the way he knew Arian liked best.

Returning to the bed, Arian gave Thomas a small smile over the gesture and climbed back in. He grabbed the quilt and pulled it up to cover both of them. "I find I am tired. That potion worked better than most."

"I'm glad to hear it," Thomas said. He curled up around Arian and combed his fingers through his hair a few times. "Aphros is quite gifted with magic. I find myself looking forward to seeing what else he can do."

"He is," Arian admitted around a yawn. He shifted around so he was facing Thomas, wrapping an arm around his waist. "Good night."

"Good night," Thomas replied quietly, though he only shut his eyes once Arian's slow, evening breathing indicated he was asleep.

Chapter Five

When Collette woke the next morning, her mood from the day prior had changed. Though no longer in a state of shock, she felt that only through sheer willpower was she able to take the next breath and keep all of her molecules clinging together. Still, bone-deep grief could be contended with when she wasn't as frozen as she'd felt all of the prior day.

Slowly, she went through her morning routine, bathing and dressing in a timely manner. She thought back to long-ago days when her old caretaker Agnes's persistent knocks on her door and commanding way of styling her hair set the tone of her day. Gisella, the young half-elf who helped in the kitchen, would bring her breakfast halfway through the process, and Collette would grumble affectionately throughout it all.

She even smiled, short-lived though it was, when she recalled the morning she'd shoved Tolan from a window. It had been the day after her birthday tournament, right before she went downstairs to meet with Jayden. Her life had been tense back then, but manageable. She couldn't say that now, nor could she reasonably expect anything resembling peace anytime soon.

Chapter Five

Not ready to go downstairs yet, or to face the looks from everyone around her, Collette wandered around her suite, knowing there was nothing to discover. Nothing to soothe the heartbreak pulsing through her. Honestly, Collette didn't know what to do with herself.

She sighed in frustration and returned to the bedroom area of the suite. Like the night before, she focused in on the travel bag belonging to Larent, and she grabbed it before returning to the bed. She expected to find no surprises. Larent freely shared everything he possessed with her upon request. She knew she'd find half-finished letters, articles of clothing he had recently worn, and perhaps empty waterskins or food packs.

The jacket he'd worn during colder months had been put away in the wardrobe, as had some other items he used frequently. Habits from traveling with Nawalya and Arian for so long had left Larent cautious enough to stay mostly packed, despite the slow spread of belongings.

Collette opened the bag and began removing items without purpose. Something about feeling a book, a weapon, an item of clothing in hand soothed her. It suggested his loss was temporary, that eventually, she would correct this terrible wrong.

Putting the items aside, Collette explored another pocket of the bag, finding a large collection of letters. He'd kept them together, neatly stacked. She smiled at the number, wondering why he might have devoted so much time to writing and not sending. She would have to ask if she managed to create the chance.

Collette selected the first letter from the stack, taking in his neat, narrow handwriting. This one he'd intended to send to Nora based on how it was addressed. Since it wasn't sealed, she unfolded the parchment and began reading.

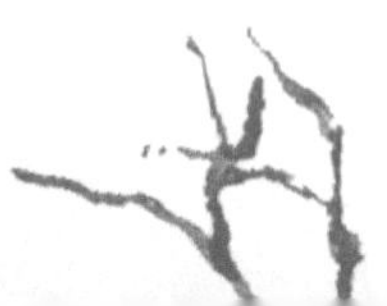

Nana and Pops,

I'm already exhausted with this mission. Quenall is a mess, and for some reason, half the people expect the very young queen to fix everything, while the other half expect her to allow older nobles to rule as proxy. I tend to favor the first option since we know where the old guard stands on every important issue. Chuckles didn't appreciate my suggestion to poison all the nobles so the queen could start over.

I've met her a few times now, much to Waya's dismay. The queen is kind, compassionate, and maybe a little too trusting. She also seems tired—worn thin. You can see it in her eyes and the way her smiles dimmed between meetings. I don't think she likes being queen. I've been told to keep my head down and mind my business. I want to help her, but there's not much I can do at the moment other than continue to spy on her brother and the other nobles.

Speaking of her brother, I genuinely don't think I've met anyone more worthless. I'm trying to take the advice from your last letter and look at him as more than an apathetic shit. He has so many resources, and even more privilege, but he lies about as though the world was designed to bother him. I never see excitement, or even investment, from him, and I just don't get why. The queen adores him, and he seems fond enough of her, but I can see him being swayed into nefarious activities if he doesn't figure out some purpose. It's obvious, when you look, that he hates dealing with the nobles, being between them and the queen. He hates court life in general, but he's unwilling to change things. I wish I knew why, but I'm smart enough not to ask since he won't talk about it. Nawalya and Arian send their love. I hope everything's well at home.

Love,
Larent

Chapter Five

Collette put the letter aside as she finished it. Larent often doubted his intelligence, at least compared to some of the others in their group, but his observations of the state of Gadleigh Palace so early in his time there spoke of someone who observed and took in details so many others would miss. It was one of the reasons they connected, because he saw her for exactly who she was from the moment they first spoke when he landed on her balcony. She picked up a second letter, deciding she needed more of him. Her brows raised as he saw her "Freckles" scrawled across the top, and she unfolded it, wondering what he might have to say.

Hi Freckles,

I know it's probably inappropriate for a servant to be exchanging letters with a queen. However, I believe we can work around that. After all, we've only really exchanged letters if you write back. So, maybe, it's less inappropriate so long as I am the only one leaving notes around.

I wanted to tell you I enjoyed meeting you the other day, and that, as a queen, you are doing an amazing job. Remember what I said: don't let the nobles get you down. Just keep doing what you're doing and you'll eventually see the changes you're working so hard to implement.

Also, if you wait long enough, my friend just might go on a murder spree throughout the castle, and that will clear up all your problems. Also, I love the way you smile, and I can't wait to see it again.

Yours,
Larent

This letter she put down as well, though she chose not to go into the rest of the stack. Unlike the first letter, which had not been addressed to her and only spoke of her in generalities, the second had homed in on her feelings at the time. The stress she'd been under. Leaning back against the ornate headboard, she felt her eyes prickle with tears, wishing she could just reach out and touch Larent once again, or hear him laugh, or have any sign at all she was going to have him back sometime soon. Resolved more than ever to bring him back, Collette closed her eyes and forced herself into a calmer state.

A soft knock sounded at the door, as if the person on the other side was worried to wake her if she was still sleeping. Collette opened her eyes, rubbed the heel of her palm against her cheeks in case any of the tears had managed to fall, and let out a deep breath. "Come in."

The door opened slowly, and Tolan entered, a small tray with a covered dish atop balanced on his right hand. With his free hand, he gently closed the door behind him before he headed toward her. "I volunteered to bring you breakfast," he said to explain his presence.

She nodded, her eyes briefly fixed on the tray. Collette wasn't hungry. As with the night before, she found the idea of food repulsive, even if she didn't voice it. "That you had to volunteer tells me people are worried."

Tolan nodded as he set the tray down on a small table near the bed. She noted he didn't remove the cover. "Yes, people are worried. There was also a disagreement as to who should bring you your food. When it started to get heated, I took the liberty to grab the tray, announce I was coming to see you, and leave." Tolan shrugged and looked around awkwardly.

She saw he'd pulled his dark wavy hair back that morning, though the dark circles beneath his eyes suggested he hadn't slept well. He lingered where he was, as though he wanted to stay but was not sure how to ask if she wanted company.

Collette sighed and moved some of Larent's items from the end of the bed, then motioned for him to sit down. "It's not like I'm suddenly out of control or dangerous."

Tolan tentatively sat down on the bed, looking at Larent's things before turning his gaze away. "They aren't concerned about that. It's more your general well-being, and there's discussion of who should be around you right now."

Collette rolled her eyes. "You can tell every person here if they insist on behaving stupidly, I'll leave. I don't have time or patience for the theatrics."

Tolan winced. "Theatrics isn't the right word. It's more them loudly voicing their concern for what we're planning to do. Some people are uncertain about how we're safely going to get you in and out of the castle."

"Not one single person is obligated to help me with retrieving or using the spell," Collette replied. "I know it's dangerous and it's not what anyone signed up for."

"I know," Tolan said, then shook his head. "We know, but the majority of us are going to help."

"Then why did you report that all of you are acting like I'm going to fall apart at any second?"

"Not all of us are. I'm fairly certain Arian isn't, at least." Tolan paused. "You've been through a lot, and this, Larent's death, is the worst of it. It wouldn't be surprising if you did fall apart. That you haven't before now speaks highly of everything Larent did for you. Also, I think the argument in the kitchen was more because everyone wanted an excuse to see you and check in. You don't need that."

She took that in, not wanting to snap at Tolan, especially when she was aware of her own sensitivity. "I'm not falling apart because I don't have the luxury, Tolan," she said after

taking a calming breath. "You've told me as much in the past, and what I want to do now has nothing to do with getting Rhoslyn and Zephraim, which means it has to be done quickly and efficiently." She looked up, meeting his eyes. "I am grieving, but that doesn't mean I'm not practical."

Tolan winced at the reminder of his own words, but he didn't apologize. "They're still worried about you. They will be for a little while at least. Though, I think Nawalya's already putting together a plan to go over with you at some point."

"I'm not surprised. I think several plans will be presented in the next few days."

"I'm willing to bet Arian already has a few ideas in mind as well."

"Probably," Collette agreed. "Arian doesn't like to sit with nothing to do." She picked up the letters she'd been reading and refolded them before, packing them and the others back into the bag.

"No, he doesn't. I've never seen him like that before. Normally he hides his feelings better. It's Nawalya that's more open, but not this time."

Collette continued packing the bag with other items now. "Arian is more fragile. We all act as though Nawalya is, because of the way her visions affect her. But Arian is, and always has been, the one in need of the most protection."

Tolan looked down at the blanket on the bed, making it clear to Collette he was thinking over her words. "You're right," he said. "She looked tired and her eyes were puffy and red, but she seemed determined to move forward."

"I wish I felt that way," Collette replied. "But I will be moving forward, no matter how I feel."

Tolan lifted a hand as if to reach out to her, before dropping it in his lap. "You'll bring him back," he said firmly.

"I hope so," she replied.

Chapter Five

"To be honest, I don't think there's a force in this world or the next that can stop you." Tolan stood from the bed and nervously rubbed his hands on the front of his trousers. "There's fruit, some bacon, and a piece of toast with some seafood on the tray if you're hungry. If you're not, leave it."

"Thank you," Collette said, though she didn't remove the dish cover yet. "I'll eat something."

Tolan nodded. "Let me know if you need anything, alright? I'm here for you."

"I know," Collette said. Even in the midst of early grief, she recognized that Tolan still cared about her deeply.

Tolan looked like he was going to say something else but, instead, just nodded and left the room.

Chapter Six

Rhoslyn, my love, my queen,

It is with a heavy heart I write to inform you that our attack on the Nereid Kingdom was unsuccessful. The force Collette brought to her side outmatched our own. Even our ships were taken down by the use of Nereid magic. We lost good, dedicated men, supplies, and ships. I can only hope to atone over time.

I will do what I can to encourage the morale of our soldiers on our return trip to Coralia. No matter our failures, they have done extraordinary work on the battlefield, and they deserve a hero's welcome upon return. I will do what I can to celebrate the achievements they managed in the meantime. I know your graciousness will be bestowed on them as well.

The good news I can report is that I killed the man I believe to be Collette's lover, something I hope will be a devastating blow to her personally. With that loss, she may be easier to take down at some point in the future. I believe she still has the support of the Nereid king and Fythias, but neither country has ever been of military concern to us.

Chapter Six

I hope and pray you allow me the opportunity to make you proud on the battlefield next we see the traitor. She is weak, and we've dealt a deadly blow, which is a victory unto itself—one I hope you will greatly value. Her losses shall always be our victories.

We should arrive back in a few weeks' time, and I will surrender myself to your judgment once more.

Yours always,
Riken

Mallan looked out at the sea as a light breeze fluttered through his brown hair, his brows narrowed in contemplation. The Azmarin regent's otherwise serene expression gave away none of the seething mood just beneath the surface. And there was no other way to describe his mood, for he was angry. They had skilled, highly trained soldiers. They had expensive, well-maintained equipment and weapons. Their ships outmatched those of every other nation. There was no reason as to why the combined forces of Azmarin and Coralia should have failed in the battle against the Nereid, yet here they were, sailing back to Coralia, defeated and with less resources to aid in any possible counter attacks.

He glanced toward the quarterdeck where Lord Riken spoke with the ship's captain. In Mallan's estimation, the man lacked the deep shame someone in his position should hold after such a terrible defeat. In truth, Riken's arrogance seemed, if not the lone reason, a big reason as to why Coralia suffered so much defeat. He fought as he existed: filled with arrogance and assumptions of his superiority. He'd never taken the threat of the fallen Queen Collette with the seriousness it required, and it would surely come to haunt the young lord in time. Like it or not, the woman had more claim to the throne than Queen

Rhoslyn ever did, and Mallan would not be at all surprised if she managed to steal it back.

He watched as Riken finished his conversation. Clapping the captain on the shoulder, the two shared a small moment of apparent camaraderie before he headed in Mallan's direction. He didn't come directly to the regent, however. Instead, it seemed as if Riken was determined to take a moment to speak with every one of the Coralian soldiers currently positioned on deck. No stop took longer than a minute or two, but Riken was attentive and reassuring with each, nodding as they spoke and making physical contact through pats on the back. Only once every person had been addressed did Riken finally reach Mallan. If Riken felt any shame over the loss they'd just suffered, he showed nothing in his walk or posture.

The lord didn't say anything at first. Instead, he leaned against the railing about a foot from Mallan to look out over the water. "The captain says we should make port within a few days without issue so long as the weather stays clear, and he's sure it will."

"Let us hope for such good fortune, then," Mallan replied, somehow stopping himself from laughing at the shallow address. He surveyed Riken, noting the overly styled black hair and the haughty narrowness of his eyes. Queen Rhoslyn's lover might as well have been on his way to a picnic rather than returning from war. "The good weather will allow you to deliver updates with swiftness. I am sure your queen eagerly awaits our arrival. I'm also certain she will have little complaint once you explain just how we lost to a group of Mers."

Riken laughed, his smile a little too bright. "Oh, Queen Rhoslyn is going to be extremely upset with this loss, as she should be." He crinkled his eyes in a way many did to convey amusement, but something in the action felt deliberate, as though Riken wanted Mallan to believe him unworried. "While she is not prone to the same punishments as King Sargarus was when such failures occurred, I fully expect to face her rightful wrath upon our return."

"You lack the distress one might expect in your position," Mallan observed.

Riken gave an abortive shrug. "What good would showing my distress do for the morale of our remaining soldiers? We've no idea how my queen might respond, and if she does so with unhappiness, it would be warranted." Riken shook his head. "No. It is best I keep a more optimistic mood in front of the soldiers. I know a happy front can be off-putting to some, but it's seemed to help many." Riken turned his gaze to the deck.

Mallan watched Riken surveying the soldiers, real concern creeping into the lord's expression. These men might very well be punished for the lost battle, and all Riken could give them now were empty moments of positivity. Queen Rhoslyn must truly rule with ruthlessness.

"Perhaps," Mallan said. "I find a more balanced approach necessary when dealing with my own people. They know of my disappointment, but I am not overly harsh with them, either. I find honesty more beneficial to all involved."

"Everyone handles these situations differently. I have been speaking with my people one on one. They know my feelings, such as they are. They fought well, and I would rather focus on that for the moment." Riken shrugged and turned his whole body toward the quarterdeck.

"And what happens when you arrive back in Quenall and your queen wishes to take her anger out on those who followed you into battle?"

"You mistake my queen for someone she is not." Riken said firmly, still not looking back at Mallan. "She is not prone to unreasonable fits of rage, and when she does become upset, she aims it at the people responsible. If she deems punishment

necessary, it will be aimed at me and possibly a few others in the chain of command. Anything she does will be reasonable and, unless she sees fit, will be done in private. One could not ask for more from their ruler."

Mallan smiled to himself, sensing annoyance, perhaps even anger and dejection, in the way Riken responded. He lacked a true understanding of the danger he bedded, but Mallan had no desire to correct the man. He doubted Riken would even listen. "No. I think I see your queen for exactly who she is, Riken. Unlike you, I lack the romantic fog through which you view her."

"You can believe that if you wish," Riken replied, as if granting the other man a favor by not contradicting him. "Regardless of our differing views involving my queen, we are now tasked with planning for any counter attacks that come. I'm fairly certain the losses on Collette's side were nearly as great as our own, and they will have to cobble together a refreshed army before they'll be ready to strike."

Mallan wasn't sure he agreed. Everyone had suffered losses, yes, but their soldiers had taken a harsher beating. Even Riken, who benefited from additional use of Mallan's healer, might have bled out or grown sick from infection thanks to the blow landed by Collette. Riken's behavior during the battle left Mallan with little choice on how he would proceed after. The healer could only help so many, so her services had been focused on the most critical of soldiers and the highest ranking. The rest would need recovery time, and even that was no guarantee of future usefulness on a battlefield. "Is that what you observed?"

Riken hesitated before answering. "I observed a lot of losses on both sides, though ours clearly lost."

"I think running away after one battle clearly communicates as much. Had we been able to, we might have remained close by, waiting to strike again," Mallan mused. He looked back out at the ocean. "There will be those in Azmarin who question the alliance after a loss like we suffered, you know."

"I am aware," Riken agreed, though he did not address Mallan's first point. Perhaps he could find no argument to counter it. Perhaps he was too angry to try. Riken simply gave off an air of disinterest, which held the equal odds of being feigned or real.

"I will do whatever I can to ward off potential withdrawals of support," Mallan added since Riken gave no further indication of speaking. "My advisors may have different opinions. I will find out what I can."

Riken crossed his arms, which could have been to ward off the chill coming from the sea. Nothing about the young lord's mannerisms gave off any discontent, but Mallan could feel it bubbling just below the surface. He wouldn't be surprised if the lord raged before their journey ended, no matter how foolish such an action would be. "If there is anything I can do to help, let me know. Otherwise, I know the queen will have to mitigate these issues."

"Of course," Mallan replied. He felt as though he'd learned quite a bit in his time since meeting Queen Rhoslyn. The trip to the Nereid Kingdom with Riken by his side had taught him more. He would have to act accordingly.

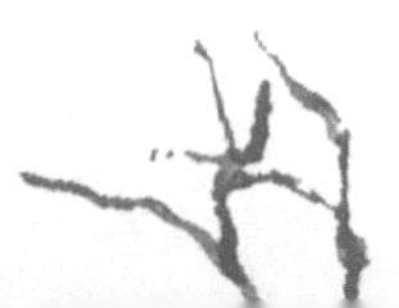

Chapter Seven

The sound of dishes being taken away and replaced echoed around the otherwise silent dining room. Rhoslyn brought a newly filled goblet of wine to her lips, sipping the sweet dark liquid as she watched servants exchange glances. No official news from the battle in the Nereid Kingdom had yet reached Quenall, but hushed rumors circulated. If one believed the whispers, Coralia had lost, and not barely. The possibility alone left Rhoslyn ill-tempered. Not that she hadn't been before. Zephraim's escape from the palace left her with another source of annoyance, and she wondered what new irritation would meet her next.

She flicked a lock of straight cinnamon-colored hair from her shoulder after placing the goblet down. "What is taking so long with my fruit?" she snapped at a passing servant.

A servant rushed into the room, past Cadan, who had done what he could to keep a respectful distance from the queen. He'd been invited to dine with her, so he sat close to the door, observing. Rhoslyn saw him side-eye the servant in disap-proval, but she knew he would keep his mouth shut unless she commanded otherwise. Cadan was very good at taking and following orders.

The servant hastily served Rhoslyn, then bowed, stepping back out of the queen's reach. "Don't make me ask next time," Rhoslyn snapped.

Cadan shook his head slightly in disapproval at the servant girl. Rhoslyn knew he was upset at the way the staff treated her. He'd even asked if he could make an example of one or two of them, but they had larger concerns, and he hadn't pressed, just offered.

"I may take you up on your offer," Rhoslyn said after she took a few bites of food. "No one around here seems capable of doing their job."

Cadan nodded. "I have one or two in mind for when you're sure." His eyes moved to the servant who'd delivered the fruit, and Rhoslyn was reminded that this was the same girl who almost spilled wine on her the day prior. "Just say the word."

Rhoslyn watched the young servant, half-elf from what she understood, look down, her hands balled into fists at her side. She was afraid. "Perhaps I shall."

Cadan bowed his head in acknowledgment, taking a drink of his wine. "You deserve servants who treat you with respect and know how to do their job. If an abject lesson is needed to get them back on track, so be it."

"There are many areas within this palace that could do with some reminders of their duties," Rhoslyn replied. "Perhaps we should discuss just how to accomplish that." Zephraim escaping had been the worst of things, and the guards would need to answer for their deficits. But kitchen girls not knowing when to bring out food? Did they have some other, more important purpose?

Cadan rested his elbows on the table, clasping his hands together just under his chin. His eyes scanned the room,

hovering over the faces of each servant. While his expression held its normal neutrality, it was his steely gaze that told Rhoslyn he did not trust them enough to be completely open. "I am available at your convenience to speak on any topic you wish." His eyes darted to the door that would lead to a more private setting.

Rhoslyn nodded. When she was finished with her morning meal, they could have a more in-depth discussion. She turned back to her meal when another servant entered the dining hall, a sealed letter in hand.

"My apologies, Your Majesty. We've received word from Lord Riken."

Cadan sat up even straighter in his chair, but that was the only indication of his interest.

Rhoslyn snatched the letter from the servant and waved him away. She broke the seal, certain of what she was going to find within. Her green eyes narrowed as they scanned the letter, and her lips thinned. "Of course," she snarled, throwing it down. "Of course he failed. Again!" She sighed. "Everyone but Cadan, out." The servants hastily retreated elsewhere, leaving the queen alone with Cadan.

When she looked at him, she saw his lips pressed into a thin white line, his eyes locked on the letter. Rhoslyn wasn't sure if he was displeased with the contents of the letter or her outburst. "You may read it," she said.

Cadan reached out, his movements unhurried. He scanned the contents, his countenance darkening as he set the letter down with more force than necessary. "May I speak freely?" Cadan asked.

Rhoslyn motioned for him to speak.

"While it is entirely possible Collette managed to gather an army large enough to beat our own," he stopped and pinched the bridge of his nose between his thumb and index finger, as if what he was going to say next pained him, "since Zephraim took the throne, Lord Riken has been more arrogant, more self-assured. He is smarter than he has been acting as of late. Though the loss of a large battle cannot be put entirely on his shoulders, he was still in charge of your troops, my queen."

"Riken has repeatedly caused problems with his arrogance," Rhoslyn replied. "He has openly challenged Zephraim and others in council meetings. He's twice been within reach of Collette and let her walk away. He shows no caution in any act, and he doesn't seem to understand how much of a problem his behavior is for me."

Cadan gave a sharp nod in agreement. "He has been so sure of himself and of you that he thinks nothing can go wrong. While I hope this will have taught him a needed lesson, I wonder if you need to punish him severely. Though not publicly, maybe."

Rhoslyn gave a short bark of laughter. "Oh, I intend to deal with him." Of course, it would have to be done in private. His position alone warranted that much respect. "It's as though he gives no thought to my tenuous situation, and I must make him understand."

Cadan made a thoughtful noise. "I think he believes the two of you are untouchable. Which is never true, but more so with Zephraim gone." Cadan sighed. "It was my own arrogance that did not spot Barris for the threat he posed. I will work on correcting that as well."

"The failure to recognize spies in the palace is a grave concern," Rhoslyn acknowledged. She took a calming breath. "Have we confirmed if Zephraim and Barris travel together?"

"Yes, a patrol spotted them together. The survivor of that patrol couldn't confirm the other two they traveled with, but he was able to confirm them." Cadan growled out that last part, upset over the loss of all but one of the patrol.

"Do we think they are dumb enough to head to Barris's estate?" Rhoslyn asked.

"I want to say no, but anything is possible."

Rhoslyn nodded and leaned back in her chair, a habit she'd once refused to ever engage in, but now thought little of. "I would think neither of them are foolish enough to head for the eastern coast, but we should be prepared in case it happens."

"I can send a few men to scout Pontus Bay and report back what they find. They can stop by Barcomb Mill as well in case one of the people who were with them was Sara Whyldon," Cadan offered. "If they were willing to take Zephraim directly from his room, they may be bold enough to return there thinking it safe."

"If you intend to send a unit to both places, you're better off sending two different groups," Rhoslyn replied. "Somehow, I doubt anyone we target will return to Galel after we arrested Sara Whyldon, but it doesn't hurt to check."

Cadan nodded. "I'll have it done by the end of day." He looked at the table in front of him, his brow creased in thought. "Not to get too far off topic, but I would like to make a show of punishing the servant girl and the guards who'd been stationed at Zephraim's door. I think calling the servants and some guards together to bear witness would drive home the point that they need to be more attentive to their duties and to you."

"Of course," Rhoslyn said. "The servant girl has the sympathy and heart of many in the palace. Take care that your punishments cross no lines."

"A light flogging, then?" Cadan inquired. They both knew a flogging, no matter how easy Cadan went, would still be extremely painful for the girl. "List off the ways she has failed over the last month and make it clear this is the punishment for those who do not perform their job in a satisfactory manner going forward?"

"I think so," Rhoslyn agreed. "Make sure Agnes is present when it happens. That old woman still struts around the palace like she owns the place. She fails to recognize that her ward is no longer queen." Agnes had raised Collette, dressing and instructing her alongside Whyldon. Rhoslyn doubted anything would sway her loyalty.

"Of course," Cadan said, his brows creased. Rhoslyn knew Cadan would make things just as painful for Agnes as he did the servant girl should Agnes choose to intervene. "The soldiers will get a harsher punishment. They should have heard something from inside Zephraim's room. Talking, the noise of him gathering a few belongings. Anything."

Rhoslyn nodded again. "Their failure to keep Zephraim confined also has wider reaching consequences for me. The punishment should reflect the severity of the mistake."

"I wonder if we could push the narrative that he's been kidnapped by those who are against the betterment of Quenall and Coralia as a whole. We could start telling the story now so should he speak out against you, the people will hopefully believe it coercion." Cadan made a thoughtful noise. "Just a suggestion. It may not work, of course."

"Hmmm," Rhoslyn replied, tapping her fingers on the chair arm. "I shall give it some thought and let you know."

"I will not act without your approval."

"Thank you," Rhoslyn said. "I need some time to reflect on how I will handle Riken when he returns." She rose from her chair. "Let me know how your dealings go. If you will excuse me."

Cadan stood when Rhoslyn did and bowed low. "Of course, my queen. Please send word if you need me."

Rhoslyn gave a shallow nod and left the room. She had much to do.

Chapter Eight

"She's authorized Cadan to issue punishments to castle staff," Agnes reported. Though the old woman's face was splotched red and her eyes bracketed in deep worry lines, nothing about her tone or posture illustrated that she was flustered or over-worried. She delivered her news factually and with a precision that often eluded those of similar age. Diana completely understood why Queen Collette had kept Agnes, her old nurse and governess, in her employ well past the need for a governess and caretaker. Agnes could be counted on.

"With Zephraim gone, she's going to have a rebellion on her hands if she's not careful," Diana replied.

"Don't I know it," Agnes said. "And it would serve her right. It's one thing to parade around the palace like some celestial being when you at least pretend to be loyal to the supposed king. With Zephraim gone, who knows how long she will be tolerated."

Crem's lips were pressed so tightly together as to be almost colorless and his arms were crossed. Diana knew he was taking in all the information, processing what their next move should be. "Is there anyone that needs help getting out of the castle before these punishments start?"

"I imagine there will be no final list," Agnes said. "I know the young girl they hired to replace Gisele is being targeted, as are the soldiers who were supposed to be guarding Zephraim."

"We have a few people in the castle that can help them escape if need be. We don't know what Cadan will consider appropriate punishment, and even then, it's not right that she is allowing this." Crem looked over at Howle, who was leaning against the cave wall a fair distance away. Since his outburst a few weeks back, he'd kept a respectable distance from Diana and Crem. "What are your thoughts?" Crem asked.

"I'm wonderin' how many people know Zephraim is gone. It seems as if the castle is doin' ah good job keepin' it hush, hush. I think we need to let more people know if that's the case."

"What you three need to be doing is finding somewhere outside of the city to set up a real home base," Agnes countered. "Ever since Zephraim escaped, they've increased surveillance in the city, and the perimeter is growing with each new wave of searches. It's only a matter of time before they come looking around these caves."

Crem forced himself into a more relaxed posture. "We've been talking about that. That none of the tunnels under the city have been discovered yet is a gift from the Mother, but Cadan is smarter than Lord Elrick and Lord Riken. If I thought we could get away with it, we'd take over a house or warehouse so we're still in the city itself. I think we might be best hiding in the nearby forest and staying on the move, but that has its own troubles."

"I agree with Agnes. We need to be outside of the city, and we need to set up a more permanent base," Diana argued. "You know she's out there, and she will come. Our queen needs to find friendly faces before she ever crosses into the city."

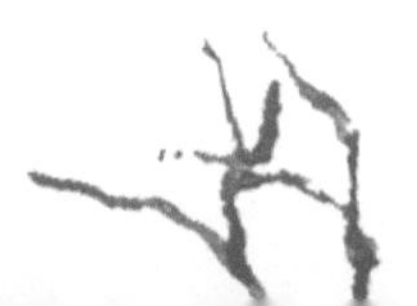

Before Crem could respond, Howle let out a large sigh, pushed off the wall, and walked over to another table. Grabbing one of the maps, he brought it over to them and unrolled it onto the table, using random items such as a cup and Diana's brush to keep it from rolling back up.

"There are several places our queen could approach from. If she has the ships and the manpower, which we assume she does, she could sail all the way around and attack Quenall directly." He pointed to the map where the port was. "Or they could land in Pontus Bay, gather more help from Barris, who we have ta' assume has already sent a letter ta' that lady of his lettin' her know what has happened. From there, they'd march around, more than likely taking Vitel and Wildrun on the way, doin' which would really piss off Her Bitchiness and that whore of hers."

Howle's finger walked down the map, tracing the possible path. "Another possibility is her sailing toward Branlin, though Queen Collette may not know she has supporters there."

"All of those make sense, but we need to stay close by so we can help anyone in trouble," Crem responded. He eyed the map. "We can trust our people in the castle to inform us if ships are seen coming directly for Quenall, but we may want to make more friends at the port just in case. We can send people to Branlin so maybe we'll get an early warning should Collette take that route. Otherwise, we will have to trust Barris to send us word should she make landfall there." The small growl showed how unhappy he was at the idea of working through others.

"We don't have enough people locally to arrange groups here and in Branlin, and certainly not as expeditiously as needed," Diana pointed out. "And given the time and resources it would take to sail from the Nereid Kingdom, around the southern border of Coralia, and back up once reaching the western coast,

I think we can assume that will not be the plan. She'd be in open water too long. They could run out of supplies or catch patrol ships from Azmarin or Coralia. And of course, seeing royal ships from the Nereid Kingdom or Fythias would give her away."

She tapped Branlin next. "Porting here would cut the trip in half and help avoid a mountain crossing, but the same concerns exist. I think we are safer to assume she will sail somewhere on the east coast, and depending on where that is, both Vitel and Wildrun might be a considerable distance out of the way."

"I think Pontus Bay makes the most sense from the options," Agnes spoke up. "She'll avoid getting too far into the heart of Galel because of the connection with Whyldon, and who could blame her? So, she'll likely land there or somewhere more southern, travel along the coast, cut around the bottom of the mountain range, and up through Myrefall."

"I was just layin' out possible options. I believe Pontus Bay will be where she lands as well," Howle agreed.

Crem was quiet. "I just want to cover all our bases. We don't know who won that battle yet, even if rumors say Queen Collette did." His eyes moved to Diana's stomach and back to her face in a quick movement. "But you're right. We don't have the manpower. I could write to Branlin again so maybe if she does make landfall there, we can still get advanced notice." He crossed his arms again. His index finger tapping against his arm. "How does the forest and mountains sound? We are moving into summer soon, and if the queen is on her way, we should be back in the city before autumn. If she's not, we can always find a new place."

"I'd think you'd have enough information in a few weeks to make more solid plans," Agnes advised. "Once she's back on Coralian soil, our dear queen won't be able to keep her presence secret for very long."

"She might be able ta'," Howle added. "We do need ta' know what she's plannin', but you're right. We'll have advanced notice. So will the Bitch Queen, but we won't be planning against her."

"It sounds like we have a plan, even if it ends up being temporary," Diana concluded. She placed a hand on Agnes's back. "Thank you for bringing this to us. Can we possibly persuade you to leave the palace before an evil hand is turned on you?"

"I will think about it," Agnes said.

"Please consider it before they implement the punishments," Crem said earnestly. "Rhoslyn has to know your loyalty is to Queen Collette. No one here wants you hurt."

"And no one would be more dedicated to protecting her legacy in the palace than I," Agnes replied with a shrug. "But I will leave should the need arise. That I can promise."

"That's all we can ask," Crem said before looking back down at the map, beginning to work out a plan for leaving the city.

"Thank you for coming to see us," Diana said, taking Agnes by the arm and leading her back toward the tunnel entrance. She knew they couldn't make Agnes do anything she did not wish to do, and her information from the palace proved invaluable. Hopefully, though, they'd be able to convince her to come along when they relocated.

Chapter Nine

Barris sat on the edge of the mattress in the small room he and Zephraim were sharing for the night at Ian's inn. Sara had her own room, of course, and he imagined it looked similar to this one. A square space with solid whitewashed walls and one window facing the streets below, the space was filled with a couple of beds big enough for one person, a dresser, and a table. The floor was made of worn, wooden planks. Though the room and its furnishings were clearly old, it was clean and everything was in good repair. Of course Ian would take pride in his inn.

They had traveled here as quickly and as stealthily as they could, especially after running into that patrol shortly after leaving Quenall. While he was grateful to have a roof over his head, a warm fire, and what felt like a comfortable mattress, Barris wished he was home already where he knew they'd be safe.

Looking across the room to where Zephraim lay on his own bed, Barris couldn't help but smile. So many people underestimated him, and yet Zephraim had handled himself well, not only during the trip here. They'd slept on hard ground, traveled on foot for long stretches of time, and experienced

51

the wilderness in a way he had not expected Zephraim to be prepared for.

It had been Zephraim who first spotted the patrol, who instructed Ian and Sara to hide while he tried to reason with them. "I'm supposed to be their king. I cannot appear as though I don't think so," he'd explained to Barris. The justification made sense to Barris, so he'd not argued against it.

Unfortunately, the patrol failed to listen to reason, and Zephraim, with some help from Barris, had to dispose of them. Zephraim's competence proved extremely attractive, and Barris knew he would have to be careful. Zephraim saw him as a friend and a married man, and he was positive Zephraim wouldn't be open to the sort of non-monogamous relationship that was the norm within the Nereid community. Zephraim had never felt truly loved by one person, and the idea of love existing beyond those confines would surely be beyond him. Barris was happy to enlighten him, but he knew now wasn't the time.

"I think my body will appreciate having a soft surface to sleep on tonight," Barris said, breaking the tired silence that had been stretching on since they entered the room.

"Have you never gone camping before?" Zephraim asked, lightly teasing him. "It's been no worse than that."

"It's been some time since I camped like this," Barris admitted. "Last time I went camping was on the beach. The soft sand is much nicer than cold hard dirt."

"Some beaches don't have soft sand. The last one I visited was covered in rocks. I doubt that would appeal."

"That would be worse," Barris said with a laugh. "I don't know why sleeping on the hard ground hurts like it does. I'm not that old."

Zephraim chuckled. "Perhaps we lie to ourselves about what is and is not enjoyable when we are younger."

Chapter Nine

Barris couldn't help but let his smile grow wider at Zephraim's chuckle. He'd been so much more relaxed since they left Quenall, more open, less apathetic. The deep sadness behind his eyes still lingered if one knew how to look. "That's possible, or we just didn't notice the pain as much because we were always too busy with our next adventure."

"Also a possibility," Zephraim agreed. "But I don't complain about the comfortable bed."

"It could also be our lifestyles. Sara and Ian seemed to have less trouble than I when it came to sleeping on the ground. Maybe when we get home, and the trouble in Quenall has been handled, I'll start helping in the fields more," Barris said. He decided to ignore the fact that he just said we and home in the same sentence. He instead asked the question he'd held off on since escaping Quenall. "How are you feeling about all this?"

"I'd rather not rehash the consequences of my choices tonight," Zephraim replied, his voice losing some of the amusement he'd held.

"I'm sorry. I just wanted to see how you're doing," Barris said, his smile dimming. He knew he could be intrusive with Zephraim's thoughts, but it was only because he so wanted to know what the other man was thinking and how well he was coping. He supposed he should dial it back. "I will rephrase," he said, trying again. "I know what you have been through must be overwhelming. You asked for very little of what happened. If you wish to voice it, even just to vent, I will listen."

Zephraim was quiet for a moment, and as the silence dragged on, Barris wondered if he'd crossed a line of some sort.

Finally, Zephraim spoke. "I appreciate that, and I'm sure I'll take you up on it at some point."

"I'm available for anything you need or want. When you're ready," Barris responded. Thankfully it was evening, and they were in beds on the opposite sides of the room. It made it easier

to hide the flush creeping up his neck and blooming on his cheeks when he realized how his words might be taken.

"Thank you," Zephraim replied quietly.

Barris nodded. Realizing this could get awkward, he quickly stood and changed topics. "Are you hungry? Ian mentioned making food. I'm happy to go grab a bowl."

"It probably is wise to stay in here for the duration of our visit, isn't it?" Zephraim asked.

"Maybe, but at the same point, I may be less recognizable." Somehow, Barris thought he might have made himself more so by helping Zephraim. So, he amended his first thought. "Though we shouldn't risk it." Barris started undoing the laces of his boots.

"Ian will probably bring something up or have someone he trusts do it," Zephraim replied as he settled back against the bed.

"True," Barris said, looking up at Zephraim as he removed his second boot. He allowed his eyes to drink in the other man for only a moment before he cast his gaze about the room. He would need something to distract himself.

Though the Nereid people allowed for more than one romantic relationship, Barris had never felt anything for anyone other than Lynessea. She'd had other partners, of course, and they had occasionally invited him into their shared beds. Physically, he'd enjoyed the experiences, but Barris had missed the personal connection with the other partner. He hadn't even been willing to sleep with Lynessea until he'd been sure that he'd fallen in love.

Knowing that made it easier to accept how he felt for Zephraim, even if he was sure the other man didn't return his feelings. He wouldn't be surprised if Zephraim couldn't, given everything he'd been through, and that was okay. That didn't stop either of them from needing a distraction, though.

Thankfully, his eyes landed on a discarded set of playing cards that had probably been left behind by a prior guest. Standing, Barris took the few steps to where they sat. Holding them up, he asked, "Up for a game while we wait, or are you going to rest for a bit?"

"We can play a game," Zephraim easily agreed. He sat up and walked to the table situated in one of the room's corners so they could play.

Chapter Ten

Faron stood facing the window that looked out toward one of the many water gardens, enjoying the sun on his face. In his hand was a letter from his and Sabine's daughter Elyn. He found the contents of the letter concerning but of no real consequence at the moment. No, he was more intent on the figure that sat hunched over on one of the benches in the garden. From this angle, he wasn't able to see much, but he was sure the figure was scribbling away in a journal. It was typical of Éric, especially when his emotions were high.

"Your son is hiding in the gardens," he called out to Sabine. "I don't think he slept at all." If there was one thing he wished his children hadn't inherited from him, it was how high their emotions could run.

"He's been doing that since the battle," Sabine replied from the desk. Their suite had been fitted with an area for Sabine to work, and his wife sat there now, reviewing documents that might very well be personal letters or items meant for King Alaoin to tackle.

"More than likely because he and Alaoin are still at odds, not that I blame Alaoin for being upset." He turned to face

Sabine where she sat, and as always, the mere sight of her was enough to take his breath away, even after all these years. Her long, caramel hair hung in silky loose waves around her shoulders, and her vivid green eyes rose to meet his gaze. He would never quite understand how he'd been so lucky to wed the duchesse. "I don't think a simple apology is going to fix the tensions between them."

"I doubt it will," Sabine agreed. "But I also think our son would serve himself well to offer one all the same. Alaoin has been quite subdued in the last few days. I've no doubt it's due to the impact of Éric's words."

"Éric thinks Alaoin a great king. His feelings just get in the way when he worries. It used to be the same for us. With luck, this will be a learning and growing opportunity for him." Faron walked over to Sabine, looking down at the paperwork in front of her. That he understood everything she was working on was proof of what nearly thirty years of practical lessons and hands-on knowledge could teach someone. "I just hope this hasn't ruined them."

"I am certain they will work their way through Éric's outburst," Sabine replied. She sat the paper aside. "I do not blame Alaoin for being upset, but I feel for our son. I know he meant to cause no harm." She looked up at Faron and smiled. "He reminds me of someone."

Faron couldn't help but smile at her words. "I have no idea who you could be referring to," he joked. "I wish they would work this out sooner rather than later, before either of them can make this worse."

"I love our son, but the tension between them is of Éric's own creation, and he will have to make amends."

Faron had hoped Sabine would volunteer to talk to Éric so the situation would fix itself before a larger rift grew between the two due to Éric's reluctance to even look at Alaoin. Alaoin

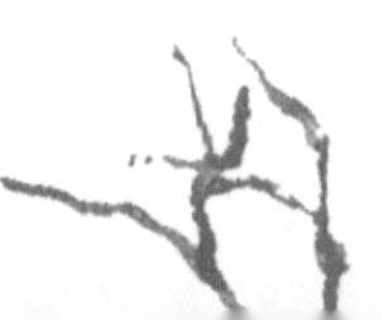

was struggling to even be around Éric, and why wouldn't he? Éric had made Alaoin feel like he was a bad king and a worse person. "We'll have to wait and see where they're at in a few weeks. Hopefully, they'll be talking again before we set sail for Coralia." Faron considered locking them in a room together if needed, though he was sure Sabine would not be happy if he did.

"Hopefully," Sabine replied. "They are adults, though, and we are not to interfere."

"Well, if we can't interfere with those two, can we interfere with this?" He held out the letter from their daughters. "Apparently, Alaoin wrote to the girls before the battle letting them know we were considering invading Azmarin. So now they wish to ready the army to march on land." Faron rolled his eyes as Sabine scanned the letter.

"They included a plan of action that says they went to Avana for assistance." Their girls were too bloodthirsty. They definitely did not get that from Sabine. He believed having the Fythian army at their back wouldn't be a terrible idea, but considering the distance they would need to cover and all their uncertain immediate plans, he thought it best they put a stop to this right away. Sabine could have a different idea.

"I will consult with Alaoin in the morning," Sabine decided as she handed the letter back to Faron. "It's probably too early to have the army at the ready, but making preparations..." She shrugged.

Faron nodded and took a deep breath, bracing himself for the next conversation they needed to have. Not that he thought Sabine would have a bad reaction to it. No, it was his own fears and concerns he needed to face. "I am thinking of writing home and asking them to send us a few things." He couldn't meet Sabine's eyes. "I think it might be helpful for Collette since she's intent on bringing back her husband."

Sabine's eyes widened in understanding, and she nodded. He'd known she'd regretted not bringing up the spell before, and while passing on knowledge now couldn't change Larent's death, it could aid in making the intended spell safer. "Of course."

"I'll need to apologize to her as well as to him should all this work out." Faron made a face. He wasn't against apologizing. He just questioned his decision to not be honest with the shifter when Larent had approached him about how to handle their differing life spans.

"You had no way of knowing what was going to happen," Sabine reminded him. She rose from her seat and wrapped her arms around him. "And he may not have wanted to know how to link their lives."

"From how he spoke, if I had told him I might know a way to do such a thing, he may have gotten on his knees to beg for it." Faron ran a hand through his hair. He still wore black wavy locks down past his shoulders. "Though we don't know how his being a shifter might affect the spell. The spell granted you my lifespan. No one knows how long shifters live. Not anymore."

"If you recall, the spell could have easily given you my lifespan," Sabine reminded him. "The life expectancy of a shifter may not matter."

"True," Faron agreed. "I wonder which they would prefer. To live a set number of years or to have the future spread out in front of them for an unknown amount of time?" He didn't know which he'd prefer, but with Sabine by his side, he'd have taken either.

"You might ask if ever you are granted the chance," Sabine replied, then she frowned. "Of course, as we came to find, with Larent, it hardly mattered how long shifters live. Someone stole those years from him."

"They did," he acknowledged. "But with a lot of luck, love, and determination, maybe he can be brought back. I lack any true worry over it."

"Then what do you worry about, my love?"

"I'm concerned about the loose plans of returning to Quenall, but only because I hate Coralia." He had lived in Coralia during the reign of King Sargarus, had witnessed some of the horrors that had been allowed to happen. Faron had faced the monster down in a different battle twenty-six years prior after the king had poisoned Sabine and their people. Most of the people on their side had only lived thanks to another friend's magic. They were lucky Collette didn't take after the man.

"I think this fight was always going to land on Coralian soil. Maybe not as soon, and with different motivations, but it is decades in the making," Sabine admitted.

"You're right, but I had tried to keep that from my mind for as long as possible. I do not want to go to Coralia, as much as it needs to be done."

Sabine reached up and cupped his cheek. "You do not have to go to Coralia if you do not wish to, you know. Even Alaoin would not defy me if I said no."

Faron considered it for a second. Staying in the Nereid Kingdom instead of traveling to Coralia was appealing, but his mind immediately reminded him that meant sending his wife, his son, and their king, who was like a son, to Coralia alone. He just couldn't do it. "No. I'm going with you."

"Okay," Sabine easily accepted. "Now, it is late, and I am ready for bed. I suggest you make yourself ready."

Faron nodded and bent down to place a gentle kiss on the top of Sabine's head. Then he walked to the washroom, stopping once he reached the doorway. He glanced over his shoulder and casually asked, "Blue or black rope tonight?"

Chapter Eleven

An arm wrapped around Collette's middle, holding her close. A hand ran through her hair as she leaned against the warm body behind her, their breaths in sync as they relaxed in the afternoon sun. A few feet from them, gentle ripples from a clear pond occasionally drew attention. Collette basked in the peaceful warmth, convinced she could never be happier.

"This is where I am happiest," she declared with a blissful sigh.

"You know, we could just stay here," he said into her hair, the tone teasing. "Screw everything else."

"I want to," Collette said, dreamy and content.

"Then we should. It wouldn't take me long to build us our own house. Two bedrooms, you think?" He kissed her hair.

"As long as you're there, nothing else matters to me."

"I'll always be here, Freckles."

Freckles…

Collette jerked awake with a gasp, her heart racing and her sleepy mind not quite aware of her surroundings. She took deep, slow breaths, fighting away the panic of waking up alone, terrified for no discernable reason. As her heart slowed, she realized what must have happened. She'd dreamed of him again. Of his smile and his laugh, and the adoring way he would look at her in the quiet moments.

If the spell didn't work, she'd never experience any of it again. Not that she'd have long to if it worked the way she suspected it would.

Taking a deep breath, Collette rubbed her eyes and swung her legs off of the bed, intent on walking around the island since natural sleep would elude her. She still felt groggy and out of sorts from a draft Aphros had given her hours ago. She needed to quit taking it, if only because eventually real, natural sleep would come to her, and she didn't want to grow dependent on potions in the meantime.

As she stood, she noticed the nest of blankets on the floor, a visual reminder that she wasn't alone. Arian's messy blond hair poked out from beneath the heavy covers, and she could just make out his face in the darkness. Arian didn't look awake, but he inevitably would be. "I'm going for a walk," she announced. "You should go to Thomas."

Arian opened one eye and looked up at Collette, the quick response confirming the elf hadn't truly been sleeping. "No, I will go with you. If you are okay with the company." He sat up and stretched, then looked up at Collette, waiting for her response.

Collette shrugged as she pulled her hair back into a messy ponytail. Usually, she would have braided it, but given the early hour, she didn't have the motivation. "When Thomas gets angry, I'm pointing him in your direction." She found her boots and pulled them on, pointedly ignoring the number of Larent's belongings she'd left out. She did grab his carved figurine and stuff it into a pocket because she didn't want to leave it behind.

Chapter Eleven

"I told him I was worried you might have night terrors or not be able to sleep," Arian reported. "He said he was alright with me staying with you so long as it did not become a regular occurrence. I think he was making a joke," Arian said as he reached over and grabbed his shoes, quickly pulling them on.

"I usually don't sleep well," she replied, unable to deny how much Larent's mere presence had done to alleviate some of the struggle. She spotted the empty vial which had contained the sleeping potion the prior evening sitting on the edge of her bedside table. "I suspect Aphros thinks I should be consistently drugged so that I sleep. He keeps offering, and I've accepted a few times, but I keep telling him his drugs won't be useful when we board a ship in a few days."

"I am aware of how little you usually sleep," Arian acknowledged. "Taking potions every evening is not the answer, though. Some people think that when one has gone through a traumatic event, drugging the person is the best thing to do. They are wrong."

"He's trying to help," she said. "Nothing does help, unfortunately, but we should appreciate the effort."

"People always try and help," Arian grumbled. "There has been a potion with my food every night as well. I had hoped it would stop when they realized I have not taken one since the first night, and yet..." Arian made a frustrated noise. "Thankfully Thomas does not push."

"Thomas knows what you need," Collette said, nodding. "If you're coming with me, come on."

Arian nodded and stood in one fluid motion. He grabbed a jacket from the floor and slid it over his shoulders. "Lead the way," Arian said, motioning Collette forward.

As they stepped into the corridor, Collette saw they were likely among the few still awake. She preferred to be left alone, to avoid pitying looks and hushed whispers, and she could

only regret the busy movements of staff and other residents come morning.

She led them outside with no particular destination in mind. In the days since Larent's death, she'd felt like she'd traveled every inch of the island. Arian walked beside Collette, silence stretching between them as they walked, but not in an uncomfortable way. She appreciated his company, undemanding and understanding of her current state.

Much of the island was illuminated, either by the moon and stars or by torches along designated pathways. Like the palace, much of the area they walked had emptied of residence. She assumed they'd gone underwater for the evening, and it was a real pity they would not ever be able to see that part of the Nereid world.

"How has Thomas been since the battle?" Collette asked. "He's been quiet whenever I am around."

"He does not think going back to Quenall is a good idea, but he understands why we are doing so." Arian closed his eyes for a moment before adding, "I do not think he expected my reaction to Larent's murder to be as overwhelming as it has been." Arian always referred to Larent's death as murder. The arrow, covered in poison, had been intentional, and the elf refused to downplay the situation by referring to it as anything else.

"At least he isn't actively working against the plan to go," Collette pointed out. She stepped over a vine, one she knew would lazily creep across the ground or around any falling in its path.

"You mean like Rion." Arian's voice was very dark as he said the man's name.

"Rion thinks I'm going to get myself killed, but he's not actively working against me," Collette explained in her former lover's defense, though she didn't think he deserved it. Rion had made choices in his life, and Collette had not spoken against the man doing what he thought was right for him. He'd had the right to leave her, especially knowing he couldn't handle the way she was treated by dissenting nobles. In doing do, he'd simply left her at the mercy of the people he claimed he wanted to protect her from. Not that she thought Rion's presence would have prevented Zephraim's betrayal and her imprisonment.

Arian gave Collette a look that was somehow both understanding and incredulous at the same time. "His opinions stopped being of importance when he left you. Showing up in the middle of our journey does not mean his opinion holds weight."

"I didn't say it did," Collette pointed out. "And honestly, even if I did care what he thought, it wouldn't stop me."

"He seems to think it does and that you will listen in the end. I believe Nawalya threatened to stab him." Arian shook his head. "I am aware not everyone supports going, but at least the others are helping. Even Tolan."

"I'm not surprised Tolan is helping," Collette said. "And in the end, Rion will go."

They found themselves in one of the many gardens near the palace, something Collette wished she'd paid more attention to when they'd been walking. She had memories with Larent here, like the time he'd spent teaching Nawalya to dance, or the many quiet moments they'd stolen for themselves. She'd bury her fingers in his russet hair, pulling him closer. Inevitably, they'd end up partially, and sometimes fully, naked, and they'd laugh and tease one another as they made love. She had to take a slow, deep breath to keep calm.

Arian reached out and tentatively took Collette's hand. She knew he meant to be supportive, and the awkwardness was very endearing. "Why are you unsurprised by Tolan?" he asked, distracting her.

"Regardless of his shittiness after we left Azmarin, he's always wanted to support my efforts."

"I just assumed he would agree with Rion. Out of fear for your safety only," Arian clarified.

"Larent thinks…" Collette paused before forcing herself to continue. "Larent thought Tolan wanted to fuck Rion, so he may have leaned in that direction had we not so forcefully shut down Rion's protest."

Arian's complicated expression became unreadable for Collette. "Tolan has rarely been swayed by his dick when it comes to what he believes he should do. That is not to say it could not happen."

"Well, it did not for now," Collette replied.

"I understand their concerns. Returning to Quenall, breaking into the palace, will be dangerous. However, it is your choice to make."

She did not answer at first as her gaze turned to the area of the garden where, the night before the battle, she and Larent had playfully danced. Collette still wasn't sure how she kept breathing without him there. "I'd have gone alone if I had to."

"Never alone," Arian promised her, his eyes on the same area.

Collette squeezed his hand, appreciating Arian's presence. She looked over at Arian. "We should head back. I have a meeting with the other rulers later this morning."

Arian nodded. "Would you like to play cards until then?"

She didn't, but she wanted to sleep even less. Besides, Tolan once told her Arian was the best card player he'd seen other than Collette. Maybe sharing a few games with Arian would be a good distraction, at least for a little while. "Sure."

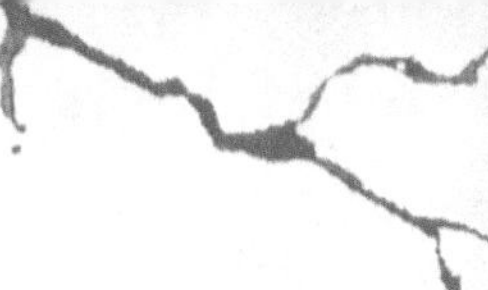

Chapter Eleven

Hi Nana and Pops,

Sounds like we'll be leaving Coralia soon. Things seem to be coming to a head with the nobles and the queen. I've gotten to spend more time with her, and I know she's going to weather this storm beautifully. She'll take some hits, though. She shows the world this hard exterior, but inside, she's soft and gentle. I feel like she'll come back stronger than before. I mainly worry about how she'll react if Zephraim ends up on the opposite side. She loves him so much.

Tolan is still around, and if things go bad and we have to flee, I think he'll come with. I'm hoping something will prevent him from coming. I do not want to have to spend any more time around him than I have to.

I hope everything's going good at the farm and you're both in good health.

I'll write again when I can.
Love, Larent

Chapter Twelve

My dearest Lynessea,

Sadly, this letter will have to be quick, but I wanted to inform you I am no longer in Quenall. Rhoslyn had Zephraim arrested for treason and leaving the kingdom became a priority. I am headed home to Pontus Bay and will write you a more detailed letter once I arrive. Know I am safe. I hope the same for you.

Your heart,
Barris

Lynessea knocked on the door to the council room out of courtesy, knowing at least a handful of people would be on the other side. Usually, she'd not be so formal, especially with a letter with such vital information. By the time Aphros called for her to enter, Lynessea had been on her toes, dancing back and forth, her indigo and sea-green streaked hair bouncing with the effort. Permission to enter granted, the Nereid woman threw open the doors and slipped inside.

Lynessea stopped a few feet from the large table that sat in the middle of the room, letting her eyes scan the space quickly before she bowed to Aphros. Ceto and Jayden had joined him, sitting on either side of the king. Ceto's bright orange hair contrasted with Jayden's inky black hair, making it seem like Aphros was flanked by morning and night.

She took a moment to study Aphros before speaking. Her brother looked tired and stretched thin. Someone who didn't know him well wouldn't see it, but she could. It wasn't as bad as when his wife, their queen, had been murdered during Sargarus's reign of terror, but it was close. Lynessea knew the position of king took a lot out of him, especially since he was never supposed to be king. Their society was matriarchal, but he'd been a good leader during the Fythian wars from thirty years prior and they had needed stability, so the Nereid had decided to keep him as their king, something none of them regretted.

"My king," Lynessea greeted. She turned and bowed to Collette. "My queen. I have news from Barris." She even turned to King Alaoin and nodded in respect despite him not being her monarch.

"What news?" Aphros asked, curious, though nothing in his response suggested alarm.

"Barris writes that he has left Quenall after Rhoslyn had Zephraim arrested for treason," she reported quickly, walking around the table to hand him the short letter.

Aphros took less than a minute to browse the parchment. "He seems rushed."

Jayden made a thoughtful noise, drawing Lynessea's attention. "Is it possible he fled Quenall because he was implicated as a traitor as well? Perhaps he wrote that while trying to evade soldiers?"

"It seems as though it would be an important thing to leave out," Aphros replied.

He handed the letter to Ceto, who passed it to Collette. The queen read it with some interest, then tilted it to her left so that Captain Whyldon could read it. When he was done, he rose from his seat and walked it to the other side of the table before handing it over to Duchesse Sabine. Her concerned expression showed that she saw the letter as more serious than King Alaoin's more neutral response when it was passed to him.

"I think he was simply letting me know about the change in leadership and location," Lynessea volunteered. "If he was in danger, I think he'd have taken the extra few seconds to let me know." She hoped so, anyway. If Barris had been implicated in Zephraim's charges, then he would not be safe even upon reaching Pontus Bay.

"It's good information to have," Faron said from Sabine's side.

"And we now know we will meet him when we arrive at Pontus Bay. I don't think it should have a large effect on our plans," Nawalya offered as she returned to the table, a chalice in hand.

Lynessea realized food and drink had been made available, and a few of Queen Collette's group had been serving themselves upon entry. Tolan now joined the table, followed by Rion.

"I think it's funny Zephraim has been arrested, given what he did to Collette," Tolan said as he sat down.

"It's not exactly an unfitting consequence, is it?" Rion asked. "He's probably questioning a lot of his choices now. Of course, Rhoslyn may wish she'd not acted so rashly in arresting him."

"I've thought about that," Faron interjected. "Other than through marriage to Zephraim, this Rhoslyn character has no claim to the throne. Could we use that against her?"

"Neither of them were entitled to the throne to begin with." Collette spoke up from her seat. Obviously tired and impatient, she didn't buffer her words. "And no one has acted like it matters. Rhoslyn will retain most of her support, with or without Zephraim's presence."

"If anything," Rion added with a dark chuckle, "arresting Zephraim was a critical error on Rhoslyn's part, and she's going to know that. She'll become more dangerous because she is going to be more desperate."

A blush flashed across Faron's features, but he moved on quickly. "Then we need to keep that in mind while we make plans," he said.

"It may make getting into the castle harder, especially if she is more paranoid. Not impossible, just harder," Arian pointed out to the room, though he cast a supportive smile in Collette's direction. Thomas, who stood beside him, nodded in agreement.

"Riken will also be there, no doubt, desperately clinging to their position," Whyldon added.

"Riken has proven deficient in most ways," Collette said.

Those from the Coralian party all made affirmative noises as Arian and Thomas finally made their way to the table.

"So, with this news, we know we must be more careful getting Collette into and out of the castle," Thomas summarized.

Nawalya nodded. "What else does this change, if anything?" she asked the group, obviously looking to steer the discussion back on topic.

"It depends on what plans Rhoslyn has for Zephraim, I think," Whyldon speculated. "And how Riken is feeling when he arrives back in Quenall."

"I would think she would have him executed, but she could have other plans. Is saving him something you'd even want to worry about?" Jayden asked.

Lynessea knew she'd be surprised if Queen Collette wished to save her half-brother after he'd been responsible, in part, for her overthrow and arrest.

"I don't think Rhoslyn will kill him," Collette replied after several long moments. "It's not impossible to prove treason was committed by a reigning monarch, but Rhoslyn wouldn't legally assume the throne."

Thomas laughed. "She may be insane enough to execute him, but I think she knows she can't. Whoever she's allowed to remain at court would pose a threat to her rule the second Zephraim ceased breathing."

"Then we don't have to move up our plans," Nawalya said. "Not that I was going to suggest we do so. Though she may try to use him as leverage."

"She can't possibly think Queen Collette would waste breath trying to help Zephraim," Ceto said incredulously.

Lynessea agreed with Ceto. There could be no way the false queen would believe that, but it seemed others had a different idea.

"I'd agree," Rion said. "She accused Joss of murdering Wrenn Almeida, but I think we all know who was behind it. Why she'd think Joss is any more benevolent…"

"It would depend on if Rhoslyn was involved or knows Zephraim attempted to use blood magic to kill Collette," Arian mused. "If she knows about it, then I would assume she is intelligent enough to know Collette will not forgive him for that transgression. However, from everything I observed, there were some who thought Collette too forgiving, too kind, too soft. While that is untrue, it may mean Rhoslyn could believe Collette would forgive Zephraim for the imprisonment, and he could, therefore, be used against her."

"Let's put it on the record that, no matter what else happens, I do not forgive him," Collette said.

Aphros smiled. "Forgiveness is a funny thing," he said as he rose from his seat to refill his chalice. "Even if you did choose to forgive him for your own peace, it does not mean you'd go help him. The question is, is Rhoslyn smart enough to know as much?"

The others looked to Collette and Whyldon for the answer.

Collette shrugged. "I think if anyone doubts her intelligence at this point, they are terribly unprepared to deal with her."

"She seems methodical, but I was rarely around her." Arian shrugged.

"Methodical under certain circumstances," Thomas reminded him, placing a hand on his shoulder. "Desperation may change her."

"Then we agree to proceed with caution where Rhoslyn is concerned," Aphros said, drawing attention back to him. "Hopefully we can get a more accurate understanding of what she's doing with Zephraim as we approach Quenall."

There were nods of agreement from those around the table as the conversation moved back to when they should leave and where they should make port. For a moment, Lynessea wondered if she should attempt to get a message to Cremisius Hawke to get more information about Zephraim before dismissing it. There was just no safe way to do so, and with as much time as it took to send and receive news, whatever she did find out might be outdated by the time it came.

Knowing she was no longer needed there and having other things to do, Lynessea caught Aphros's eye, bowed her head, and left the room. She hoped they would nail down a plan soon.

Chapter Thirteen

Nawalya stood at the end of the main dock in Pontus Bay, slightly to the left of the gangplank, the rest of their traveling companions and the ship's crew were also exiting. Ignoring the bustle around her, Nawalya looked out over the sea at the multitude of ships that had followed them to port and knew Quenall would know of their arrival soon if they didn't already.

A fleet like theirs would have been easy to spot from miles out. Her eyes dropped from the horizon to the shore where some of the Nereid that had accompanied them were rising from the sea before she returned her eyes to their original point. She was sure she could watch their transformation from Mer to human without censure, but it felt wrong to do so, and not just because a few were naked as they emerged from the water.

Turning her head, she looked over at the town of Pontus Bay, which teemed with life, more so than the last time she'd been there. That had been when Barris's father and older brother had been alive. Then, the seaside town had seemed subdued and quiet. Today, from what she could see, the streets were full of vendors selling what looked like every kind of seafood imaginable, with craft and weapons booths mixed in.

A small smile crossed her lips as she remembered Arian's rant about wishing to kill the old Lord as he had Lord Riken's father. It had taken both Nawalya and Larent to stop him from going after Barris's father.

The smile fell from her face as quickly as it had come at the memory of Larent's laughing eyes, the mild panic when he realized Arian was serious about running off to kill the lord. It hit her like a punch to the gut, making her feel like she couldn't breathe before she forced herself to compartmentalize and push the memory aside.

Turning her gaze back to the ocean, she took several deep breaths, her mind going over their plans for getting to Quenall.

She was slightly surprised when, a moment or two later, Arian stepped up beside her. That Tolan was with him was more surprising. The two men hadn't been hovering over Collette. She would never have allowed it, but she knew Arian had been splitting his time between Thomas and Collette fairly equally, while Tolan had been present in whatever area Collette was in when she wasn't in her bedroom. The elf had to assume that their queen would be joining them soon since Arian and Tolan were with her now.

"It still surprises me that the Nereid do not have tails," Arian mused.

"Same," Tolan replied.

"Many do, though, and some of them refuse to ever come to the surface again after what Sargarus did to them." Nawalya turned to face the two, her dark brown hair whipping around in the breeze, and she tilted her head as she tried to remember what those Mers were called, but the name slipped her mind.

Arian nodded his head in acknowledgment. "Possibly, but I still find it interesting that people who do not work directly with the Nereid believe similarly. I would expect the less obvious signs, like their elongated hands and scales and the webbing between their fingers and toes."

"It's just too bad Sargarus viewed those scales as reason to maim and kill them," Tolan spit out with a low curse.

Nawalya opened her mouth, either to add on to the curse or continue the conversation with Arian, when both men's heads snapped up. She knew without looking that Collette had made an appearance. Turning around, she found she was correct. At the top of the gangplank stood Collette, Whyldon by her side.

The air of sadness still clung to Collette. Every step she took looked heavy, every nod took more effort, but she walked down the plank, speaking as matter-of-factly with Whyldon as she ever did.

"How is she today?" Tolan quietly asked Arian.

"She is the same as she was yesterday and every day since his death. Quiet, sad, but fiercely determined," Arian said with a hint of annoyance in his voice. Nawalya knew he was trying to hide how often Tolan asked the question.

Tolan let out a sigh, and Nawalya wondered if he had somehow thought Collette's grief would lessen over the last few weeks. She'd known it wouldn't. Every single day Collette woke up alone would only add to her sadness, no matter how often she went through his things. Spirits, she and Arian had only just started recovering from their own decades' old grief.

The three grew silent as Collette approached them. Whyldon, it seemed, continued to join a distant discussion with Ceto and Aphros. "The captain was informed Barris is at his estate," she reported.

Nawalya was a little sad that Whyldon didn't join them but quickly brushed it off. The two were becoming friends, but it was still a work in progress. "Do you think he will come greet us?" Nawalya asked, though she was sure the man would. He seemed a strong supporter of Collette's.

Arian leaned back a little to get a better view of the gangplank, a small frown on his features, and she knew it was because Thomas hadn't left the boat yet. She reached over and gave his hand a quick but gentle squeeze.

"Probably," Collette guessed. "He's all sunny disposition. He'd want to be a good host, even in the middle of war."

Arian groaned as if in pain at the reminder that Lord Barris's nickname was "The Golden Lord" because he was so fucking happy all the time. Nawalya couldn't help but grin at his response.

Tolan chuckled lightly before sidestepping the two of them to stand closer to Collette, offering her his arm. "Would you like an escort?" he inquired.

Nawalya felt her eyebrows rise as she wondered if this was Tolan being Tolan or something more.

Collette gave Tolan a brief smile but shook her head. "Thank you, but I think someone needs to go fetch Thomas before Arian declares war against the ship. He was inside, speaking with Alaoin when I left."

"I will go and check on him," Arian volunteered with a wry smile before he moved to head back up the gangplank.

"I'll go instead. I must grab a few other things, and we don't need you glaring at another monarch," Tolan said. "I should also find Rion."

Nawalya was grateful when Arian didn't argue but instead offered his own arm to Collette. Thankfully, Collette accepted it, but given her increasing reliance on Arian, there was little doubt of the response. Nawalya knew there were small concerns with how much the two were coming to depend on each other, but Nawalya understood. Right now Collette needed someone who would support her unconditionally, and Arian,

when it came to grief, needed someone to take care of lest it drag him under. She also knew if—no—*when* Larent was back, it would lessen. Not right away, but it would.

As they moved away from the ship and into the busier area of the docks, the smell of fish became more prominent, though it wasn't unpleasant, thank the Spirits. Nawalya kept her eye on the crowd as they went, looking for any possible danger, which is when she spotted the Merscales on display. It had been so long since she'd seen them on open display that Nawalya stopped for a moment to stare at the items. Earrings, necklaces, and other decorative pieces just sat out in the open, twinkling in the sunlight. She felt her anger rise until she met the yellow slitted eyes of the shopkeeper and she realized it was a Nereid selling the scales. Seeing the Nereid who smiled warmly at her instead of a human behind the stall got Nawalya moving again. Though she didn't miss the fact that Collette and Arian had also stopped to take everything in.

When they caught up with her, Collette was frowning, but no anger rested in her expression. "The Nereid selling them likely means the scales were given willingly," she said quietly. "But they still shouldn't be on sale. Willing trade is how we ended up with genocide before."

"She would see it as the Nereid agreeing with the trade as a whole, or she would say as much," Nawalya said as they continued walking, their destination the large estate on the far side of town.

"I doubt she'd give thought to what the Nereid thought or did, but she'd point and use it as justification," Collette said.

The closer they grew to Barris's estate, the more people from their small fleet joined them. Collette very much resembled a supported, though stoic, queen who had little doubt of her position and right.

Chapter Thirteen

As they neared the estate, the crowd seemed to spread out as raised voices were heard coming from the direction of the main gates. "I had wanted to meet the queen at the docks. Since I was unable, I will meet her on her way here, as is right." The voice was firm but friendly and very obviously belonged to Lord Barris.

"Yes, my lord. I just thought you would like a group of soldiers to accompany you with everything going on," said an older female voice.

"Thank you, but no," he replied, his voice firmer.

Lord Barris moved as if to sprint down the street to find Collette, only to stop upon seeing she was almost at his gates. Barris closed the distance between them quickly, dropping to one knee, his head bowed, once he was in front of Collette. "My queen, I am sorry I didn't meet you sooner. Welcome to Pontus Bay."

Nawalya couldn't help but nod her approval of how he greeted Collette. It seemed Arian agreed as well.

"From what I understand, it's probably not wise for you to leave the grounds, so it's understandable for us to only meet up now," Collette replied. She motioned for him to rise with an upward flick of her fingers.

Barris looked up at Collette, his smile wide, and Nawalya could almost hear Arian's internal groan.

"Everyone keeps telling me that, and yet we haven't seen a single soldier from Quenall. I also thought it a worthy risk to come out and meet you."

"The risky welcome is appreciated, but I think we'd all be safer going inside your estate." Collette motioned around her. "As you can see, I come with supporters, including the King of the Nereid Kingdom and the King of Fythias."

Barris stood at Collette's words, bowing to Aphros and then turning to bow to Alaoin, which surprised Nawalya, as she hadn't recognized them joining the group.

She noted Lynessea stood near to the King of Fythias and had obviously pointed him out before moving through the group to stand next to Barris. "Hello, my wife," Barris said softly to Lynessea, who gave him a warm smile in return before she pressed a quick kiss to his lips.

"Let us get our guests situated," she suggested, and Barris motioned for Collette to join them.

Chapter Fourteen

After taking time to settle in her allotted room, Collette joined Barris in his quarters where they were to share a meal. A table had been set up on the large balcony off of his sitting area, facing the city and, more distinctly, the blue line of the ocean. Collette imagined it would be peaceful to come out here and enjoy the light, fragrant breeze and the view.

One of the side doors of the room opened and Barris walked in. From where she stood, Collette could see it was a bedroom, and she could almost make out Lynessea inside, pinning up her hair, before Barris gently closed the door behind him. She found herself a little jealous and wistful, wishing she could retreat to her own room and find her husband there. But it was not to be. At least, not here, not now.

Hopefully, she'd given them sufficient time to reunite before arriving for a meal, though Collette couldn't feel terribly distressed about arriving at the time and location she was asked to.

Barris crossed the room in a few quick strides to stand near Collette, giving her a quick but deep bow before rising. He'd chosen a more casual ensemble for their meeting, choosing a blue cotton shirt and black pants, paired with worn but well-cared-for boots. Her own outfit was similar, but only because she'd not had the desire or energy to pick something more befitting her station. She very much doubted Barris cared, either way.

As she studied him, Collette found that Barris wore a more serious expression than she was used to. She supposed he could be worried about the fate of Coralia, but she suspected something beyond that bothered him.

"Have you settled in well?" he asked, starting the conversation.

"As well as I can," Collette replied. She doubted she would ever feel anything resembling settled until she was able to revive Larent, but she didn't want Barris to think she was putting down his hospitality. "You look well for someone who recently arrived from Quenall."

"A change of clothes, a warm bath, and a soft bed will do wonders for one's disposition," he admitted with a soft, wry chuckle. "I have discovered that I may not have the disposition for long-term camping."

Collette let out a huff of a laugh. "I've slept on the ground quite frequently over the past several months. One grows accustomed to it."

"I will take your word for it and hope that, from here on out, any traveling I will need to do will include inns whenever possible." Barris's eyes drifted from Collette's toward the sea.

Collette imitated the motion, watching gentle waves rolling in. Truly, Barris had a peaceful setup. She was almost tempted to abandon their plans to dine together and allow him time to continue recuperating with his wife from his own recent trip. She couldn't though. He'd been in Quenall and inside the palace, and he could provide details others could not.

"What were things like in Gadleigh Palace in the days leading up to your exit?" she asked.

"Stressful and extremely tense, and that was before I had to escape the kingdom." Barris raised a hand to rub at the back of his neck. "Riken is overconfident, and Rhoslyn thought me an idiot, but Cadan… He's Riken's guard commander and close confidante. Him, I was worried about."

"I do not believe I ever met Cadan, but I have heard many things about him. I would think he brought about a new form of horror when he came to Quenall."

"He was smarter than Elrick when setting up his trap. He didn't take my smiles at face value. Had we not had a solid plan and help, I think getting Sara out of prison might have been next to impossible. He is more loyal to Riken than the servant Rhoslyn killed. He also shares similar beliefs, but he lacks Riken's arrogance. I think Crem and his people are in a lot more danger now than they were before."

"It sounds like we can't linger here very long, then," Collette replied. She looked back to Barris, a question she wanted to ask since arrival making itself known. "I understand Zephraim escaped Gadleigh Palace at the same time you did," she prompted. "Did he travel with you?" The question of her brother left her wary, since his intentions and location remained unknown to her.

Barris tensed for a moment before his shoulders relaxed. He looked down at the estate grounds before he looked over at Collette. His brows were furrowed and he winced before speaking. "Zephraim is here, as is Sara Whyldon."

Collette felt the rage fill her, as though someone was physically pouring it into her. She felt the red-hot temper circulating around her toes, in her fingertips, and up her neck. Still, when she spoke, her voice sounded oddly calm. "Where, exactly, is he?"

Barris swallowed hard, and she could see the hesitation in answering. "I think he's in the library."

Collette did not respond. She turned from the balcony, walked through the room, and out into the corridor. She knew where the library was. The steward had pointed it out when she'd been shown to her suite. She heard Barris call out first to her, followed by Lynessea, but the voices quickly faded as she stormed through the estate.

She would have Arian deal with Barris. How dare that fool allow the whole of their organized support to occupy the same space with that traitor. She couldn't believe he could be so stupid. So careless! No. The only thing to do with Barris was to follow up with appropriate punishment. Perhaps then he could see why his actions had been so wrong.

When she reached the library doors, she found none of her anger diminished, and with great satisfaction, she shoved the doors open.

Zephraim looked up as his sister entered the library, though he supposed he'd lost the right to call her sister the moment he taunted her with a layer of prison bars between them. Though she did not run, Collette's quick, determined steps had her closing the distance from the door to where he sat in a high-backed chair. Zephraim rose to his feet, not wanting to feel quite so vulnerable sitting down.

Collette paused at the edge of the ornate area rug, just out of reach. His eyes widened, seeing her current state. She didn't look well: pale, leaner than he'd ever known her, and plagued with bruise-like circles beneath her eyes. Zephraim couldn't help but look down, ashamed of his actions.

He said nothing, waiting for her to choose when she spoke. If she even thought him worthy of conversation. The long pause hanging between them suggested she had nothing to say. He was beyond her pity, her use of personal resources and energy, and he couldn't even argue against the treatment. He'd behaved abominably, and nothing he could do would ever atone for his crimes against her.

Zephraim finally lifted his gaze, meeting Collette's dark brown eyes with his own. He nearly gasped, seeing the absolute sadness lingering there. He wanted to hug her, to assure her everything could be okay again, but he knew he'd be offered no open arms. He took a breath and decided he must say something. "Collette," he began.

"Don't," she said, cutting him off, the single word clipped and icy. "You had me arrested, and you used Larent to try to kill me."

"I know," Zephraim replied, glancing down in renewed shame. Rather than flushing, he felt the color drain from his face. "I don't—" He paused and shook his head. "I cannot begin to express my regret for everything."

Collette scoffed and rolled up the hem of her shirt, revealing pink scars that would forever mark her. "You made Larent do this to me, and you want me to believe you're sorry?" she asked, her tone almost hysterical with disbelief. "These scars are probably the least serious of the offenses attributed to you, though I admit I didn't know you could use magic."

"Not very well, given how ineffectively I used the magic on Larent," he replied to her, his voice strained with emotion. "I thought you were behind Wrenn's murder. I believed you were a liar and a murderer, Collette. I was angry and I wanted revenge."

"Your revenge cost me everything!" she screamed, her words echoing off the stone walls, her eyes shining with enraged tears. "My home. My family." She took a shuddering breath, trying to regain composure. "The people who have died and suffered from your revenge do not heal because you are sorry."

"I didn't want anyone to die," Zephraim replied. "Even as king, I didn't have the sort of power to prevent those deaths."

"Oh? Was being king hard, Zeph? Did you not enjoy it?" Collette mocked. She approached him, her strides deliberate and quick, until they were face-to-face, separated by inches. She was a tall woman, and though her height did not match Zephraim's, there was no questioning how intimidating she was just now. "You're lucky you survived the absolute chaos you single-handedly brought down on all of Coralia." She pointed at him, a threatening finger in his face. "I fought, every single second, to keep things intact. And look what took you less than a year to accomplish."

"I know," Zephraim replied. He did not argue against her accusation, and he could only wish she were wrong. He had caused so much pain and turmoil. "Once I came to my senses, I did what I could to fix things. I know I can't repair everything, but I want to try."

Collette glared at him. "Riken killed my husband," she said flatly, a dangerous tone from her. "How do you possibly plan on repairing that?"

Zephraim's brows narrowed. "Husband?" he asked, confused. Then it sank in. "Larent was actually your husband?"

She looked down at that, lips pressed tightly as though she was restraining a scream. "Not when you used blood magic on him, but he was my husband," she confirmed quietly.

"Riken killed Larent," Zephraim repeated in abject disbelief. He had no doubt Riken would be cruel enough to kill someone like Larent, especially when he had such a close connection to Collette. "How?"

"An arrow covered in Veinfire. Riken had him shot, and it went through one of his lungs." Her voice went hollow as she explained, as though she couldn't quite face what had happened.

Zephraim's insides turned cold. Of all the people who deserved to get hurt in the conflict, Larent wasn't one of them. He regretted the blood magic all the more. "I am sorry," he repeated, knowing how lame the apology was in light of what he'd done to Larent in the past. "He didn't deserve Veinfire."

"Don't talk about Larent to me," Collette said quickly. "After what you did to him, you don't deserve to discuss him." She crossed her arms, diverting her glassy gaze away from him.

"Of course," he agreed. He could obey her request, such as it was. "Whatever you want."

"I can't have what I want," Collette mumbled. "Not right now, anyway." She closed her eyes and took a breath, then let her crossed arms drop. "I hope you're happy Barris is here protecting you. He's not popular with a lot of people right now, including his wife."

Zephraim shook his head and walked over to the window, creating more distance between them. The reminder of Barris's wife left him feeling strange in a way he didn't want to examine too closely. "I don't wish to cause trouble for him, but I also can't force him to do anything."

"You don't have to take advantage of him," Collette said.

"He's not taking advantage of me," Barris said from behind them. "I had to guilt him into leaving Quenall, even with the threat of death hanging over his head."

Lynessea stood next to Barris, a kind look in her eyes as she studied Zephraim.

Collette looked over her shoulder at Barris. "For your sake, I hope his contrition is real."

"It is," Barris said, his voice certain. "And I know Zephraim will do whatever he must to prove that to you."

Lynessea's eyes gleamed.

"Zephraim isn't my problem," Collette said simply before looking back at the man she had called brother for so many

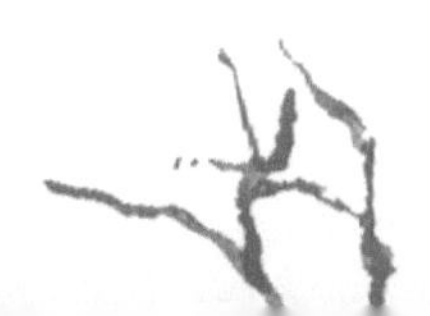

years. "I am sorry Rhoslyn used you in all of this. Truly. But what you've done to Coralia, what happened to Larent… I don't have it in me to forgive you." She didn't wait for a response and instead left the library.

Barris and Lynessea watched Collette go, both with considering yet sad looks on their faces, before they turned to Zephraim. Before Barris could do anything, Lynessea held out a hand to Zephraim. "Would you like to get a drink?" Her smile was warm, kind, and inviting.

Zephraim actually didn't feel up to drinks. Sadness and guilt permeated every pore at seeing how much Collette suffered, but he knew, at least for now, he could not fix things with Collette. So he nodded and accepted Lynessea's hand.

Chapter Fifteen

Jayden walked down one of the many hallways that spanned the length of Lord Barris's estate. Despite Barris's more atypical appearance—at least for humans—of gold piercings and intricate tattoos against tanned skin and dark brown hair, Jayden found the estate rather traditional. The marble, granite, plush rugs and hangings, and bold, rich color, while beautiful, did little to distinguish itself from other estates he'd visited in Coralia. The Nereid had to assume the furnishings had been reflections of Barris's father rather than his own.

As he took in more details, he realized little touches had been sprinkled throughout which were more representative of both Barris and Lynessea. Every vase he'd come across held flowers that Lynessea would find favorable. The walls were painted in light colors, both complementing the darker surroundings while also creating rooms that felt lighter. Jayden thought, with more time, Barris and Lynessea would create a home which would feel likable and welcoming instead of the status symbol it had once been.

He stood admiring a landscape painting in a large corridor, a pair of large double doors only a few feet down from him leading to the garden. Hurried steps caught his attention. Turning, Jayden saw Queen Collette marching toward him, a fierce, angry look sitting on her features.

"Did you know Zephraim is here?" she demanded of him.

Jayden was taken aback by the statement, enough that it took him a moment to process and answer her question. Even as he replied, he knew his golden, cat-like eyes were wide with shock. "No, I had no idea. I assume Barris is behind this?"

"Of course he is," Collette replied. "And I wouldn't be surprised if Lynessea knew or had some inkling."

Jayden reined in his shock and anger at the idea that the man who'd allowed a legal establishment of the Merscale trade to be restarted was sharing the same roof as himself, as well as his king. Even now, he still retained the title of Nereid Ambassador, and as long as he held it, he would take no action which could embarrass Aphros. "No, Lynessea would have warned us had Barris told her. While she is one of the best spies we could ask for, she would have given us warning, if only so no one killed her husband."

"He very well may be killed once I talk to Arian, Nawalya, and Whyldon."

Jayden thought Whyldon may not be as bloodthirsty as the other two, but he certainly wouldn't stop them from causing harm. Not after everything Collette had been through. "Do you think they'd kill Barris or Zephraim first?" Jayden tried to joke, only for it to fall very flat.

Collette's expression did not change. "You realize they are both guilty of treason? Someone much less kind than I would not continue to stand here entertaining their continued breathing."

Jayden considered that. He knew Zephraim had committed treason of the worst kind and should be punished for it, if not outright executed. Barris though… Jayden wasn't sure treason was the right word, but he also wasn't stupid enough to say that out loud. Admittedly, Zephraim being here did answer the question as to why Barris had fled Quenall so quickly. "No, I suppose someone like Rhoslyn would have had them beheaded within moments of seeing Zephraim. Since he's here, and we know he was arrested, we can assume that was more than likely her plan."

"I don't care what reason he had. He brought Zephraim with him, and he was obligated to hold him as prisoner until I could decide what I wanted to do with him, at minimum. You think he isn't going to stand against me over that? Or that Lynessea will not defend her husband?"

"Honestly, I don't know," Jayden answered. "I have no idea what caused Barris to even extend a hand of friendship to Zephraim. In all honesty, I would have thought he would be one of the first to spit on him, considering Zephraim put his wife, his family, and his adopted people in serious danger."

"Barris has put himself in quite a perilous position," Collette allowed. "He and his wife are Coralian with ties to the Nereid kingdom. I don't doubt Aphros needs to be told about what Barris has done."

"Oh, he very much does," Jayden agreed.

"You might as well go tell him that I will need to speak with him about what to do. They are my subjects, but his opinion holds some weight here."

"Of course. I'll go now." Jayden looked around to get his bearings. He would need to go left down the next hall to get to Aphros and Ceto. Another realization hit him. "Maybe make sure your grumpy elf and his friend don't run off to kill them before Aphros can arrive." There was a smile on his face and humor behind the words, but it was an honest concern.

"I will make sure the intent is for everyone to stay alive until Aphros and I consult about the most appropriate actions," Collette replied.

Jayden nodded. That was all he could ask for, and he split off from her to go find his king and best friend. He ignored the decor that had caught his attention the first time he explored these halls, his mind too lost in thought over the possible ramifications the revelations of Zephraim being in the estate could cause their groups. He didn't feel Barris warranted as severe of a punishment as Zephraim did.

He almost didn't realize he had reached Aphros's door because of his rambling thoughts. With a steadying breath, he knocked.

Ceto answered, looking initially surprised to see him, but she stepped back and motioned Jayden inside. "Just in time. Aphros and I were talking about meeting with King Alaoin and Queen Collette later today."

"We are going to need to do that sooner rather than later. I'm afraid I have news," Jayden replied, his tone more serious than it had been as of late.

"What's happened?" Aphros asked from his seat at the desk just inside.

Jayden stepped past Ceto, bowing his head in thanks as he entered the room before speaking. "Zephraim is here, and it's looking as if Barris left Quenall with him. Queen Collette is…" Jayden searched for the right word to describe how upset she'd been. "Livid."

"Ah," Aphros said, rising from his desk. "I think she would have a right to be livid if Zephraim is here. I would think most would, but not more than her."

"She has every right to be angry. Especially after Zephraim threw her in prison and used blood magic to try and kill her. She is, however, including Barris in her call of treason."

"Is she wrong, though?" Ceto asked. "If Zephraim is here, Barris has an obligation to hold him and turn him over immediately upon her arrival. He didn't do that."

Jayden shrugged. "I don't know, but accusing him of treason feels wrong. We all know Barris is a resourceful man, but he's also a well-meaning idiot," he pointed out. "Though, I will make no complaints should she decide to punish him."

Ceto looked at Aphros. "What do you think? We can't make an argument over Barris at all and only marginally over Lynessea, who will argue over a charge against Barris."

"I think granting Barris an opportunity to explain himself would be warranted," Aphros said. He rubbed at his neck, something he did whenever he was thoughtful or worried.

Jayden understood. "I can't say I'm not interested in how all this came about. Barris and Zephraim becoming friends was not something I ever thought could happen."

"Yes, but there is a difference in foolishness and intent," Aphros said. "And that should hold some weight."

"Unless there's something more going on that we don't know about." Jayden gave a casual shrug, but his tone revealed his doubt.

"One would hope, but even so," Aphros replied.

"Should we find Queen Collette and talk about this or go find Barris?" Jayden asked.

"I think speaking with Queen Collette first is prudent," Aphros decided. "Barris is her subject, and the offense was rendered against her. In truth, if he was not married to Lynessea, I think we'd all have a much harsher view of him right now."

"On the other hand, he didn't get his markings for, or even because of, Lynessea. He earned those on his own," Jayden pointed out. "He was a strong supporter of us before they married. I think we would still have sympathy for him."

"Another fair point," Aphros said.

"Perhaps their shared markings might make Queen Collette more understanding?" Ceto said, the statement more resembling a question.

Jayden shook his head, unsure. "I wish I knew, but despite our shared time together, I can't even begin to guess at her thought process on this."

"Given her very recent loss, I think even those who know her best would have a hard time guessing at what she wants to do," Aphros said. "Ceto, will you please visit her and request a meeting? She likes you. She might be willing to listen."

"Certainly," Ceto quickly agreed. She hurried out, leaving Jayden and Aphros alone.

"Would you like me to find Barris so you can question him prior to the meeting?" Jayden asked.

Aphros shook his head, the waves of salt and pepper hair swaying. "No. You might warn him, however."

Chapter Sixteen

Finding the others after leaving Jayden proved difficult, although part of Collette supposed it was for the best. She was too upset to make choices right now. Too angry. Too many conflicting, swirling, terrible emotions threatened to bubble over at any second. Larent was dead, and Zephraim was here, and everyone expected her to solve the world's problems on top of keeping herself moving forward. It was a lot, and it suddenly felt all too much.

When Whyldon appeared in the random corridor she resided in, she half suspected someone must have summoned him. "Did you hear?" she asked, hating how emotional and … squeaky the question sounded.

"About Zephraim?" Whyldon asked, his voice as calm and soothing as ever. "I did. Ceto came to request a conference with you and Aphros."

"Of course," Collette replied. "They'll want to make sure to offer defense of Barris's actions, I'm sure."

"Perhaps so," Whyldon said. "But there is no rush to meet or make decisions. You should take the time you need." He motioned down the hallway toward a door at the back. "Come.

We'll retire to my quarters for a bit, have something to drink, and talk it over."

Collette nodded, not having it in her to argue against her father, and she allowed him to lead her down the corridor, taking in nothing other than the sounds of their boots against the stone floor.

Whyldon opened the door to his suite and motioned for her to go inside, and though Collette didn't spend much time looking around, the arrangement and colors reminded her of the bright, peaceful room she'd been allotted. She found a chair in the sitting area and sank down into it, finding it more plush than supportive. Perhaps intentionally so.

She watched as Whyldon went to a table against the wall and poured a drink from a crystal decanter. A whiskey of some sort, assuming each guest suite had been given the same drink. Collette's knees were bouncing by the time Whyldon handed her the drink, and only then did he sit across from her.

"So," he began. "Zephraim being here was something I know you didn't anticipate. You didn't plan to contend with him until reaching Quenall, I think."

Collette shook her head and rubbed a clammy hand along the knee of her trousers. The other hand was still occupied with the drink, though she found she didn't want it. "Yeah," she responded. "I didn't think he'd be here."

"No one would," Whyldon said. "Take a few sips," he directed.

She did, the usual burn of the alcohol registering dimly in the back of her mind. Again, she rubbed the palm of her hand against her trousers. "I don't understand why everything has to be so hard," she explained.

"I don't either," Whyldon replied, his blue eyes carefully settling on her. "You've gone through more than most people would be able to handle. It must feel like even more is being asked of you now."

She nodded, blinking as the room started to feel dimmer somehow.

"Take another drink," Whyldon encouraged, and she did, noting it affected her even less than before. "What do you want to do about Zephraim?"

She took a breath, finding it more difficult to fill her lungs than it should have been. "I…" she began, then paused to breathe again. "I don't… I don't know."

"That's understandable," Whyldon said. He gently took the drink from her hand and put it aside. "Regardless of what he did the night you were arrested—and what he did to Larent—at one point, you were both close. Righteous anger over his sins against you doesn't erase everything from before."

Collette shook her head. "It doesn't," she agreed. Breathing harder now, she felt like she was gasping. Her chest felt tight, and the bouncing in her legs had slowly transitioned into a full body tremor. Whyldon just sat there, talking as though she wasn't dying in front of him. Was he crazy? How did he not see?

Tears formed, but she didn't bother with them, as they were not as pressing. Her chest ached and her breathing felt near impossible.

"You're right," Whyldon said, drawing her gaze up at him. "And you can take the time to figure out what you want to do about him and about Barris. If anything. You know you will have the support, no matter what. I don't think even Zephraim would argue against the severest of retaliations if you decided that was necessary."

A startled laugh left Collette's mouth. "No," she said, shaking her head. "Undergoing a punishment would require him to do something."

"It would," Whyldon agreed, the corners of his lips turning up. "And punishment would require more of him than drinking wine and lounging in whatever chair is closest by."

Collette gave another huff of laughter as her chest seemed to relax and her breathing slowly grew steadier. Whyldon made for a good distraction, enough so she'd avoided the worst of what promised to be overwhelming anxiety. "He wasn't that bad."

"No," Whyldon agreed. "But he had his moments." Silently, he handed the glass back over, and she thanked him before taking a sizable sip.

"He did," Collette agreed. She cradled the glass between her hands, letting the calm flood over her. She didn't yet feel normal, but she did feel like she'd been pulled back from the ledge at the last moment. "I've never felt like that before," she said after a few beats of silence.

Whyldon nodded. "I've seen many suffer from anxiety and panic after battle. If you had nothing else to worry about, this would have happened at some point. It may happen again. I can try to intervene when I see it if you would like."

"That's probably for the best," Collette replied. She brushed away a few of the fallen tears and sighed. "I think people already suspect I'm losing it."

"Some might, those who don't know you. But I suspect the important people on this quest understand your motivations and trust your judgment. I would not worry about the rest." He shrugged. "You do what you feel is right for you. That's going to Quenall."

"And what about Zephraim and Barris?"

"You've always thought Barris was an idiot, and I am inclined to agree. I think he acted for reasons that have nothing to do with his loyalty to you."

"What reason could he possibly have?" Collette asked.

"I cannot say," Whyldon replied. "But he was in the palace more recently than anyone else here, and his reasoning might be just. I think it wise to speak with him at the very least before making any decisions. His reasoning is a separate issue from what Zephraim did, and even there, you have options." He shrugged again. "Zephraim aside, Barris has done us a kindness."

"How so?" she asked.

"Sara is here. Not only is she out of the prison in Quenall, but she is in a place where she can remain safe and well cared for. I was speaking with her before Ceto showed up. She is eager to see you."

Collette nodded and finished her drink, feeling some excitement about seeing her aunt. "I suppose I should speak with Aphros, as requested, before saying anything to Zephraim. Once that is done, I'll see Sara."

"Probably a wise move," Whyldon agreed.

"Okay," she said, then she hoisted herself out of the seat. Her hands remained a little shaky, but she could walk. "Come with me, then?" she asked.

"Of course," Whyldon agreed, and he rose to join her.

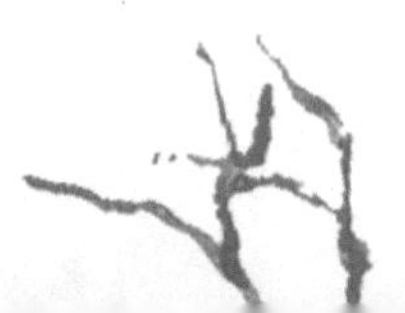

Chapter Seventeen

Barris closed his eyes and took a deep breath to center himself. Since Collette had confronted Zephraim, Barris knew his life was about to get interesting. When Jayden showed up while he, Zephraim, and Lynessea had been having a drink, his suspicions were confirmed. He put on a smile, hoping to comfort Zephraim, who'd allowed himself to be consumed with guilt and moroseness. While he'd been quiet and thoughtful, Lynessea tried to keep any kind of conversation going by sheer will alone.

Barris had spent the time between Collette leaving and Jayden arriving having trouble quieting his mind from the whirlwind of thoughts that had taken over. No, he hadn't told Collette the moment she'd arrived that Zephraim was there. He hadn't even thought to. He had planned to tell her once he belatedly realized he needed to. He'd just planned to do it after dinner when he hoped they could sit and talk over why Zephraim was there.

Now he was being summoned before Collette, Aphros, and who knew who else to explain his decisions. Decisions he still believed in. Taking another breath, he thought about his goddess Galene and her teachings. Teachings about second chances, about regret, guilt, and forgiveness. His shoulders relaxed as his mind slowed down. He understood what he did wrong, but he believed that helping Zephraim, befriending Zephraim, was the right choice.

Now he just had to convince everyone else. After all, he'd promised to keep the other man safe, and so he would. As best he could.

Opening his eyes, Barris raised a hand and knocked on the door.

"Enter," said a female voice unfamiliar to Barris.

Plastering a smile on his face, Barris entered the room, wondering who was inside.

Queen Collette, King Aphros, and King Alaoin sat in luxurious armchairs surrounding the hearth to the left of the door. With them stood their closest companions. Ceto and Jayden for Aphros, Whyldon and Arian for Collette, and a pair Barris recognized by sight and not name with Alaoin.

Barris fought to keep the smile on his face and keep it genuine. He had been expecting Aphros and Collette. He'd also assumed Jayden would be there, and Whyldon, but the rest? No. This was not the audience he had anticipated, and it made him all the more nervous.

Stopping in the middle of the room where he could see everyone, Barris bowed to the three monarchs and then waited. He knew if he started talking, he might just start to ramble. Rambling seemed easier than looking at the stern-faced Whyldon or the blond elf who looked ready to lunge at him any minute.

"Thank you for joining us," the woman spoke. One of King Alaoin's party, the woman looked in her early forties, and she had ample caramel hair. "I'm Duchesse Vassetre, Sabine of Fythias. Their majesties felt it prudent for a neutral person to

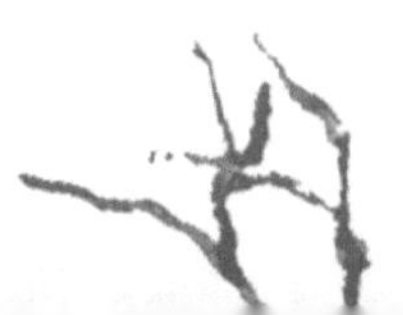

speak with you about how you came to have Zephraim Villot in your home.”

“Of course. It’s nice to meet you,” Barris said honestly, and he felt himself relax, finding something about her manner soothing.

“Thank you,” Duchesse Sabine replied. She motioned to the tall elf beside her. Of course, tall felt an inaccurate adjective given his stature. “This is my husband, Faron. He, too, will have questions, I’m certain.”

The very, very large elf who practically dwarfed Arian made a noise of assent that sounded more like a threatening grunt and undid all the work Barris had done to help himself relax. “I’m open to any questions,” he said.

“I’m glad to hear it,” Sabine replied. “Let us start with the basics. How did Zephraim find himself in your home?”

Barris reminded himself to stick to facts only. Answer the questions being asked and try not to say anything unimportant. He didn’t need to deflect here. “By invitation, though I had to twist his arm to accept.”

Sabine gave no indication that she saw Collette roll her eyes in exasperation. She remained poised and focused. “What caused you to issue the invitation?”

Barris bit down the need to apologize to Collette as he answered Sabine’s question, trying to go into as much detail as possible without rambling or overexplaining. “Zephraim was arrested and put under guard in his quarters. I was uncertain of what Rhoslyn’s plans were for him, but I thought it a bad idea to wait and find out. She’s not the most rational or reasonable person. Then add in Cadan, who considered Zephraim a traitor after Sara Whyldon escaped from the prison there.”

He paused as he saw Collette and Whyldon exchange looks, though Barris saw no surprise there. “She’s here, too, but it looks like you may have seen her already.” He cast his gaze away when Collette glared at him, but he continued. "With Riken serving as an ever looming threat, and his obvious connection with Rhoslyn, I just didn't like Zephraim's chances of living much longer."

"Given what we know he is guilty of, why did you not leave him in Quenall to face the consequences of his actions?" Sabine asked.

Barris knew this question was coming and looked away for a moment to gather his thoughts. "Because he showed regret for his actions prior to being accused of treason. Because he became a friend to myself and Diana Hawke. Because he was willing to pardon Queen Collette had Rhoslyn not gotten in the way of it. Because we would not have been able to save Sara Whyldon without him. At least not without losing people." Barris looked over to Aphros and those with him. "Because Galene says that if someone shows genuine remorse and sorrow for their action, we should give them a second chance."

"So he showed contrition for his actions when it might have been to his detriment to do so, and certainly before the others had turned on him?" Sabine summarized.

"Does that matter?" Collette interjected. "Zephraim had no cause to arrest me and nothing to pardon me for, and it seems as though every other thing you named, Barris, resulted from his stupid decisions."

Barris felt the anger in her words, though she did not shout or chastise as he had expected of her. Indeed, she seemed reasonably calm. He also noted that Arian, who was standing behind where Collette sat, had placed a hand on her shoulder in a comforting gesture.

"He had no reason for any of the things he did to you, and he has admitted as much," Barris replied. "Every decision he made was brought on by a multitude of emotions, but that doesn't make what he did to you right. In any way."

"Then why did you bring him here, and what exactly are you hoping I do with the two of you?" Collette demanded. "Because I am fairly certain no one here would fault me for having him executed for treason. Real treason which has cost untold lives."

"I didn't know you were coming here, but I do believe he is remorseful and deserves a second chance to live. Since we started talking, and more so since leaving Quenall, I have seen a very different man. One I believe deserves a chance to live his life. Do what you wish to me, but him, I promised protection in my home. So, I will take whatever punishment you wish to inflict." He ignored Jayden's harsh intake of breath.

Aphros, thankfully, chose to cut in on the heavy silence. "Queen Collette has every right to charge and punish Zephraim for his crimes, which are numerous and deadly, no matter his remorse now. She will have my support should she make that decision."

"And mine," King Alaoin spoke up. Despite his golden curls and overtly handsome face, the youngest monarch's words conjured something darker in his expression. "Every person in here has suffered at the hands of tyrants like Rhoslyn and Riken and people like Zephraim who make selfish, spiteful choices enable the King Sargaruses and Queen Rhoslyns in their tyranny. And you stand before your queen and openly deny her right to deal with her brother while knowing of the hundreds and thousands of people's blood staining his hands?"

Barris closed his eyes. "No. I know it sounds as if I would, but no. I would ask for mercy, but I understand should she choose otherwise. I understand what he has done hurt everyone in this room, but Queen Collette especially." Barris rubbed the bridge of his nose and wondered how he could fix this. Collette had every right to her anger, her pain, and her sorrow, and while he had promised to protect Zephraim, he realized he could not protect him from her decision.

"Barris, you've made your stance quite clear," Collette said, rising from her seat. "You and Zephraim may stay here and enjoy one another's company. I will issue neither punishment nor so much as a chastisement for the two of you. I also know I cannot rely on you for support. So, I'm going to seek alternative lodging for the duration of my time here and be on my way from this village once my people are ready to move on."

"You have my support. You've always had my support, and I am sorry if my current actions make you feel as if you don't. You are welcome to stay here for as long as you wish. I will ensure you see neither myself nor Zephraim for the remainder of your time here." Barris hated that Collette felt this way, but he did understand.

"If I may," Aphros said, looking to Collette. "I know we all heard what very much sounded like Barris promising to intervene should you choose to address Zephraim's crimes, but I do not believe it was his intent. Barris is one of the reasons I agreed for Jayden to visit Coralia when you requested to open talks between our people. I cannot wholly believe his loyalties would have changed so drastically since."

"They haven't, and I realized I've misspoke here more than once. My loyalty is to you," Barris said, latching on to the help Aphros was so obviously giving him. "Goddess, if it wasn't for you, I don't know where I would be in my life. Queen Collette, you are the reason I reached out to the Nereid, the reason I worked so hard to protect them and work with them."

Barris looked away for a moment, hoping honesty would aid him. "When we were much younger, you told me something that changed my entire life. Without your guidance, my father would still be in charge here. Or my brother. The Nereid wouldn't have a safe haven here, nor anyone else. My loyalty is to you, and I will do anything you ask to make up for my mistakes."

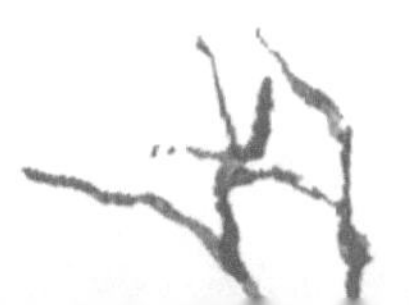

He liked Zephraim. He felt terrible for Zephraim, and he wished the other nothing but happiness. Hopefully here on Pontus Bay with him and Lynessea. But he had more than made a mistake in trying to force others, especially those Zephraim had hurt, to try and see what he had. He just wasn't sure he could fix any of it now.

"Thank you for the clarification, Barris," Aphros said. "If Queen Collette wishes to deliberate further on what to do about Zephraim, I think the prudent thing would be to keep him away from any official discussions." He kept his gold eyes focused on Collette. "Would that be acceptable?"

"Zephraim should be kept away from official business," Collette agreed. She had not resumed her seat, nor had she made any indication her announced plans had changed, but she was discussing how to proceed, which gave Barris hope.

"I will not discuss any official business with Zephraim, and unless I am needed, I will keep myself away if you so desire, so there can be no doubt that he is learning anything of use," Barris offered. "Pontus Bay's guards and what soldiers we have are yours to do with as you will in the coming battles."

He watched as Collette exchanged unreadable looks with Captain Whyldon, but he didn't know what the exchange meant. She did sit back down, though Whyldon leaned over to whisper something imperceptible to Arian. He wondered what had been said but knew it wouldn't be shared with him. So instead, Barris let his eyes wander to the others.

Again, Sabine spoke. "Thank you for speaking with us, Lord Barris. I believe the monarchs are satisfied for now."

Barris bowed deeply to each monarch. "Thank you for your time," he said before making a quick exit to go and find Lynessea … and maybe get very, very drunk.

Chapter Eighteen

Although he knew they no longer relied on less than a dozen people, Whyldon still felt it best to call their party together after the confrontation with Barris. He called the group into the sitting area of his suite, and Sara was amongst the first to arrive. She smiled upon seeing Collette and went to give her a hug. Whyldon was struck by the similarities between his sister and daughter, so much so he'd have believed them mother and daughter. Other than age differences, the only distinguishing feature between them was Sara's blue eyes, a common Whyldon family trait, and the deep chocolate color of Collette's, which she'd inherited from her mother.

"My dear," Sara said as she put some space between herself and Collette, though she did not relinquish her loose hold. "It's so good to see you," she said. She didn't mention Larent, which was probably for the best, given the meeting they'd just left.

"You as well," Collette said. "Honestly, everything I've heard…"

Sara waved it off. "You know these matters will never be pretty, and I survived without lingering scars. I am lucky in so many ways."

Whyldon left the two to catch up, hoping Sara's presence would further soothe Collette. He watched Arian and Thomas enter the room, their heads bowed close together as they spoke softly. Arian had been assigned to gather the others, and Whyldon expected to see the others trickle inside.

Nawalya quietly entered behind them, and while she looked as sharp and alert as always, it was apparent she hadn't been sleeping again. She seemed paler than usual, and he saw the shadows of sleeplessness under her eyes. There had been a time when he'd have gone to comfort her, and even though they were easing into a friendship, he thought it was not his place now.

Still, he saw no reason to remain aloof. "Are the others coming?" he asked.

Nawalya stopped walking and gave him a small smile. "Tolan and Rion weren't too far behind. I'd give them another minute at most," she replied.

"Did Arian fill you in on what happened?" he asked.

"Yes, but it was a very bare, brief explanation. That Zephraim is here at Barris's invitation, walking free as if he has done nothing wrong. Collette is upset about that, and he has not been given permission to stab either of them."

"Did he tell you Barris essentially told her she'd have to go through him to get to Zephraim?" Whyldon asked. "He only rephrased after Alaoin and Aphros intervened."

Nawalya was silent as she took that in. "No. That would explain why Thomas is insisting he cannot go out and stab Barris."

"I would have no objection if he did," Whyldon acknowledged. "And she has more patience than I would, listening to someone explain why their suffering did not matter because the guilty party was sorry."

Nawalya shook his head. "I'd always heard Barris was a hopeful, optimistic idiot, but this is… I have no words."

"I'm choosing to believe he didn't act maliciously because Aphros trusts him, but that does not mean he did not offend." Whyldon sighed and shook his head. He would never understand the level of privilege Barris must feel when making such decisions.

Nawalya sighed and shook her head. She started to reach out a hand as if to comfort Whyldon, only to drop it as Tolan and Rion entered the room.

"We were summoned?" Rion asked as the door behind him and Tolan was closed.

"Yes," Whyldon said. He looked at Collette, who folded her arms across her chest. She nodded for him to continue. "For those of you not in the know, Zephraim is on the grounds. Lord Barris brought him here after Zephraim was arrested for treason."

Moving across the room to stand near Collette, Tolan came to a dead stop. He turned slowly to face Whyldon and then Arian. "You just said we were needed urgently. Why isn't he dead yet?"

Arian's look was cold. "Because our queen hasn't given the order."

"I think we would make ourselves unpopular with the Nereid if I acted without giving it more consideration," Collette added by way of explanation. "They generally trust Barris, and as Barris brought him here, no doubt they would believe he had good reason."

"And what reason did he give?" Rion asked, his eyes wide in disbelief.

"He believes Zephraim is sorry," Whyldon supplied.

"There must be more to it than that," Nawalya guessed.

Tolan and Arian had a stare down, only for Tolan to finally sigh and find a place to sit near Collette.

Sara raised her hand. She'd taken up a place near the fireplace, though she remained standing next to Collette, the other hand resting on her shoulder. "I believe I can provide a more detailed explanation," she said.

"Please," Whyldon encouraged.

"As some of you may know, Zephraim is the one who put himself at risk to get me out of prison. I also traveled a great distance in his company. In that time, I came to the realization that, while he made a terrible decision to arrest my niece," she paused and squeezed Collette's shoulder, "a decision with dire consequences, he never intended for most of what followed to happen."

"And yet, he is still responsible for what has happened. Being regretful, not wanting something evil to befall others, matters not when you helped that evil along," Arian said.

"I don't disagree," Sara replied. "But there is a difference between acting maliciously and what he did. The way it is addressed would need to be different."

"And others outside of our group would consider his intent in addition to the outcome," Collette added.

"I'd say arresting you for a crime you did not commit to be pretty malicious, Joss," Rion said.

"Oh, it was," Collette replied. "I will never forget how he treated me when he came down to the dungeon to gloat. Still…"

"No one expects you to forgive him," Nawalya pointed out. "In fact, no one here would be surprised if you did have him jailed and executed."

"I'm not nearly benevolent enough to consider forgiving him. Too much has happened. I've been through too much, and so have countless others. That said, I don't think I can morally have him executed."

"If you need a moral reason, I can help you find one," Arian offered.

Tolan rolled his eyes before saying, "Whatever you want to do here. We support you."

Collette nodded, though Whyldon felt she would be indecisive for some time. He understood. Despite everything, even the blood magic and Larent's death, she'd once loved Zephraim. Perhaps she still did. "No decisions need to be made now," he added.

Murmurs of agreement sounded from around the room. "Are you going to have to see him? To deal and speak with him? Zephraim, I mean?" Tolan asked.

Collette shook her head. "No. In fact, I said he was not to be given any official information at all."

"We'll follow your lead with this one," Rion promised her. "But I think Sara's assessment is probably right. He never wanted to create the mess that resulted from his original actions."

Whyldon's eyes widened. Of everyone present, Rion had been the least compliant. However, he recognized it was not because he wanted to control her. Protecting Collette had always been a priority for him.

"You mentioned looking for another place to stay while in that meeting. Is that still the case?" Arian asked.

"Probably not, if only because of Aphros." Collette gave a short, bitter laugh. "I must admit, I enjoyed shaming him in front of everyone by questioning his hospitality."

"It's important to take joy in the little things," Nawalya said. "However, should you need a break from all this, from being here, I can think of a few safe places in the town we can retreat to for a few days. Your safety and your health are important to us." Her tone was serious but comforting.

"I'm not worried about myself," Collette said, though she offered Nawalya a brief smile. "I was more interested in publicly shaming Barris for his stupidity."

Nawalya nodded in understanding, and the two shared a small smile.

"Other than Barris being a moron, have we learned anything new about the state of Quenall, or is it too soon to know?" Tolan asked.

Collette sighed. "We can safely assume they've hit the worst-case scenario in Quenall. Rhoslyn will have unchecked power as long as Riken's devotion remains intact. I can't imagine anything that would change it."

"Unfortunately, Riken had already been dismissed from court when we arrived in Quenall, so we have little information on him. But if he is anything like his father, you are correct. He will remain faithful to Rhoslyn to a fault," Arian said with a grimace. "I regret dismissing Rhoslyn as quickly as I did when she and Wrenn arrived in Quenall. If anything, I thought him more of a threat."

Whyldon laughed this time. "Even without the alcohol, Wrenn Almeida never had much intelligence. He was, however, a man who believed himself to be as cunning, resourceful, and clever as Rhoslyn proved to be."

"He lacked the drive for power Rhoslyn has, though," Collette said. "He'd have been content to remain in Veitel, driving up debt, neglecting those in his care, and continuing on in his casual misogyny. That's why Sargarus never considered him a real match for me."

"That Sargarus even considered him as a match for you truly shows how insane that man was," Nawalya said with a shake of her head.

"Would you allow me to question Zephraim?" Arian asked. "I wish to see what information he may have to help us in our upcoming endeavor."

"How do you plan on questioning him, my dearly loved brother?" Collette asked.

"Not with my knives if that is what you are worried about," Arian returned. "Not unless absolutely needed."

"I'll say yes if you keep your knives to yourself," Collette replied. "If he's as changed as Sara reports, he'll not need the motivation. If not, we'd likely create tensions with the Nereid, and we can't afford that."

"If he hasn't changed, may I suggest Thomas be there too? It can't be Tolan or me, given our feelings toward the man. I don't think Thomas would allow for torture," Nawalya said, addressing the fletcher standing quietly next to Arian.

"I'm still firmly against using torture," Thomas said quietly. "And might I also suggest Sara be present? I believe Zephraim would trust her."

"I'm willing," Sara said.

"By all means," Collette agreed.

A rather disgruntled look crossed Arian's face before it was wiped clean. "I'm happy to have the assistance."

"Good," Collette said. "Whyldon, will you arrange for us to meet with Zephraim tomorrow for questioning? I think giving everyone time to cool down is in order. Oh, and Barris will not be permitted to be there, especially since Sara will be present."

"Of course," Whyldon said with a nod.

Chapter Nineteen

Evening settled in, and with it, calmer moods. Zephraim had agreed to a discussion the following day, and as much as Collette hated to admit it, she could feel herself softening to his plight with every passing hour. She doubted she and Zephraim could ever repair their relationship. Still, she was willing to enter a more peaceful understanding and opinion of him should Barris and Sara's observations be accurate.

Although she was not hungry, Collette agreed to meet with the others outside, where drinks and food were being passed around. Unsurprisingly, Ceto had pulled Collette over to share a table, and the bright, bubbly Nereid did everything she could to lift Collette's mood. "I think you'll enjoy the drinks," she shared as she pulled her long, ginger hair into a messy bun. Collette watched drops of water slowly fall from the locks, it seemed Ceto had returned to the sea at some point between the earlier confrontation with Barris and now.

The clatter of nearly a dozen liquor bottles hitting the table between Collette and Ceto drew both women's attention. They looked up at Lynessea, her colorful tresses tied back from her face. Hands now on her hips, the Nereid woman stood there with a large, friendly smile, almost bright enough to match her husband's. "I don't know about anyone else, but I feel the need to get very drunk." she asked.

"Sure!" Ceto answered brightly. Collette merely shrugged.

Lynessea grabbed a bottle and opened it using the small tool she pulled from her pocket, only to pause mid-movement. "I should ask, are you alright with me being here? I can understand if you don't wish to see me with everything Barris has done, not to mention any talk of him and Zephraim that may come up."

"Is there something else regarding Zephraim and Barris I should know about?" Collette asked, eyebrows raised.

"I am not completely sure. Barris and I haven't had much time to talk about Zephraim other than telling him to explain his thought processes to me better than he apparently did to you." She took a long drink from her bottle. "However, from how he talks, Barris has developed feelings for Zephraim."

"Of fucking course," Collette grumbled as Ceto gasped in surprised delight.

"Well, obviously," Ceto replied as she grabbed a bottle. "Why else would he have him here?"

"I don't think Barris knew until recently. Very recently," Lynessea said, concern and slight confusion crossing her face. "My husband is a wonderful man who's much more self-aware than most men I know. When it comes to emotions that lean more toward romantic or even sexual, he doesn't often recognize them. It took me almost bashing him over the head for him to realize and acknowledge his feelings for me. He thought I was just very friendly."

"Have you pointed out your observations to Barris?" Ceto asked with interest.

"Yes. He attempted to deflect at first before, after some back and forth, he admitted I was right. It was as adorable as it was pathetic," Lynessea told Ceto as she glanced at Collette from the corner of her eye.

Ceto's gaze followed Lynessea's, and she gave the tiniest of shrugs. "So," she prompted, "is Barris going to do anything with his feelings?"

"I don't think so, at least not without my permission. I have no idea how I feel about it at the moment. I always hoped he would find other partners, but for it to be Zephraim... I will need time. I did, however, recommend Barris go and speak with Zephraim about how relationships among Nereid work and see if he can broach his feelings as well." Lynessea took another long drink as she shrugged her shoulders. "I have no idea how that will go."

Ceto also drank and nudged Collette's bottle closer to her. Collette complied, picking up the bottle and taking a sip. "He must see something in Zephraim the rest of us have not," Ceto said.

"Zephraim has only ever craved one thing," Collette interjected. "And it appears you believe Barris provides for the craving."

Lynessea's attention shifted to Collette. "What is it he craves?"

Collette raised a brow. "To be loved. He's shit at recognizing it when he has it, though. That's one reason he chased Rhoslyn for so many years."

"I don't think that woman can love anyone but herself," Lynessea said with a shake of her head. "I thought you would say something else, but love makes sense." She held up her bottle in a mock toast. "Here's hoping he recognizes what Barris offers, then."

"I'm angry with him, but I'm not unfair. I know what he has always wanted," Collette said with a shrug.

Chapter Nineteen

Lynessea offered an understanding smile. "You should be angry with him, after everything he's done. The Goddess knows he threw away every good thing he possessed." Lynessea took another drink. "If you want him executed for treason, I would have it done by the hour."

"I have no plans to execute him," Collette replied. She took a sip from her bottle and placed it on the table. "There will be those who think I should, however."

"Well, you're the queen," Ceto replied. "Fuck what your detractors say."

"If anyone tries to tell you what to do or disrespects you, you just point us and your angry elf in their direction and we'll handle them for you," Lynessea said, agreeing with Ceto. "That includes my husband."

Collette nodded in response. She had no intention of serving in the way she once had, where she'd been left vulnerable and far too kind regarding insults and threats. Collette would be more fully insulated and supported when it came to who she surrounded herself with. She doubted those who wished her ill will or disrespect would be able to express it.

"When you take back your kingdom, if you need help with your guard, spy work, assassins, I am more than willing to help," Lynessea said earnestly. "Ceto would be willing to help too."

"Absolutely," Ceto confirmed. "Whatever you might need, we will be there."

"You're not alone, and I was serious about Zephraim should you change your mind."

"I know," Collette said. She took a breath, knowing she had a duty despite her misery. "And I appreciate it."

Lynessea opened her mouth to respond when a loud shout and the sound of soldiers running came from the other side of the garden wall.

"Stop it! Stop that thing!" yelled one of the shoulders.

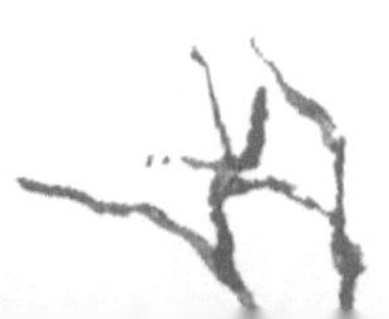

Lynessea and Ceto stood, pulling their weapons, as an enormous spotted cat jumped the tall garden wall. The cat was beautiful, golden with black spots covering its body, but the eyes were very intelligent, almost human.

Collette stood as well, though unlike the others, she was struck by familiarity and comfort rather than fear. She approached the giant cat. "Lower your weapons," she instructed the others present.

Lynessea looked at Collette confused but stowed her daggers away, Ceto doing the same with her own. "That is a huge cat! Is that a cat?" she exclaimed in a low voice.

The large cat just sat on its haunches and looked at Collette, its expression growing stern.

Collette's gaze remained steady on the cat's. The returned expression confirmed her suspicions, and her sadness over her loss rolled through her. "Hello, Nora," she greeted softly.

The cat disappeared, morphing into an older woman with tan skin and silver hair wearing worn travel leathers. "Oh, my dear girl," Nora Leassitor said, holding her arms open for Collette.

Collette hesitated only a moment before striding into Nora's arms.

"I've got you," Nora said as she wrapped her arms around Collette. "I'm here."

Chapter Twenty

Nora glared at the kitchen staff, hands on her hips, eyes narrowed dangerously. Although the people present hadn't been responsible beyond preparing food for those currently residing at Pontus Bay, she couldn't help but hold them partially responsible for the lack of care they'd given her daughter. Of course, it was entirely possible everyone had tried and failed to help Collette.

The young queen retained all of the intelligence, observation, and wit Nora had observed when she and Larent visited months before. She also looked pale and exhausted, and her clothes fit much more loosely than before. Larent had been able to sway her to eat and rest when needed. Nora had watched everything her grandson did to ensure Collette was well cared for. Larent was not here now, so she would have to do what she could.

She snapped, dismissing the kitchen workers without another word. When just she and Collette were left, Nora pointed to a chair near the middle counter. "Sit, please. I'm going to figure out this mess of a kitchen." Thankfully, Collette obeyed without protest.

Nora moved around the kitchen, throwing open cabinets and pulling out what she needed or thought looked interesting. Cleaning and preparing were good, busy work for her daughter, who genuinely needed help. The work lessened the giant hole in Nora's heart and stopped tears, which had intermittently flowed since she received the letter from Nawalya detailing Larent's death.

"Did you leave Pops behind?" Collette asked, quiet and subdued.

"Yes, someone had to watch the farm, and the goats only listen to him. He'll likely spend most of the time in bear form." Nora kept an eye on Collette. Nora immediately changed her plans for her meal, deciding on something easy to eat but simultaneously nutritious and hydrating.

Collette nodded. Her arms settled on the countertop before resting her chin on them.

"So, tell me what's been going on. Nawalya's letter was sparse on details." Looking around the kitchen, Nora realized the cooks she had thrown out had been working on dinner. Though undoubtedly delicious, she thought the preparation less than healthy, especially since most of the manor's residents would soon be fighting in a war. Nora put together a new plan and started on a more extensive meal while keeping an eye on what she was cooking for Collette. Her daughter came first, her daughter's army second.

Collette sat up with a sigh. "As you know, Larent was murdered in battle," she said, her words careful, almost hesitant, as though distancing herself from the words. "I tried to save him, but when we examined the arrow that hit him, we saw the Veinfire. I couldn't help him." She went quiet, taking several slow breaths before continuing. "Aphros put Larent's body in a stasis spell so we could bring him to Galel. So, he is here with us." She looked down. "We're waiting for the Coralian army to further retreat, and once they have, I am going to Quenall."

Nora had to pause at the news of her grandson's—no, son's, body in stasis and that she could see him. The news Collette was going to Quenall was another concern, the more pressing one. Stirring the pot with Collette's meal, she turned to look at her. "Why are we going to Quenall?" she asked.

"To get a spell to bring him back."

Nora once again paused, but only for a moment as she went over all the spells she had heard of that might be able to bring her boy back, and none of them were good. Instead of expressing her thoughts, she asked, "How does it work?"

"From what I remember of it, the spell is straightforward enough. A potion and a ritual that can be completed by one person."

Nora made an affirmative noise so Collette knew she was listening. "I assume they're in Sargarus's library or wherever he squirreled away the magic the rest of us were forbidden from using?"

Seeing water boiling over the fire, Nora finely diced up mushrooms and potatoes and added them to the pot. She planned on a thick stew and meat and vegetable hand pies, which would be tasty and filling.

"I found it in his library after he died," Collette confirmed. "And I hid it."

"Smart move," Nora said as she swirled a wooden spoon around the pot. The items would need a few more minutes. "Tell me about everything else. Who's with you on the mission? If you would, daughter."

"Whyldon doesn't call me that, you know," Collette said, the observation factual more than anything else. She detailed those who had agreed to go with her to retrieve the spell and those who would follow her to Quenall for other reasons. Each

person's motivation was revealed as she spoke. "Then again, I don't call him 'Father.'"

"I'm not Whyldon, and you are my daughter. If using the term bothers you, let me know, and I'll stop," Nora said. Leaving the stewpot alone, she began making the dough for the pies.

Collette shook her head. "It doesn't bother me," she replied. "Just an observation, really."

Nora nodded, grabbed a load of baked bread, and warmed it in the oven before stepping over to the door. Opening it, she spotted the head cook waiting nearby and waved her over. "I will be finished in twenty minutes. You may have the staff come in then to gather food and send it to the residents. If you try to return after, I will turn into a cat and eat the lot of you."

The woman gave her a wide-eyed look before nodding and stepping away.

Turning back to the kitchen, Nora made up a small bowl of mushroom, potato, and sausage soup for Collette. She returned to the oven, pulled out the bread, and carefully sliced it, setting it near Collette's bowl. Nora presented the meal to her. "Do you like tea with honey or lemon?"

"Honey," Collette said as she looked at the food.

Nora nodded and made a cup of tea for Collette. She soon set the cup and a jar of honey in front of the younger woman before making a bowl for herself. Nora sat and ate a few bites, noting that Collette mostly swirled the spoon around the bowl rather than eating. She motioned to the bowl in front of Collette. "The soup was his favorite when he was younger."

"Before or after he decided he would live as a sheepdog?" Collette asked. She lifted a spoonful to her lips and ate.

Nora laughed. "During, actually. He wanted to eat with the other dogs when we could talk him into being human. The soup was our compromise. He didn't have to use cutlery." She took another bite of her food, pleased to see Collette eating a little.

"You must have loved raising him," Collette replied. She put her spoon down and picked up a slice of her bread.

"I did. We had been considering having another when my good-for-nothing son contacted us and offered us a beautiful bundle of joy who couldn't keep one shape for more than an hour." Nora grinned. "Larent is amazing. Always has been."

"He is," Collette said, a brief smile forming before fading. She put the uneaten slice of bread back down. "He's like a bright light in the middle of every room he enters. Nothing dark can touch him."

"He always has been, and considering everything, I've always thought him to be a miracle from the Lady." Nora laughed. "It seemed like nothing could bring him down, even having to drink soup from a regular bowl instead of one of the food troughs."

Collette nodded again and picked up the bread slice she'd abandoned. She tore a piece off and dunked it into her soup before popping the bit into her mouth. "What do you believe happens when you die? Where, theoretically, would he be right now?"

Nora paused as she considered how best to respond. "Our belief isn't too far off from the elves. Shifters are wild things at heart, so we join the Lady in her evergreen forest, running and playing with all the shifters who passed before us, family and strangers alike. The only ones who do not go there are those who have committed atrocities considered unforgivable. There is no barren place when it comes to the Lady. She just erases your soul as if it never existed. But take heart, he is with those who love him until we bring him back to us."

"But he might not want to return if the afterlife you describe is real."

"Oh no, he would. Trust me. He would. You're his, and he is yours, and even there, he'd know he's missing a piece of his heart."

Collette looked down at her food, her brows knitting together in silent contemplation. Nora had no idea what she thought or believed, but the question presented some uncertainty in her decision. "I suppose he can tell us what he thinks when he's back."

"Ask questions whenever you have them. I'll tell you anything you want to know," Nora swore. She ignored the kitchen staff as they quickly scurried in, grabbed the food she'd made, and left.

"I'm not sure I have anything to ask, honestly," Collette replied. "I feel like I'm all over the place."

"And that's alright, dear," Nora replied with a soft smile. She was happy to see Collette was eating, at least a little. She would have to take over the kitchen and ensure Collette continued to eat.

"You should check in on Arian. He's not doing well," Collette said after another few spoonfuls of soup. "Nawalya isn't either, but she hides it. Even Tolan is upset."

"I will. They're family, too, but you're my daughter. You come first."

She gave a brief smile. "I am," she confirmed.

Nora smiled at her. "Speaking of Arian, I may need help wrangling him. He doesn't like to be taken care of. Did he get with the young scholar Nawalya mentioned?"

Collette nodded as she set down her spoon, a third of her meal eaten. "He did. Thomas takes good care of him despite Arian's protests."

"Good to hear," Nora said with a feral smirk. Finding things to be happy about numbed some of the pain.

"Funnily enough, even with all the self-neglect, he's been trying to take care of me. He's a good brother."

"You adopted him, then?" Nora asked. "Because if you did, I can say he's mine too." Nora laughed. "I'm glad he's been trying to take care of you. You'll need all your strength to pull it off," she said softly.

Collette nodded, her gaze fixed on her uneaten food. "I know what could happen."

"I'm not saying eat all of it. Eating and sleeping are the first things to go when times get hard. Just eat what you can. I'm going to take over the kitchen, so if you have any requests, let me know. I'll even just bake cakes and pies if you ask."

"I can't sleep," Collette said simply. "I've tried."

"With everything you've been through, I'm not surprised. I know some remedies. They won't keep you trapped in sleep, they'll just help you relax. I'd be happy to put something together if you're interested. Otherwise, we can play cards," Nora offered.

"I'm having nightmares when I can sleep," Collette explained.

"I can find something harder to prevent dreams if you want," Nora offered.

"I'll think about it," Collette said.

"That's all I ask," Nora said as she finished her bowl. Glancing around the kitchen, she wondered if she should get some things prepped for breakfast.

"I told Aphros and Alaoin I would meet with them after dinner. I'll see you after."

"Of course, my dear. I'll get things cleaned up, and I should probably find Lord Barris." Nora gave her a soft smile. "I'll be nearby if you need anything."

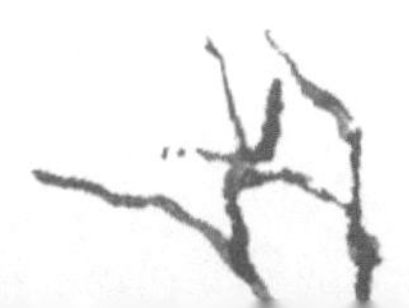

Chapter Twenty-One

Barris stood in the middle of his bedroom, his earlier conversation with Lynessea repeatedly playing in his head. He was rather upset with himself, not just for how he'd handled the discussion with Collette and the other monarchs but also for denying what he felt for Zephraim when Lynessea had asked. Hadn't he told himself that he would talk to Lynessea about what he'd begun to feel for Zephraim? Didn't he want her approval? Was he not interested in her opinion of Zephraim's interest?

Thankfully, his wife was wiser than he. While he didn't have her approval to pursue Zephraim, Lynessea did permit him to talk to Zephraim, both to let him know of the polyamorous nature of many Nereid relationships and of his feelings. Her permission to do that much had been better than expected, though he was uncertain about how to proceed. Barris recognized the worst possible outcome of speaking with Zephraim would be making an ass out of himself and having to apologize. Okay, no. The worst outcome was losing Zephraim's friendship completely, but he'd learned significant risk sometimes came with great reward.

Walking to the other end of his quarters, Barris grasped the handle leading out to his and Lynessea's private garden. Barris found himself pausing once again then laughing at himself. Of course Lynessea had known his feelings before he'd spoken them; he'd given Zephraim the only other suite with access to his favorite sanctuary, a place only a handful of people had ever seen. Those actions alone would have given it away immediately.

Pushing the door to the lush green garden, Barris couldn't help but stand there momentarily and watch Zephraim. The former king relaxed on one of the two lounge chairs, his normally red-gold curls seemingly more blond in the fading sunlight. He sat reading a book, looking relaxed despite the tension pulsing throughout the estate.

Barris strode over to him, stopping within arm's reach. "Enjoying your evening?"

Zephraim looked up from his book. "As much as possible, given I might be ordered for execution at any moment. You look well for someone who's undergone two sessions with my justifiably angry sister."

"It wasn't that bad, though I did not do well explaining my point of view of our current situation. I will likely need to grovel at Collette's feet for how I handled things and find a way to show my gratitude to King Aphros for coming to my rescue." Barris looked down, his face thoughtful as he considered the best way to go about both of those things. If Collette would even see him.

"Collette has been forgiving in the past, but I cannot guess how she will react now. She's been through too much. Lost too much." Zephraim sighed, closed his book, and put it aside.

"She's upset, and rightfully so. At the moment, though, she mainly wishes not to see you, and you are not to be informed of any plans being made," Barris explained. "She has not asked

that you be imprisoned or anything like that." Barris knew that this was the best outcome. She could have asked for Zephraim to be killed, and she would have been right to ask, but Barris was so glad she hadn't.

"Whyldon visited me earlier. She wants to question me come morning. I imagine it's going to be less than pleasant." Zephraim didn't shrug, but his easy acceptance of the decree left him seemingly resigned.

"Are you worried about torture? I can say with complete certainty that Collette wouldn't allow it." Even as he said it, Barris found a small ball of doubt in his mind. After everything Collette had been through, if Zephraim offered any resistance to questioning, it was possible Collette could consider it.

"Not really, but I imagine it will be unpleasant all the same."

Barris nodded. He wanted to make a joke to try and lighten the tension that had taken over the other man, but he knew better. "I think it will be okay. They just need more information for whatever they are planning, and you would know a lot more than I."

Zephraim gave him a slight smile. "Your ability to remain positive is an asset."

"It's a gift. Or a curse. Depends on who you ask." Barris moved to sit next to Zephraim as he contemplated how to broach the subject of his feelings and where he hoped things would eventually lead. It just didn't seem like the right time, though. Not with everything else going on.

Still, as he looked at Zephraim, his light gray eyes, his red-gold curls, and the silent acceptance of the hatred and anger directed toward him, Barris wished to do something, anything, to bring him comfort. Barris found himself reaching out and taking Zephraim's hands in his own. "It's going to be okay," he said, leaning forward.

He watched as Zephraim's gaze slid from his face and down to their hands, wishing he could read the thoughts running through Zephraim's mind. Was he confused? Disgusted? Or did the fact that Zephraim didn't pull away from him suggest something else? Something more positive?

Barris tilted his head to the side and studied Zephraim before saying, "Did you know Nereid have multiple partners? Single pairings are rare." And that hadn't been what he wanted to say at all. He either needed more tea or more sleep.

Zephraim slowly shook his head, eyebrows raised in confusion. "I did not."

Barris nodded. "The Nereid celebrate love in all forms and believe that if you feel something for another, as long as other partners agree, then having additional partners is okay. Lynessea has had a few partners over the years, one of whom comes and goes occasionally."

Zephraim blinked a couple of times before speaking. "Why are you telling me this?"

Barris let out a harsh breath and struggled to meet Zephraim's eyes. "Because I have developed feelings for you," he admitted, bracing himself for Zephraim's reaction.

"Oh," Zephraim said, the word taking on a surprised, higher pitch than his usual tone. "I didn't..." The corners of his lips twitched upward before falling. "I somehow doubt Lynessea would ever approve of me."

Barris's grip on Zephraim's hands tightened in an attempt to be reassuring. "She's the one who told me to come see you and to make sure you understand how our relationship works. Though, I know I would have come to see you either way. She asked for time, and I don't blame her. You're the first person I've ever been interested in outside of her. She doesn't disapprove, but she would like to get to know you better." He smiled at the possibility, then realized he needed to clarify. "Should you decide you'd like to pursue something, you don't have to have a romantic connection with her. I don't really involve myself with her other partners, though we are friends."

Zephraim nodded, and they sat silently for a few minutes. "I have never been involved with anyone who has another partner before," he explained. "I'm not even positive I could be."

Barris understood Zephraim's answer, and while it wasn't a no, he still found himself slightly disheartened. He didn't show it, though. Instead, he considered the answer and remembered how unsure he'd been at first with Lynessea, and he'd known for years how relationships between the Nereid worked. "If you can't, that's okay. But if you want to try, I'm more than willing to help you navigate this."

"Can I think about it?" Zephraim asked.

"Of course," Barris said, his tone reassuring. "Take as much time as you need." He gave Zephraim a soft smile. "Have dinner with us tonight?" Lynessea had joined the others outside for an evening meal, but she would probably agree to dine with him and Zephraim if asked.

"Okay," Zephraim replied, the answer coming much quicker than his prior decision had. He even smiled again, a true, lingering one this time.

Barris's smile grew at the agreement, and he released Zephraim's hands, less anxious now that maybe this could work out. "So, what were you reading?"

"Just a collection of essays on the histories of various world religions," Zephraim replied, gesturing toward the book.

"Sounds interesting," Barris replied as he settled in more. "Finding anything that catches your interest?"

"The whole thing, really. So many different interpretations of nominally similar belief systems."

"I didn't know you had an interest," Barris said, enjoying how Zephraim lit up as he spoke. "We have many more books like that when you've finished that one."

"Then I will probably look at some of those next," Zephraim replied.

Barris nodded and smiled again. Even if the romance part didn't work out, he knew he'd made a good friend.

Chapter Twenty-Two

Walking down one of the many hallways of the Pontus Bay estates, Thomas by his side, Arian did everything he could to ignore the feeling of wrongness surrounding him. Before leaving their room, Thomas had convinced him that the best way to handle Zephraim's questioning was to avoid using phrases like "interrogation." Doing so would distance everyone, himself included, from the inherent violence in that form of questioning.

He'd left all his weapons back in their room except for the two daggers Thomas held for him. Arian understood Thomas's need to hold them. Arian's emotions—customarily kept under tight control—had not been as they should following Larent's death. The chances of Zephraim upsetting Arian enough that he simply slit his throat were much too high to risk. Still, it left Arian feeling off-balance and unprotected. Thomas must have noticed because he reached out to take Arian's hand.

"She doesn't want harm to come to him," Thomas said quietly. "If Collette was going to strike out against Zephraim, she would have done so by now."

"I am aware, but it is still disconcerting not to be armed," Arian responded, trying not to sound upset. "Thank you, though, for watching out for my well-being."

"Someone needs to, especially since you have spent all your energy looking out for hers. If Collette succeeds in her current quest, Larent will owe you."

Arian hadn't considered that. It hadn't even crossed his mind—that Larent would be grateful once brought back. "Do you think he will let me stab him for putting all of us through this? Somewhere non-vital, of course," he half joked.

"I'm relatively certain he will probably allow it for whatever happened prior," Thomas replied. He squeezed Arian's hand.

Arian smiled at Thomas, glad he had gone along with his jest. "I just want him to be back and okay," he said softly. He had planned to say more, but he spotted Whyldon ahead, waiting for them by the room where they had agreed to meet Zephraim. "Is he already inside?" Arian asked.

"He is," Whyldon confirmed. "As are Ceto, Éric, and Sara." He rested a hand on his belt, revealing that he was still armed even though Arian was not.

Feeling more relaxed, Arian nodded and motioned for Whyldon to enter. "Let's go talk to him, then."

Upon entering the room, Arian found Zephraim seated at a table, with Sara occupying the seat to his right. Éric, the son of Duchesse Sabine and Faron, was seated a little farther down the table, parchment in front of him and quill in hand. The man looked slightly uncomfortable being there, and Arian wondered what he thought was going to happen.

Food and wine were placed along the table as though this were a meeting rather than an interrogation. Arian frowned as he took in the scene, finding the meeting room overly cheery for questioning, but he somehow thought Barris wouldn't have anywhere more suitable. He spared a thought to see if they

might have a dungeon. Lynessea seemed like the practical sort who would have one, and he wondered if it was too late to move the meeting, before banishing the thought.

Arian let Thomas take a seat before standing behind the seat next to him. Sitting just didn't feel right at the moment. He assumed Ceto felt the same, as she leaned against the wall farthest from Zephraim, her arms loosely crossed.

"How have things been going?" Arian asked Sara.

"Well enough," she replied. "Barris's people are welcoming and accommodating." She smiled at her brother when he came to stand by her chair.

Zephraim, meanwhile, kept his gaze locked on his clasped hands, which sat on the table before him.

Arian nodded in acknowledgment of Sara's words before his eyes moved to study Zephraim. He had expected anger and disgust at the sight of the other man, but now, taking him in, all Arian felt was pity. He finally took a seat. "No one here is going to hurt you. We just want to know if there is anything you can tell us that may help Collette with her endeavors to take back Quenall," Arian found himself saying, his voice gruff, but there was a promise in it.

Zephraim looked up, meeting Arian's gaze in what the elf assumed was assessment. Finally, Zephraim sat back in his chair. "I'm not sure what you will find important, but I will gladly share what I know."

Arian nodded and leaned against his chair, slightly raising the back legs off the ground. "Tell us about Rhoslyn and her mental state. She was dangerous before, but we can only assume the worst now with how much she's lost." Arian glanced over at Éric as the sound of quill scratching against paper reached his ears. It seemed he was going to document the entire meeting, and Arian didn't mind. Notes might prove useful.

"My assessment of Rhoslyn is that she will glom herself on to whoever she thinks is strong enough to keep her safe," Zephraim answered without considering it. "She tolerated Wrenn because it was necessary. She played at loving me because she thought my position would shield her from accusations of his death. Now she's glommed on to Riken because he has an army and followers willing to get their hands dirty."

"With Riken's loss to Collette in the forest at the labor camp, and now against the Nereid, do you believe she will cast him aside for someone else?" Arian asked. The only person he could think of who might benefit Rhoslyn was the new Azmarin regent. They'd heard a king hadn't been selected yet, but they hadn't managed to find out much about the person. Arian made a note to see what Zephraim knew about them next.

"It's possible," Zephraim said, hesitating more this time. He only spoke again once Sara placed a comforting hand on his forearm. "I do believe she loves Riken, but she isn't motivated by love."

Arian considered this information. Rhoslyn seemed to be a very self-motivated woman, and if she truly loved Riken, her affections could prevent her from discarding him, if not outright killing him, for his failure. Arian was not sure which option was best for them. He looked to Thomas to inquire about his thoughts on the matter.

"How did she respond to Riken's failure the night he apprehended Collette?" Thomas asked.

Éric interrupted. "This was the night she saved the people at the labor camp, correct?"

"Yes," Zephraim confirmed. "And she was rather severe." His fingers uncurled from one another, and he pressed his palms on the table. "She forced him to his knees, knowing one was shattered."

Arian despised the fact that he found himself impressed with Rhoslyn for doing that. "His devotion must also be strong if he did not fight against that order. Was there anything more to the punishment?" Another issue came to mind. "You were still king at the time. What changed to make her punish Riken and not you?"

"I was not the one to let her escape," Zephraim answered. "And I suppose she was still observing some faux regard for my position."

Arian wanted more details about what had made Rhoslyn decide to sideline Zephraim but felt it was less important than knowing more about Azmarin and its new regent. "We know the new Azmarin regent was in Quenall. Is there anything you can tell us about them?"

"He's not lovesick the way Riken is," Zephraim said with a huff of wry laughter. "But he's just as ruthless. Rhoslyn won't be able to sway him as she does Riken, which makes him more unstable."

"Is she aware of that?" Ceto asked, still positioned against the wall. She'd been so still and quiet that it had been easy for Arian to forget the presence of the Nereid.

"I think so," Zephraim replied. "But she keeps her thoughts to herself."

That concerned Arian. Not that Rhoslyn may be unable to attach herself to the new regent, but that the man was more ruthless. That could make him the most dangerous person in that group, especially since he was an unknown. It was a relief that Collette, Aphros, and Alaoin had already spoken about how to handle Azmarin when Quenall was dealt with. However, another war so soon after taking back Quenall was not something to look forward to. "Who else is in Quenall that we may need to be careful of?"

"Riken has a host of people he's brought to the palace from Wildrun," Zephraim said. "All of them are ruthless. One tried to assault Rhoslyn. The person he's most relying on now is a man known as Cadan."

Sara nodded, her brows furrowing. "He thinks a lot of himself," she cut in. "He'll act as viciously as possible, but he's practical."

"The man who assaulted Rhoslyn. What became of him?" Arian asked, though he thought he knew the answer.

"He's dead," Zephraim replied.

Arian nodded. "Was this before or after you let Riken loose to burn down an elven village and attack Collette?"

The scratching of Éric's quill ceased.

"Arian," Sara said, her voice stern.

Arian couldn't help the slight smirk that crossed his lips. "I am only establishing a timeline." Éric quickly began scribbling notes again.

"Do you really think I would approve of someone burning down a village?" Zephraim asked, sitting back in his seat.

"You approved restarting the Merscale trade," Whyldon said, calm and factual, as he usually came across.

"John!" Sara exclaimed. She'd swiveled in her seat to look at her brother in disbelief.

"No, he's right. I did that," Zephraim said, crossing his arms. "In Pontus Bay, overseen by Barris. I believe he was in the room during some of those discussions, and I agreed to the limitations he thought best."

"You also arrested Collette," Ceto accused.

"Arresting my sister is not the same thing as signing off on what Riken attempted."

Arian's face went expressionless. "No, you told those men they were right by arresting my sister, their hatred for Collette and the people she wanted to protect was just, and the money

lining their pockets was more important than our lives. You are too intelligent not to know that by allowing one noble to reopen the trade, others would assume they would eventually be given the same rights and start early. By opening the door to one, you opened the door to all. We will not discuss that you also allowed them to reopen camps." Arian's voice was flat. "You saw what you wanted to see, what she wanted you to see, until she was no longer pretending to be interested in it, and you cannot pretend otherwise."

Arian took a breath to get himself back under control. "Speaking of, when exactly did that happen?"

"You're too smart to wrap the whole thing up in a pretty bow like that," Zephraim replied cooly. "I'm aware of what I did and what came from it. I don't deny anything I am guilty of or what it led to. So I don't understand why you're talking to me as though I have tried to push away my responsibility, unless it feels good for you to do so."

"Nothing about anything we've experienced these past months feels good, Zephraim," Whyldon interjected. "But you know that. You know Collette is fragile, no matter how good she is at hiding it. You knew what turning on her would do to her."

Zephraim hung his head. "I did," he agreed.

"And yet, you still did it," Arian said, before snapping his mouth shut at Thomas's look.

Thomas turned his attention back to Zephraim, though he caught the eye of others in attendance. Éric, it seemed, disapproved of the way the questioning was going based on the deep frown he wore, though he voiced no concern.

"I believe we have sufficiently established culpability for what happened under Zephraim's watch," Thomas said.

Ceto nodded and moved from the wall to stand on Sara's other side. "I am willing to believe you allowed for the Merscale trade as you did because it would be reestablished anyway. You saw an opportunity to reduce harm," she said. "Someone who hates Mers and wished them harm would not be here."

Arian looked down at his hands, quiet for a minute. "If Larent were here and he felt you were being honest, he would not ask Collette to forgive you, but he would work toward a better understanding of this entire situation and eventual forgiveness on his end. Much like he has with Tolan." He sounded slightly bitter at the next part. "I do not think forgiveness is something I will ever grant you for what you have done to Collette. But Ceto is right."

"I'm not asking for forgiveness," Zephraim replied, shaking his head. "I don't deserve it from anyone, but I am asking to help right the wrongs I have caused. That's why I ultimately came here with Barris instead of accepting the fate I had sitting in Gadleigh Palace," Zephraim replied.

"From what I have heard, Barris had to convince you to leave with him," Arian retorted.

"He did."

"Hmmm." Arian glanced over at Ceto before looking back at Zephraim. "What did you think to accomplish by staying?" He was honestly curious.

"There were a couple of possibilities." Zephraim unfolded his arms and rested them on the table. "Some would not have accepted Rhoslyn and Riken's authority if I were still present. It might not have been enough to stop them, but it would delay their actions." He gave a shallow shrug. "Additionally, despite knowing remaining there would eventually lead to my execution, I cannot say the outcome would be unjust."

"Yes, it would," Sara said. She stood up, closed the distance between herself and Zephraim, and put an arm around his shoulders. "You made grievous errors, but your sincerity in trying to set things right tells me your intent was, mostly, not

selfish or hateful. There would be no justice in the truly wicked using their power to silence you."

Arian wasn't about to argue against the point. He may believe Zephraim deserved to be punished, but being executed at the hands of those two monsters wasn't something he deserved. "Is there anything else you can think of that could help Collette, no matter how small?"

Zephraim rubbed the back of his neck as he thought. "Many of the staff directly connected to Collette have fled the palace. Agnes was still there when I left, and she communicates with the Hawkes."

Arian looked to Whyldon. "Agnes was Collette's personal maid, correct? If so, one would assume Rhoslyn would have had her removed already."

"She was her nurse as a child, and Collette kept her on as a lady's maid," Whyldon said. "She has spent time with Collette nearly every day of her life. She's older, though, and quite loved, even among those who thoroughly disagreed with Collette. Rhoslyn may not know what to do with or about her."

"We will have to hope for her safety. As Rhoslyn starts to run out of options, she may start to truly lash out at those she believes would betray her," Arian said thoughtfully. His mind went to any elves who would have been too stubborn to leave the city and the humans who couldn't leave but had never believed in the atrocities Sargarus had committed. Everything was going to get worse for them if this plan failed.

"Have you gathered enough information from this meeting, Arian?" Sara asked, her arm still around Zephraim's shoulders.

Arian thought over everything they had learned and couldn't think of another question. Zephraim had proved compliant, willing to answer questions and accept the blame, which he had not expected. It left him feeling disconcerted. "I think so. However, should any other questions arise, we may need to meet again," he told the room before looking over to Ceto, Thomas, and Éric. "Do any of you have questions?"

Thomas shook his head. "I feel like Zephraim has been cooperative."

"He has," Ceto agreed. "I think we should plan to speak again soon. Queen Collette may want to be involved."

Arian bit back his automatic response. He knew Collette wasn't going to be around Zephraim ever again. He'd hurt her too badly, and since Larent had died, she wasn't up for finding the patience she'd need for Zephraim. Arian would stand by her side if she changed her mind for any reason, not in her way. "I will go find her and advise her of what we have learned," Arian said as he stood. He moved toward the door, stopping only when Éric spoke.

"I will make copies of what I wrote down so Queen Collette can read them over."

Arian gave him a nod of thanks before seeing himself out.

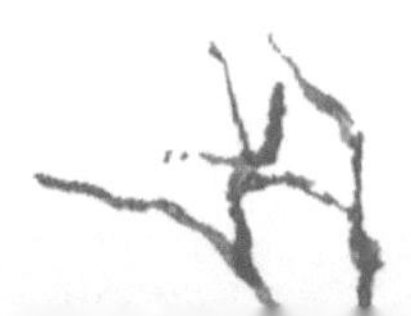

Chapter Twenty-Three

Dear Nana and Pops,

I wish I could say everything's going great here, that we found all those who stand against Queen Collette and have saved the day, but you know how these things go. We have an idea of who we need to be looking into, but nothing we can say for certain will make a difference. It's making Arian jumpy. Nawalya has decided to bring Whyldon, the head of Queen Collette's guard, into the fold. I'm unsure how that will work out, but I believe in the Lady.

Good news, though Arian wouldn't think so: I've gotten to see Collette again. I'm worried about her. She looks more tired and worn down each time our paths cross, but her smile remains warm. It's still the brightest thing in the room. I would ruin the lives of every noble in this kingdom if it kept her smile bright. She truly is amazing, and I pray to the Lady every night she will watch over Collette and keep her safe.

I must go. I've apparently done something to bother Arian. I'll write to you again soon.

Love,
Larent

While Arian and some of the others had spent the afternoon questioning Zephraim, Collette accompanied Nora to the wing where Larent's body was kept. He'd been given a small bedroom, and his body, still in stasis, remained colder and paler than the living but warmer and in possession of a more natural pallor than the dead.

Collette hadn't been able to stay long. Other than the period immediately following his death, she hadn't wanted to be near his body, not when he wasn't there. Not when he couldn't laugh and smile and ask her to tell him something.

Spirits, she missed that.

After returning to her suite, Collette had fallen onto the sofa by the fire where she'd left Larent's travel pack. The figure of the Lady lived in her pocket most of the time, but the letters … she kept those safely tucked away until she was by herself. She was still browsing one when a knock sounded at her door.

"Come in."

The door was gently pushed open, and Arian stepped in. He closed it just as gently behind him as he joined her. Collette noticed he looked grumpier than usual. This was confirmed when he gracelessly sat in the chair across from her and said, "Zephraim is a pain in the ass."

"He is," she agreed as she folded Larent's letter. "Why now, though?"

Arian reflected for several long seconds, and Collette allowed him time to collect his thoughts. "He was reasonable,

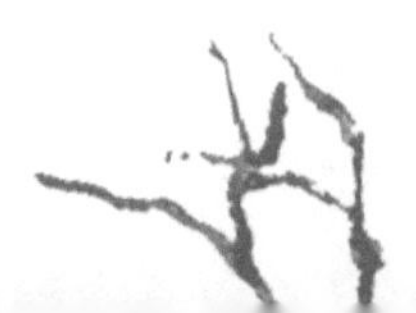

accepted the blame for what has been done, and refused to do anything that would allow me to remove him from this life."

"How dare he," Collette half-heartedly joked. "Did he at least provide good information?"

"He advised us on the state of those in Quenall, how each person is likely to react to the loss in the Nereid Kingdom, and how unstable Rhoslyn has grown. It appears as if she shut him out of ruling before he was arrested, so there might be things only she and Riken know," Arian answered sullenly.

Collette took that in but nodded as she accepted Zephraim had been of some use. "How did the others respond?"

"Sara is very, very sympathetic to him. Éric did not care for me taunting Zephraim. I could not get a good read on Whyldon and Ceto. Thomas refused to let me enter the room armed."

She nodded. "What would Larent have thought?"

"He would have felt pity for Zephraim," Arian answered. "He would never invalidate how Zephraim makes you feel or tell you to forgive him, but he would pity him and try to move past his own hurt feelings because Larent could be ridiculous like that."

Collette gave a brief laugh. "Larent enjoyed being ridiculous."

"He did," Arian agreed. "And he was kind, but not in the idiotic way Barris appears to be. Though, Barris appears to have only the best of intentions."

Collette rolled her eyes. "I'm sure he means well, but I was not wrong about Barris. Not when I was in Quenall and not now."

"I heard you always considered him an idiot. The Nereid seem to agree, except they seem to expect his way of thinking." Arian cast his eyes around the room before they landed on the wine carafe on the nearby table. "Would you like a drink?"

Collette almost said no. As depressed as she was, she recognized how easily she could turn to drink for solace. But she'd never been one to drown sorrows, at least not for long. "Sure," she agreed.

Arian rose and went to grab the carafe, along with two glasses, which he carried back to where they'd been sitting. They sat in comfortable silence while he poured each a glass.

Wine now in hand, Arian sat back in his chair once more. "I am interested in something King Aphros said during our meeting with Barris, though."

"And what is that?" Collette asked. No one had sided against her during that meeting, but she'd walked away from it feeling far less support because of how soft the response toward Zephraim had been.

"They contributed their willingness to meet with you to Barris. I would like to know what he said to them and what you did to cause him to push them the way he did. Not that I doubt your ability to talk someone around to your point of view. I just did not think you spent much, if any, time around Lord Barris if you could help it."

"Oh," Collette said. "I just assumed they couldn't trust me given my connection to Sargarus and Barris convinced them otherwise." Collette took a drink of her wine after grabbing the glass. "I've made no secret as to where I stand on the mistreatment of Mers and others from the beginning. And after whatever he said or did, the Nereid soon trusted me enough to send Jayden right before the events leading to my arrest."

"True, but it was implied you had done something. I may make inquiries. I find myself interested." Arian took a sip of his wine, the disgruntled look appearing back on his features. "Éric took notes on the meeting and said he would transcribe a copy for you. You will note that I did attempt to goad Zephraim into a fight."

"Naturally you did," Collette said. "I'm sad he didn't rise to your bait."

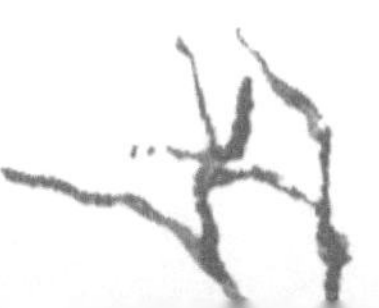

"As am I." Arian paused again and braced himself for what he was about to say. "Zephraim seems honest in his regrets. I cannot help but wonder though. If Rhoslyn had never turned her affections to Riken, would he still feel the same?"

Collette looked at her wine as she tried to, fairly, figure out what Zephraim would have done. She sighed, hating the answer she came to. "I think many of the worst atrocities we've seen wouldn't have happened. I also believe he would have willingly given the throne back at some point."

"Truly? Even with Rhoslyn fully behind him?" Arian asked, his brows knitted in confusion.

Collette nodded. "You have to have a level of ambition, of command, and a willingness to be disliked that he so thoroughly lacks. No matter how much support Rhoslyn gave him, no matter how much she'd try to guide his hand, he would not be up to the work in the long-term."

She put her wine glass aside. "Rhoslyn and Riken worked in tandem, it seems, to lead him into the atrocities we know about. But outside of the blood magic he used on Larent, I believe he wouldn't want to harm others. He's not naturally cruel."

Arian tipped his head back to stare at the ceiling, and Collette knew he was thinking over her words. "So, what you are saying is, if I had taken the time to find and kill Riken the same night I killed his father, we would not be in this situation?" It was said in a mostly joking but more wry tone. "What do you intend to do with Zephraim now?"

"I don't know," Collette replied. "I need to do something. I need to make it clear that his actions won't be tolerated, but … he is my brother. Others will expect some level of mercy."

"You could banish him from Quenall," Arian said after a moment's thought. "Make a decree that he will stay here, in Pontus Bay, and work with the Nereid to help improve the relations he has helped to damage."

"I plan to move the capital from Quenall when I get the throne back," Collette said, but she tilted her head as she let the idea swirl around her mind. "It's not a bad idea, though." Zephraim would be happy in Barris's home, no doubt, and he would have something useful to do.

"Truly?" Arian said with a raised eyebrow. "Where are you considering moving the capital to?"

"Somewhere in Galel, I think." The decision had come to her, not out of a selfish desire to be close to Barcomb Mill and the farm belonging to Larent's grandparents, but because Veitel and Wildrun had clearly needed more oversight. "It's more central, and it will give me the ability to keep watch on the different estates. My mistake from before was trusting reports."

Arian made a thoughtful noise. "You could move into Wildrun. Riken's family has cultivated a culture of bigotry and hatred within the town surrounding the estate. You living and ruling there would demoralize any supporters he and his ilk still have once you are queen again. It would also allow you to keep a better eye on Veitel, and you'd be closer to your supporters."

"I'd also be in the home of the man who murdered my husband."

"I did not consider that fact, and I should have. I apologize," Arian offered.

"Just don't be angry with me when I slowly kill Riken and we'll be fine." Arian had been right about playing with Riken in their encounters. Had she been more decisive and deliberate in killing him, Larent might still be there.

"I would hand you my dagger to use if I did not already know you had one of your own," was the easy, accepting reply.

Collette smiled. "I know. I'm going to make his last minutes horrific."

Arian's returning smile was all hard edges. "Good. He deserves no less. Just let me be there if possible."

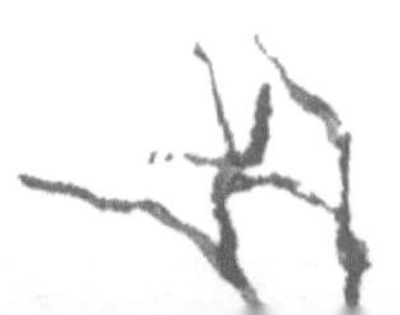

"Of course," Collette agreed. She could imagine few others by her side at such a moment.

Arian looked at the empty wine glass in his hand and then down at the carafe. "How upset will Thomas be if I decide to drink until I can sleep only this once?"

"I think he would understand," Collette decided. She was reminded of the evening after Tolan had abandoned her when Larent had made sure she got nice and drunk. He'd understood her need to step away, to have a moment of selfishness. She thought Thomas would feel the same. "With that in mind, drink up."

My Darling Alexander,

While I am glad you're safe at home tending to our animals, I do wish you were here. Your quiet, steady strength would be nice to lean upon as I try to take care of our daughter and the others. Collette is barely holding on. She has a plan to resurrect Larent, and only the promise of bringing our son back is keeping her moving. Even then, I watch her search for motivation to keep going. She barely eats or sleeps, and when she does, it's because I'm telling her about our Larent as he grew or she's taken a potion to keep her nightmares away.

Oh, I wish I could spirit her away from all this. Either to hide her on our farm or pack everything up and take her as far away as possible. But I won't take away her agency by doing so. No, I will just be here and be as supportive and encouraging as possible.

Arian is showing signs of the same stress and brokenness he was when his clan was murdered, but it's not as desperate as it was. He has found support in Thomas that he didn't have in Nawalya, and it keeps him going. I also think if he let himself wither away, Collette would never forgive him. They're good for each other, I think.

Nawalya is doing what she can to keep busy and help with the plans while also dancing around Collette's father. It's rather sad to watch, but I've decided not to interfere.

Chapter Twenty-three

Tolan is trying to be helpful, and Collette has seemingly forgiven him the worst of his offenses against her. She's shown him grace Larent struggled with. We'll see how that turns out. He always was a good young man when he didn't overthink things.

Write to me when you can, though you should know we are moving out of Pontus Bay here soon.

All my love,
Nora

Chapter Twenty-Four

Éric sat at the desk in his room, lights low, a quill in hand as he penned a letter to his sisters he wanted to send out the next morning. He'd finished copying the meeting notes earlier in the evening, having chosen to eat his dinner in his room. He liked being there where he could think and stay out of Alaoin's sight.

He sighed, putting his quill down, knowing the letter to his sisters could wait, even with their constant demands for updates. When they complained, he could lie and say he was too busy to constantly write. After all, the meetings between the monarch left him believing that they would all head further into Coralia in the coming weeks, which would require quite a bit of time commitment from him.

Of course, he wouldn't be surprised if his sisters called him on his lie. No doubt one or both of their parents had shared the ever-widening chasm between him and Alaoin. They would offer advice and admonishment, prompting him to talk to Alaoin and resolve the problem. How he was supposed to do that, Éric didn't know. He hadn't even spoken with his parents about it yet.

Chapter Twenty-four

A knock sounded at the door, and Éric couldn't help but glare at the door as if it was the poor thing's fault. Knowing the late hour, he assumed it was one of his parents, so he called out, "Come in," before going back to his letter.

Sabine let herself into the room, smiling warmly at her son despite the hour. Her long caramel hair was down. And no doubt, his father would come looking for her if she remained long. "I saw light," she explained. "And it is late."

"Hello, Mother," Éric replied. "I lost track of time." Which wasn't entirely true. He'd been struggling to sleep since the battle.

"You have lost track of time quite frequently," she observed.

"There's been a lot to do and take care of," he explained. "I spent the afternoon in a tense interrogation, you know."

His mother, naturally, did not call him on his partial truth. "You have been busy, but you have been worried and anxious. Your father has wanted me to speak with you for weeks."

"Father worries more than is necessary." Éric gave a careless shrug. He hadn't truly spoken to his parents about what had happened with Alaoin. He hadn't needed to. His father had witnessed his shouted shaming toward their king, and Faron would have shared it with Sabine without hesitation. "Of course," he said, deciding to divert the conversation, "there is much to worry about. We will soon move into another battle, a much larger one. I worry for Queen Collette, given the state she's in."

"I cannot imagine the pain Queen Collette is in," Sabine acknowledged. "But I understand the fear. I think all of us must be considering what we would feel like if we were in the same position."

"I think you would burn the world to ash should someone take Father the way Riken has taken Larent from Queen Collette," Éric said with conviction. He knew, despite everything, he would have broken had it been Alaoin.

"I would be devastated," she acknowledged. "And I think possibilities about other losses weigh on you."

"They do," Éric said with a nod. "But we were lucky. Those we care for are safe. For now at least."

Sabine put a hand on his shoulder. "I know you are worried for Alaoin. He did well in the last battle, but that does not make future possibilities any easier."

"Yes, he did," Éric admitted. "There were several close calls, but he handled himself very well on the battlefield." Those close calls haunted his sleep.

"From what I understand, you had some as well."

"Nothing too bad," Éric insisted. "Not like Father. Did he tell you he lost his sword at one point and there are now rumors he beat several men to death using another of the enemy's soldiers?"

"He hesitated to tell me about his lost sword," Sabine said, shaking her head.

"What about the fact that he waded into the middle of the other army without backup?" Éric thought he should feel remorse for telling on his father, but if it stopped Mother from asking questions about Alaoin, he would tell her all his father's misdeeds.

"I am aware of your father's many misadventures on the battlefield," Sabine replied. "And he's aware of my displeasure."

Éric internally cursed. "Sometimes I feel Father is a little unhinged. Would you like something to drink?"

Sabine shook her head. "He is a little unhinged," she agreed. "Did you want to talk about Alaoin?"

"No, but I have a feeling you will not allow me to avoid the subject forever." He motioned for her to start.

Sabine nodded and took a breath. "I understand you were quite unkind to him before the battle."

"Very much so. I've apologized several times since then, but it doesn't make up for my words."

"How has he responded?" she asked.

"His answers are very neutral, as if he accepts my words but they are viewed as meaningless."

"Why do you believe he is responding as such?"

"Because through word and deed, I have convinced him I do not believe him to be a good and responsible person or king." Éric knew his mother was aware he didn't believe as much. What he thought didn't matter in the face of what he had done.

"And how are you planning to reassure him you do not believe those things?" Sabine prompted.

"I don't know if I can," Éric admitted, giving a thoughtful glance at the letter drying on his desk. "I have broken both our professional relationship and whatever personal one we had."

"From what I see, I think it's reparable, but you are going to have to consistently demonstrate how you feel without letting your fear and worry dictate your actions," Sabine advised. As always, she delivered her words with a gentleness reserved for those she loved, but Éric felt he didn't deserve her kindness now.

"Don't forget jealousy and insecurities. But mostly jealousy."

"Yes, yelling at him about his sexual habits wasn't the best call," Sabine agreed.

"No, it wasn't, just like it's none of my business if he's more than likely slept with a good portion of the Nereid women on the island, or that he's probably at a tavern tonight picking up another one." Éric knew his face had taken on an unpleasant twist, so he motioned to it as if to say, *See the problem?*

"He's in his suite, actually," Sabine said.

Éric made a noise of surprise. "He's spent so much time out, I just assumed."

"You're letting your jealousy concoct stories to be angry about," Sabine corrected.

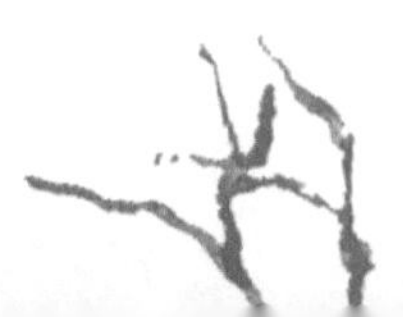

Éric raised an eyebrow. "He has spent many a night at the tavern surrounded by beautiful women since we arrived. We both know he would rather stay up all night and sleep the morning away."

"Staying up all night is not the same thing as the free debauchery you describe," Sabine said. "Nor does your response invalidate my words. Alaoin is lonely. Even in his position with people so often around him, he is lonely. Finding ways to connect with people will happen. You've told him how you feel, but given the context of the conversation, I'm not sure he believes you."

"I've always tried to be there for him, to show him I cared. It's only been the last year or so that things have changed between us, and not for the better. Since he took Lady Linora's marriage proposal seriously, I've just been so … so jealous and upset. It's ruined everything." Éric paused, reaching for the calm he had learned from his mother. "I am considering resigning my post," he finally admitted out loud. "I think I am doing more harm than good, and I do not see a way to fix anything without creating more harm."

"I think resigning would make everyone unhappy," Sabine said after a surprised pause. "But you are a grown man. You have the right to make whatever decision you deem necessary."

"I just do not know what else to do, Mother. Things feel hopeless and broken. What am I to do? Spend years trying to make things right only for him to marry someone else?" Éric hurt at the mere thought.

"No one is saying there is an easy solution, but the two of you should have an actual discussion about your feelings. Do not embrace your instincts to act like your father on this one."

"But Father has done so well for himself," Éric joked. He looked up at his mother, wishing for all the world his problems were small enough for her to resolve, even if he knew his wish wasn't possible. "Do you think I should go now or at a more reasonable hour?"

"I doubt he is sleeping if you wanted to speak to him now."

"I don't even know what to say to him." Éric looked away from Sabine and back to the unopened letter on his desk. "I think I will wait, let us both get some sleep and try tomorrow. Hopefully he will speak to me."

"Just tell him you want to talk," Sabine suggested.

Éric couldn't help but think how intimidating that sounded, but closing his eyes, he fortified himself. The worst Alaoin could do was tell him to go away after all. "Alright. I will try tomorrow." He stood and reached out to hug his mother. "If this goes badly, I'll tell Father where you hid those treats he's been complaining about missing from back home. How he doesn't know you have an entire stash, I will never understand."

"I am not afraid of your father," Sabine quipped. "He is of me, though."

"As he should be," Éric agreed before moving to escort her from the room.

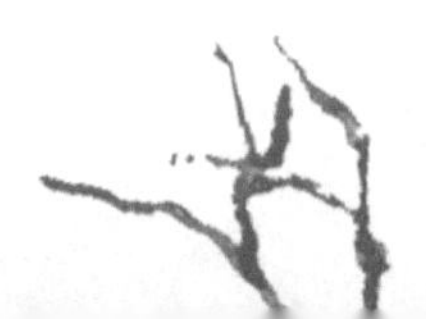

Chapter Twenty-Five

Riken wished he could say their return to the city had been full of cheers. The army triumphant with Collette either in chains being dragged along the city streets or rotting on the Nereid beach. He would have accepted either outcome over the empty streets and the absolute disappointment Rhoslyn had radiated when she met them. She had responded as he expected with the troops, and he couldn't be prouder. Her words had been firm but fair, reassuring but honest as she discussed the consequences of their loss against Collette's forces. Collette would push forward, and they would need to be ready.

If she blamed the troops, they did not know. Their morale would grow and they would stand ready to defend should Collette show up at the gates of Quenall. What hurt, however, was that she had not glanced his way for more than a second. She had, in fact, discreetly held up a hand to stop him when he had gone to join her on the steps the way Mallan did. She'd later sent Cadan to tell him she would call on him at her leisure as she walked off with the Azmarin regent.

So he stayed with the soldiers, helped with what wounded they had left until finally, after several hours, a servant had been sent to fetch him. Now here he stood, not outside her bedroom door, or even her regular study, but the king's study. Riken couldn't help but wonder what she had planned and if Mallan would be there. Raising a hand, he knocked and waited for her command.

"Enter," Rhoslyn called from behind the door.

Riken straightened his shoulders and prepared himself for the worst. This would be the second time he'd faced his lover, his queen, after losing to Collette. And this time, the loss was so much worse, he reminded himself. He deserved whatever punishment she dealt him. Pushing the door open, he felt relief that Rhoslyn was the only one in the room. Hopefully, no one else would see his punishment.

Rhoslyn's eyes didn't rise from her desk where she read over what looked to be a report of some kind. "Explain to me why I do not banish you from this city, much like Collette did, and send you back to live out the rest of your miserable days in Wildrun."

Riken almost moved to stand at rest, as if he was facing his father or one of his trainers from his younger days. However, this was Rhoslyn, and facing her like this was so much worse than facing them. So, Riken went down on his knees and bowed his head in supplication instead. "My queen, I can offer no excuse for my loss against that bitch. I can only submit myself for whatever punishment you see fit. I underestimated her and her support once again and lost."

"Cease your theatrics. We are beyond begging. You cannot complete the simple task of ridding Coralia of its biggest problem when she is in your reach. What good are you to me?"

Riken raised his head to look at her, though he noted Rhoslyn still did not look up. He felt desperation start to bubble in his chest. "She had more forces than we anticipated, and the Nereid water magic overwhelmed our ships. This should

have been a much simpler victory, but it wasn't. I have to take responsibility for that, even as I ask for another chance." He thought about the arrow that had surely killed the man who was Collette's lover if his desperation to get to her meant anything, but he felt this a bad time to bring it up.

Rhoslyn lifted her gaze, icy green eyes glaring at him. "Did you know we have reports that she is back in Coralia?"

Riken couldn't help the frustrated noise he made. "No, I didn't. I had thought we may have slowed her down, giving us more time to prepare if she didn't just give up. I am positive we killed her lover."

Rhoslyn slammed her palm against the desk. "So you angered her, gave her a reason to be vengeful, and didn't kill her," she summarized. "Tell me, Riken, what are we to do if she comes strolling into Quenall in the coming weeks?"

Riken had not considered how Collette could attempt to strike out so quickly in vengeance. He should have. "We hold," he said, though he knew it wouldn't be that simple. "The walls are tall enough to give them pause without something that can tear them down. We have the supplies to hold out for months. We can still be victorious."

"That woman managed to escape the prison, walk across the grounds and over the bridge into the city without being stopped. Without anyone noticing," Rhoslyn reminded him. "She made it to Azmarin without being discovered, and only then because she revealed herself to Brath. What makes you think she wouldn't, or couldn't, be as stealthy in a return?"

Riken hoped that they would be better prepared should something like that happen, especially if it was of great concern for Rhoslyn, but he knew that was impossible. There were just too many ways in and out of the city, and they couldn't possibly know who might be working with that little rebellion run by the Hawkes.

"It's entirely possible that she could. But if she is back in Coralia, at least we have some notice and can prepare." He hated how tentative he sounded, how unsure, but he still felt like they could win this. "I'll give my life to protect yours."

Rhoslyn continued glaring at him. Her anger almost never struck out in heated rage. No, it spiked out, icy and calculated, and Riken swallowed nervously. "You may not act without running ideas or plans by Cadan or me. You will stay close to Cadan or Mallan when acting in any official capacity. Do you understand?"

Riken understood running all his plans through her, but Cadan was his man. Mallan was a conniving snake whose presence he hadn't even felt on that battlefield, though he'd had reports that the man had fought. Her decree felt like an insult, and yet, he couldn't deny that his plans as of late had been foolhardy. He never should have lost to Collette when he met her in the forest. He would accept this, despite not truly wanting to. He would also go and pray to the Mother for guidance. Then he would start anew and not lose again.

"Of course, my queen," he said, making sure his tone was nothing but respectful when he said it.

"Good," Rhoslyn said. She took a breath, and he watched as calm and patience settled across her expression. "You of all people should be aware of how tenuous our positions are. People question Zephraim's absence, now."

"Wait, he's gone?" Riken asked, confused. When he'd left for the battle, they'd had plans to watch him and arrest him for treason if Cadan's hunch was correct. How had they gone from that to him missing?

"Oh yes," Rhoslyn said, giving a wry laugh. "We placed him under house arrest, and Barris somehow helped him escape. I'm surprised no one here told you before now."

"I received no letter, and other than the soldiers, you are the first person I've spoken to since arriving." Rhoslyn's anger made more sense now. She only held the throne through marriage to Zephraim, and it was possible people would think she had disposed of him or worse if they didn't do something soon. "Does Mallan know?" he found himself asking.

"I haven't told him, but I imagine he will be told by someone, and soon."

"I don't trust him," Riken admitted. "I worry for your position when he finds out." He didn't mean to deflect from his defeat, but he couldn't help but express his concern.

"He's not been made king in Azmarin and he could be replaced at any moment. I'm aware of the danger he poses here, especially in light of the problem with Zephraim."

Riken's mind immediately started making and discarding plans before he forced himself to stop. After all, in the position he was currently in, anything he suggested would more than likely be outright dismissed if he wasn't more careful. Especially since he didn't have all the information yet. No, Rhoslyn was not only better informed but also better placed to handle things. So, instead of making suggestions, Riken asked, "What are your plans?"

"In the short term, I plan to act with confidence and authority. Show respect to his position while maintaining mine. Cadan thinks Mallan cares little for the religious points you do, and that alone has Cadan willing to do dirtier work should it be deemed necessary. Mallan may require that sort of handling in the future."

Cadan had always been practical like that, and now Riken wondered if maybe he, with all his religious convictions, had been holding Cadan back from doing what was necessary. "I'm glad to see you two working so closely together after what happened before."

Chapter Twenty-five

"There is work to be done, and Cadan has proven himself reliable."

Riken barely held back a flinch at her words, knowing they were picked specifically to hurt. "Is there anything that I can help with?"

"As I said. Help Cadan with planning and keep Mallan close. Mallan is as likely to turn on us as he is to help against Collette."

Riken nodded before realizing Rhoslyn couldn't see it because she had gone back to whatever she was working on. "Of course," he said before slowly rising. There was one more question he wanted to ask but he was worried about the answer.

"Is there anything else?"

"How does my failure impact us?" he asked.

"Right now, I'm hoping your foolishness doesn't get me killed," Rhoslyn said. "My claim here doesn't have much legal backing, and Collette will be out for blood."

That was better than her saying what they had was over. "I will do everything I can to ensure your safety," he said, knowing she wouldn't trust his word.

"I hope so," Rhoslyn said. "Despite my anger over your failures, with Zephraim gone, we have possibilities before us."

Riken felt his heart lighten that she still held out hope that this could go their way. "What possibilities are you thinking of?"

"Our future, of course," Rhoslyn replied.

Riken wanted to ask for more details. He wanted to be trusted the way he was prior, but that would take time. Time they hopefully had. "I shall leave our future in your perfectly capable hands, then." He made to leave, not wanting to overstay his welcome, but he paused as she spoke.

"My future has been in yours. Do not forget it."

Riken nodded and left. He was disappointed and upset, but more hopeful than he had been. After all, he hadn't been banished. Yet.

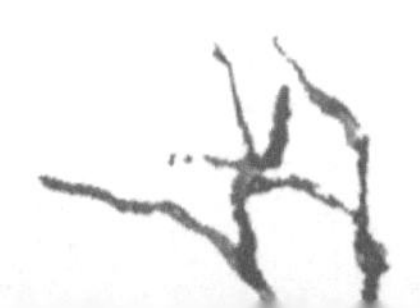

Chapter Twenty-Six

Cadan's brows narrowed as Riken gulped down an almost full glass of what he thought was whiskey. The remaining golden colored liquor swayed back and forth after Riken sat the glass on the table at which he sat with a loud *clunk*. Instead of their usual meeting places, Riken had chosen a private study in a hidden corner on the second floor of the castle in which to drown his sorrows. The lord patted the table, a silent invitation to join, and Cadan complied.

The study, small and stuffed with a table and overly stuffed chairs, provided solitude from the bustle of palace life, though Cadan could not remember it being in use since his arrival. He thought his lord might be too ashamed of himself to go elsewhere.

As Riken eyed the nearby decanter, Cadan spared a thought to stop him. The drink held by the decanter was meant to be savored, but Riken seemed determined to turn himself into a stupid, drunken mess. He didn't want to think about Rhoslyn's wrath if she found out he intended to be more foolish than he'd already been.

He decided to say nothing. Cadan wasn't really up for an argument, not with everything else he was trying to accomplish. His most pressing concern had been locating the new headquarters for Cremisius Hawke's rebellion. Only days before, he'd located old maps in the library showing ancient tunnels leading out to the caves near the beach. Following intuition, her and his people arrived to find a recently emptied cavern. Though he'd been proud to have the lead, the abandoned space vexed him. They'd been so close to possibly ending the rebellion, and they needed a win right now.

"So, you've managed to get yourself in Rhoslyn's good graces," Riken said, drawing Cadan's attention.

He decided to respond, though he intended to ignore the undercurrent of jealousy. Cadan had no time or patience for that level of interpersonal theatrics. "I only did what you asked me to do, my lord." Cadan felt that was the safest reply he could give.

"Even though you let Zephraim escape? That doesn't seem like something she would approve of." Riken refilled his glass with a barely perceptible stiffness. He was angry, and he intended to get drunk.

Cadan held back a sigh and refrained from rubbing the bridge of his nose. Sometimes he forgot how bitter Riken could get when things didn't go his way. He liked his lord when the man was being reasonable. At times like this, though, he was reminded of how his lord could be when things didn't go his way. He recalled Riken's sulking in the weeks following Collette's banishment of him from Quenall. Knowing he had to be the better man here, Cadan was, again, careful with his response.

"Zephraim escaped out the window, something none of us could have foreseen. We were not aware of how devoted some within the palace remained to the Gaillane family. As soon as

his absence was noted, I informed Her Majesty and took full responsibility." Cadan had faced many terrible and memorable moments in his life. Notifying Rhoslyn of Zephraim's escape would remain with him until his dying breath. "She was appreciative of the quick notice and my foresight to send troops out to look for him right away."

"You always were good at taking responsibility for your mistakes," Riken muttered as he took another drink. At least he only sipped for now.

"A lesson your father taught me well," Cadan replied, pretending he didn't see Riken wince at the mention of his father. The deceased lord would have beaten Riken within an inch of his life for his recent failures, and they both knew it. There was no tolerance for such mistakes, especially with the critical stakes on the line.

Deciding to cut his lord a break, Cadan inquired about another matter. "I've heard rumors that you and Regent Mallan do not get along. Perhaps the rumors have exaggerated some minor friction. The troops I've spoken with seem uncertain."

"We don't get along," Riken bit out before taking another drink. "The man is a charlatan—a snake who's only here for his own benefit. I believe if it profited him, he would hand Quenall back over to Collette or try to take it for himself."

Cadan raised an eyebrow. Those were some interesting allegations, but Rhoslyn had expressed a similar sentiment. Their queen was smart enough to never put her full trust in someone she'd only recently met. She'd admitted there was no given reason to think Mallan would turn on them, of course. He'd not be a welcomed guest were that the case, but he was self-serving and incredibly smart. A smart political mover would understand taking advantage of the weaker opponent was simply part of the process.

Riken, unfortunately, made for a weaker opponent with all of his recent failings. Because of his connections to Rhoslyn, the weakness cloaked them as well.

"Is this a gut feeling, or did he do something specific?" Cadan asked.

"Not anything in action, but in word," Riken said as he ran the pad of his thumb along the edge of his glass. "He speaks negatively of Rhoslyn and her position, and he seems to know that Zephraim is not in charge despite how Rhoslyn handled his brief visit. I'm also sure he knows, or suspects, our relationship. There are some veiled threats in the way he speaks that do not sit right with me." His forehead creased and his jaw worked, frustration radiating from the lord.

"What is it?" Cadan asked.

"I do not recall seeing Mallan on the battlefield once we made landfall."

Cadan sat back, surprised. "You're sure about that?" What Mallan knew, or thought he knew, about Coralian affairs was concerning, but if he hadn't fought with his troops and for Coralia, Rhoslyn could use the information to protect herself, surely.

"No," Riken replied with a shake of his head. "The battle was large and chaotic. There were so many titled and royal individuals on that beach, and I tried to keep an eye out for him, but I never saw him."

Cadan felt his hope fade. Mallan might have been on the Nereid beaches along with the others and gone without detection because Riken had been engaged with Collette. "I will have to see what I can find out, then. I'll speak amongst our soldiers and see what they have to say. Then, I will approach some of those from Azmarin."

"Going to take some of his soldiers out to get drunk and question them?" Riken asked sarcastically.

"No, but I will assign some of my men to tail them when they go drinking. They could use a night on the town." He stood, brushing imaginary lint from his tunic.

"Good luck with that. I think I'm going to stay here and read unless Rhoslyn calls for me," Riken said, formally dismissing him.

Cadan took little joy in knowing Rhoslyn wouldn't call on Riken. Her displeasure with him remained greater than her need. At least, he hoped so. It was the least Riken deserved for getting ahead of himself. Cadan wouldn't ever voice such thoughts out loud to anyone, though. At best, such thoughts would be considered treason. At worst, some might assume he had developed feelings for the queen, something which would never happen. He respected Rhoslyn and her intelligent ruthlessness, but it would never be more than that.

"Have a good night, my lord," Cadan said before exiting.

Chapter Twenty-Seven

The bright office made for a cozy afternoon. Sunlight streaked through the large windows and a salty breeze fluttered through the light curtains, creating an atmosphere that very much felt like home. Under different circumstances, Faron might have taken a seat across from his wife, enjoyed some tea, and simply appreciated a peaceful day.

Faron didn't get to have that sort of day, though. He wasn't pacing, not exactly. The office acquired by his wife wasn't large enough for someone of his stature and stride to pace. Additionally, the heavy oak bookcases placed along the wall didn't hold books but delicate looking trinkets which trembled at even the daintiest of steps. Faron found himself concerned that his pacing could result in those figurines crashing to the floor around him, and he did not want to embarrass his wife in Lord Barris's home.

So no, he was not pacing. He told himself he was ensuring the security of the room while they waited on Queen Collette's arrival. He knew the queen would share what they had to tell her with her closest companions, but that didn't mean they wanted any others to overhear.

Sabine's silvery laughter broke through Faron's thoughts, and he stopped not pacing to look over at where she sat behind the ornate desk, a few papers she had taken from Éric in one hand. With a raised eyebrow he asked, "Is my dear wife laughing at me?"

"Frequently," Sabine replied, a fond but teasing smile on her face. "Can you blame me?"

"Only when it's at my expense." Faron took the four steps needed to reach Sabine and laid a kiss upon her lips. They were quickly approaching nearly thirty years together, and the only thing that had changed about his love for her was the ever-growing intensity. "I may be slightly nervous," he admitted.

"I feel the same," Sabine said. She stood and brushed her long caramel hair over her shoulder. "I think the information will be taken in good spirits, though."

"I hope so, but the poor woman has had to handle so much. She may not be understanding as to why we didn't share this sooner."

"I know," Sabine replied with a sigh. "I don't think what we have to say will be of much comfort, but I don't think she'll take it poorly either. The ritual wouldn't have saved his life."

"No, it wouldn't have," Faron admitted, though it didn't help him feel any less guilty. He could only pray to the Spirits that Collette would understand why they held the information back. He leaned down to kiss Sabine again, only for a knock at the door to interrupt them.

"You better go let her in," Sabine directed.

Faron grumbled but pulled away from Sabine and headed to the door. He opened it with no hesitation, showing no nervousness. "Good afternoon," he said in as friendly a manner as possible and stepped inside so Collette could enter.

Everything about the way she entered the space showed how much strength she truly had. Like the others, Faron had noticed the lack of sleep and the slow loss of weight, but none of her pain showed in her confident, deliberate stride or the straight set of her shoulder.

"Thank you for joining us," Sabine said, bowing her head respectfully to Collette. "Please have a seat."

Faron moved to stand next to Sabine. He had wanted to be the one to tell Collette, to take responsibility for not telling her sooner, but Sabine had decided they were going to do this together. So he deferred to his wife. She would handle this more diplomatically, whereas he just wanted to blurt out the information. In all their years together, he still hadn't developed anything close to his wife's natural consular charms.

Sabine only resumed her seat when Collette did. "Would you like some tea?" she offered. "Faron had some brought up not long ago."

Collette shook her head. "No, I'm fine."

Faron tilted his head, taking in the young queen once more. He felt so awful for her and how hard her life had been. "Would you like some alcohol?"

She shook her head. "I agreed to some training this afternoon with Alaoin and Whyldon. I think it best to keep myself sharp."

Sabine nodded. "Alaoin is looking forward to training with you. He admires your footwork."

Collette gave a short laugh. "Good footwork is a thing worthy of admiration."

Faron was glad to see her smile and to hear she was spending time with Alaoin. Their king hadn't been in the best of spirits since the altercation with Éric, and though Sabine had spoken with their son, he had yet to try and fix anything. "It is, and you have a way with a sword that he doesn't. He'll learn a lot from training with you and Whyldon."

"Hopefully so. No matter how good one is at combat, there is always someone who is better and something more to learn," Collette said.

Faron nodded in agreement. Hadn't he learned those throws he'd shown Collette in the Nereid Kingdom from his wife who was mostly a non-combatant? As much as Faron would rather talk about fighting tactics, he knew they'd asked Collette there for a reason. Looking down at Sabine, Faron brought up a hand and rested it on her shoulder, grateful when she raised a hand and placed it over his own. "As much as I would like to continue to talk about training, we have an important matter we need to speak on."

"Which is what?" the queen asked.

Faron looked down at Sabine again, and she gave him an encouraging smile as she silently gestured for him to continue. He thought to start with an apology or maybe a full explanation of the situation, before deciding that wasn't the way to handle this particular conversation. "We have in our possession a spell that might be useful in your upcoming ritual. It could also be a hindrance, but we won't know until we see the ritual." He reached a hand into one of his pouches and held out a folded piece of parchment for Collette to take.

Collette accepted it with some hesitation, but she unfolded the paper, sat back in her chair, and slowly read through the spell. "It could help," she said after several long minutes of silence. She looked up. "How did you come by this?"

Sabine took over now. "Faron and I decided, long ago, that linking out lifespans was something we needed to do. We did not like the idea of Faron spending decades without me, as I would age and die more quickly than he." She smiled up at her husband before turning her gaze back to Collette. "Eventually, we came across the spell you have in hand, and once our children were a little older, we performed the ritual.

"That's why neither of you look old enough to have three grown children," Collette replied.

Sabine laughed. "Indeed, though Faron made us wait so long I threatened to not do the spell at all. As one might imagine, I did not want to possibly subject myself to a prolonged life in my fifties or sixties while my husband barely looked thirty-five."

"We should have told you sooner, and I apologize for not," Faron added. "You're now one of a handful of people who know. I worry for Sabine's safety already, and larger numbers only make me worry more."

"There's also the danger associated with the spell," Sabine said. "There has to be pure, honest love between the people engaging in it. Otherwise, participants might die."

Faron nodded, then smiled down at Sabine. "There is no guarantee of how the connection will form. We were lucky the spell linked her lifespan to mine. I could have just as easily gained the life expectancy of a human."

Sabine squeezed Faron's hand, but she kept her gaze locked "There are other protections in the spell. Stronger defenses against magical harm. That sort of thing. It could make the resurrection spell less dangerous for you."

"When you bring your shifter back, the spell could just as easily match him to your life, or you to his. We don't know how long his race lives, so you should take that into consideration if you use the spell," Faron added, then took a breath. "I think I know you would accept either scenario, though, as long as he is brought back to you."

Collette folded the parchment and tucked it away in a pocket, her brows furrowed as she did so. "Do you know how his current state might affect the spell?"

"The texts for that spell were vague at best, unhelpful at worst. But having a second person to anchor you might help."

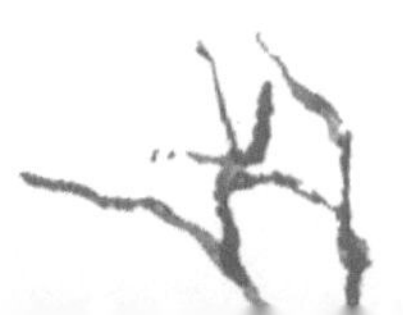

"So finding a third person?" Collette asked.

Faron nodded. "We requested our girls send us all of the information we kept on the ritual. Most of it is useless, but there are some gems hidden away in the tome. There is a passage on performing the ritual on someone close to death. In those cases, an anchor, someone who cares for you both, can stabilize the ritual. I have no idea how that translates when one of the parties has already passed or how it will interact with your ritual since we didn't need a third. However, we are willing to provide you with any information we have. Anything that might help." Faron wished he'd brought the book with them to this meeting. He wasn't sure why he hadn't other than his worry over how the entire meeting would go. "I'm happy to get it for you when we're done here if you'd like."

"If I could get it before we depart for Quenall, I would like the opportunity to go through it," Collette replied.

"Of course," Sabine said. "We will have it delivered to your quarters once this meeting has concluded." She stood when Collette did, bowing her head once again in respect.

"We hope this helps, though I know having this spell beforehand would have made no difference. I am still sorry we didn't tell you sooner," Faron couldn't help but say once more, though he was sure Collette understood his hesitation.

"I'm sure it will," Collette said, and without any further discussion, she left the room.

Sabine let out a sigh. "I think that went well."

"Better than I had hoped," Faron admitted, though he didn't feel particularly wonderful. He suspected Collette might be more upset, or worse, hurt than she had let on. Not that he blamed her. They were still basically strangers, and she would have likely kept her guard up. "How much do you have to do today?" he asked Sabine, knowing she still took so much on her shoulders despite not being regent anymore. "I think we both need a distraction."

"You heard, same as I, that our king had plans. I can make myself free for whatever you like."

"I have a few ideas," Faron said, a gleam in his eyes as he casually strolled to the office door and clicked the lock.

Chapter Twenty-Eight

Dear Nana and Pops,

After months in Quenall, getting to sleep on mostly comfortable beds, I have to say that sleeping in human form on the ground is for the birds. So, I've been spending several nights a week as a bird, under the guise of that form helping me to spot anyone who may be trying to find us. It's even mostly true. Arian, and I'm pretty sure Collette, both know I'm full of it, but neither have said anything.

Nawalya would have noticed, but she's too busy making eyes at Whyldon, that personal guard of Collette's I've mentioned before. I really hope her romantic desires work out for her, but I have a bad feeling about it. She and Whyldon came together so quickly, and I know she hasn't told him everything. Not that I can talk.

We are getting close to Azmarin, and so far, it's been uneventful, which is a good thing. However, I would love it if someone was trailing us just so I had someone to take my growing frustrations on.

Tolan is being a dick any chance he gets, and not just to me, though I have been the cause of some of his issues. He's just so easy to piss off. Sometimes, I watch him with her, with Collette, and I see her shoulders tense because he's put so much on her. We all have, even myself. I don't even know if he realizes how much he's adding to her stress by holding her up as if she's unbreakable, unstoppable, a perfect queen instead of a person. I don't get how he doesn't see her breaking a little more each day as she's forced to pretend to be okay with what's happened to her. With what Zephraim did to her. I'm trying to take some of that off her shoulders, to help support her, but I don't feel like there's much I can do other than just be with her and support her. I hope it's enough.

I hope things are good on the farm. I love you and I miss you.

Larent

Collette didn't return to her suite after leaving the meeting with Sabine and Faron. Instead, she slowly made her way down to the gardens where she knew some of her party were spending the afternoon. With plans to depart Pontus Bay approaching, they'd increased discussions and time planning, but staying indoors for hours every single day had been taken as repugnant by nearly everyone.

Rion sat on a bench just off the walkway, his weapons and tools spread before him on a leather mat. He picked up a dagger from the mat, examined the blade's sharpness, and removed a whetstone to use on it. Whyldon stood nearby, observing and commenting in a light chat.

"There are several ways into Quenall that won't see us trying to sneak in the front gate. Not that some of us couldn't go in that

175

way if needed to help the others enter the city," Nawalya said from where she lay on the grass looking up at the sky.

"We should also see if we can get in contact with Cremisius Hawke and his people. They will have the most updated information on Rhoslyn and the rest," Arian added from where he sat on the ground, leaning back against Thomas's knees since the fletcher was seated on a bench adjacent to Rion's. One hand played with Arian's hair in an obvious attempt to help him relax.

Thomas smiled as he spotted Collette and waved her forward. "How did your meeting go?" he asked.

"It was … interesting," Collette replied.

Arian's head snapped to where she was, his eyes narrowing. Collette also felt Nawalya's attention move to her. Tolan, who she hadn't spotted at first as he'd been partially hidden behind a bush, gazed at her curiously.

"Define 'interesting,' please," Arian said.

"There's a reason Sabine looks less than forty and has children nearly as old as I am," Collette replied. She took a seat next to Rion on his bench, and he began putting his weapons and tools away. "Have any of you ever heard of a life linking spell?" Collette didn't feel especially guilty about asking the question or giving away Sabine and Faron's secret. They'd given her the information without swearing her to silence. Besides, she doubted any of her people would run off with the information.

"So Sabine linked her life to Faron's. That makes sense," Tolan mused.

"She looks just old enough that the grown children were plausible," Whyldon added. "But I've been suspicious. She's wise beyond her apparent years."

Nawalya sat up on her elbows. "I've heard stories of them. Most require blood magic or a sacrifice of sorts." She looked mildly concerned.

"They gave me a parchment with the spell, and they have a book they are loaning me with more information. What I've read so far doesn't seem like blood magic." She retrieved the folded parchment from her pocket and handed it to Nawalya.

She sat up fully to accept the paper and read it over. "I've never heard of a ritual like that. It looks simple," she said as she absentmindedly handed the paper over to Arian, who scanned the content, Thomas looking over his shoulder. He handed it back to Collette.

"What are your thoughts on it?" Arian asked as she handed the spell to Whyldon.

"Sabine said doing this spell would possibly make the resurrection spell less dangerous because of how the linking works," she explained. "Though, Faron sounded like he thought I'd need an anchor, given Larent's current condition."

"An anchor?" Tolan asked. "An item, something personal to you or Larent, to ground you and pull you back if something goes wrong? Or something else?" He looked as if he was thinking it over and wondering what the anchor could be.

"I took it to mean a person," Collette replied. "Though, I think I'm going to do this, anchor or not."

"If you need an anchor, Joss, I'm in," Rion said as he casually tossed his repacked items on the grass beside his feet. "I don't care what it requires. If it reduces risk to you, there's no question."

Arian tilted his head, his eyes narrowing. "Oftentimes, spells will have specific requirements for what is needed, even for an anchor. We'll have to wait for more information before any decisions are made."

"Arian has a point, but based on what Faron and Sabine mentioned, you might actually be a solid choice for an anchor," Collette said, her tone carrying a rare note of aspiration. She felt something stir within—a flicker of possibility. It wasn't

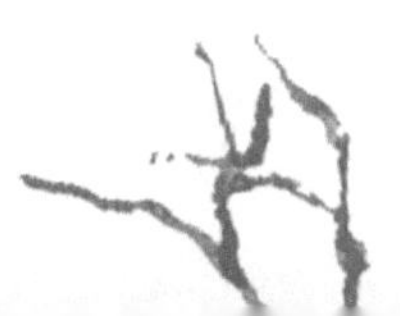

excitement exactly; it was subtler than that. Hope. A feeling she'd almost forgotten how to recognize. For so long, she'd kept it buried under layers of anger, grief, and doubt, but now, it nudged its way to the surface, tentative but insistent. Larent might be revived and she might survive the ritual.

"If I can do it, I'm in," Rion said with a shrug. "No one has outright said it, but we're on a dangerous path. If I can do something to lessen that danger for you, there's no question as to what my actions will be."

Those in the garden nodded in agreement. "I assume we're not to discuss that spell with anyone beyond those of us here?" Nawalya asked.

"I think it for the best," said Collette.

"Might I suggest one exception?" Whyldon asked. "Sara might be helpful in discussing magic. She is well-versed, as we know."

Collette nodded. "Once I have the book, I'll meet with her and see what she thinks."

The group's murmur of agreement rippled through the air once more. Nawalya stretched out on the grass, and Arian leaned comfortably against Thomas again.

"Are we resuming arguments over planning?" Tolan asked, glancing between Arian and Nawalya.

"We're not arguing," Arian said calmly. "We're having reasonable discussions."

Tolan raised an eyebrow. "I've heard that one before. But Collette already laid out the plan we're supposed to follow. Repeatedly."

"And first plans always run into some sort of issue. You are more than aware of how Arian and I process these things."

"Might I suggest that most of what is decided here will have to change on the go once we're back in Quenall?" Whyldon said. "Having discussed numerous options can't hurt, even when a path has been determined."

"Arian and Nawalya get like this when they have an upcoming mission. Larent—" Tolan's voice caught on the sound of his name before he continued on. "He would cause some sort of scene to distract them, otherwise they do this for hours, even though Arian will always end up deferring to Nawalya's judgment."

"Then figure out completing this mission without Larent's distraction so that he can distract and deflect in the future," Collette said. She looked over to Whyldon. "Are you still overseeing training with Alaoin later?"

"Unless one of you has requested a change," he said.

"Okay. Then I'm going to get ready," Collette replied, and she turned back toward Barris's estate.

Chapter Twenty-Nine

Alaoin lay on his bed, staring up at the ceiling and doing nothing in particular. Candlelight flickered from the desk, and he contemplated getting up to extinguish it from time to time. He never did quite muster the energy or enthusiasm for the required follow-through. He was tired, of course. The afternoon of combat training took a lot of energy, but that was not his problem.

Nothing in particular phased the young king, or rather, nothing new. The weeks following the battle with Coralian traitors and Azmarin opportunists had left him down a friendly figure, and though Éric had spent the past months turning into a prickly fuck, he missed their chats. He just didn't know how to talk to the man after the insults thrown on the battlefield.

A knock sounded on his bedroom door, soft enough that, had he been asleep, he would have missed it. Alaoin sighed and sat up. "Come in."

The door opened slowly and Éric stepped in. He closed the door behind him, but he remained as close to the exit as physically possible. "Hello."

Chapter Twenty-nine

Alaoin was tempted to sigh out loud at Èric's visit. He did not. Instead, he met the other man's gaze. "Hello."

"I was hoping we could talk," Éric started. Only to tack on, "Only if you want to."

"We can talk," Alaoin said with a shrug.

Éric's shoulders slumped for a moment before he straightened up. "I'm sorry for what I said on the battlefield and for the way I've acted and treated you the last year and a half. I believe you are a great king and an amazing person, and I will do anything and everything in my power to show you that."

Alaoin looked down as Éric spoke, believing him. Sort of. "You know, I know your actions are influenced by your father and the way he treats what he views as threats of danger. Over the years, I've seen him treat your mother similarly."

"It's a testament to how much she loves him that she puts up with him. And it speaks ill of me that out of everything I could have taken from my father, it's how I handle someone I love when jealous or worried."

"I have far less emotional stamina than your mother," Alaoin said simply.

Éric's shoulders sagged again. "I thought I was smarter and emotionally stronger than my father."

"If you want to be with me, you don't get to grow angry and yell at me because I've done something you don't like."

It was obvious by the way Éric stared he hadn't expected Alaoin's response. "Wait, what?"

"You heard me."

"I … I thought you didn't care for me like that." Éric gave a self-deprecating laugh. "You've never shown even the slightest bit of interest in me. Ever."

"You've been acting like your father for the past year or so," Alaoin reminded him.

"What about before? Before I started acting like a complete ass? I told you I was in love with you, and all you did was stare at me for a moment and then comment on one of the passing noble lady's breasts? I thought you were being nice and letting me know you weren't interested," Éric said, his voice laced with confusion and hurt as he leaned back against the door. "Then six months later, you informed me you were seriously considering marriage, and I knew you would never pick me. Boring Éric, too stuck in his books and papers." He looked down at his ink-stained hands.

"I genuinely don't remember you telling me how you felt, but I know you must have because you've told me that many times now," Alaoin replied. "I'm not so heartless as to ignore a confession like that if I'd heard it, regardless of how I felt."

"I didn't consider it heartless. I considered it a kindness," Éric said, not looking up.

"So you thought I was ignoring your confession to be kind?"

"Yes."

"I did not hear, nor do I remember, it."

"Well then." Éric looked up at Alaoin. "I love you. I've been in love with you for years. I'm sorry I've been a jealous, unthinking asshole."

"You're like your father. You can't help it," Alaoin said with a shrug. "I love you too."

Éric took a step toward Alaoin then burst into tears.

Alaoin rose from the bed and walked over to Éric, wrapping his arms around the other man. Éric stiffened at first before relaxing into Alaoin's arms, still crying. This close, Alaoin could see the toll the lack of sleep was taking on Éric. Alaoin simply held him closely, a hand going up to Éric's hair as his fingers gently pulled through the short, light caramel hair.

"Sorry," Éric said as he got himself back under control.

"It's okay," Alaoin said soothingly. "This has been a heavy conversation."

"Everything has been hard," Éric admitted, making no move to pull away from Alaoin.

"It has," he quietly agreed.

"I should clean my face before I make more of a mess on your shirt."

"Okay," Alaoin agreed. He carefully unwrapped his arms from around Éric but let the other man determine when he wanted to let go. He felt Éric take a deep, slightly shaky breath before pulling away. Taking a step back, Éric gave Alaoin a small smile before retreating to the washroom.

Alaoin took himself back to his bed, sitting on the edge while waiting for Éric.

It took a few minutes for Éric to emerge from the washroom, his face clean but his eyes red and a little puffy. He approached the bed, stopping within arm's distance of Alaoin. "Sit with me," Alaoin invited, sensing the need to issue the invitation.

Éric sat down next to Alaoin, hands in his lap, his fingers nervously tapping against each other. "I don't know where to go from here," he said.

"Where do you want to go? I assume it's not me walking around with visible bite marks," he lightly teased.

A muscle flexed in Éric's jaw at the thought. "I would not be opposed to it." He looked at Alaoin. "Or if I had the bite marks."

"You want to leave bite marks on me?" Alaoin asked with a teasing grin. "That, I would very much like to experience."

Éric looked like he stopped breathing for a moment. Then he moved, straddling Alaoin's lap in one fluid movement. "May I kiss you?" he asked, his voice deeper than normal.

Alaoin looked up at Éric and nodded. Éric leaned in close to Alaoin, his lips inches away, but he didn't kiss Alaoin, not yet. "I never thought I'd get to do this," he whispered.

"And how are you feeling about it now?"

"Like I'm going to wake up any second now in my own bed," Éric said.

"Maybe you should kiss me and see if that happens."

Éric closed his eyes and leaned in, gently kissing Alaoin. Alaoin returned those kisses, slow and soft at first. Éric pulled away enough to take a deep breath before deepening the kiss, his hands moving to encircle Alaoin's shoulders.

Alaoin teased at Éric's lips with his tongue, fingertips trailing down his side. Éric opened his mouth, allowing Alaoin access, his hand moving to play with Alaoin's hair as he unconsciously rocked against the other man. Alaoin groaned softly at the movement, his kisses growing hotter and needier. Éric smiled against Alaoin's mouth as he purposely rocked against Alaoin this time, deepening the kiss even more. Alaoin groaned again, and this time, he responded in kind, kissing the other man hungrily.

Éric reluctantly broke the kiss. "We should—" He swallowed. "We should stop."

"Should we?" Alaoin asked, a little dazed.

"No," Éric said, then corrected, "Yes." He gave a small breathy laugh. "I don't want to, but should we talk first? Establish what it is we want from each other."

"Right now, I'd like those promised bite marks," Alaoin joked.

Éric lowered his head, his lips brushing Alaoin's lips, the corner of his mouth, his cheek, and the lower portion of his jaw, before whispering in his ear, "I can do that." He kissed down to the junction where Alaoin's neck and shoulder met before biting down, carefully at first.

Alaoin tilted his head back and closed his eyes, focusing on the delicious way Éric's mouth traveled along all of his most sensitive points. He let out a soft hiss as Éric bit into him, but as he breathed out, his pleasure in the mark made itself known.

Éric released Alaoin, kissing the now darkening mark before he began nipping and sucking at the surrounding area, while one of his hands ran down Alaoin's back.

Alaoin spoke soft words of encouragement, his hands now resting on Éric's hip. "You may have to stop if you don't want to go much further," he confessed.

Éric rested his head on Alaoin's shoulder, his breathing heavy. "Spirits, I want you. I want to ruin you or have you buried so deep in me I feel you for the next week."

"How do you want to ruin me?" Alaoin asked, his voice heavy with need.

Éric laughed. "Tease," he whispered against Alaoin's skin between nips.

"How is it a tease?" Alaoin asked.

"Because I'm not sure we should. Not yet. But if we continue… If we continue, I will peel these clothes from your body and worship you the way I have wished to for years."

Alaoin groaned again, motivated both by the feel of those delightful teeth and Éric's words. "As good as I know it would be to share that with you, I think you're right. We probably need to wait."

"Then I need to get up," Éric said, though he made no move to do so.

"Your plan seems to be working well," Alaoin teased again.

"Oh, hush. I just need a moment to convince the blood to go back to my head."

"It feels like you don't have that particular problem at the moment," Alaoin replied with a grin.

In revenge, Éric ground his hips against Alaoin, muffling a moan in Alaoin's neck.

Alaoin gasped. "Who's a tease?"

"Definitely you," Éric said, repeating the action once more.

Alaoin moaned again, and his hands went to Éric's ass. "I guess you aren't getting up."

"No, I'm getting up," Éric said. "Even if it seems you wish to let me up as much as I wish to get up."

"I wish to build a situation with you which makes you comfortable and happiest in the long term," Alaoin said with a shrug. "You grind against me, though, and I'm going to grab your ass."

"In the short term, that sounds like a wonderful idea," Éric said as he finished pulling himself off of Alaoin. He sat next to the young king, hands clasped in his lap. "For anything long-term, I should leave and hope to the spirits I can get some sleep tonight so we can discuss this more tomorrow in a room without a bed in it."

"You could always stay," Alaoin suggested, looking over at the other man. "I promise to behave."

Alaoin could see Éric considering the option. "I don't know if I could," he admitted.

"Then go to your room and we shall talk in the morning," Alaoin promised.

Éric obviously did not want to go but forced himself to stand anyway. "I will see you in the morning."

"I will see you when I wake up," Alaoin replied.

"Sleep well," Éric said, and he slipped from the room.

Chapter Thirty

Your Majesty,

You will find the promised spellbook enclosed, along with the most important chapters and pages marked below. Someone with a magical background may be better able to sort through the information for additional support. Please do not hesitate to ask any questions you may have. We wish you the best.

Respectfully,
Sabine, Duchesse Vassetre

As promised, the book containing the life-linking spell was handed over to Collette less than a couple of hours after the meeting with Faron and Sabine. Although she'd spent the afternoon training, Collette wasted no time diving into the old tome. Instead of admiring the fine leather or the smooth, creamy pages, she consulted the spell immediately, using the letter as a guide.

Lien de la Vie sat scrawled across the top of the page in intricate gold lettering. "The bond of life…" Collette said out loud. A list of ingredients had been handwritten on the left side of the page in the margins, hitting up against the printed text: oil, powdered obsidian, sage, oil, black spider lily, a collection of precious stones, and human blood. All were common ingredients they could easily access. Most were relatively harmless on their own or combined. Only the black spider lily gave her pause but not enough to linger more than a few seconds.

Prepare the oil by mixing with a drop of blood from those to be linked and a sprinkling of powdered obsidian. Warm and stir until reaching the consistency of a salve.

Innocuous thus far, each line had Collette's heart beating faster in anticipation. Nothing looked too difficult. Oil, a potion, and some chanting, and she could link her life with Larent's. It seemed too easy. Too inviting. Of course, as she reached the next page, she realized everything assumed the participants were living, and though Larent's body remained in stasis, and thus appeared cooled and sleeping, he was dead all the same.

She closed the book, stood, and picked it up, deciding to consult with Sara. She found her aunt in her quarters, sharing an evening meal with Nora. The two women got along well, or had from Collette's observations, though they'd known one another long before this particular quest.

"I have a spell I want you to look over," Collette announced after entering the suite.

Nora's face lit up, and she reached out, making a grabby motion with her hands that was so reminiscent of Larent, Collette felt her breath catch. If Nora noticed, she said nothing, but she did give Collette a warm, motherly smile as she handed over the book. "It's been so long since I've gotten to look at new magic. Well, new magic for me."

"What sort of spell is it?" Sara asked. She peered over to look at the book as Nora opened it and began browsing.

"One that links two lives," Collette explained.

Nora shuffled through the pages until she found the spell in question, then moved the book so Sara could better see it. They both browsed the page, eyebrows rising at parts, with hums of curiosity and concern sounding. Nora finally spoke. "It's not like any other spell of this type I've ever seen. This one is simple, almost too simple to be honest, but those usually hold the highest of consequences."

"The spiritual component seems to serve as the foundation of the spell," Sara added before looking up at Collette. "Do you intend to use this with Larent?"

Collette nodded.

Nora's head tilted to the side as she turned the page and reread the spell again. "That could be an issue with Larent, with his spirit currently not being one with his physical self. Did Sabine and Faron have any suggestions for that?" she asked, though it was obvious to Collette she had drawn her own conclusions as to how to make this work.

"They mentioned having an anchor, and Rion has volunteered. From what I've read, there's no reason he couldn't be."

Sara hummed again. "You may need two, given the state of Larent, and even then, it might not be enough. That said, if you are determined to proceed, I see no reason not to."

"I don't know if Rion would work," Nora said hesitantly. "The spell would work perfectly if Larent were still present because the love the two of you share. While you were with us, that love showed in everything you and he did. It was— *is*—a gift and a real thing. The anchor would need to have an attachment to both of you, and from what I understand, Rion and Larent spent little time around each other."

"He loves her, though," Sara said, brows furrowing as she went back to browsing, stopping to tap her finger on some passage. "His presence and love would help keep her safe, but a second anchor, one with an attachment to Larent, and preferably both, would also be useful."

"Would it?" Nora asked and looked up from the book to Sara. "From what I've heard, his love comes with more strings than Tolan's, and that will not be helpful here." She turned back to Collette. "Sorry. I shouldn't say that without all the facts, but it might be better to have one person with a connection to both of you. It could be Arian, who loves both of you, or me. Unless you have another idea?"

"Theoretically, your life would already be as long as Larent's," Sara pointed out. "That, coupled with the familial link, would weaken the power of an anchor." She looked at Collette. "Arian might work, but I don't know if he'd agree. Rion would work to protect you. If you go with him, because he has volunteered, do you believe he truly loves you?"

Collette considered the question, but she found she just didn't view Rion in the way many others did. "He does. He hasn't shown it the way I might have wanted or others have expected, but he does."

"Arian would do it if asked, as would Nawalya, I believe. If you think Rion will serve well as an anchor, we will plan for him. Who else would you use?" Nora asked.

"I'm not asking Arian. He is already facing decades without Thomas. I'll not put more on him," Collette decided. "And I don't know that I'd want to ask anyone lest it come off as a command."

Nora nodded in agreement. "While I don't think they would take it as a command, it's best not to chance it."

"Perhaps present your findings to the group, and you can go from there," Sara suggested. "You may get more volunteers or even more information from the wealth of experience surrounding you."

Nora nodded in agreement as she began to look at the other spells inside the book. "Sara's idea is wonderful, and no one will be able to mistake it as a command."

Grateful for a path forward, Collette felt her shoulders relax. Nora and Sara carried a wisdom about them that the others—save for Whyldon—simply lacked. She'd needed to hear their ideas and concerns and to work through them. "That's what we'll do, then."

"Good," Sara said. "Would you like us to go through the spell with you? That way we can identify any potential problem areas."

"Yes," Collette replied. She saw herself into a free seat across from the two older women, and they spent their evening studying the tome.

Dear Nana and Pops,

So apparently, I still get turned on being pushed around by Tolan in abandoned alleys. Apparently, he still gets turned on when I return the favor. I will no longer be going off alone with him, even if Collette asks really nicely, lest we accidentally fuck or kill each other. It's going to go one way or another, and neither option is okay.

On a happier note, I got to spend some time with Collette later that night. Kind of ratted Arian out for going off on a few "errands" around the town. It was good, spending time with her. Except, toward the end, all I could think about was how much I wanted to kiss her. I think—no, I know I'm falling for her,

and hard, which makes what happened in the alley even worse. I'm kicking myself so hard right now for everything.

> Love—oh, who am I kidding?
> I'm never sending this letter to you.
> I should just burn it.
>
> Larent

The next morning, Collette found herself in better spirits than she'd experienced in weeks. She'd risen early, eaten a larger breakfast than anticipated, and had sought out Rion. He'd volunteered to serve as anchor before they had a spell in front of them. Now, she wanted to check in with him and share what she'd learned. She also wanted to make sure he was still willing to help. Magic could be dangerous, and what she ultimately wanted to accomplish was even more so.

She found Rion outside, enjoying an early morning stroll along the grounds. He'd always been an early riser, restless with energy to go out and do something. When they'd been together, she'd sleepily complained about him waking her before dawn, and he'd chuckled, kissed her hair, and left her to fall back asleep.

She'd been young then, perhaps too young for the seriousness of their relationship, and certainly overwhelmed by responsibility at the end. She'd also been stupidly in love with him. How could she not have been? He'd openly adored her, easily teased and bickered with her, and had she not become queen, she was certain she'd have married him, spending her life traveling the world, working in the same trade he had before joining her cause.

"You look excited this morning, Joss," he commented as she fell in line with his stride. She was tall for a woman, but Rion was practically a giant, and she took two or more steps for each one he took, just to keep up.

"I spent the evening reviewing a spell which will help me in bringing back Larent," she explained. "It's made me feel like I can actually bring him back."

"Well, of course, you can," Rion said with a nonchalant shrug. "I never had any doubt about that."

"I know," she replied. "But the others still behave as though you've been kicking and screaming the whole time. You haven't been, unless I'm missing something."

"Some of the people you travel with are dramatic, and others don't like me because I didn't tell you that your idea was perfect and reasonable. I still don't think it is."

"It's not," Collette conceded. "But I'm not doing it because it's reasonable."

"I know, and I know there is no stopping you." He looked at her, his lips curved up in a knowing smile. "So that means I will follow you in this quest and do whatever I can to make sure you survive."

He hadn't needed to confirm it, as Collette knew how Rion would choose to act, but the confirmation was reassuring all the same. She would have to do more to make sure the others were nicer about his initial objections. "I take it that means you're still willing to be my anchor?"

"Of course," Rion confirmed. "You just tell me what that requires, and I'll do it."

"Let's make time to go over the spell this afternoon so you can start preparing," Collette suggested. "There are risks—"

"Which I knew."

"And your lifespan might grow by a lot."

"I'm not complaining." They came to a stop, and he scratched his chin through his gingery beard. "I made the choices I did because I couldn't protect you from the bullshit the people at court put you through. Some people might not understand that. This, however, is something I can do and something I want to do."

Collette put her hand on his forearm. "I have never judged you for deciding to leave Quenall, you know. It's difficult, watching someone you care about suffering and knowing you can't do anything about it."

"I should have tried harder."

"You tried, and you were not happy," she reminded him. "But I have to ask, did leaving make you happier?"

"In some ways, I think it did." Rion was a man of action. His natural restlessness would have been exacerbated by being confined to palace walls for long periods of time. Becoming a furrier had fulfilled that part of him. "But I never stopped regretting leaving you behind."

"You came back at the right moment. I could ask for nothing more."

Whether or not he agreed with her, Rion still nodded. They resumed their walk, going nowhere in particular. "Have you decided what you're going to do about the Nereid woman who wants to fuck you?" he asked, grinning playfully when she shot him a look.

"Ceto does not."

"Oh, she does," Rion said. "And I don't think she's been especially subtle about it. She might have a word with Larent when he's back. I'd bet it will be quite the amusing conversation."

"Why do I put up with you again?" Collette asked, amused. The subject, though seemingly out of nowhere, had foundations of truth. Collette had no intention of doing anything about Ceto's desire, but she could laugh about it.

Chapter Thirty

"Because I am an excellent example of masculinity," he joked. "And you think I'm handsome."

"I think you need more hobbies if a man your age is that hung up about being handsome."

Rion laughed and slung an arm around her shoulders as they continued on their walk.

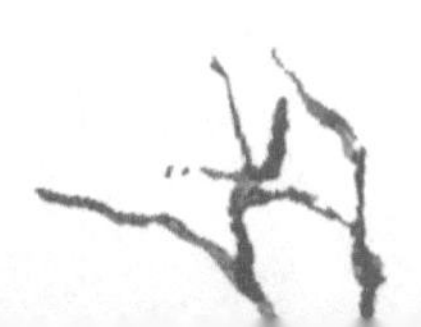

Chapter Thirty-One

Although Barris had promised Collette to stay out of her way, Zephraim had not needed to make such a promise. After everything he had done, the least Zephraim could do was grant his sister her request for peace and distance. He still saw her from time to time, through a window or from a balcony. He heard her speak and laugh in those moments, but even from a silent distance, he noted the distinct lack of engagement, of the silly expressions she'd make when conversing, of the teasing which had once been a hallmark of her demeanor.

He was responsible for that change. Maybe not directly, but arresting her had sent her down a path which had caused so much heartache. He wished, more than anything, that he could set things right, but knowing that he couldn't change the past, that meant working on correcting what he could.

In between sightings of his sister, Lynessea had been spending time getting to know him. She had a way of interrogating him without attack or provocation, and though Zephraim deserved both, he'd been appreciative of her effort. In truth, Zephraim didn't know if he wanted to pursue anything with Barris. He'd been burned by following his treacherous heart in the past, and the sort of arrangement Barris posed sounded complicated and scary.

He supposed it didn't really matter right now. Barris did not want to act without Lynessea's approval, and as far as he knew, Lynessea had not given any. So, he did not ask about or follow up on that particular subject for now.

Since he was trying his best to remain out of sight, Zephraim had tucked himself into a chair in the library that morning. He doubted any member of Collette's entourage forgot he was in the building, but they didn't have to see, hear, or speak to him, and he hoped that was good enough. On a few occasions, he'd come across someone by accident, and though no words had been exchanged, the glares had more than communicated their feelings.

Because of his reception by everyone other than Barris, he did not look up when he heard the door to the library open, nor when the sound of steps came to a halt. The person stood in silence for several long moments before finally clearing their throat. Zephraim glanced up and saw Collette standing there, a large book held in her arms.

"Collette," he greeted with a nod, uncertain what she could want or how to respond. Perhaps she had meant for him to depart wordlessly, or she wanted him to know she was there and not to bother her. His sister had always been vocal about her thoughts, but that had been the case before his betrayal.

"I didn't realize you had been using this library," she replied without greeting.

"It is the one Barris suggested," Zephraim explained. "Relatively few people come and go, and I wanted to stay out of the way since it's what I understand people wanted."

She nodded, ignoring the chocolate strands of hair that fell into her face. "Well, I won't bother you. Supposedly Barris has another book written by the person who wrote this, and I want to see it." She emphasized the heavy book in her arms by lifting it slightly.

Zephraim couldn't see what sort of book it was, but it looked older. "What sort of book is it?" he asked. "Barris keeps things organized by type," he added quickly. The last thing he wanted was to accidentally anger her.

"A spellbook," she said, her tone suspicious.

Zephraim pointed to the shelving in a corner to his right. "Spellbooks are back there. I haven't looked at them much, but if they are anything like other parts of his collection, Barris will have items from all over the world."

Collette's expression relaxed—a good sign. "That could be useful." She looked over her shoulder toward the corner, eyes narrowed as she scanned the larger titles. "I'll leave you to it," she announced before walking away.

Zephraim thought he should be pleased that she'd spoken to him. She didn't trust him, obviously, but the few words he'd gotten were more than he expected. He actually smiled to himself as he retrieved the book he hadn't really been reading before.

He wasn't sure how much time had passed before he heard Collette rise and walk back toward him, though judging by the amount of progress he'd made in his book, it might have been an hour or more. "Yes?" he asked when she stopped in front of him, her spell book still in hand.

"I think you should come back to Quenall with us," she said, her voice steady, with no hint of jest in her demeanor.

"Why?" he asked, his brow furrowed in confusion.

"Because if you are with my people, it will show your support and lend validation to my rule. Rhoslyn will lose whatever remaining claim she has."

Zephraim opened his mouth to respond, but the words caught in his throat. Collette's logic was sound—strategic, even—but he couldn't shake the image of returning to Gadleigh

Palace, the halls heavy with the weight of betrayal and loss. The few who still clung to Rhoslyn and Riken's fractured regime wouldn't be swayed by the presence of two ousted royals.

"Are you certain the others would agree?" he asked finally, his voice quieter than he intended.

Collette's gaze hardened, though her lips curled into a faint, knowing smile. "I'm their queen. I have the right to make decisions, and my inner circle will back whatever I say."

The finality in her words reminded Zephraim of why she had survived this long in the chaos of power struggles. She wasn't asking—she was telling him. He simply nodded. "Of course. I shall do as you ask."

"Good," Collette replied. "I'll notify Barris that you're coming with us. If he decides he cannot be away from you, we can figure out him joining."

Zephraim didn't have any idea about what Barris would want to do, but he trusted Collette would handle things in accordance with her preference. "Of course," Zephraim said again.

Collette nodded and turned from him without further discussion, her footsteps echoing through the vast library as she disappeared into the dimly lit hallway.

Zephraim remained seated, absorbing his newly assigned task. With a resigned sigh, he put his book aside then stood, abandoning the library for his assigned rooms.

Barris strolled through the halls of his estate, a small stack of books held carefully in his arms as he headed toward Zephraim's room. He had thought to meet his friend in the library, where he'd noticed Zephraim had taken to spending the majority of his time. However, upon arrival, he'd been informed by one of the library's keepers that Zephraim had left not more than ten

minutes prior after having an accidental meeting with Collette. More for his own peace of mind than anything else, the man had assured Barris that the meeting between the two had seemed cordial and lacked any of the hostility of the first meeting. As such, Barris felt no need to rush to Zephraim's side. Though, he hoped if Zephraim was distraught, he would seek Barris out, if even just to talk. Arriving at Zephraim's door, he gave a soft knock and waited to be invited in.

Zephraim's footsteps sounded from the other side of the door, and within a few seconds, the handle turned and the door opened. Zephraim looked well and certainly not like someone who had encountered Collette's wrath. "Hi," he greeted.

"Hi," Barris responded. He didn't bother trying to keep the fondness from his voice. "You mentioned you wanted to read the rest of the tomes on magic from the southern continent the other day but couldn't find it." He did his best to hold up the books he held. "I found them in my office and thought you might appreciate them." Barris could have kicked himself. He sounded too eager, like a young man with a crush instead of a fully grown man with deep feelings. Though, he didn't know if there was much difference.

Zephraim chuckled and took several books from the top of the pile. Those, he placed on the table closest to the door. "Thank you for bringing them, but I won't have the opportunity to read them. Collette informed me that I will be traveling back to Quenall."

"Oh. That's unexpected news," Barris said. To say he was surprised was an understatement. He had assumed the queen would leave Zephraim behind in Pontus Bay. He wanted to ask about her reasoning and why Zephraim had said yes, but he also didn't want to push. Maybe that made him a coward, because there were a lot of things he hadn't been pushing on lately. "Are you okay?" he finally managed to ask instead.

Zephraim shrugged and took the rest of the books from Barris. "I agree with her that my presence lends legitimacy to her claim," he said. "But I didn't think I had much room to argue against it. She is the queen."

Barris made an affirmative noise because, really, what else could he say to that? If Collette wanted Zephraim there, he had to go, especially if she'd made it an order. That she asked him to go with to help make her claim over the throne stronger than anything Rhoslyn could hope for was also a very smart move. "How upset would she be if I asked to accompany the group?"

"She told me you could come as well," Zephraim said. "But that seems like a discussion you should have with Lynessea."

Barris was quick to answer. "She's been talking about going with Collette to Quenall for a while. We just weren't sure what I should be doing. This clears that up—so long as you're okay with it."

"Of course I'm okay with it. You'll likely be the only friendly face I'll encounter."

"You have Lynessea as well," Barris assured because he knew it was true. Lynessea was slowly warming up to Zephraim, faster than Barris had anticipated, but Zephraim was an easy man to like when not around those at court.

"Perhaps. She could always decide not to like me, you know."

"I view you differently because I'm willing to look past your misdeeds to see who you really are. If more people were willing to do that, and not just for you, the world would be much brighter," Barris pointed out. He meant it too. People didn't just have one side to them, and they shouldn't be defined by past actions if they were trying to atone in good faith. He didn't believe Rhoslyn and Riken were redeemable, because they didn't see what they were doing was wrong. Zephraim, on the other hand, was trying. The others would see that eventually.

"You are unique, then," Zephraim murmured, his voice soft. "Not that I would ever dream of complaining."

Barris's smile bloomed with happiness. "I would rather be unique in your eyes than fit in with everyone else," Barris said, his gaze fixed on Zephraim's with unwavering warmth.

Zephraim's expression softened further, his eyes alight with quiet affection. "You are that, no doubt. I think it would be quite impossible to view you any differently."

Barris melted at the look in Zephraim's eyes, and it took everything in him not to reach out and touch Zephraim. Not to draw him close for a kiss. He wanted to, but he wanted to be sure it was what Zephraim wanted without pushing him more. He opened his mouth to deflect, to move the conversation to safer territory. Instead, what came out was, "May I kiss you?"

Zephraim nodded before he spoke, stepping a little closer to Barris. "Yes."

Barris lifted his hands, resting them lightly on Zephraim's hips, hesitant, as though he might scare Zephraim off. Or worse, reveal it to be a dream. Slowly, he closed the gap between them, stopping just a breath away from Zephraim's lips. He paused, letting the new closeness settle as he inhaled Zephraim's scent. A mix of ink and parchment, sandalwood from the library candles, and something softer, elusive, just beneath it all. Finally, Barris leaned in, brushing his lips gently against Zephraim's, giving the other man time to pull away if he chose.

Zephraim stepped closer, returning the kiss without hesitation. Barris wrapped his arms around him, pulling him flush against his body as he deepened the kiss. It never grew heated, as the moment was calm, affectionate, and intimate. But even as it ended, Barris found himself breathless with pleasure.

He pulled away just enough to rest his forehead against Zephraim's. They stood there in silence, catching their breaths, before Barris let out a still slightly breathless, "Wow."

Chapter Thirty-one

"Indeed," Zephraim agreed. "I don't think anyone has ever made me feel so…"

Barris waited with bated breath to see if Zephraim would finish that sentence. He had a feeling he knew what Zephraim would say, but he didn't let his hopes get too high. "So?" he softly prompted.

"Adored," Zephraim finished.

Barris let his small warm smile grow. Zephraim's response was better than he'd hoped for. "Good. You should be adored."

"Why do you think so?" Zephraim asked, his voice still soft.

Barris raised a hand to caress the other man's cheek. "You are an amazing person, Zephraim. You have been through so much, and yet, you have a kind soul, even though it's been led astray. You're trying to be better, and I believe you will succeed. That's not even touching on your intelligence."

A smile spread across Zephraim's face, something that seemed to happen more and more often as time passed. "I think, if Lynessea approved, I might be willing to try having something with you."

Barris couldn't help himself from kissing Zephraim again at those words—a soft, fleeting touch of lips that lasted only a few seconds. "Lynessea has said only positive things about the time the two of you have spent together. If I let her know you want this, that we want this, I don't think she'll have any objections."

Zephraim gave a thoughtful nod. "Hopefully. But you should probably talk to her first before we go any further than this," he suggested.

Barris let out a soft laugh. "Very true." Barris took a small step away from Zephraim, showing what he felt was an astonishing amount of restraint. "Lynessea had a few things to get done. When she's free, I'll let her know your decision, and we can go from there?"

"I think that's the best path forward. You made it clear her approval was necessary, and I'd hate to lose potential approval because we moved too quickly."

Barris nodded, his smile widening. "Her approval is important. I would have no rifts or issues between any of us. I think open communication will only serve to strengthen us in the long run."

"True," Zephraim replied.

"I'll leave you to enjoy your reading. I'd offer my company, but that may not be the best idea at the moment," Barris said, his tone slightly joking. "I'll stop by later, though, if you'd like."

"I would," Zephraim decided. "I suspect I might need to consider getting my limited things together since Collette intends to head out in a matter of days."

"I'll need to do the same since I am accompanying you. I'll see if I can get an exact date." He would need to know as well, and he was sure Lynessea would have some idea, as she had been preparing their soldiers. If she did not, he would approach Collette.

"Okay," Zephraim replied. "I'll let you go about talking with Lynessea."

Barris nodded, flashing Zephraim a bright smile, before he spun on his heel to go find his wife.

Chapter Thirty-Two

The departure to Quenall came sooner than Collette had anticipated, but she was more than eager to be back on the road. After weeks of sitting idle in Pontus Bay, trapped in a cycle of tedious meetings filled with nothing but endless debates and petty squabbles over strategy, her restlessness had reached its peak. Collette found herself growing increasingly impatient. Movement, she decided, was action—and action was what she craved.

The larger collection of Nereid, loyal Coralians, and Fythians decided the wisest move was to divide into two groups, with Collette's group traveling northwest toward Quenall. The journey would pause briefly on the other side of the mountain range, where the group would split further into two smaller parties, making it easier to enter Quenall undetected.

Aphros would take the second party south, around the southern tip of the mountains, securing Wildrun and possibly Veitel along the way. Though the stop risked resources and lives, Collette couldn't help but feel a sense of satisfaction. This approach would guarantee bringing Riken to his knees, and it would increase the chances of total success since those in Quenall would not suspect a counter-attack within the city.

She'd hugged Aphros before leaving Pontus Bay, promising to greet him upon their arrivals in Quenall. For now, Collette turned her attention to the immediate task at hand.

Unlike their travels out of Quenall and into Azmarin, this march west was not done in secret. They'd traveled in the open, commanding the respect of those they passed. As with the secret, rushed travels of the prior year, the rumors of her death had also passed. Each new village brought forth happy faces greeting the true queen, and more than once, Collette's battalion grew with eager volunteers.

They were two weeks into the trip when it was decided to settle into a makeshift camp for the evening. Fires were started, hunters hunted, and what little shelter or comforts might be needed were attended to. As night settled in, Collette sat, her back resting against a tree trunk while her gaze locked in on the small, orange fire before her.

The sounds of leaves crunching underfoot reached her ears as someone approached her from the left. The deliberate, heavy steps made it clear to her that the person wanted to be heard, but somehow, she hadn't expected Tolan to appear in her line of sight. He took a seat on the ground near to her, but not close enough to touch. "I'm tired, but not enough to sleep," he said awkwardly.

"I'm exhausted, but I have no desire to sleep," she returned.

"Mine comes from being travel weary. I assume yours comes from other things," he said softly, looking up to meet her gaze with his deep brown eyes.

Collette knew he was offering to let her unload if she wished, to unburden herself of the hurt. Ever since Larent's loss, she'd tried to keep those thoughts to herself. Most everyone was grieving in their own way, and they didn't deserve to deal with her sadness on top of their own. But she nodded. "The ache of missing my husband never goes away," she admitted.

Even now, his body, still under Aphros's stasis spell, had been secured in one of the covered carriages that made up their party. Nora visited frequently, though Collette couldn't bring herself to do so. "See what happens when you let people sneak around my castle?" she said in half-hearted jest.

Tolan's laugh was honest, if barely there. "Next time, I'll just drag them to the dungeon and throw away the key. Save everyone the thought of any type of heartbreak."

"Really, it's the only option," Collette added, laughing softly. She smiled as a memory rose in her mind. "It seems so hard to believe how long ago all of that was. I remember Arian showing up in the guard one day, a recruit Crem was really excited about. I'd been out, observing the guards with Whyldon, and I kept wondering who made Arian so angry since he looked like he was going to stab someone at any moment."

Tolan made a sound between a snort and a laugh at her words, and he looked around the group of people with them until they landed on Arian, who was pressed up against Thomas. "I can picture it. It's nice to see him slightly less murder driven." Tolan shook his head. "Nawalya found me before I ran into any of them. That ended up being a good thing, because turning a corner only to run into Larent robbing one of the nobles' wives while she thought he was flirting with her would not have gone well otherwise."

"Don't you know, they came on to him," Collette joked. It had been the claim Larent made when they first met and he'd told her stories of his dealings with Lady Elrick.

"You would be surprised how often that statement wasn't a lie," Tolan said as if he knew what she'd been thinking of. "He refused to take those types of missions when we were …

whatever we were, and yet women and men still threw themselves at him. He hated it."

"I know he did," she said. "He rarely voiced it, but he hated being reduced to a handful of physical attributes. It led to friction with Arian for a time once we were on the road, and I told him he didn't have to put up with how he was treated."

"Larent always wanted those he was closest with to be happy, and sometimes he made himself less to ensure that happened." Tolan sighed. "I never really understood why he did it, but he did. I'm glad he started standing up for himself more."

"He deserved to be celebrated for all the wonderful things he is," Collette said as she rested the back of her head against the tree trunk. "And he will be celebrated again, soon enough."

"You know, I didn't think I'd miss him as much as I do," Tolan mused as he looked up at the night sky. "I know I wasn't in his company for years, but I knew he was out there causing some sort of havoc. I'm hopeful to see him causing trouble again soon."

"I'm going to do my best to make it happen." There were so many questions about feasibility and safety, but Collette could do nothing else until he was back. "Nora thinks he'd want to be back, so I've decided to believe her." She glanced over at Tolan and wondered how much Larent's death must have hurt. Tolan had taken up the responsibility of pushing them forward. She knew he was grieving, probably at least as much as the others. "I know, no matter what the two of you have said in the midst of fighting, there is some connection between you two."

"Trust me, I am more than aware of that," Tolan said with a laugh that was slightly bitter and self-mocking. "I've had a lot of time to think over our relationship, both the almost one and the antagonistic one later. Though, really, our altercation in Azmarin should have been an eye-opener more than anything."

"I don't think it's one-sided if that makes you feel better. Larent's heart is big, and I don't think his feelings ever truly dissipate."

"They changed more than dissipated, into anger and loathing. Maybe the fonder feelings were still there, but it wouldn't matter. He loves you more than he's ever loved anyone or anything. It was obvious to anyone with eyes," Tolan said. His tone was accepting more than it had ever been before, as if he were at peace with that now.

"To be loved in the way Larent loves is an addicting thing," Collette replied. "And for a long time, it felt as though the only person who looked at me and understood what I was feeling was Larent. I don't love him because of that, but it made it damned easy to let the sparks between us ignite in those moments of recognition." She shrugged and took a breath. "I think it's more visible now, how I'm feeling."

"I think he was the only person who understood you and your feelings completely. He didn't put some sort of expectation on you to be anything but yourself. Sometimes though, I think the two of you were made for each other. You just fit so well, and your feelings were always obvious to anyone who looked."

"I think I ended up being somewhat of a disappointment to you, all the same," she said, though no accusation echoed in her words. "I was not what you expected me to be."

Tolan opened his mouth to respond then shook his head. She'd noticed he'd started doing that before Larent had been killed, perhaps as a way to prevent further arguments. Finally, he spoke. "You never disappointed me, because you never tried to be anyone but who you were. I think I forgot about Joss from the tavern and replaced her in my mind with Collette, the perfect, unshakable queen. I didn't remind myself that you're a

person like the rest of us. I'm the one who made the mistakes there, who let you down. You never let me down."

She gave him a smile, placed a hand on top of his, and gave it a squeeze. "I wish I could be Joss from the tavern again. I think she got lost in the chaos of war and death. Sometimes, I think Rion still calls me that because he wishes that was who I could be."

"You're still Joss. That part of you just got buried for you to survive the things you've gone through. Some of which I put you through when I left. Joss is still there, though. Larent wouldn't have been able to pull that side of you out otherwise. I'm sorry Rion was the only one to see it for a while."

"Everyone is so down on Rion, but he's a smart guy," she playfully complained, laughing lightly all the while.

"He was the loudest voice against your plan, but he knows you would just go off without us if you thought you had to."

"I absolutely would run off if it was needed."

"No need. Arian and I have said nothing against your plan. In fact, Arian is probably the only person who has supported you from the moment you expressed your decision to go to Quenall." He gave her a self-deprecating smile. "I like to think I'm smarter than I used to be. Rion… I know he means well, but I think he needs to become more vocally supportive of you instead of taking every step with a scowl on his face."

"He hasn't said anything lately," Collette protested. "In fact, other than when I first announced my intentions, he hasn't objected."

Tolan held his hands up in surrender. "Okay. Point taken. He's not as bad as he was in the beginning."

"He's not," she agreed. "And he volunteered to be my anchor when I cast the life linking spell. That's hugely supportive."

"I'm glad he did, but if you need any more help with the ritual, I'll help in whatever way I can, even if it's just to fetch water or something," Tolan volunteered.

Collette debated the question that came to mind. She didn't want to leave anyone feeling as though they were being forced into something, but Tolan had offered. Given Tolan's history with both Larent and herself, she felt she could ask. "Would you want to serve as a second anchor?"

Tolan's eyes widened in surprise, but his smile showed some pleasure. "Of course; whatever you need. Though, I guess I should ask what that entails."

Collette learned forward, having not expected such easy acquiescence. "If it works, it could possibly extend your life to that of a shifter or shorten it to match mine, assuming it works at all given Larent's lack of life."

"If it helps to bring Larent back, who cares what lifespan I end up with? You'll be happy and he'll be with us again. I don't think the rest matters." Tolan gave Collette a warm smile and a careless shrug that reminded her of better days between them. She couldn't help but return it.

"Then tomorrow, we can start going over the spell in more depth."

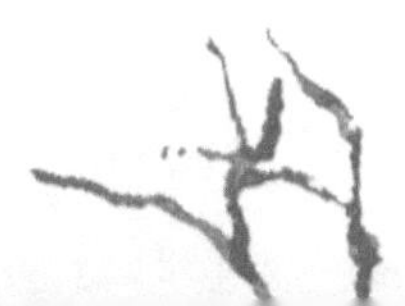

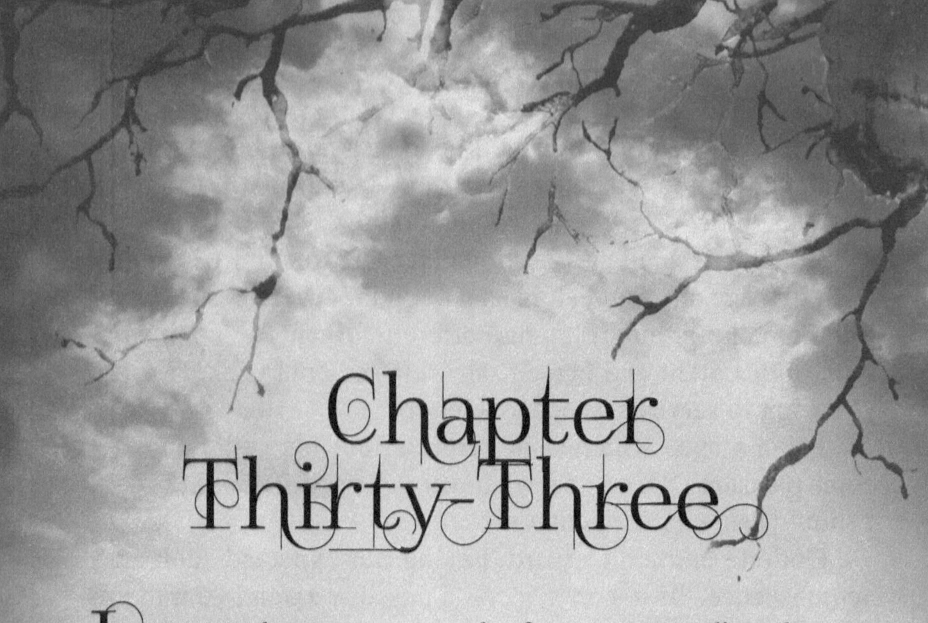

Chapter Thirty-Three

Lynessea kept an eye on the forest surrounding them as they made their trek across the mountain. She'd intentionally positioned herself close to Queen Collette's group but with enough distance she couldn't overhear any discussions held between the queen and her inner circle. Lynessea hadn't been banned from knowing about plans, but Barris and Zephraim had, and she was eager to show loyalty and compliance. Thankfully, she thought Queen Collette had no true concerns about people listening in when they were not wanted.

Traveling with Collette's half of the army had not been Lynessea's original plan. Aphros, being both Nereid and her brother, seemed the most logical choice. Even until the night before departure, her intention remained unwavering. Only when Aphros pointed out she would better serve Queen Collette's more immediate goals did she change her mind. She'd more recently been inside the castle, after all, and perhaps she could provide information she hadn't thought important.

In truth, Lynessea thought her change of plans were ultimately for the better. Zephraim would be kept under Collette's supervision, and with that being the case, Barris would follow.

Barris had already proven himself a nuisance to Collette, however unintentionally. In his hopeless naivety, his implication that their queen would have to go through him to get to Zephraim had been nothing short of damaging. Although, she knew he meant no harm, as it was something her loving and sweet husband would say without considering the interpretations of others. Because Lynessea knew others wouldn't understand his intentions, she decided she couldn't take a chance of anything happening to him.

With a sigh, she decided she had to extend the same protective watch to Zephraim, who'd been walking beside her in quiet contemplation for about an hour since Barris had wanted to check in with some of their men who were with this group. Deciding maybe some conversation would help the time go faster, as it felt like they'd been on this mountain pass forever, she asked him, "Nervous about going back to Quenall?"

"I don't think I am, actually," Zephraim replied, his voice so soft Lynessea could hardly hear his response over the solidly paced crush of underbrush beneath hundreds of footsteps. "I find myself feeling quite peaceful about the prospect."

Lynessea nodded as she moved closer so they could converse more easily. It had been a long time since she'd been in a group this large, and she'd forgotten about all the noise. "Does it help knowing the people who helped bring all of this about will soon be facing punishment?"

"Perhaps, though I tend to think it is because the world is being righted, now. I've felt, almost since the beginning, that things have been unbalanced, even if I were foolish enough to not recognize the feelings for what they were early on."

While Lynessea felt like she understood exactly what Zephraim meant, she didn't want to assume, and so she asked, "What did you think it was early on?"

Zephraim shrugged. "I can't say I did much thinking early on. I had what I thought I wanted: a wife and lots of praise from those around me. Dissecting the reality I'd created didn't have much appeal."

Again, something Lynessea understood. Why, when everything should feel amazing, when everything seemed perfect, would a person look at the flaws? Lying to yourself was easier at times than finding the strength to face what you knew to be a lie. She'd had friends and colleagues do that, and she admired that Zephraim had eventually found the courage to do so. "It had to have been hard, when the reality of everything sank in." Her words held no pity, only compassion and a want to understand if not help.

"Looking back, I don't truly think I found even a second of what I created to be easy. The subtle digs from Riken, Crobán's attempts to lead, and Rhoslyn never being quite happy with me… I think I knew, to some extent and very early on, that I'd made some serious mistakes."

"It's hard to see all that when you just want to be happy. To justify what's happened, you often feel as though you have to say, 'This is what I wanted, and therefore, it has to be perfect.'" Lynessea glanced over to check on Barris, who was laughing with one of their people. He shot her a glance, his head tilted to the side, and gave her an inquisitive smile. She returned it with one of quiet confidence and joy.

"I think that's exactly it," Zephraim said. "You have to say what you wanted is, in fact, what you wanted."

"That sounds like it would be both incredibly easy and hard at the same time," Lynessea replied.

"The more you realize you must do it, the harder it becomes."

"I'm grateful I've never been in that position, but it sounds terrible," she admitted.

"It is," Zephraim replied, shrugging.

They continued walking alongside one another, occasionally hearing pieces of conversations from those around them. The Fythian crowd who'd remained with Collette's half of the party marched along in a jovial mood, in part over their king's turn of good spirits and because they were still intoxicated by their own success in the battle back in the Nereid kingdom.

Lynessea couldn't help but let out a small laugh at hearing some of their conversation. Sabine gently teased Alaoin about Éric but in such a way those around her wouldn't have caught it if they didn't know what Lynessea had accidentally discovered.

Not wanting to keep discussing such difficult things with Zephraim, as it seemed like the few times they had spent time together that's all they did, she leaned over and whispered, "I caught Éric and Alaoin together in one of our less used rooms. It appears very new, but it's cute. Not you and Barris cute, but similar."

"Barris and I haven't found ourselves in cute situations," Zephraim replied with a soft laugh.

"Well, not in the way those two have, but you're still adorable. It's the way you look at each other."

"Perhaps. I don't have the benefit of observing the two of us from another's perspective."

"True," Lynessea said thoughtfully. She wondered if Zephraim and Barris didn't notice the exchanged glances or the way they watched the other whenever they were in the same room. She knew Barris could be that oblivious. There were many times when she'd caught him watching her, a besotted smile on his face, and he didn't know until she pointed it out.

Zephraim, on the other hand, had been too hurt not to realize he was doing it on some level, which could explain the way she'd seen him blush when he would quickly look away from Barris. She'd wondered if he'd done the same thing with Rhoslyn when they were younger, but Lynessea doubted it. She thought Zephraim had very much only believed himself to be deeply in love before now.

"You and Barris have kept different circles and friends for as long as I've known him. I must say, if I was a betting woman, the two of you together would never have occurred to me, as friends or otherwise. But I'm glad it's happened."

"As am I," Zephraim replied. "Barris has been a real surprise in my life."

"It was the same way for me. Though, it took him much longer to recognize how he felt about me." She couldn't help but laugh.

Zephraim chuckled and nodded. "I believe I've heard that before."

"I'm sure you have." She studied Zephraim, uncertain if she wanted to be with him in the way Barris did, but she liked him. He was so different from the man she thought she knew in the palace. Perhaps one day she would want to join them. The goddess Galene only knew for certain. "If you want to be with him, you have my approval."

Zephraim's surprise proved nearly imperceptible. His gray eyes didn't widen, nor did a brilliant smile bloom at the news. He didn't appear worried or panicked, which was good. "Do you wish to share that news with Barris?" he asked.

"I will when I'm ready." She gave him a mischievous smile. "I thought I would give you time to adjust to my 'yes' first." She thought Barris's enthusiasm might overwhelm Zephraim if they found out at the same time.

"I appreciate it." Zephraim returned the smile. "And I will bide my time until you speak with him."

"It sounds like you don't feel you'll need much time to adjust," Lynessea said.

"Your speaking with him does not push up my timeline."

Chapter Thirty-three

Lynessea nodded in understanding. "I'll talk to him when we have some free time, then."

"Of course."

It was the easy answer and the small, barely-there smile that convinced Lynessea to give Barris no more than an hour before pulling him aside to talk. Maybe she shouldn't push it, but Zephraim truly had grown on her.

Chapter Thirty-Four

Nora slowly made her way through the camp, looking for a particular queen after having spent the last several hours putting Arian through his paces. The young elf had generously referred to it as training. Nora secretly referred to it as ensuring he'd sleep that night. Nora had wanted to invite Collette, but she'd been busy with Whyldon and Rion at the time.

Thomas, who had found himself a useful role in writing up plans, minutes, and letters, had been asked to convey the invitation to Collette if she had free time later. Collette never showed, but Thomas stopped by an hour in to watch. Clearly Collette had not been up for some jousting, or she'd remained too busy—both of which were possible.

That Nora was slightly disappointed Collette hadn't shown was something Nora kept to herself. She'd seen how well Collette handled herself against Alexander when she and Larent visited months ago, and she'd been looking forward to sparring against the kind of strength and agility Collette brought to the field at some point during this trip. The only reason she hadn't offered while they'd been at the farm was that Larent needed the type of structured training only Alexander would give him.

Not the back-alley, bar-fighting style Nora was known for. She could be a disciplined fighter when needed. She just preferred to win all her fights.

Finally spotting her prey, Nora stalked gracefully through the rest of the camp before reaching the spot Collette had chosen on the outer edges where she had set up. Collette sat alone at her campfire, hunched over a piece of parchment in her hand. Nora waited until she looked up before taking a seat next to her on a log that had been drug over.

"Hello, dear," she said softly, waiting to see if Collette was in the mood for company.

"Hi," Collette returned. She placed the parchment she been holding on top of a leather pack beside her.

Nora looked at the pack, certain she knew who it belonged to with the state it was in, which made her curious about the letter. However, she wasn't here to pry but instead to check on her daughter. She could pry later if she really wanted to. "Are you feeling alright? You missed me teaching Arian the meaning of humility."

"I'm as fine as possible," Collette shared. "I wasn't really up to anything physical, so I contented myself with invading my husband's privacy some more." She motioned to the pack where the parchment sat.

Nora's eyes lit up. She loved when she was right. "When it involves your husband, it's not really an invasion of privacy so much as information sharing," she said jokingly. "Alexander tells me that's not the correct way to view things, but he's often wrong."

"I think Larent would willingly hand over the whole thing if he thought I was considering asking, so I think we can say it's a three against one scenario right now."

"As it should be, especially when one is as observant as Larent." Nora glanced back at the letter sitting on her son's pack,

once more pushing away her grief. "I have to ask, is the letter addressed to Alexander and me? Do you have a stack of them?"

Collette nodded. "Well, this one is addressed to Tolan, believe it or not, but there is a sizable stack, and many of the letters he wrote are to you."

Nora laughed, though it faded as the grief over Larent not making it to the end of his latest adventure tried to swallow her joy once again. "That was a habit of his: writing letters to us and not sending them until the adventure was over. He claimed it was so we didn't worry. We could read about the pain, the hurt, the joy and peril and know he was okay because he waited to send us the entire stack." She brushed some tears from her lash line. "I will say, had he sent some of those letters on their own, I would have tanned his hide."

"Having read some of his letters, I can see why. I've been a bit amazed, reading through all of the experiences we've had through his eyes."

"What catches your attention the most?" Nora asked, interested to see more of her son through Collette's eyes.

"I think it's that he allows himself to be honest in ways he doesn't always show to others."

"I've found that to be true as well. I've always thought he just let himself feel his emotions more in these letters. Sometimes, it made them harder to read."

Collette nodded. "Some of the letters have been hard to read. Others make me laugh."

"That sounds right. The letter from after Tolan left him may have been the hardest for us to read, and that's including the letter that only said 'I was stabbed.' That was it." Nora could not hold back the disgruntled look that crossed her face, and that incident had been years ago.

"That would be devastating," Collette agreed. "Feel free to slap him when he's back. I might."

Chapter Thirty-four

"I'll give him a day or two and then do it. After you've brought him back, I doubt anyone will see either of you for a few days." Nora kept her tone knowing instead of teasing. After all, Collette and Larent would likely spend days sleeping, unable to do anything else.

"I might let him go long enough for you to do it."

Nora laughed. "We both know you wouldn't, but I appreciate the offer." Nora studied her daughter for a minute before asking, "Do the letters make him feel closer?"

"Sometimes," Collette replied quietly. "Sometimes, they make the loneliness worse. Like when I read about how much he worried about me, I just wish I could reassure him."

"You can do that once he's back here with us," Nora said, as if she had complete confidence that Collette's spell would work. She didn't, if only because it was unknown magic, and she was terrified she would lose her daughter when she'd only just truly gotten to know this amazing woman her son had married. But she had faith in the Lady, even if she had let Larent be taken from them.

"I will," Collette promised. "There are a great many things I will share with him when he's back."

Nora nodded in understanding and sent a silent prayer to the Lady that this would work. Not for herself, but for the woman sitting next to her, who Nora truly believed wouldn't last long afterwards if the spell failed. "Have you eaten today?" she asked, trying to get her mind off such thoughts.

"This morning, I think."

"Would you like something to eat? I have a few snacks in my pack, and tonight's meal is rabbit stew. I ensured it was cooked in a way you would like. Though your cook gave me some grief." Nora had to admit she liked Diana, but there were a few bad habits the woman had that would need correcting in Nora's opinion.

"I guess," Collette said. She glanced toward the camp then back at Nora.

"I'll go get you a small bowl. You can stay. Would you like a small piece of bread as well?"

"Sure."

Nora patted Collette gently on the leg in what she hoped was seen as a comforting gesture before rising to her feet, making an uncomfortable noise at the way her knees cracked. She made her way quickly through the camp to where Diana was overseeing the food distribution and went for one of the wooden bowls. "I'm making Collette some food," she said, feeling the blonde's eyes on her.

"Good," Diana said. "She needs to eat. She's far too lean."

"I do what I can, but sometimes she just can't stomach anything," Nora explained as she made up a bowl, making sure there was an equal portion of vegetables with the rabbit and that the pieces of meat she received were easy to chew. "I find if you sit with her and make conversation, she will absentmindedly eat." She wasn't sure if that was helpful for the cook to know, but if she wasn't around, maybe Diana could help her eat.

"Would you like me to share that with certain people around camp?" Diana asked. She looked over in Tolan's direction before turning her gaze back to Nora.

Nora considered the idea. Tolan had been treating Collette well since they'd lost Larent and not in a way that said he wanted to be with her again, but more the way a friend should. "Yes, please. She needs to eat more."

Diana nodded. "I will do it, then," she promised.

Nora gave a decisive nod, grabbed two pieces of warmed bread, and headed back to Collette. She noted Thomas, Arian, and Nawalya had moved closer but still hadn't joined Collette, who had the letter in hand once more. "I have food. Let me know if it's to your taste."

Chapter Thirty-Five

Riken sat in the office Rhoslyn had given him, his eyes trained on the letter in his hands, though he wasn't really seeing it. At this point, he had read the words so many times he had memorized them—not that there were many words on the piece of parchment. What words there were, however, were devastating.

Lord Riken,

Wildrun has fallen to Collette's invading army.

Commander Shalen

His home had been taken. The estate his family had resided in for generations had been taken by that bitch and her mindless followers. Followers who didn't understand the Mother and all she offered. Followers who had no respect or care for what Coralia could be. The only consolation he had was that his people would never tolerate the unlawful occupation. They would find a way to fight back. The knowledge didn't make his loss any better, but very little could at the moment.

Riken rose from behind his desk, folded the letter carefully, and headed out of his office. As much as he wanted to rip the parchment into pieces and throw it in the fire, he couldn't. This was something Rhoslyn would need to know about if she didn't already.

He headed first to her office, only to find it empty, and then to her rooms, only to again find them devoid of his queen. Not allowing his frustrations to get the better of him, Riken thought to find Cadan before he remembered his—no, Rhoslyn's second was performing another punishment on the servants. This time on one who had been caught talking ill of their queen. While Riken approved of flogging, he never had much stomach for it, even when he was the one issuing the punishment.

Knowing not all the servants would have been called to the courtyard to watch, Riken took a moment to find one of the available ones, only to be told Rhoslyn was in the garden with Mallan, which just darkened his mood. That man was spending too much time with Rhoslyn, and he truly disliked it, especially since he knew Mallan didn't have a real interest in Rhoslyn.

It was a matter of moments to head to the garden and locate the two strolling amongst the flowers. Rhoslyn noticed him first, her eyebrows raised in question upon seeing his distress.

"What is it, Riken?"

Riken thought he had done an alright job hiding his distress, but Rhoslyn could always see through him. It was one of the reasons he loved her. However, he hadn't wanted to show weakness in front of Mallan, who was looking more interested than he liked. "I received a letter from the commander Cadan left in charge when we came here." He moved so he was closer to her and held out the letter, finding saying the words out loud too difficult.

Rhoslyn unfolded the parchment, and her brow furrowed as she read the one line. "Mallan, if you will excuse us. I need to speak with Lord Riken."

Mallan looked like he wanted to protest but, instead, inclined his head, wished Rhoslyn a good afternoon, and left. Riken noted offhandedly that Mallan had ignored him completely, but he wasn't in the mood to handle it. "I am going to write back and see if I can get Shalen to send a scout to get troop numbers and ensure Collette is with them."

"Good idea," Rhoslyn replied, her voice filled with quiet sincerity. Without another word, she wrapped her arms around him in a gentle, comforting embrace.

The moment he felt her arms wrap around him, offering the comfort and love he so needed in that moment, Riken felt his carefully constructed wall of strength crumble. He allowed himself to be weak, to let out a shaky breath and shed several silent angry tears at the loss of his home. At the insult this so obviously was. "They could have come over the mountain to us directly, but no. She had to point her army at my home. Had to take that from me, purposefully."

Her embrace tightened, her presence an anchor in the storm of his emotions. "We'll get it back," Rhoslyn promised. "We have the manpower. I could have an army out within days to take it back for you."

Riken wanted to say yes. He wanted to strike back against those that had done this. But Rhoslyn's words from when he first arrived back in Quenall after the battle rattled inside his head, making him stop and question his first instinct. "I want that more than I can voice, but I want to make sure she's there first. Because you're right. No matter how many guards we have, no matter how many secret entrances Cadan finds, it's still too easy to get into the castle. I can't have her sneaking in

here and murdering you while we are distracted. Losing you would be worse than losing Wildrun."

Rhoslyn lifted her chin and drew Riken in for a kiss, a sign of affection she'd denied him since his return. "Then I suggest we send out scouts as soon as possible. Taking Wildrun was intentional. A warning of what is to come. Perhaps we'll learn the fate of Veitel as well."

Riken initiated another kiss, grateful for the attention she was giving him, then immediately felt guilty. "I am so sorry. I hadn't even considered Veitel. I will get scouts out right away. If Veitel hasn't been taken, I will send what remains of my soldiers from Wildrun there to help keep it safe."

"With the two estates being so close, I wouldn't be surprised to hear more bad news," Rhoslyn said, her voice soft. She reached up and touched his cheek, delicate fingertips brushing against his dark stubble. "No matter what happens, we will make it right. You and I."

Riken nodded and his eyes narrowed in a determination he now felt instead of the pain he'd so acutely suffered before. "We will make it right, and we will make them suffer," he vowed.

"Indeed," Rhoslyn agreed. "Now, please, go direct Cadan to act, then return to me. I shall make sure you are properly distracted this evening."

"I'll go now and make sure everything is taken care of." He kissed her softly. "Thank you again, my love."

Chapter Thirty-Six

Jayden stood at the front gates leading into the Wildrun estate, taking in the sights before him. The town sprawled out like a drab, lifeless shadow, especially with all the people voluntarily sequestered in their homes. Behind him, the imposing estate loomed—its cold, stone walls threatening and unwelcoming, contrasted with the warmer manor at Pontus Bay. By the Goddess, even the castle in Quenall had been more inviting.

Wildrun exemplified coldness and oppression. He couldn't imagine living under these conditions. At least taking Wildrun had been easier than they'd anticipated; a small victory which would hopefully precede bigger ones. Their scouts had reported a sizable group of soldiers and guards stationed at Wildrun, something both he and Aphros had questioned, having assumed Riken would all but empty Wildrun in his attack on their kingdom. Perhaps the survivors had returned after hearing Collette and her army had made landfall in Pontus Bay.

When their army of Nereid, Fythian, and loyal Coralians had arrived at Wildrun's outskirts, they had been met by the steward of the estate. A young man, whose rounded cheeks and lack of facial hair only made Jayden feel sorry for him, held out a letter of surrender when approached. Upon questioning, he admitted the remaining soldiers had fled upon seeing the approaching army.

Jayden remained astonished at their luck. They'd taken one of the oldest and largest estates in Coralia without shedding a single drop of blood. It was a victory, and yet, it didn't feel like it. The townsfolk were terrified of them, the Nereid specifically, as if they were monsters instead of the victims of a decades' long attempted genocide by these very same people. It left him feeling sick and unhappy, and he hated that.

"I've seen you in better spirits," Aphros commented, drawing Jayden's attention.

Jayden turned his head to look at Aphros and tried to muster a smile for him. "This victory feels … hollow," he said after a minute's thought.

"Do you think so?" Aphros asked. "I have an entirely different take."

"I'm sure I'll be fine in a little while. I think the way the townsfolk reacted just caught me off guard," he admitted, managing a real smile. "Let me hear your take."

Aphros chuckled and pointed his thumb back at the manor. "The man who is helping to take Coralia back to their darkest days is inept enough to leave his home unprotected. I think I feel much more optimistic about the plans in Quenall."

Jayden couldn't help but concede the point to Aphros on that one. "You are right. Did they think we'd just go over the mountain and not cut off potential escape routes?"

"I think they know Collette's reign is legitimate, but they doubt her support," Aphros said as he ran his fingers through his salt-and-pepper hair, pushing it back from his face. "Or they are ignorant to it."

Chapter Thirty-six

"Willfully ignorant," Jayden said after a moment's thought. "While Wildrun may be full of those who hate or don't understand us, the rest of this side of the kingdom is not. When I was here as a diplomat, I remember hearing things about Veitel."

"Oh?" Aphros inquired.

"Their former earl was quite negligent in his duties. When the people there needed help, it was the elves who stepped up first. Once Collette found out, she sent help as well. I doubt the people there will soon forget that."

"Let us hope," Aphros said. "Now, I think we need to investigate the estate and see what information we can find. You never know what might be useful."

Jayden nodded. "It also allows us to see what type of alcohol the lord liked best," he couldn't help but joke.

"Then let us see if we find something in which we'd like to partake."

Jayden laughed. "Let's. I'm willing to bet a man like Riken has a full cellar."

The two made their way into the large estate, and Jayden found himself shocked upon entering. Although the decor was not to his taste, he understood how someone could appreciate the dark wood, deep mahoganies, reds, and greens that featured in the great entryway.

"Lord Riken is a man of certain tastes, is he not?" Aphros commented, pausing in front of a portrait which greeted them immediately to the left side of the doors. The man, tanned with dark curly hair and darker eyes, held an arrogant pout on his lips.

"He most certainly is, though I wonder if these tastes are of an older family member now long gone." Jayden returned his gaze to the painting. He decided he didn't like the young man or his petulant demeanor. The figure depicted would likely be a man willing to do whatever he felt necessary to get his way.

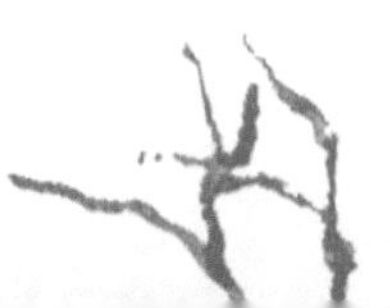

Looking at the name plate at the bottom of the portrait, he suddenly knew why. "Oh look. It's the lord of the estate."

"These old family homes tend to remain quite the same, generation after generation." Aphros pointed up at the painting. "This is likely the newest thing you'll find in this estate."

Jayden imagined the cost for remodeling an estate this size would be astounding and not worth the cost. Unless one didn't care about your people, which it seemed was not the case for Riken. He wondered if the lord would have felt the same if his people didn't share the same beliefs he did. "Remind me when we are drunk, or at least less sober, that burning items like these are not a good idea."

"I shall tell you Queen Collette will likely appoint someone to take over this title and estate and oversee the redistribution of wealth as needed," Aphros promised. "Shall we continue our tour?"

"Which is why a less sober me cannot burn anything. While I doubt anyone will buy a portrait of that man for any significant amount, you never know," Jayden replied and motioned for Aphros to go first.

Aphros continued from the entry hall into the heart of the first floor. They came into a wide, circular room with portraits similar to the one of Lord Riken placed in even intervals along the wall. Jayden could see the family resemblance among them, though the current lord was probably the handsomest amongst them.

It didn't help that every other painting of the lords and ladies who were pictured all wore scowls and haughty gazes. Jayden understood how Riken came to be, knowing nothing beyond those expressions.

As they continued along, they experienced more of the same decor and furnishings. Jayden chose to focus on the path ahead of them until they reached the kitchen. It was empty of staff, as was the rest of the estate—the servants having apparently fled upon their arrival. The kitchen itself was open with a lot of room to move around. It was also a bit more bright and cheery than the rest of the house. He wondered if one of the former ladies of the house had enjoyed cooking and baking enough to, at some point, make the financial investment that had obviously been used there.

Spotting a door on the far left side, he pointed it out to Aphros. "We can start there and hope," he said as he continued looking around. "I think I like this room best so far."

"I doubt Lord Riken ever set foot in this room," Aphros mused. "That could be why."

Jayden snorted. "Cooking is for the servants or for the wife. Though, I can't picture Rhoslyn in the kitchen," Jayden said as he opened the door. It was a fully stocked pantry that had enough food to feed their people for quite some time.

"Women of this social status would not do their own cooking," Aphros commented as he poked around.

"True," Jayden remarked before motioning toward the overly stuffed pantry. "This is a bit much for a steward and the staff alone." He took note of a second door and strolled toward it, betting alcohol would be found there. "How do you think Collette is doing?"

"She's surviving," Aphros said after a pause. "But I doubt much more than that."

"They should reach the other side of the mountain soon if they aren't there yet. I hope this works. I know you would have done anything to bring back…" He let the words trail off. They never talked about Aphros's wife, taken from them too soon.

The Nereid king shook his head. "No, I don't think I would attempt to resurrect the dead. I believe those who have moved on are happier where they are."

"Do you not support Collette's plan, then?" Jayden asked. They hadn't had much time to truly talk about how either of them felt about this quest to bring her husband back from the dead. Jayden, while having been fully supportive, had mixed feelings about everything.

"I did not say that," Aphros replied as Jayden finally opened the door to what appeared to be a cellar. Without pause, they started down a short staircase where they were met with a nearly bare supply of wine. "I think each person has to determine what is right for them and those they care about. She would know better than I if Larent would want to return, and certainly if the path is right for her."

Jayden nodded in understanding. "I've never been in love the way you or Collette have. I like to think if I had that type of love, I'd go to the ends of the world for that person, but who knows." Jayden gave a disgruntled look at the wine.

"And I hope you will never have to know what you might do in the most dire of circumstances."

"Same, which is why I may just continue to bed hop until my hips give out." He read a few of the labels and grabbed two bottles of the ones he knew and a bottle of one he didn't. "Grab some glasses?" he asked as they headed from the wine cellar.

Your Majesty, Queen Collette,

I am pleased to inform you that we have secured Wildrun in your name. I am also pleased to say this was accomplished without bloodshed. Lord Riken appears to have neglected his home in his pursuit of your head, power, and influence.

I have secured a report of our findings for your use. At this time, we have chosen to forgo backtracking to Veitel in favor of meeting you sooner in Quenall.

Chapter Thirty-six

I did send scouts in that direction so we have some idea of the status of that estate. I expect it will not be an improvement over Wildrun.

Yours,
Aphros

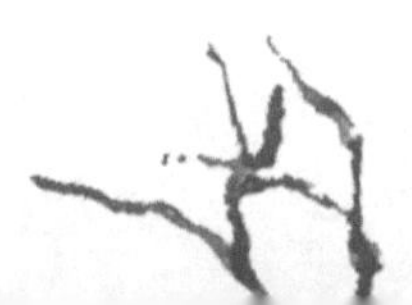

Chapter Thirty-Seven

Cremisius Hawke looked around the small clearing he and some members of the ever-growing resistance had claimed as their own in the forest outside of Quenall. Soon after leaving the tunnels, Crem and the other leaders of the Quenall resistance decided to spread out into factions. That way, should Cadan or his ilk find any of them, the others would remain safe and free.

Of course, Crem suspected an encounter with Cadan would come at some point. Though it had taken months, Cadan eventually found the tunnels, and he had done so within half an hour of the resistance's departure. The sizable force accompanying Cadan suggested arrest, or even death, had been possible.

"They came ta' kill us," Howle had insisted. Crem disagreed, at least when it came to the swiftness of the death. He thought Rhoslyn would want to make a spectacle of bringing them in and having them executed. That Diana agreed with him didn't make everything better for once.

Looking up from the table displaying the map in the center of camp, Crem glanced around for his wife, finding her and Howle engaged in a good-natured debate near the fire.

He didn't know what she'd said or done, but shortly after they'd set up this camp, Diana had pulled Howle aside and managed to change his attitude, which had gotten better since his outburst some time back. He was still grumpy but in better spirits, and the two of them were getting along again. Crem decided it was an upside to living in the forest.

He still had no idea how to handle Howle's confession of attraction, but it didn't seem that important at the moment. Not when Collette had made landfall and, within a few short weeks, her army had taken Wildrun. No. Right now, seeing what they could do to help her seemed like the best thing to focus on.

Diana smiled as their gazes met, and his eyes traveled to the swell of her stomach. She would grow rounder in the coming months, and Crem couldn't help but contemplate his mix of joy and fear. Fear seemed to win out most often. He tried to combat it, but the idea that they were going to bring new life into this world, especially with the threats they currently faced, scared him more than anything else ever had. Diana did her best in helping him keep that fear at bay, even if she still refused to remove herself from active danger. It was still her choice, and he wasn't going to take that from her.

Running a hand through his dark hair, he pushed away from the table, intent on going to his wife and best friend, when noise from the northern section of the camp drew his attention. He was sprinting toward the noise before it even registered. "Hide!" he mouthed to Diana. Whatever it was may be coming at them from the mountain-facing side of camp and not Quenall, but that meant nothing, and they knew it.

Thankfully, the members of the camp knew what to do, with the more vulnerable going into hiding and the others taking up strategic positions. As they waited, the distinct sound of multiple pairs of boots reached Crem's ears. That was a lot more people then he'd expected Cadan to bring, but it mattered not.

They would win the day or go down ensuring their families escaped. "We hold this line, if for nothing more than to give our loved ones time to escape," he said loud enough for the handful of men and women at his side to hear him. A quick glance showed they wouldn't run. They were just as determined as he was.

"There are people nearby," a deep voice sounded from the trees. "I think we might have found what we were looking for."

Crem thought he recognized the voice, but it was just far enough away that he wasn't sure. There was also the fact that the voice belonged to a person he was sure was in Wildrun with the queen's army where he belonged and not sneaking through the trees to give him a heart attack.

"Did ya hear that?" Howle asked from beside him, a large broadsword in his hands.

"Keep your sword ready. Just in case," Crem said firmly.

"Crem, you big-eared idiot, are you out here?" a distinctly familiar female voice asked. "I swear to the Spirits, why do I have to do everything?"

Crem felt his arms relax of their own volition as Howle burst into laughter next to him.

"That is most certainly our queen. Lower yar weapons, soldiers, and greet yar queen," Howle called out through his laughter.

"Yeah, laugh it up, you giant idiot," Crem said as he put away his weapon, ignoring the laughter of those around him and what he was damn sure was his wife's laughter in the background.

The queen soon emerged through the trees, flanked by the familiar faces of Whyldon and Arian on either side. Behind her, several followed, though Crem suspected they didn't begin to represent her forces. His heart raced with dual forces of relief and anxiety. Relief because she had returned and she would right the wrongs in their world. Anxiety because he knew she didn't want the responsibility and he could only imagine what else it would cost her.

Crem let out a sigh as he took in their queen. Collette stood in her travel leathers, similar to the outfits she'd once worn when they'd go hunting. Though the outfit was clean and in good repair, there was no hiding the frequent use. No doubt it had accompanied her to Azmarin and back. Her hair, which had once hung down her back in loose waves or the occasional braid, now rested just on her shoulders. She also looked thinner, as her cheek bones stood out more prominently beneath her dark freckles.

The changes in appearance weren't the only things that struck him. He'd known a bright, talkative, and, at times, crude woman who exuded strength. She had little apprehension in pursuing the passions she held. He saw flickers of all of that in her expression, but a cloak of sadness seemed wrapped around her now, and he was left to question what right he and the rest of the rebellion had to demand her leadership.

After all, her rule had been full of people telling her what she could and couldn't do. How stupid and naïve she was. How her policies would ruin Quenall. It had been full of bullies and fear mongers and worse. And it had ended with Crobán trying to humiliate her and her brother betraying her. Collette had no reason to be there, and yet, she was.

A tentative smile tugged at the corner of his lips as she stepped into the clearing. Shouts of joy issued from others in the camp, cementing this moment as a culmination of their work and hopes. He took a step forward and bowed to Collette. "My queen," he began before rising. "Permission to hand over command of the soldiers to Whyldon? I could use the break."

"Permission granted," Collette replied as she came to stand in front of Crem. She crossed her arms and took him in with

a wry expression which reminded him of the days before the overthrow. "You look like you need a break."

Crem laughed and nodded, though the humor left his face as he studied her up close. He was able to really take in the queen now that they were this close. Her exhaustion and weight loss were all the more prevalent, though he imagined, had he faced the same hardships, he'd suffer similarly. "As do you. Thankfully Diana is also here to keep me sane," he said as his wife appeared by his side.

Collette's gaze turned to Diana, and her eyes dipped to Diana's pregnant belly. "I'm surprised he allowed you to stay so close to Quenall."

"It was not his choice," Diana replied, nodding her head in respect.

"What she said," Crem agreed. He thought of offering his arm to Collette so he could escort her to the command tent, but Howle beat him to it.

"Would ya like ta' sit down and have a cup a tea before y'all get down to business?" he asked, offering her his arm.

Crem was surprised he'd do that. After all, Howle had been King Sargarus's lapdog until he suddenly quit when she was still a child.

Collette accepted Howle's offer. "Of course. My party could use some rest, and I'm certain Crem and Whyldon would like the chance to catch up." Howle nodded and led Collette away with Diana, leaving Crem, Whyldon, and their respective camps.

Both leaders dismissed their people before Crem turned to Whyldon. "How has your vacation been?" he asked, laughing as Whyldon raised his eyebrows, unimpressed. Like Collette, Whyldon had seen better days. A year had passed since they'd last seen one another, but Whyldon had aged beyond that.

Whyldon gave a tired sigh. "There are no words to describe what these past months have been like, though I'm sure we'll give it a try."

"I'm happy to hear you try, and while you're at it, I'll try to come up with my own explanation for what's been happening here." Crem shook his head. "Things have been … shit." He ran a hand down his face. "I'm happy you're here."

"I'm glad to be back, but I fear what that means," Whyldon confessed. "She's planning to break into the castle."

Crem found himself surprised by Whyldon's words. Collette had arrived with what looked like a sizable chunk of her army, and wasn't that going to be a bitch to keep hidden? "Is she planning on using the army as a distraction so she can break in and assassinate Rhoslyn?" Crem joked.

Whyldon, however, didn't dispute the idea. "It's one of the plans, depending on what we find out about the state of Quenall. I can't imagine, though, that there would be lax security, especially after Zephraim escaped."

"No. It's gotten much tighter since then. That's one of the reasons we don't have a base in the city anymore. Cadan is smarter, more resourceful, and patient. I think he took it as a personal affront when both Sara and Zephraim got out. Especially when he was right there."

"That makes sense," Whyldon said. "She'll want to do reconnaissance in the city before she makes a decision, but any information we can provide beforehand will likely be appreciated."

"There are a few entrances and exits we can use that haven't been discovered yet. I suggest sending people who aren't well known in town or people who are good at going unseen." Crem looked back at the group who'd followed Collette here. Amongst them stood Zephraim, though he paid Cremisius and

Whyldon no attention. "Well, I'm not unhappy to see Zephraim, but I'm surprised he's here with you."

"Collette told him to come," Whyldon said. "Though I suspect he would have requested to come along."

"He's a good resource, and he helped us out," Crem said, though he was sure Whyldon heard a bit of hesitation.

"I don't doubt his sincerity. If he was just saying what was needed to survive, I think we'd know by now. Still, his betrayal has irrevocably changed her life." Whyldon glanced at the tent Howle had taken Collette to. "She's never going to be the same."

"That's why I don't trust him. No matter how much good he does now, he can never make up for the harm he caused for so many," Crem admitted, and while he did feel bad for saying it, it was true.

"Perhaps he can be useful in righting those wrongs, and afterwards, he can be left to lead a quiet life. Hopefully it will be more in line with what he's truly wanted for himself."

"I wonder if he ever knew what he wanted for himself before recently," Crem said. There had been tension between Barris and Zephraim before they'd left. Given that Barris stood close by Zephraim now, perhaps it had been resolved.

"Who knows," Whyldon said. "Why don't you and I get a drink and catch up?"

"That sounds amazing, and we just had a delivery of some good ale too." He didn't need to say more for Whyldon to know they'd taken it from some noble who didn't support their queen.

Chapter Thirty-Eight

Nawalya closed her eyes, letting the sounds of the forest at night close in around her. She leaned against one of the many moss-covered trees a little ways from camp, having let Thomas know she needed some peace.

"Of course," Thomas easily replied as he closed up a book he'd been jotting in. "I'll let the others know if they ask. Try not to stray too far. Quenall will have scouts out looking for a camp."

She'd agreed, as the request was reasonable. Nawalya only went far enough away that the consistent low-level buzzing from the camp almost disappeared beneath the rustling of trees and the trickle of a nearby brook. She could make out one of the nearby campfires. Both the scent and sight of it called her back to the safety of the group. She would return, eventually.

Nawalya hoped being away from everything, if only for a little while, would help her relax, releasing the tension in her shoulders. A small part of her knew it wouldn't. She'd been carrying the tension for months, ever since the first time she'd had the vision of Larent attacking Collette. That she hadn't had a single vision since Larent's death only served to make her feel worse. Not knowing if the ritual Collette planned to do would work or not worried Nawalya, but there were no answers, and the tree was dark.

One would think sleep, which eluded Nawalya many nights, would be easier to come by because of it, but now she just had nightmares. Nightmares of Larent with an arrow through his chest, Collette's screams, and Arian's sobs repeating over and over again when she tried, making sleep even less appealing than it had been when she had seen an arrow over and over again.

She had hoped to try sleeping again tonight at some point, but for now, maybe just not being around such a large group of people would help. The cracking of branches to her right drew her attention, though she wasn't concerned. Cremisius Hawke had patrols around the camp based on what they'd been told around dinner. What did surprise her was to see Hawke and Whyldon conducting the patrol.

She was glad the two were reconnecting. From what Whyldon had told her over the past several months, he and Cremisius were good friends. While he got along well with the majority of their travel group, she hadn't felt like there was anyone he'd truly call a friend. Well, except maybe Rion. Seeing them spot her as they moved closer to where she was, she raised a hand in greeting, fully expecting the two to continue on.

"Hello, Nawalya," Whyldon said as the two men came to a stop near her. "Do you intend to spend the evening so far from camp?"

Nawalya considered the question. She hadn't intended to spend the entire evening away from camp, but she did tend to lose track of time when lost in her thoughts. "Not the entire night," she finally answered as she casually observed the two men. Whyldon looked as put together as he always did. Crem, she noted, had turned his body slightly to keep an eye in the forest. She approved that he was so vigilant.

Whyldon nodded. "You may want to head back soon enough. The next on patrol are some younger men Crem says are a bit jumpy."

"More than a bit," Crem said under his breath. Nawalya found herself wondering why they were on watch if they were so anxious.

Nawalya wondered if it would be worth climbing a tree to hide before dismissing the thought. With her luck, they'd think her a wild animal or something. "Thank you for the warning. I'll take a few more minutes and then head back."

Whyldon nodded and his shoulders relaxed from a soldier's posture. "We'll leave you to it. I imagine getting away from everything for a bit feels nice."

"It is. The camp can be very … loud." Nawalya gave him a soft smile, and not wanting to worry Whyldon more, nor risk losing track of time, Nawalya stood from her spot by the tree. "I'll head back now, just to be safe." She knew he was under enough stress, and she refused to add to it by making him worry over her or Crem's men.

Though sudden raucous laughter from the camp had her reconsidering that stance. "I'll go see about it," Crem said with a sigh before jogging off.

"It's good they are taking time to enjoy themselves now," Nawalya said, smiling to herself for once. Only youth could usually find such humor in the midst of a war camp. "I'd truly forgotten what it was like to be with such a large group."

"It will be even bigger once Aphros's half rejoins us here," Whyldon pointed out, his blue eyes crinkling in amusement. The guard captain motioned back toward the camp, and they began walking.

"Don't remind me," she said, enjoying his amusement. "I keep trying to convince myself that the noise will disperse into the open area, but I know it won't."

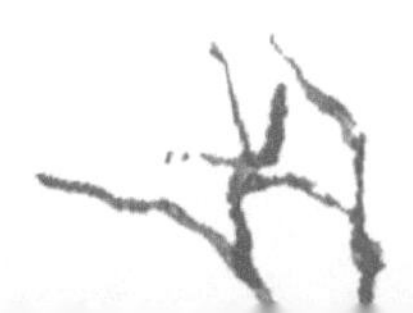

"In truth, there isn't much one can do about the hum of a large group. You'll adjust soon enough."

"I will. It's just a lot right now. The lack of sleep isn't helping," she said wryly as they continued their slow walk back toward the camp.

"No. Lack of sleep intensifies every annoyance. I've been in many a camp such as this, unable to sleep and grinding my teeth because a fellow soldier talks too much or snores too loudly. Dealing with it while grieving feels impossible."

Nawalya nodded. Losing Larent had been difficult, and his death touched every subsequent experience. "I had to teach myself to ignore Arian's snoring in the beginning. He used to make a strange whistling noise as well. We were dealing with enough back then without me trying to smother him." Nawalya shook her head.

"He still snores from time to time," Whyldon pointed out.

"Yes, but not the way he used to. Trust me, it was much worse."

"I do," Whyldon said with a chuckle.

Nawalya laughed with him before venturing to ask, "How are you handling all of this?"

"Better than I expected. I didn't have the same connection to Larent, and the pain of death does not strangle me the way it does others."

She nodded. He'd barely liked Larent in the beginning, and Nawalya was sure he wished Collette had picked anyone else to fall in love with. "I don't know what she and Arian will do should this not work, which is why it will."

"I fear she would give up."

"I do as well," Nawalya agreed, her voice quiet as they reached the camp. "I don't pray much anymore, but I've been praying about this." She looked around the busy camp that was starting to wind down for the night. Crem stood with the group of younger people she assumed had been the cause of loud laughter from a few minutes earlier.

She sighed, knowing she should go find her tent. As much as she wished to prolong her time with Whyldon, she couldn't come up with another topic of conversation to keep him around. She was tired of talking tactics and didn't want to dwell on the ritual and the very bleak future they had in front of them if the spell didn't work.

"I know you've been silently suffering since the battle," Whyldon spoke up, his voice quiet. "I understand why, but I know it's been difficult."

"Grief is never easy, but Collette and Arian need me to be strong right now."

"You are still allowed to mourn, even if you are being strong for others, you know," Whyldon said.

"Thank you," she said softly. "I just worry I'll get caught up in it. I've been trying to mourn in smaller, healthier ways than I used to. Like when my village was massacred. Sara and Nora have both had good suggestions." Nawalya gave him a small, shaky smile. "I appreciate your concern, but I will be okay."

"I know you will, but that does not mean someone shouldn't check on you."

"Thank you," she said earnestly. "It means a lot, especially after everything." She immediately regretted that she brought up not telling him about her visions, even if she knew they were past that.

Whyldon nodded, though he didn't immediately speak. Nawalya couldn't blame him. She still regretted the choice to keep the vision of Larent and Collette between herself, Arian, and Larent, but she'd accepted she didn't have the ability to change what had happened.

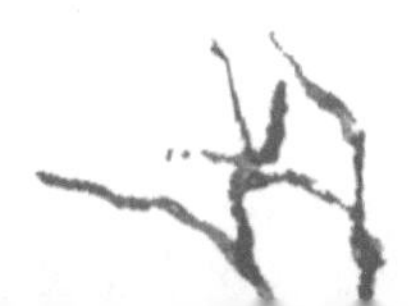

"I can imagine that, given the dynamics between you, Arian, and Larent, it was more than easy to convince yourselves it was best to stay quiet back then."

Nawalya looked away from Whyldon as she considered her next words before deciding to just admit the truth. "It was fear that prevented Larent and I from saying anything, though I tried to convince myself otherwise. Larent couldn't bear the thought of losing Collette, and I was so afraid to act. Arian wanted to tell you, though, and he planned on it if I'd had one more vision after Larent and I begged him not to say anything."

She was ashamed of that now; she should have trusted Whyldon more. Larent's fears weren't a lack of trust in Collette, but a fear of abandonment, a fear he would always hold thanks to his parents. Nawalya felt she had no excuse.

"Truthfully, I see that part. I see the fear, and while I disagree with what happened, I think I've come to understand that the dynamics at play are much more complicated than my initial anger allowed me to acknowledge."

"Your anger was warranted no matter the circumstances." Nawalya glanced around quickly to make sure there was no one who might be listening in. She still lowered her voice when she said, "I put your daughter in danger. That you said you wanted nothing to do with me anymore was the least I deserved."

"I meant that at the time," Whyldon admitted, his gaze falling to his boots. "And I took my anger out on those who did not deserve it." He sighed and lifted his gaze. "I would like to move past what has happened."

Nawalya's smile softened. "I deserve your anger, but I am more than happy to move past this if that's what you want," she said, tilting her head to the side. She'd thought they were already working toward friendship, though the renewal process had been disrupted by literal battles. She also recalled telling Arian she wasn't sure if she had loved Whyldon before, not the way she should have, not in a way that overrode her fear. But she knew she could, and she wanted that chance. This—this was a good start.

"Good," Whyldon replied, and he pointed in the direction of the camp. "Should we head back? Collette has insisted she go into the city come morning to see the state of things for herself."

Nawalya let out a breath as she once again thought about the implications of Collette going into the city. She hadn't spoken up against it, but she had concerns. "We should head back so you can get some rest. I think you'll need it if we're to help keep an eye on things."

"It's not even the most dangerous thing we will do while here." He offered his arm, despite the short trek back.

"No, that will be getting in and out of the castle without raising the alarm," she half joked as she accepted his arm.

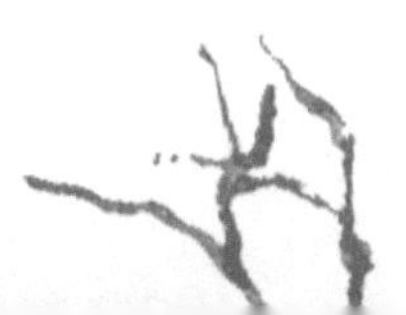

Chapter Thirty-Nine

Collette could hardly remember the last time she'd stepped foot in the castle, yet it seemed as though just yesterday she'd walked the streets leading toward Gadleigh Palace. The earthy, mountainous scent lingered in her memory, as did the carefree days spent losing herself in the woods on hunting trips. The same cluster of buildings still stood in the distant market, and the little homes remained scattered along the worn paths and streets. Life carried on—people hurried from their homes to their work, just as they had always done.

A pang of nostalgia tightened her chest, a bittersweet ache for a life that had once been hers, one that would never return. Even if she reclaimed the throne, she couldn't undo the experiences that had shaped her during months on the road. Most of which, she admitted, she wouldn't want to forget.

If she were successful in her quest, in getting inside, grabbing the spell, and getting out, she would never forget the feelings of horror and grief that accompanied Larent's death. But, she told herself almost constantly, if the spell worked and she lived through it, she planned on punching him square in the face before he had a chance to speak.

As merchants were in their shops and farmers in the fields in the middle of the day, she and her companions were more easily able to navigate their way through the city. Fewer people meant fewer sets of eyes falling on them, and that meant a greater chance of escape once they'd obtained the spell. Still, she pulled her cloak a little further over her face, making sure to hide her identity as much as possible.

As they neared the market, the familiar scent of spices and fruit invaded her senses. Collette was not one who required much luxury in her meals, but the nostalgia of being in her former home served to remind her of the way the kitchens would smell as Diana cooked while Tolan pretended to be helpful.

She almost smiled at the memories but paused as her gaze was drawn to a glittering display in a nearby booth. Instantly, her eyes narrowed as she recognized the familiar gleam and shape of Merscales, and she might have gone over to investigate—and exposed herself—had Arian not grabbed her arm and hissed, "Keep moving," in her direction.

Collette listened, but she made a note of the merchant. When she was queen again, she might very well take Zephraim's advice from long ago. Examples often created lasting memories.

As they moved away from the market, Arian directed them down a side street, still part of the economic district but away from the main route. The change was smart, theoretically, but no guarantee of safety came from it.

"I think it will be best if we stay off the main street," Arian said in a low voice. "I would hate to see you start flipping tables if there are more merchants selling Merscales."

Collette turned her gaze to Arian, an eyebrow raised. "Oh, you aren't going to do that for me?"

"Would you let me?" he asked seriously

"After I get the spell out of the castle, you can treat Merscale traders with all the respect they deserve."

"I had assumed you would handle them before I could," Arian said, his smile sharp. "But I will be glad to show them all the respect."

"And you will do a lovely job," she replied. It had been decided for the group going into Quenall to break up into smaller factions. Arian and Collette, naturally, had branched off together. "Other than the Merscale traders, have you spotted anything else of note?"

"There are a lot more guards walking the streets, some not in uniform. It is possible they are from Azmarin, but they are watchful. We are lucky none paid attention to us. I think we were only missed because most were paying attention to the general populace—most of which were walking with their heads bowed and as quickly as they could. The air of fear is almost as bad as it was under Sargarus," he said quickly.

"Don't you half wish someone would mess with us?"

"If you were not here, I would have already been arrested." Arian's words were delivered as factual with an edge of steel.

"I'd prefer we both get out of here without arrest," Collette said. They'd made it solidly into the middle of the market-place, which teemed with shoppers despite the near tangible atmosphere of fear. The castle, though partially obstructed, could be viewed from their little corner of the marketplace, and Collette found herself overwhelmed with the desire to approach. Larent's salvation seemed so close.

As if sensing her need, Arian gently placed a hand on her forearm. "If you truly wish to do this right now, we can. I will support you, but it may be better to wait." He motioned to the guards that could be seen near the castle.

"I know," she said with a nod. "Now is not the time. At least, not at this immediate moment."

"If you wanted, I could set up a beautiful distraction," Arian offered.

Collette knew he would do whatever she asked him to, and she did want to break into the castle now. She felt like she could figure out how to sneak inside with the same amount of urgency as when she escaped. "The others will be angry."

She could see Arian struggle with himself for a moment before the word, "And?" left his mouth, as if all their planning didn't matter.

She raised an eyebrow, all the encouragement she needed having been given. "Don't pretend to fuck me this time?"

Arian gave a pained laugh. "No, I would not. No." He pointed to an inn across the way. It was a two-story building and had a great view of the castle. "I am going to climb onto that roof, do my best impression of Larent giving a motivational speech, murder some guards, and hope to start an uprising. While I do that, you can get in and out. Nawalya is only a few streets over. She will help. As will Tolan. The rest will help for no other reason than they have to. Spirits willing, we all get out alive."

She nodded, moved to take a step, then paused. "Whyldon does not go near the castle, no matter what else happens."

Arian nodded and took a determined step forward, heading into the open area. "Go now," he said as he started to undo his cloak.

Collette did as instructed, moving her feet as quickly as possible without drawing attention to herself. Putting distance between herself and Arian was critical, especially when he planned on attracting less than welcoming glances.

She ducked into a side street off of the center of the market-place then paused when she heard an intake of breath. Turning, she saw Tolan. She let out a silent curse, telling herself she had to be more vigilant in listening for danger.

"What are you doing?" she hissed.

"I got separated from Rion and ended up here." He looked past Collette and his eyes got wide. He held out a hand for her to take. "I assume we are headed for the castle. Right now?"

She took his hand without hesitation. Tolan couldn't stop her, and they both knew it, which meant he was volunteering to help. "It's right there," she said.

Tolan nodded, and together, they started toward the castle. "I had a feeling this was going to happen," he admitted as they both heard Arian start to shout out to the crowded square.

"Thomas is going to kill me," she muttered to herself. "If we don't get ourselves killed first."

"As long as Arian survives, I think you'll be fine." He pulled them down another side street as several guards ran past them headed in Arian's direction. "He'll be fine."

"I hope so."

From their new position, Collette could make out the bridge leading to the castle. Though she would classify it as heavily guarded, there was more scrutiny of those passing to and from than the night she'd escaped. "I see five."

"Seven. There are two standing a little ways off talking to a merchant." He pointed to the left. "I wish there was another way in." Collette could hear the frustration in his voice. "Nawalya would set something on fire to distract the guards," he muttered to himself, and she knew that no matter what it took, Tolan was going to get her inside.

"If there are two major distractions, they'll know something's up." She shifted so she could better see the merchant and guards.

Glancing around, she took in the old path running parallel to the bridge which ducked beneath it in some places. It had long gone unused, though it had once been used to bring in people and supplies to the castle while the current bridge was built. That had been some twenty years prior, and though she doubted there would be land passage all the way across, it was the best option they had. "We might have a chance to go unseen that way."

"Let's give it a try."

They moved quickly, but not fast enough to attract attention. Tolan took a deep breath and held it for several beats, probably trying to calm his nerves. Once they were back out in the open, they kept to the side of the crowd, their movements purposeful but unassuming. Another couple of soldiers, these ones in official Coralian uniforms, brushed past them without looking back, running in the direction of Arian's voice.

"Spirits, I hope they're okay. I know Larent said Arian really wanted to fight the castle, but…" Tolan's voice was low so no one else could overhear.

"He sounds okay," Collette said. She subtly gestured for Tolan to step from the road into the grass and rock strewn area that would lead to a hill.

"If they're sending more people, he must be," Tolan said as he followed her instructions. "What's the plan for when we get inside?"

"Do you remember the large, unused estate rooms on the highest floor?" Collette asked as they descended down, the tall grass creeping higher and higher.

Tolan made an affirmative noise. "I remember. Are we climbing walls, or is there an entrance I don't know about?"

"There's an old entrance down there we might be able to get into," Collette said as she carefully made her way down the hill. The closer they got to the water passage, the slicker the ground grew. "I don't fancy scaling walls in broad daylight."

"Whoever you put in charge of Quenall is going to have their work cut out for them to ensure palace security. There are just too many ways in and out," Tolan said, his grip on her arm

tightening slightly. She noted he kept carefully checking their surroundings, ensuring they hadn't been spotted.

When they reached the bottom of the hill, Collette looked around, studying their options. A small entry gate sat directly beneath the bridge, its existence invisible from the bridge above. Though clearly well made, its orangey coloring and rough edges suggested a general lack of use for the last several decades. In truth, she doubted anyone residing in the palace now knew about it. Most had always used the bridge above.

Granted, its usefulness would render the entrance unimportant. It looked big enough for only a handful of people to walk through at any given time, and the surrounding stream, though shrunken, probably never allowed more than a dinghy to pass by with whatever wares it could hold. "Think we can lift that?" she asked.

"Yes, but the amount of rust could make it difficult."

"As long as we get in without notice." She moved forward, taking care to stay out of the water as much as possible. In some places, the stream looked deep enough to nearly reach her knees, so she used bits of stone and the old walkover bridge as much as possible.

Reaching the other side in as dry of a condition as possible, she waited for Tolan to join her. Up close, she could peer through the gate to the inner chamber. On the far wall, a door stood, which she was positive would lead into the servant's quarters based on their location.

Tolan examined the hinges for the gate, scraping a fingernail against the rust. "This doesn't look so bad up close. You take that side and I'll take this side, and we can see if it opens."

Collette placed the palm of her hands beneath the horizontal bar which rested about chest high on her. Thankful for her incredible strength—which may or may not have been due to Nereid blood—she looked to Tolan. "Go on three?"

Chapter Thirty-nine

Tolan nodded before grabbing the same bar. He shifted his weight and placed his right foot back in order to get a better grip. "Whenever you're ready."

She signaled for both to try lifting, and surprisingly, the metal budged, creaking loudly from the effort. Collette commanded a brief pause so they could listen for responses. When none came, she beckoned Tolan to help her continue. Slowly, the gate lifted from the ground, orange particles of rust floating around them.

In total, it took them about a minute to get the gate up and out of their way. Tolan let out a labored breath once they were done. "That would have taken several of us if it weren't for your strength," he said, resting his hands on his knees.

"You're no slouch, Mister Arena-Fighter," Collette replied. She brushed the rust and debris from her hands, noting the little imprints left in her palms.

"It's been a little while since I had an arena to fight in. A new person came into power and did away with the sport." He gave her a small grin as he referenced their first meeting.

"I hear that bitch was ousted if it's any consolation," she joked as she took in the next door. "Come on. We have a lot to do."

Tolan let out a startled laugh at her words. "Lead the way," he said.

They reached the door in a few quick steps, and surprisingly, when Collette took the handle, the door clicked open with no resistance. She glanced back at her former lover, then carefully pulled the door open and stepped inside, Tolan following behind.

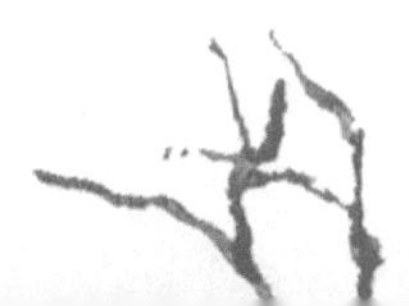

Chapter Forty

Arian grumbled as he made his way across the town square. He did not regret sending Collette to the castle, but he was concerned that his makeshift plan could go horrifically wrong. He'd had little choice though, especially once he had seen the look of longing on Collette's face. He'd had to do something.

That still did not stop his grumbling and cursing, especially toward Larent, who'd had the audacity to be murdered, leading to Arian doing something that would get him killed. If not by the guards, then by Thomas, who was sure to be upset when he found out they'd done this. Whyldon might also murder him if Thomas did not.

Reaching the halfway point of the square, Arian lowered his hood, ensuring those who were watching him—several guards, three on the right, four on the left—knew he was an elf. One of the four made a movement to catch the attention of an eighth guard who was harassing a poor stall woman some ways away, the movement becoming more frantic when Arian dropped his cloak completely, revealing his leather armor. A short sword rested on one hip, and several daggers were scattered along his body.

Chapter Forty

As he reached the building he had pointed out to Collette, Arian noted the eighth guard was finally paying attention and running off to get help, while the seven began to advance on his position, not that they would get near him before he reached the highest part of the roof. It was the work of seconds to jump onto the first-story roof, using an empty box one of the stall keepers had left on the ground to give him the height needed to reach it, before pulling himself up and moving quickly to the next portion. Once there, he looked out onto the square, noting that he already had many eyes on him.

A noise drew his attention to the ground where two of the soldiers were trying to lift a third onto the roof, the armor they wore making it difficult to lift him. It was also clear the man they were trying to lift wasn't a climber, as his hands and feet scrambled to find a secure holding.

Cursing Larent again, and then Nawalya for letting Collette and him be alone together when her objective was in reach, he called out to the people. "People of Quenall! See me! Hear my words! I am Arian Tal'Dela, survivor of the A'lierdeen massacre. I am not one of you, but I have been in your position: oppressed, terrified, unknowing of what horrors may come next! I refused to be in that position again, and so I fight. I fight against a tyrant who keeps you scared, who threatens your family and friends, your very lives! If you wish to be free, then you too must fight! Join me now, stand up, fight for yourselves, your kingdom. Your queen!"

He was out of time. During his speech, two of the guards had managed to get onto the roof and were almost within arm's reach. With one hand, he flicked a dagger into the throat of the closest one, pulling out his sword and made quick work of the second. Using his momentum, he slid down the second story roof and onto the third guard, bringing his sword down through the man's chest before kicking the fourth from where he attempted to lift himself onto the roof, sending him sprawling over the ones under him.

Noise from the far side of the square announced more guards coming. Arian counted to ten, even as he cast a quick glance at the people standing still, as if in shock at both his words and action. For a moment, Arian felt hopeless. He was never good at speeches, and so he had failed to rally the people.

Still, Collette needed a distraction, so he would give her one. He just hoped Nawalya was as close by as he had told Collette she would be. He was confident in his own abilities, but he knew, without help, he would eventually fall trying to give Collette as much time as possible.

Sending a silent apology to Thomas, he took a deep breath and readied himself to jump from the roof and onto the soldiers below who were slowly rising to their feet. With luck, he could make quick work of them before engaging the other ten.

He was about to jump down when a loud crash drew his attention to where the other soldiers were coming from. Two of the young men from a stall that sold pottery had pushed over the boxes stacked next to their stall, knocking over some of the guards and stalling the rest. Arian couldn't hear what the men said, but he heard one of the guards yell, "Arrest them!" And in that one moment, with that one small act of defiance, it was as if the square came to life.

A large man with a sword stepped in front of the two young men and engaged the guards, while others grabbed whatever was on hand to help. Arian glanced down at the four guards on the ground beneath him, who watched as the people turned on them, slow horror dawning on their faces as to what this meant.

"Get moving! We have to stop this now," said an older looking guard.

Arian picked him as his next target. Sheathing his sword, he next drew two of his longer daggers and jumped from the roof onto the man, his blades sinking into the man's shoulders. Bringing up his legs, he used the dead man's downward momentum to push himself up and off, daggers and bloody bits of the man coming with him.

The group of soldiers now consisted of three men. Daggers out, blood splattering his armor, and a crowd behind him that were attacking the only help that had arrived so far, Arian knew he looked frightening. That said, he was still surprised when one of the three decided running was the best option. He moved to throw a dagger at the man, only to end up having to take on the other two who had decided death was better than cowardice and tried to attack him together. Arian appreciated the effort, but they were clearly not used to fighting together, getting in each other's way and making Arian's job much easier.

Once dispatched, he turned back to the crowd, noticing that in the short period it took to handle the guards, more had joined in the fighting, but so had other townsfolk. As he looked around, he noted members of Crem's group had joined as well, though he didn't see the old commander or Howle.

Arian itched to stay and fight, but he also wanted to see if he could catch up to Collette, or—and this was more important—get to the nearest of Crem's camps and request help be sent to the town. They would need to keep as many of the townsfolk as safe as possible once the uprising started to die down, and if they could kill a large amount of Rhoslyn's or Azmarin's guards, even better.

Seeing more guards, a lot more guards, enter the square from the direction of the castle, Arian knew he had to get more fighters. He moved through the crowd as quickly as he could, killing all guards that crossed his path and garnering a lot of attention from the oncoming soldiers before he broke free from the mayhem into a less crowded area.

He glanced around, reorienting himself with where he was and what the fastest route to Crem's camp would be, when noise behind him caught his attention. Glancing back, Arian growled as a large group of guards pushed through the crowd. He knew he could take them, but the townsfolk needed help more than he needed their blood on his hands. Taking off, Arian kept his eyes open for an easy way to get to the rooftops. The fighting had spread outside of the town square into the narrower streets and areas between buildings, making his escape much harder.

Spotting a cart he could use as leverage, Arian changed directions, speeding up as much as his tiring body would allow. Hearing what sounded like a string being pulled taut, Arian glanced back and pivoted just in time for an arrow to fly past his face, cutting his brow as it went. Cursing that he'd missed the arrival of archers, rendering the rooftops no longer safe, Arian slid to a stop and turned to face the men. Only then did he see the group had broken off, with three of them coming for him from his left.

He dodged another arrow, moving around the long sword that came at him from the left, making it so he couldn't dodge the guard that decided ramming into him in the wall was a smart idea. He knew his ribs were not broken, but they were badly bruised by the way they protested as he brought a dagger down into the man's neck, barely turning his face away in time to avoid getting blinded by the spray.

Having expected the other soldiers to be on him already, Arian looked up, pushing the body off of himself and preparing for another attack in one fluid motion, only to almost sag in relief as Nawalya danced between the remaining guards.

"Go," she called out. "Tell Crem we need everyone now!"

Arian nodded and climbed up the cart and onto the roof above it, holding in a wince as his ribs screamed at him.

Glancing back at the town below him, he took a moment to take in the absolute chaos that was unfolding as the city of Quenall rose up to fight for its freedom. Larent would have been proud.

Arian took another moment to catch his breath and let the pain in his ribs reside before he started across the rooftops once more. With luck, it would take him less than twenty minutes to get through the town, into the woods, and to camp. Picking up speed and ignoring the pain, Arian was halfway through the town when he caught sight of a small group moving toward the town square at a decent speed. Recognizing Whyldon amongst them, Arian considered jumping down to them for a moment before changing his mind. Dropping down into the middle of an armed group without warning would be sure to get someone injured, so instead he let out a sharp whistle that drew their attention upward to him. The group slowed to a stop as Arian climbed down to them. "I am glad you're here. We could use the help," he said dryly.

"I see you're alone," Whyldon shot back. "Where is Collette?"

"If everything went as she planned, she should be leaving the castle soon, spell in hand," Arian answered and held back a flinch at the look in Whyldon's eyes.

"Why did she go to the castle, let alone by herself?" Whyldon asked, his calm demeanor forgotten.

Arian thought back to the longing look she had sent to the castle, the pain that had been mixed in. "I am fairly certain I heard Tolan join her. I did not go because she needed a distraction."

Whyldon cursed uncharacteristically, his hand going through his hand in frustration.

"Joss isn't stupid, Whyldon," Rion spoke up. "If she went in, she saw an opening."

"Rion's right," Crem said, placing a comforting hand on Whyldon's shoulder. Arian was grateful none of them asked him for confirmation, because it had been a spur of the moment decision, and he truly did not want to fight Whyldon.

Whyldon shook his head. "So, I take it all of this," he paused to motion to the surrounding chaos, "was a distraction."

Arian looked around at the seemingly ever-growing uprising. "I did not think the people were this ready to revolt," he admitted. "Though it is a good distraction."

"Then let's go help with it," Rion suggested. "They can't go find Joss in the castle if they are dealing with us."

Crem let out a sigh, which somehow got deeper when Howle whooped, and said, "Let's go kill us some traitors!"

Chapter Forty-One

As predicted, the door led into a corridor just off the servants' quarters. Thankfully, they'd entered the castle during the day, and the servants would surely be scattered throughout the palace, working on their various assigned tasks. "We need to get upstairs without being spotted," she warned in a nearly imperceptible whisper.

"I find myself wishing I'd spent less time in the kitchen and a bit more time exploring." Tolan glanced over her shoulder. "If it wasn't a waste of time, I'd suggest looking for servants' clothes, but our best bet I think is going to be moving as quickly as we can. Maybe we can use one of the hidden passages to get around. Which room did you hide the spell in again?"

"The old royal estate rooms at the top. I never used them for myself, given some of the very evil decisions that came to be there." She motioned them down the first corridor past servant doors, not pausing to look into open doors, before ducking into a stairway that was used primarily for the comings and goings of palace staff. "We might run into someone this way, given how I bet the nobles here view staff."

"Crem said Rhoslyn has allowed Cadan to beat servants for even the smallest of mistakes now, so hopefully, if we run into someone, they'll be on our side." Tolan let out a breath and removed a dagger from its sheath. Collette had no doubt he would handle anyone who even appeared to be a problem for them if he had to.

They ascended the stairs, their steps light and careful. Now and then, they paused as they heard distant rumbles of conversation at each landing.

"I hear a fight has broken out in the main square," a female voice was heard saying.

"Truly?" asked another, her voice scandalized.

"Yes. There aren't many details yet, but the *queen* sent her dog out to deal with it."

"Be careful when you say that. Cadan has ears everywhere," the second woman replied, sounding more gleeful than upset.

"I heard he arrested several people on counts of treason just for speaking ill of her or Lord Riken," the first woman scoffed.

They weren't able to hear the rest of the conversation as the two moved out of hearing range, though they exchanged worried glances with one another. Collette vowed to rid the world of Cadan if they crossed paths.

As they reached the top floor, Collette took a deep breath and stepped out of the landing and into the corridor. She listened intently as she took a few hesitant steps forward. She could feel Tolan close behind her as they moved toward the correct door. The quiet around them conjured unnerving feelings, given the castle had once been bursting with life.

The royal estate room sat at the end of the corridor, and while they'd been lucky to encounter no one thus far, Collette wasn't certain they'd remain so. Having assessed no one was currently on this wing of the floor, she hastened her steps until she'd closed the distance. Taking the handle, she turned it halfway before meeting resistance. "This door always stuck," she muttered. "How could I forget?"

Tolan moved to stand next to her and braced himself against the door. "Let's push and hope. If it makes too much noise, we'll lock the door behind us or just hide once inside. If there's anywhere to hide."

Collette agreed, and together, they pushed against the door, Collette cringing when it made a loud scraping noise. Thankfully, the door could open all the way now, and she slipped inside and made sure to shut it behind them once Tolan joined her.

Tolan stood with his ear against the door, listening to see if anyone might head up to check on the noise. Being half-elven, he would hear approaching footsteps before her. "Go find your spell. I'll let you know if someone is coming."

Thankfully, it looked as though no one had used the room since her arrest nearly a year ago. Dust coated the floor and the unused rows of books on tall, built-in shelves surrounding three of the four walls. She hurried to the shelf on the left, recalling exactly where she'd hidden the spell.

A library ladder sat at one end of the unit, a light tan color that contrasted with the deep oak shelving. She pushed the ladder to the appropriate place about a third of the way down the unit, then carefully ascended, glancing back at Tolan to make sure he heard nothing.

Once high enough, she began removing the books from the shelf, placing them haphazardly on the shelves above and below until the space was cleared. Then, she popped out the faux back, stifling a triumphant cheer when she saw the old wooden box, left untouched.

She glanced down at Tolan, who was giving her an amused smile but made an approving hand gesture. Turning back to the shelves, she opened the box long enough to confirm the spell

was still inside. Satisfied, Collette placed the old wooden box in one of the pouches on her belt before placing everything back where it had been. While she knew no one would suddenly decide to use this room, it was best not to leave anything out of place.

She descended the ladder in more joyful spirits than she'd been in months. After moving the ladder back in place, she frowned, seeing footprints on the dusty floor. Not much they could do about it now. "Let's find a way out."

"We should probably stick with the way we came in. Just a bit more carefully this time," Tolan suggested as he slowly started to pull the door open.

After detecting no sign of others, they crept back out into the empty corridor. Collette was surprised; she'd expected more from Rhoslyn's regime.

"We should have been caught, or at least seen more than a handful of people," Tolan said low, shock lacing his voice.

"We're not out yet," Collette reminded him. "And when we get out, we may have to intervene in the chaos Arian caused."

"There's a good chance Nawalya convinced him to flee already. I didn't work a lot of jobs with them, but they were always good at knowing when to leave," Tolan said as they started toward the first landing.

Once inside, Collette took a hurried pace down the stairs, listening out for voices and steps not belonging to them. Just above the third landing, Collette held an arm out as people entered the stairwell below.

"Cadan's back. Go warn the others," an older woman commanded. "He's in a foul mood, having not caught the elf in the square."

"Yes, ma'am," a younger woman replied.

"That sounds like Agnes," Tolan whispered against the shell of Collette's ear.

Chapter Forty-one

She nodded, and though it was probably stupid, Collette took a couple more steps down, hoping to see that Tolan was right. When she laid eyes on the older woman, her chest constricted and her eyes filled with tears. Agnes had been the closest thing to a mother she'd had growing up, given the loss of her own mother when she'd been a very young child.

Without thinking, Collette descended the steps toward the woman, who turned to see her when a half dozen steps separated them.

"By the Mother," Agnes whispered, pressing a hand to her chest. She hurried up the remaining steps and threw her arms around Collette, crushing her in an affection hug. "What are you doing here?" she said as she pulled away. "If Lord Riken or Cadan find you—"

"I can handle them," Collette said quickly. "But I'd like to get out of here without detection. I have something I need to do before I can take them on."

"Of course," Agnes said. She looked up and spotted Tolan. "You let her come here where she's in the most danger?" she chastised in a harsh whisper before taking Collette's hand. "Well, come on. We need to hurry."

"You act like she wouldn't have come without me had I protested," Tolan hissed back, his tone more jovial.

"Excuses," Agnes said as they continued down the stairs. "Was the elf in the square one of your people?"

"He is," Collette confirmed. "It sounds like he got away?"

"He did from what I heard. Cadan returned red-faced only a few minutes ago."

"Do you know if his plan to rally the people worked?" Tolan asked, his brow furrowed with worry.

"They were planning on going back out with more soldiers, but I don't know how they plan on combating the crowd."

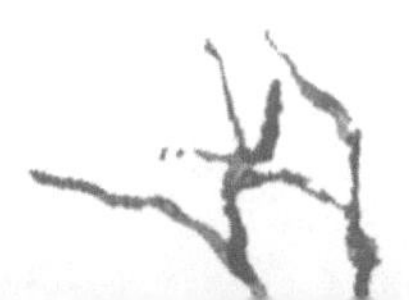

"I hope the townsfolk are okay when all this is over," Tolan said. "Crem may end up with new recruits or having to do a large-scale jailbreak."

"Someone needs to," Agnes said. "It seems like half the palace is in there."

"Then we have a new mission to plan," Collette said.

"Are they sending the people to labor camps or holding them until something worse can be decided?" Tolan asked.

"Holding right now," Agnes replied, looking back over her shoulder. For someone her age, she moved down the stairs with seemingly little effort. "Riken has been wary of the camps since he last encountered our queen."

"As he should be," Tolan muttered, only to motion them to halt as servants passed by, moving quickly and not looking around on the next landing. "After this, they might move to make an example of anyone in prison."

"We'll get them out," Collette promised. "And quickly. I can't get them all out with just the two of us," she said, then she thought about it. "Right?"

There was silence for a moment from Tolan before he said, "It's possible that if Cadan has had to go back into town with more soldiers, this might be the best time." He let out a harsh breath. "They could also have doubled the guard on the prison if they thought Crem and his people would take advantage of the chaos."

"Your Majesty, the people would be with you if you acted now," Agnes said hesitantly. "But is it for the best?"

Collette couldn't say it wasn't, and for that reason, she knew what they'd have to do. "I've gotten myself out of the dungeon before. I could theoretically do the same for others."

Tolan laughed, and if there was a slight edge of hysteria, Collette decided to ignore it. "So how do we get to the prison from here?"

"It's outside and on the opposite side of the building," Agnes said.

"We'll just have to be extra careful?" Tolan asked Collette, waiting for her to give the go-ahead.

"Looks like it," Collette agreed. "Let's go."

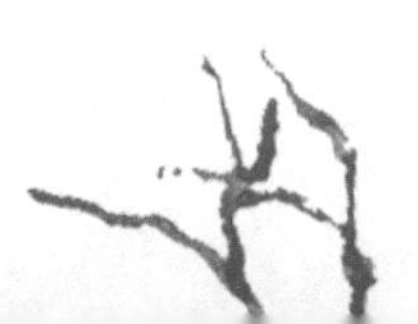

Chapter Forty-Two

Knowing there was no possible way to get a whole group of people out of the prison without notice, Collette sent Agnes away with instructions to go into town as though running errands. In the chaos Arian caused, she hoped the older woman would go without interruption. If she was successful, she could let the others know what Collette and Tolan were planning, and Spirits, Collette hoped she was successful.

Just the two of them again, Collette and Tolan made it to the bottom landing once more, but instead of taking the way back out to the old entrance, Collette led Tolan in a different direction, one that would take them by the kitchens. They were officially more likely to be seen now that they weren't hiding in stairwells, but going through the castle was safer.

After passing the kitchens, they had to cross the great hall, which had once been filled with people, laughter, and drinks. Now, no one sat at one of the long tables.

"I would have thought this place would be full of Rhoslyn's supporters. It seemed like so many stood against you. Have they all been killed or locked up? I can't picture them seeing the error of their ways. That type of greed rarely does."

"I think they got exactly what they asked for, and now, some of them have fled, some of them are dead, and a small contingency have likely been arrested."

"I'm still surprised Barris got away with everything he did. Even if the plans were Lynessea's, he still got away with so much." A bit of surprise and admiration leached into his voice. "Only Larent could have done better."

"Larent didn't get in trouble with me because I found it amusing," Collette reminded him. She took Tolan by the arm and pulled him along as they dashed past the great hall.

"Most people never saw past his smile or good looks."

"They are hard to miss, but they weren't the reason I allowed him to remain on my balcony after he mysteriously appeared."

"Why did you do that?" Tolan asked.

"Because when someone appears on your balcony and is too flustered to come up with a good reason, you have to torture them a bit." She paused as she heard footsteps. Grabbing Tolan, she pulled them both against the wall, hoping the person didn't further approach.

Tolan's laughter was cut off, replaced by a pained sound as he was pushed against the wall. He gave her an apologetic grimace for what she assumed was getting too caught up in their conversation to pay as much attention to their surroundings as he should have. Together, breaths held, they waited for the person to appear, hoping they'd pass by quickly.

"What do you mean you've lost him?" Rhoslyn's voice echoed off the walls. "He's an elf! How did you lose him?"

Tolan's hand grasped Collette's upper arm gently but firmly, as if to stop her from doing something they both might regret, before another voice, one neither of them recognized, joined Rhoslyn's.

"He started an uprising before the guards could get to him, and then he killed many of those already present in the town

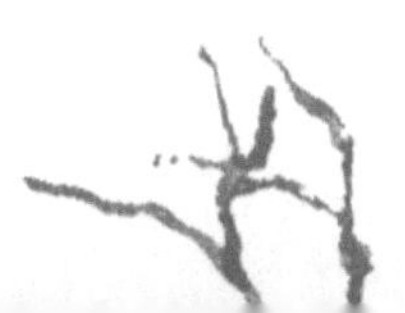

square. By the time the rest of the guards got there, they were fighting armed townsfolk, and only a few of the soldiers were able to get near the elf. Most of those died before he took to the roofs to escape. A small group of about eight were able to follow him to try and catch him. The report from those who survived that encounter report an elven woman descended on them, giving him time to escape before she also fled, leaving only two alive. I'm going back out, but I needed more soldiers. There are jumbled reports that Cremisius Hawke and his people are helping to keep the uprising going. I need to see if that's true. Lord Riken is also out there fighting."

"Good. The last thing we need is a successful uprising, Cadan," Rhoslyn replied.

"Something about this feels wrong, too well planned out."

"What do you think might be happening then?" Rhoslyn asked.

"I'm unsure, but I intend to figure it out. It could be a distraction, or Hawke could have been emboldened by her army having taken Wildrun. Either way, we will subdue this uprising and order will be restored." The man sounded firm in his belief and deadly in a way that did not bode well for the townsfolk or any of their people that might be caught.

Rhoslyn cleared her throat and, in hushed tones, asked, "Do you think she might be nearby?"

"It's possible. We haven't been able to confirm if she's with the army or not. The only people we've confirmed for sure are the Nereid and Fythian royals. They could be keeping her out of sight but..." Now frustration laced Cadan's voice. "Lord Riken asked me to verify if you are armed?"

"I'm always armed," Rhoslyn replied curtly. "You both know that. And if she is nearby, we're going to need to prepare for what's to come. She is not getting this throne back."

"No, she won't. She doesn't deserve it. Let me put down this uprising, then I will see to the castle's defense and anything else you wish." There was a pause. "Would you like me to make an example of anyone in town once the uprising is quelled?"

"If you find either of those elves, I would be quite pleased."

"As you command," Cadan replied, then they heard his footsteps heading in the opposite direction.

Collette glanced back to Tolan, a new burst of inspiration in mind. "I'm taking her," she warned in a barely audible whisper.

Tolan's eyes widened, and Collette was sure he was going to protest. Then he closed his eyes tightly for a moment before reopening them to focus on Collette and gave a decisive nod.

"She's carrying a weapon. Be careful," he breathed.

"Watch my back," Collette returned, and with a deep breath, she emerged from her hiding spot.

Rhoslyn didn't notice her at first. The petite woman stood in the corridor, dressed in lace and silks usually reserved for royalty. The dark green complemented her fair skin and long cinnamon hair. Unlike the last time Collette saw her, Rhoslyn now wore much of her hair up in an intricate style, and upon her head sat a delicate silver tiara glittering with matching green emeralds and bright diamonds.

Without a plan, Collette stepped forward and grabbed Rhoslyn from behind before the woman had any chance to react. Securing her arms with one hand, Collette covered her mouth to prevent her from screaming.

Tolan moved into Collette's peripheral vision, ensuring Rhoslyn couldn't see him, and hit the end of his dagger hilt to his palm, quietly asking Collette if she wanted him to knock Rhoslyn unconscious. When Collette nodded, Tolan followed through. The dagger hilt slammed into Rhoslyn's temple with a little more force than might have been necessary, breaking the skin.

"That's going to bruise," Tolan said through his teeth as he helped Collette support Rhoslyn's weight. "We can leave her here somewhere hidden and come back for her after we get everyone out. I can also throw her over my shoulder and we can hope we don't run into anyone. Unless you have a different idea?" Tolan's voice was calm and measured, letting Collette know he might not be completely comfortable with what they were doing.

"We could also split up," Collette said. "If we leave her here, someone might find her and the castle would go on alert."

"I'd prefer not to leave you. Just in case," Tolan said, but from the press of his lips, Collette knew he was thinking about it. "Let's get outside then discuss our options." He motioned her forward as he threw Rhoslyn over his shoulder like she was a sack of grain, taking little care to make sure her limp body didn't hit anything as they made their way quickly to the outside courtyard.

Unlike the nearly empty castle, the voices of soldiers, servants, and others filled the area, and Collette proceeded with caution as she crept around an outer wall. She didn't look back to check on Tolan, knowing he was behind her despite his near silent footsteps. The *thud* of Rhoslyn's body hitting the wall here and there did almost cause her to laugh.

She pointed in the distance. "You know the prison is over there."

"I do," Tolan agreed. "I'm still not alright leaving you alone on the castle grounds."

She knew he would go if she told him to, but his concern was strongly welcome, considering. She was about to tell him to go anyway when the rustling of a nearby bush caught her attention. It wasn't a large bush, but Collette braced herself anyway, only for a small tabby cat to appear. It walked over to them, sat on its haunches, and proceeded to judge them with its eyes.

And Collette knew exactly what she was dealing with. "I got the spell, Nora," she insisted.

The cat looked from Collette to Tolan, tilting her head to fully take in the body hanging from his shoulders before finally turning into the older woman. "It seems you got more than just the spell," she said, the glint in her eyes both teasing and concerned.

"I took a prisoner."

"Is that what we're calling this?"

"What else would I call it?"

Nora thought for a moment before saying, "I don't know. So taking prisoners it is."

Tolan cleared his throat to get their attention. "Since you're here, I'm more content with Collette's plan to send me back to camp while she stages a prison break."

"A lovely woman by the name of Agnes mentioned that when she arrived at Crem's camp. Why don't you see yourself off while I get myself caught up on our plan?" She looked back to Collette. "If my daughter is alright with that."

"I am," Collette confirmed. She put a hand on Tolan's shoulder. "Be safe. Drop the baggage if you have to."

"If I drop her anywhere, it will be in a body of water deep enough she can drown in," he answered before he leaned forward and brushed his lips against her forehead. "Be safe." And then he was off.

"That boy is an idiot," Nora said from beside her.

"Yeah," Collette agreed, her heart beating a little faster with anxiety now that Tolan had run off with Rhoslyn. She was putting so many people in danger. "So," she said, looking back at Nora. "Want to help me free the people being held in jail?"

"Sounds like a good time. Lead the way," Nora said with a grin that reminded Collette too much of Larent.

Collette nodded and once again motioned toward the prison. "That's where they'd hold anyone," she explained. "The courtyard is within hearing distance, and the old training yard is also nearby."

"I'd be surprised if there's more than a handful of guards left on the castle grounds. Arian always says Larent was the one who was good with words, but apparently Arian convinced more than half the townsfolk to rise up to fight by his side." Nora's voice was fond. "Thankfully everyone ignores cats, so I was able to get through while the soldiers were going after everyone, including the children."

Collette scowled. "I may have very little trouble taking back the throne, given what we've encountered here," she said. "Can you go see how well guarded the prison is? We can make a plan from there."

"Of course," Nora answered, and from one step to the next, a small tabby replaced her. The tabby cat gave her a small meow before running off toward the prison.

Collette watched Nora intently until she disappeared. Then she was left waiting. Collette couldn't help but compare this moment to the night she'd escaped nearly a year prior. It had been dark then, and those on the grounds had been largely drunk and celebratory. Now, gloom choked the atmosphere. Diana had crossed the main bridge with her, snapping at a disrespectful guard before they'd parted in the marketplace. Then she wandered upon Arian. It had been the mark of life-changing events which had nearly killed her time and again.

Before Collette got too caught up in memories, Nora was back, changing shape between one blink and the next. "There are two guards at the main gate, and four more inside. I couldn't see or sense any others, and from their topics of conversation, all but one is new to the guard."

Six total guards, most of whom were new. She could take on six, but she worried about drawing attention. "So drawing them away probably would bring more attention to the breakout."

"That or killing them," Nora said simply. "Together, we can definitely handle them, but if you want to go the other route, we can."

Collette didn't like the idea of killing without knowing where the guards stood. "Since I don't know if they were conscripted or not, I'd say dispatch them."

"I can do that." Nora tapped her index finger to her chin. "Scared woman is overdone. I could start a fire or turn into a more menacing animal," she mumbled to herself, another habit Collette knew Larent had.

"Menacing animal is probably the best bet, but appear somewhere other than the prison. Perhaps come in from the west."

"Give me five minutes, ten at the most. There will be a lot of shouting if this works out." Nora strode off in the opposite direction but stayed human as she went. Collette knew an older woman dressed as Nora would be taken as a servant, and that she was more than likely waiting until she was closer to her destination before changing. She settled in to wait, counting the minutes in her head.

Finally, there was shouting from the prison, a loud roar followed by shouting, and then the sound of several people running the opposite direction.

Pulling her hood closer around her face, Collette used the chaos to sprint from her hiding place over to the prison. She found the door leading down unsecured, and she hurried down the steps into the interior, grabbing the spare keyring hanging at the bottom step.

The space hadn't changed since her escape, and she was certain if she examined the cell where she'd been locked up, she'd find the hole she'd left in the ceiling. She scanned the

interior room, finding no other guards, and she methodically approached each of the cells. "Stay quiet and listen to orders," she told the occupants.

She sorted through the keys at each cell door, silently counting the people behind them. Some of the faces she knew, and Collette doubted they had done anything to warrant being imprisoned.

"Your Majesty?" one of them whispered in astonishment.

"Yes," Collette confirmed. She stepped to the final cell, releasing the last four people. In total, she had just short of a dozen people to guide out, a difficult but not impossible task. "Now, we are going to head back up the steps. If there is something in here you can easily carry and use as a weapon, I suggest you get it. When we reach the top, you will follow me until I tell you to flee." Nods and murmurs of compliance came, and with that, Collette turned and headed back up the steps, her people following behind her.

Arian was waiting at the entrance to the prison. His clothes were torn in places, his hair was in disarray, and there was a cut on his upper left eyebrow that was bleeding sluggishly. Otherwise, he looked alright. "Nora is leading the guards on a merry chase on the other side of the castle. If we hurry, no one should spot us."

Alarmed with Arian's close proximity to the castle, Collette couldn't help her response. "Keep your head down while we move. Cadan's looking for you," Collette replied. She turned to the prisoners. "You stick with me or him," she instructed before giving the signal to move.

"Is he now? You know, I would not mind meeting him." Arian's grin looked more intimidating then she was sure he meant it to be, but he also gave a nod of confirmation that he would take her advice before helping to usher everyone out of the prison.

Collette would never be able to explain how they'd managed to get this far so easily, but thankfully, everyone was mostly unscathed. The group quickly filed out onto the grounds, and with the remaining guards distracted, they headed for the same valley beneath the main bridge Collette and Tolan had used to break in. "Is Nawalya okay?" she asked Arian after directing the others down.

"Last I saw of her, yes." His answer was laced with concern but enough confidence that she knew Nawalya was alright. "She and Ceto had decided the best use of their time was to ensure Rhoslyn's people could not take any prisoners. Whyldon seemed to agree."

"Any major losses on our side?" she asked as the last of the former prisoners descended. Only then did she and Arian follow.

"No, but there have been heavy injuries that could have led to losses if not for Crem and his people." Arian paused as if not wanting to add the next part. "Zephraim appearing and declaring the crown for you caused some of the soldiers on their side to lay down their weapons and surrender. In his rage over this, Riken was seen killing two of them. Riken then gave chase after Zephraim."

"Shit," Collette said. She paused the conversation long enough to direct some people on how to walk through the stream without submerging themselves. "Sara and I can heal whoever needs it when we are back," she picked up as they moved. "Do we know if Zephraim is okay?"

"No. I left camp the moment Agnes arrived to announce you would need assistance with a prisonbreak." He addressed both the group behind them and Collette. "The uprising is still ongoing, though it is slowing down, so we will need to be careful and be ready to fight."

"I'm ready," she assured him. They started up the hill again, still without being bothered by guards or opposing groups. "I got it, by the way."

"Good," Arian replied.

As they moved carefully through the streets, they could hear fighting nearby and the screams of those who were injured. They passed a street where two soldiers were cornering some children. Before Collette or Arian could do anything, two of the men with them broke off to handle the soldiers, motioning for the group to continue on.

"I saw Tolan as I was coming to assist. He was carrying something? Someone?" Arian questioned.

"Rhoslyn," Collette explained.

Arian didn't stumble, but it was a close thing. "Explain please."

"She was there. I took her."

Whatever Arian was going to say was cut off when he held up a hand, causing the group to halt right before several soldiers ran past without taking time to look around. Once gone, the group started off again. "What will you do with her now that you have her?"

Collette snorted. "You act like I had a plan."

"I am aware we did not when we started this," he answered. "I'm just wondering if you are considering torture or something else when it comes to her."

"I don't torture," she replied. "You should remember that."

Arian made a face that Collette would call petulant. "One could make an exception for her."

"You and I are better than her, and that's exactly what she would do if the roles were reversed."

"You are better than her," Arian clarified. She knew it was because while Arian was trying to do better—for her, for Thomas, and for himself—he didn't consider himself there yet.

Collette wouldn't argue the point for now. "Come, my brother. Let's get these people to safety."

Arian nodded and the group continued on in watchful silence.

The marketplace was now filled with people, so much so, moving through became increasingly difficult. People were afraid, or outraged, by the conflict between her people and the castle. No one around them currently fought, but the sounds of shouting and weapons echoed from just one or two streets over.

"I think we may have to intervene," she said.

Arian looked around and let out a tired sigh. "I had been intending to cause a distraction, not a overthrow. It appears that the villagers had other ideas."

"It does," she agreed. "I suppose I should make myself known."

Arian held out a hand for her cloak. "I am glad to be by your side for this, but we are both aware of who should be here with you instead."

"I'd still want you here," Collette replied. "And he will be here for everything else."

Arian nodded and motioned her forward. "He will be, and he will be horrified by this entire situation."

"I'll let you catch him up," Collette said, and with a breath, she stepped forward into the crowd. Whatever response Arian gave, Collette missed it as she was spotted first by a woman holding a bloody pitchfork, then by a man tending to the wounds of another who had been complaining they didn't need help. Slowly, the crowd quieted, though low rumblings of, "It's the queen," could be heard.

"You've returned?" a voice called out, desperate and relieved at once.

"I have," Collette replied. "With support and plans to correct the harms Rhoslyn Almeida and her ilk have brought to Coralia."

If Collette had planned to say anything else, it was drowned out by the sounds of the crowd which slowly got louder and louder until the cheer was deafening, drowning out even the sounds of the fighting that were still going on. Her presence had reinvigorated the no longer subdued populace, and she didn't have to entice them into fighting.

All around her, people surged with renewed energy. They picked up weapons, and they charged out into the streets, finding the remaining soldiers who fought for Rhoslyn.

Arian stepped up by her side. "Was your intention to make the fighting worse?" There was amusement in his voice as he took in the scene before him. "How does it feel to be queen again?"

"I'm not quite sure," she replied honestly. It amazed her that she'd not raised a weapon one time today, and yet, there was no denying the meaning of this moment.

"I think we should gather some of the others and head to the castle." His gaze swept the crowd. "If we can find them."

"Yeah, that's an impossible task," Collette acknowledged. "And Aphros and his group haven't even arrived in Quenall, yet."

"Aphros is going to enjoy this entirely too much," Arian said before his smile slipped from his face.

A second later, Nawalya dropped down next to him. She was splattered with blood and viscera but, other than a few shallow cuts, appeared fine, though Collette noted Arian's eyes scanned her from head to toe twice before being satisfied she was unharmed

"Did you two have fun?" she asked, pushing sweat-slicked hair from her face.

"I got what I came for, freed some people from prison, and Arian started a rebellion. It's been a good day."

"I'm fairly sure that was the overall plan, but today was only for reconnaissance," Nawalya said, light and teasing. "Congratulations."

Collette didn't feel celebratory, even though so many around her felt as much. She couldn't blame them. These people knew Collette would do whatever she could to protect them. To eliminate the atrocities in their world. Even now, she felt her freedoms and choices, and even the lingering remnant of happiness, being stripped away. The idea of returning to that castle and walking those halls for the rest of her days felt nauseating. But she had no choice. At least, not right now.

"The others should be informed. It's time to take back the palace. Then we can worry about the ritual."

She caught Arian's eyes on her, taking her in before his gaze switched to Nawalya. "You're queen now," he told her seriously.

Nawalya stared, confused for a second, before she looked over at Collette. "I can make my hair darker and hide my ears," she agreed.

"Go help round up the others, please," Collette directed.

Nawalya nodded and quickly vanished into the crowd.

"She could do it, you know. Pretend to be you. Or we could put someone else in charge."

Collette shook her head. "No. Restoring things is my responsibility. I'm going to see it through." She glanced back toward the palace. "Well, come on."

Chapter Forty-Three

Riken raced through the streets of Quenall, ignoring the burning in his lungs and the sweat beading down his forehead as he chased his prey. It mattered not to him that he'd lost the four men that had chosen to accompany him in his chase several blocks back. No, all that mattered was getting his hands on Zephraim, who had managed to stay just several steps ahead of them thanks to his head start. Zephraim had gotten that head start because of Riken's deep rage at seeing his own men put down their swords and side with the bastard. Collette had been a traitor. Zephraim certainly was, and now, those who sided with him were among the ranks of treacherous behavior. After all, what else could someone call the lie of Collette being the rightful ruler?

"Face me, you coward!" he roared as Zephraim turned another corner, leading them into the warehouse district.

Zephraim stopped and turned, drawing his weapon in one fluid motion and pointing it directly at Riken. "You don't want to face me," he warned.

"Oh yes, I do," Riken almost purred as Zephraim finally stopped running. He pulled his own sword, which he had sheathed before taking off after the traitor, blood coating the blade.

Zephraim scoffed, though he looked at Riken with lazy amusement. "You're emotional, erratic, and a consistent failure."

Riken laughed, though the reminder of the very things Rhoslyn had so recently accused him of did hit home. "You're a traitor to your sister, your wife, and your kingdom. How long until you betray Collette again? What will sway your loyalty next time?"

"I've grown, Riken," Zephraim replied, motioning Riken forward with a mocking *come here* gesture with his free hand. "Even after all your failures, you're still the same little boy, desperate for a pat on the head."

Riken took a measured step forward. He would not make the same mistakes he had with Collette. He would take Zephraim in and see him hanged for his crimes. "You and your sister consistently throw out that sad, tired refrain. It wasn't true when she said it, and it's not true now. What is true, however, is that no matter how many times you tell yourself you've changed, you're better than you were, it remains a lie."

He took another step closer. "But please, tell me how you've changed. How the apathetic drunkard with no drive or real beliefs, who willingly overthrew his sister over a flimsy lie and affections so fake everyone else knew about it, has changed."

"I owe the likes of you no explanations or justifications, Riken. I am sorry you do not understand that, but it continues to speak to your inherent flaws."

"You're right. You don't, but your answer and the look on your face tells me you know I'm right. You're worthless, unlovable, easily manipulated, and if your sister has learned anything with her fruitless endeavor, she will toss you away like rotten fruit when she no longer has need of you." Riken went for a shallow lunge, making sure not to leave himself open for attack as he did so.

Zephraim dodged it, his show of easy athleticism surprising Riken. "She took Wildrun without lifting a blade, from what I hear."

"I had the majority of my soldiers here. A mistake I will easily correct after I take my home back," Riken said with a casualness he did not feel as he did his best to temper his anger. He took in Zephraim's form, and while he couldn't remember the last time he'd seen the other with a sword in hand, he reminded himself that Zephraim did enjoy sporting activities.

"Nice thing to tell yourself. Comforting, I'm sure," Zephraim mocked.

"What comfort do I need? I have the truth on my side. What do you have?" Riken went in for another strike, hoping to throw Zephraim off.

Again Zephraim missed his blade. "Acknowledgment of the truth."

"Oh, you accept you'll never be anything? To anyone?" Riken had to tamper down his frustration once more. Was Zephraim just going to dance away from him, or would he actually engage?

"I have no reason to argue with you or take your words to heart, Riken," Zephraim said, still refusing to engage beyond countering and dodging attempted strikes.

Riken growled in frustration, wanting Zephraim to feel as he did, wanting him hot and clumsy with anger. "Is there a reason you're refusing to engage?" Riken bit out, and it hit him suddenly; this could be a distraction. The little weasel could have led him from the uprising on purpose. Riken lowered his sword from its defense position just slightly as he contemplated this.

"Other than you not being worth my effort?" Zephraim asked.

Chapter Forty-three

Riken's sword dipped even further as his brows scrunched together. He felt his shoulders begin to shake as laughter overtook him. "This was a distraction so Crem and his cronies, or maybe even your bitch sister, could cause trouble while I was busy. I should have known. You could never win in a fight against me." He raised his sword and began to slowly back up.

Zephraim let out a laugh. "Perhaps, for your sake, you will be right."

"I know I am, or you would have at least tried." Still facing Zephraim, because he wouldn't put it past the other man to attack him when his back was turned, Riken sheathed his sword, his hand quickly moving to the dagger just above it and flicked it out, throwing it at Zephraim, his intent not to kill but to at least harm.

Zephraim dodged it again, but then he was advancing on Riken, his movements smooth and precise, leveling the blade at Riken's throat.

Riken stilled, holding back even the growl that threatened to leave his throat. He had made an error in judgment this time. It would cost him his life.

"A quick death would be too good for you," Zephraim said, his voice level. "You know that don't you?"

"Have you ever killed someone, Zephraim?" Riken asked, doing his best to control his voice so it wasn't trembling.

"I have," Zephraim replied. "Admittedly, you don't live up to that person."

Riken would have tilted his head in question had he not been sure the blade would have cut into his skin even more. "Truly? Who was it."

"Do you recall the rumors of my sister's death?" Zephraim asked, his gray eyes narrowed dangerously. "Who do you think did that? Who do you think made her bleed out?"

Riken felt bile rise in his throat at the very idea that Zephraim had used magic, let alone blood magic, on another person. Even if that person was Collette. He fought it down and answered as calmly as he could, making sure his tone was dismissive instead of horrified. "Considering she's not dead…" Riken made a show of trying not to shrug. He had to pretend like this didn't matter, like it wasn't important. Once he escaped this obvious madman, he could figure out his next steps. How Collette could let him around her, Riken didn't understand. Unless she didn't know—something Riken filed away for use later.

"Magic is the coward's way out. You've never had blood on your hands, and I doubt you're strong enough to do so now." Riken lifted his chin, showing more of his neck to Zephraim. He knew it was a risk, but he hoped Zephraim would turn away from the idea of taking a life while the person was there in front of him.

He was mistaken in his beliefs, as he felt Zephraim respond by pressing the blade harder against Riken's neck. He could feel the sting of the blade piercing skin and the trickle of blood running down his neck.

It hit him then that he was going to die. He was going to be killed by the least worthy person in the kingdom, and he couldn't even fight back. He let out a harsh breath and closed his eyes, waiting for the death blow.

"Step away from Lord Riken now," a familiar voice said, and Riken's eyes shot open. Cadan stood behind Zephraim, his blade pressed to his back. From this angle, he could see Cadan looked murderous, and Riken slowly leaned back, away from the blade.

Zephraim, though, didn't look afraid. He even laughed, humorless though it was, at the threat. "If it's not me, it will be her, and I doubt my sister will be so kind."

"It won't be either of you. Not while I breathe. Lower your sword!" Cadan shouted.

Riken took the chance to move back further, his relief at not having the blade pressing into his throat showing on his face. Only once he was out of reach did Zephraim lower his blade.

"Riken, go," Cadan ordered.

Riken wanted to run, to get away from Zephraim and his admittance of using blood magic. He couldn't run, though. His honor was on the line. "No," Riken snarled. They would end Zephraim here.

"Two-on-one. That seems a little unfair," a light female voice called out.

Riken's head snapped around as a woman, obviously Nereid from the indigo color of her hair and cat-like eyes, stood there, sword in hand, the blade slim but sharp and coated in blood. "Let's make this more even."

"Riken's never liked to play even," Zephraim replied. "He likes to have people around so he doesn't get his hands too dirty."

Riken was done. He had been humiliated and treated like a dog by this man who was beneath him. Ignoring Cadan's shouts, Riken lunged at Zephraim, his intention to maim, to hurt, to kill, only for another blade to intercept his.

"No, you don't get to touch him. Only my husband gets to do that," the woman said.

The way the Nereid woman spoke was dismissive and so uncaring that it only served to enrage him further. Without much thought or finesse, he attacked the woman before him. He heard the sound of Zephraim engaging Cadan, but he ignored it for the moment, his focus on the woman before him and cutting her down so he could get to Zephraim.

It took Riken a minute before he realized that the Nereid woman was toying with him. That while he was putting his aggression and rage into his strikes and making an attempt to

kill her, she was … amused. All this did was serve to enrage him more, making his attacks even less coordinated. He knew he was leaving himself open for her to end his life, and yet she didn't deliver the obvious blow. She was just parrying his strikes, defending as he attacked.

He knew he had to rein himself in, to fight smarter. He was wearing himself out fighting like this, which could be what she was waiting for, but he was having trouble reining himself in. He was about to disengage when a foot connected solidly with his chest, sending him sprawling to the ground, his sword slipping from his grasp. Glaring up at the woman whose posture was relaxed, he was about to lunge for his sword and engage once more when she called out to Zephraim, who appeared to be winning his own battle with Cadan.

"I'm bored. Want to switch opponents? This one is no fun."

His pride pricked hard. *No fun?* He would show her no fun. He moved for his sword, only for her foot to come down on his chest, pushing him back down. "No, no, no, the adults are talking," she said to him, only to turn her face back to Zephraim.

It was then that Riken realized Cadan was bleeding, and heavily, from the chest and torso. Cadan, who should have been able to deal with Zephraim without effort. Cadan, whose pale face would never see another moment beyond now.

"I'm afraid my opponent will be less enjoyable," Zephraim called to her.

"It's been so long since I've had a worthy opponent. Looks as if you've run into the same problem," she quipped.

Riken tried to push her off, tried to rise from the ground, anything, but he could not.

"I think we should just kill them," the woman said and turned back to face him, the smile gone from her face. Riken attempted once more to reach for his sword which was just out of reach. She didn't wait for Zephraim's approval or denial of her desire to kill Riken. She just brought her sword down.

Riken knew she would hit his heart. He knew this was his end: murdered by a filthy creature. And yet he still attempted to defend himself, tried to deflect the sword with his arms. All this earned him was a deep slice to the bone in his right arm before the sword went through his lung instead of his heart.

"I had been hoping to make this a clean kill," the woman said as she pulled the sword from his body. "But it seems you wanted to die slowly, so I'll grant that to you." She turned her back to him but kept her foot on his chest. He turned his head to look at Zephraim and Cadan. The man wasn't going to make it long. The coloring of his skin and the way he was holding the wound on his torso said as much. Yet Riken still prayed that Cadan could rally himself and kill Zephraim. No matter how unlikely it was.

He barely registered the thump of Cadan's body hitting the ground, nor the brief exchange of words as Zephraim and the Nereid left him to die. For what felt like hours, Riken blinked in and out of consciousness, the voice of his love ringing through his mind. Would she mourn him? Would her grief cause her too much pain? He hoped not. Of all the beauty he'd experienced in the world, Rhoslyn surpassed the rest.

He breathed out, shallow and weak, choking on his own blood, as he heard steps approaching him. At least two people had come across his dying body, though neither sounded like the Nereid or Zephraim. One let out a deep laugh of shock, and the other a concerned, "Hmmm." As they leaned over him, he could not make out the blurred faces. Then his world went dark, and Riken knew no more.

Chapter Forty-Four

From Thomas's perspective, the aftermath of the uprising was more chaotic than the actual riot had been. The injured sat around the great hall of Gadleigh Palace, each being attended to by healers and medical workers. Having never been in the palace before, Thomas took great pleasure in looking around the space.

Rows of tables lined the floor, ornate and in such good repair that he might believe them brand new had he not spotted the emblem of a king long-dead. The walls were lined with tapestries, though he'd overheard Rion pointing out that many were missing from the last time he'd been in the great hall. Thomas wondered if Collette had them removed or if they'd gone missing in the time she'd been gone.

Thomas sat beside Arian and the far end of one of the long tables, holding a clean cloth against the gash above his lover's eyebrow. The blood flow, sluggish and thick, indicated it would quit bleeding on its own, but Sara had called out for him to tend to the wound until he could be seen, and he intended to listen.

"Took you long enough," he joked when Collette approached. She looked exhausted, more so than usual, having been running around since returning to the palace.

"I no longer own my time," Collette quipped. "I'm surprised you got Arian to sit."

"Sara did not give me much choice," the elf grumbled. He waved his hand in the direction of the awaiting crowd. "I am not gravely injured. Go help someone else. I hear Howle took a sword to the ribs."

"Howle isn't my brother," Collette replied.

"Your brother is not bleeding out," Arian said, the defiant tilt of his head clearly stating he thought he won that argument with that logic alone.

"I believe Sara was tending to him earlier," Thomas reminded Arian. He removed the cloth from Arian's forehead. "Now, let Collette do what she wants. She's not going to stop bothering you until you do." He looked up at the queen. "Right?"

"Right."

Arian looked petulant for a moment before finally nodding for Collette to go ahead. "There are still those who are more wounded than I, and you need to rest," Arian said softly. "My wound is shallow, and my ribs are only slightly sore."

"And you are still my brother," she replied as she pressed her fingers against his cut.

"And you are my sister," he said, but he still rolled his eyes as one of his hands moved to take Thomas's.

Arian's cut knitted together as the seconds passed, and Thomas studied the spot where the wound had been, amazed as always to find it looked like Arian had never been injured.

"Where on your ribs are you sore?" Collette asked.

"He's been holding the left side toward the bottom," Thomas volunteered.

Arian looked grumpy for a second before nodding. "Thomas is correct," he said, lifting his shirt to show off the giant bruise forming on his left side.

"I don't know why you insist on hiding things," Collette murmured as she pressed her fingers on either side of the bruise.

"Because my wounds are not as important as others. They are superficial at best," he explained, wincing slightly at the pressure.

"Everyone who needed immediate attention has been seen to," Thomas pointed out. He gestured across the great hall, emphasizing the steady work that had been done. Of course, Thomas knew Arian would argue and grumble his way through the attention, regardless. "He is right, though. You look in serious need of rest."

"I will get some," Collette replied as she withdrew her hands. "Agnes promised to get my old bedchambers ready for me. Apparently, no one used them in my absence."

Arian scowled, at least until Collette said they were unused. "Good. Will you have guards posted close by or others staying in the wing as well in case something happens?"

"Whyldon said he'd make sure someone was up there, and given the people who need rooms, I'm sure many in our party will be close by."

"Good. While I need sleep after the uprising, I do not like the idea of you being alone or so far away from help."

Collette slid her gaze back to Thomas. "Make sure he gets rest."

"Oh, I plan on it," Thomas promised. "Starting an uprising takes a lot of energy."

Arian looked away from Thomas, not that it did any good. There was no hiding the guilt crossing his face. "I already agreed," he pointed out quietly.

"Thank you," Collette said. She took a breath. "I'm going to help with the others. Let me know if you need anything."

"We will," Thomas said gently. "Take care of yourself."

"You should lay down soon as well," Arian added. "But if you feel you cannot, please at least take a moment to eat a little something and drink some water. Your day was just as busy as mine."

"I will," she promised, pausing long enough to squeeze his shoulder affectionately before wandering off.

"She's delighted to be here," Thomas observed wryly. "I find myself feeling a little guilty, even though she chose to be here."

"She only made that choice because she feels it is her duty. Had there been someone else, someone better to take the throne, or any other choice, I have no doubt we would not be here right now," Arian said as he rose to his feet. Thomas could read the relief on his face from the lack of pain.

"Then once things are stabilized, we have a new mission." He gave Arian a softer smile. "Come on. You need rest."

"Larent told her several times that she should crown you king and be done with it," Arian informed him as they started down the hallway toward their room.

"I think I will forgo that suggestion," Thomas replied. He put an arm around Arian as they walked, knowing his partner was exhausted and troubled. "But there would be options."

"Such as?" Arian asked, leaning into the contact, something he never would have done in the beginning.

"That is the unknown that will have us focusing on a new mission once things are settled," Thomas repeated.

Arian nodded. The two continued in comfortable silence until they reached their room. They had been placed near Collette's, and upon opening the suite door, they found a large, well-furnished sitting room with two doors on each side. One a bedroom with an attached washroom, and the other a study

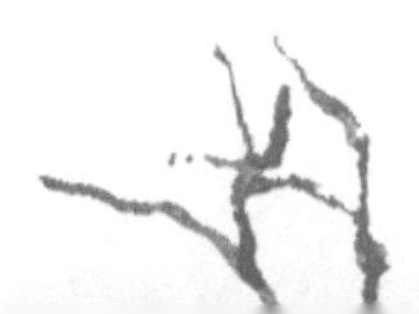

Agnes had told Thomas about when she'd given him their room assignment.

With how tired Arian looked, Thomas had expected him to head to the washroom and then to bed. Instead, he leaned against the main door after closing it, quietly observing Thomas. "How upset are you?" he asked, his eyes intent.

"I don't think upset is the right word for what I feel," Thomas decided after a few seconds of internal debate. "I'd have rather there been more of a plan, but I understand the impulse to act."

Arian looked away from Thomas, though his posture grew more relaxed. Still, Thomas could see the tension in the lines of his body. "What word would you use if not 'upset'?"

"Annoyed, maybe," Thomas replied. "Though that doesn't feel quite right, either. I suppose whatever the right word is doesn't matter. You're safe."

"We had truly meant to just scout out the town, the castle. But there was an opportunity, and we could not waste it."

"And she got the spell while regaining the throne. So it was not a wasted opportunity."

"It was not. Still, I did not mean to worry or upset you." Arian hadn't moved away from the door, as if the wood pressing against his back was grounding for him.

"I think I have accepted there are certain realities about our life together. You will take the risks you feel are necessary."

"I did not know if it would work. I just knew she wanted to go, and I needed to buy her time."

"I'm aware," Thomas replied. He took a seat in one of the chairs and watched Arian. "I've accepted that you're going to do whatever is necessary to support her, and most of the time, I don't blame you."

"Most of the time?" Arian asked with a raised eyebrow.

"Yes. Most of the time, I can see the risk is outweighed by the reward, so I support the rash decisions."

Arian finally pushed off the door and approached Thomas, lowering himself to his knees in front of him instead of one of the chairs. "Other than when I tortured those men, what other decisions have I made that you disagreed with?"

"I've told you every time I've disagreed with your actions. The torturing of those two guards was the most egregious."

"I wanted to be sure. I would have no issues between the two of us." He leaned forward and rested his head on Thomas's knee. "I am glad today worked out." They both knew that, despite his belief in Collette, he'd been worried he would not make it through the day.

"You had doubts, though."

"I walked into a town square with guards who have little issue throwing their own people into the dungeon. Killing an elf, especially one proclaiming Collette queen…" Arian's laugh held no humor. "I knew Nawalya would come, and I have faith in my own abilities, but there was still concern."

"Did you volunteer, or did Collette ask?"

"I told her to go to the castle. I encouraged her to break from our plans." Arian took a breath. "I think she would have stayed on course had I not encouraged her."

Thomas began running his fingers through Arian's hair. "Why did you encourage her?"

"Because she wanted to go. Because I saw an opportunity for her to get Larent back without having to wait another day, another week, another month."

"She has been miserable without him. There is no doubt about that."

"She has been, and I wanted to help correct that. The only thing that gave me pause was the thought of not returning to you."

"You did, though. That's what matters."

"I did. Though had Nawalya not arrived when she did…" He raised a hand to touch his forehead where the gash had been.

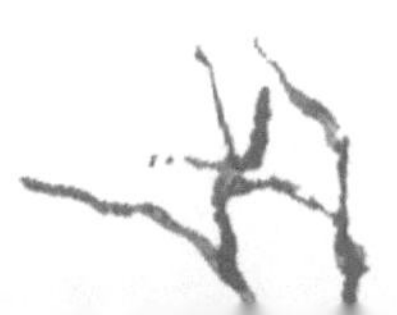

"And she got there," Thomas reminded him. "There's no reason to worry about what might have been."

"True." Arian lifted his head and took a moment to just look at Thomas before rising up to gently kiss him. Thomas kissed him back, slow and gentle, his hand cupping Arian's jaw.

Arian sighed into the kiss, his hands moving to rest on Thomas's upper thighs as he moved to deepen the kiss, prompting Thomas to move his hand upward, letting his fingers tangle into Arian's blond hair. In response, Arian let out a sound of contentment, his hands tightening on Thomas's thighs. This kiss broke, and Thomas's mouth traveled over to Arian's jaw and down his throat as he gently tugged on his hair, guiding his head back. He heard Arian's breath stutter as he gave himself to Thomas's control, his hands slowly sliding up till they rested on Thomas's hips. "Tell me what you want," Thomas whispered against his skin.

"You. Just you," Arian said.

Chapter Forty-Five

Aphros and his party arrived in Quenall three days later, surprised to see Collette and Arian had stumbled into getting the young queen back on the throne and sad to have missed it. Between the two sides of the collective army and the large rebellion overseen by Crem, securing the palace had been almost too easy.

Rhoslyn had been imprisoned in a room with no windows. Two guards stood just outside the door at all hours, with visible check-ins every two hours. The treatment, though kinder than anything Rhoslyn would grant to others, still emphasized Rhoslyn's status.

Lord Riken and Cadan were assumed dead, given reports from Zephraim and Lynessea. Collette appreciated their efforts. She still thought she'd never trust her brother again, but he'd proven a willingness to atone.

As the entire party had settled in and out of the castle, the injured had been examined by Sara, Nora, and Collette. The gravely injured had been magically healed, while lesser injuries had been cleaned and dressed.

Collette wouldn't say things had calmed any in the time they'd been back, but she felt they were more organized. A small group of their people now sat around the table in the old war room, discussing immediate plans and longer ranging concerns.

Faron placed an elbow on the table, his brow creased in thought. Sabine was turned to him, while Éric took notes from his seat beside Alaoin.

The Fythian king quietly reviewed the map someone had placed on the table. "Veitel was easy to put back under your rule. They were just waiting for a reason to rise up."

"Veitel was already facing troubles before the overthrow," Whyldon reminded them. He sat to Collette's right, across the table from Arian, the two serving as her closest advisors. Thomas sat on Arian's other side taking notes, and Rion, who'd never liked traditional meetings, leaned against the wall behind Whyldon, his arms crossed. "I'm not surprised by the political alignment."

"Wildrun, however, will have to be watched, looking at the reports," Crem, who had a black eye and several obvious bruises, interjected. "Branlin is on your side. They say they never recognized Zephraim or Rhoslyn, whereas Myrefall may still be a problem."

"Then get me the needed intel from Myrefall, and we can decide how to act," Collette replied.

"I still have contacts there," Faron said with obvious reluctance. "Some should be willing to share information. Others not so much. But with how willing the people there were to side with Sargarus originally, I feel we will have to watch the situation carefully."

"You're originally from Myrefall, aren't you?" Jayden asked from where he sat between Ceto and Aphros.

Lynessea was next to Ceto, and the two women had been talking about the uprising. Barris was missing, having excused himself from the meeting so no one would question what he might be telling Zephraim, who was also absent.

"He is," Sabine confirmed for Jayden. "Many from Myrefall relocated to Fythias under Sargarus's reign."

At an inquisitive look from a few people at the table, Faron added, "Hatred for magic users and those not human were at an all-time high. My father was murdered, and my close friend's house was set on fire because she had magic." His tone let those around him know there would be no further explanation.

"We should send scouts, then—people who can blend in and gather information," Nawalya said.

"Shouldn't be too hard to find those," Rion added. "I was in Myrefall for a bit before the overthrow. I got the sense people had more mixed beliefs than they did even a decade ago. Still, for safety's sake, Nawalya's idea is best."

"I would agree," Collette said. "We are in the early days of my second reign. No need to cause undue harm."

A murmur of agreement sounded around the table. "What are your general goals at this point? Excluding invading Azmarin," Éric asked, looking up from his parchment. Like Thomas, he also took notes, though Éric tended to provide full transcripts of meetings rather than a general outline. He gave Alaoin a pointed look, presumably because Alaoin had been talking about Azmarin again. The king seemed driven to rid them of that eventual problem.

"There is the general reestablishment of my legitimacy to other countries to think about," Collette said.

"Fortunately, I think you can count on both the Nereid Kingdom and Fythias to back your claim," Aphros offered.

"Absolutely," Collette agreed. Having other nations acknowledge her rule only served to pressure others into doing the same.

"Speaking of Azmarin, has anyone figured out what happened to Mallan? There have been no reports of his whereabouts, though he was residing in the palace," Alaoin reminded the group.

"Ah' few of ours reported they saw his people fleein' the city before ya officially took back the castle," Howle said from his spot next to Crem. Diana would have been with them, but she had decided it was less stressful retaking the kitchen than it was to deal with unending planning.

"He had a small military unit with him, smaller than what he brought to the Nereid Kingdom. We'll need scouts to verify that he's fled," Collette continued.

She saw a nod from Éric, who scribbled more on his parchment, and she wondered if he ever stopped taking notes. At least she didn't have to worry about that with Thomas.

"You're going to need to appoint new title holders, aren't you?" Tolan asked. He'd been quiet since they took back the castle. She might need to talk to him about that.

"Yes," she confirmed. "And before doing that, I have to ascertain what estates are most in need."

"Is that something you wish to assess yourself, or do you need to send people out?" Nawalya asked.

"It will be a bit of both. I can't possibly visit and assess every estate," Collette replied.

"Though I am sure you would try," Arian said softly, causing those who could hear him to laugh.

Collette gave a brief smile. "Not right now. I have too much else to do."

"Speaking of having things to do," Nawalya interjected. "When are you thinking of doing the ritual? I know being queen again wasn't part of the plan, but I doubt you want to hold off on that for too long."

"I've been going over the new spell with Sara and Nora," Collette explained. "There were some ingredients we needed, and they are working on gathering them. I anticipate it being soon, though."

"Do you need Tolan and I for anything yet?" Rion asked.

"I can meet with both of you later to go over the spells," she offered.

"Excuse me, but what is going on?" Crem asked, looking very confused, as did Howle.

"I'm using a dangerous spell to bring my husband back from the dead," Collette explained with no hesitancy. "Riken murdered him on the battlefield, and King Aphros placed a stasis spell on his body."

Crem's brows narrowed in confusion as he processed her words, while Howle just ran a hand over his face, looking a lot more tired than before. "Ya got that spell from the old bastard, didn't ya?" Howle asked, reminding her that he had worked closely with Sargarus for years, before, one day, he'd up and quit.

"I did, and I'm not going to be talked out of it," she added, just in case Howle needed to be informed.

Howle shrugged. "Wasn't goin' ta' try. Ya at least have ah' good reason ta' use it. We can both guess why he kept that spell around."

"Wait—you weren't planning on taking the kingdom back yet, were you?" Crem asked, though he looked a lot more amused than upset.

"The plan was a reverse of what has happened," she admitted. "But you know me: I got here, and problems in need of solving appeared in front of me."

Crem looked up at the ceiling as if asking a higher power for help. "I should probably be upset, but honestly, this is just like you." He chuckled before pulling himself together. "You said the spell is dangerous, so I'm going to assume from the grim look on this one's face that it means deadly?" He elbowed Howle, but gently, thankfully. The man had taken a sword to the ribs during the battle, and even after magical healing, he was still sore.

"It is, but we've a way to mitigate some of the danger," Collette assured him. She wouldn't divulge what that was. Keeping Faron and Sabine's secret seemed important and respectful.

Crem nodded. "May I ask—just in case the worst happens, and Mother willing it won't—that you please choose a successor. I cannot fight another rebellion."

"I've already thought of that," Collette replied. "Both Aphros and Alaoin would be here to oversee an adjustment, and we have options. Like Thomas, for example."

"You do remember I'm the one who stood outside of the palace criticizing you," Thomas said, his quill poised in hand, though he smirked with amusement.

"You're also not a noble, and you have a good head on your shoulders," Collette said with a shrug.

"He didn't just criticize you. If I'm correct, he called you a whore," Crem pointed out, causing Howle and several others to laugh.

"Oh, he's perfect, then," Howle said through his laughter.

Arian reached out to place a hand on Thomas's. "You will never live that down, I do not think."

"I think it will be one of my proudest moments," Thomas replied.

"There you go. We have a plan." Collette looked to Crem. "No more rebellions for you."

"Thank the Mother," Crem breathed.

"So, we shall do the ritual first and then plan out how to handle Azmarin while stabilizing your rule?" Faron asked.

Chapter Forty-five

"I think so," Collette replied.

Faron nodded. "When we are ready to take Azmarin, the rest of the Fythian army will be ready as well. They will approach from the other side. Our daughters have been putting their own plans in motion since Alaoin let them know this was a possibility."

"And they are quite adept at military strategy," Alaoin added. "They are simultaneously too much like their mother and father. It's an extraordinary thing."

"And they have a bloodthirsty aunt back at home who's more than willing to help them," Éric added, his tone mildly annoyed.

Collette nodded. Things seemed well in hand for the immediate future, and she was eager for progress. "Why don't we take a break from discussions and resume this afternoon? I know we've covered a lot."

Murmurs of consent sounded from the room, and the group began gathering anything they brought with them and started to head out.

"You need anything?" Whyldon asked quietly amid the shuffling of papers and sliding of chairs.

Collette shook her head. "No. I'm going to try to get some rest. These last few days have been a lot."

"Okay," he said. "Sara told me before the meeting that they've gathered everything, so you just need to decide when you are ready."

"The clearing we camped in with Crem and the others may be a good place for the ritual," Arian said thoughtfully, having lagged behind the others as well.

"I think that would be perfect," Collette said. "Can you arrange getting Larent safely moved there?"

"I will speak to Aphros and arrange everything." Arian gave her a half smile before turning to say something too soft for her to hear to Thomas.

"Thank you," Collette replied. She excused herself from Arian and Whyldon and hurried to catch up to Tolan, who'd already made it outside of the war room. He still wore an expression she found hard to define. Uncertain, perhaps? Maybe guilty?

"What's wrong?" she asked quietly.

Tolan was obviously caught off guard by her by the slight jump he gave. "Hmmm, what?" he asked.

Collette knew he'd missed her question entirely due to whatever was going on in his head. "What's going on with you?" she asked. "You looked, I don't know, upset, maybe?"

He looked thoughtful, as if he were putting his words in order. "I'm not upset with you, but myself," he finally admitted.

"Why?"

Tolan glanced around before motioning with his head for them to move down another hallway to have more privacy. Several corridors later, when it was just the two of them, Tolan finally stopped. "I have been a complete ass to you."

He shook his head when she tried to say something. "I have, and coming to an understanding over drinks doesn't make up for what I've said and done. I've thoroughly ruined every apology I've tried to make. But since we took back Quenall, you've been even more miserable than you were before," he explained.

"Ah," Collette replied. She crossed her arms in a protective hold and nodded. "I know this is my responsibility, and I've accepted that. I intend to do everything in my power to be a good ruler, but I don't want any of it. I don't think I ever will. Being out in the world with all of you only made me realize it even more."

"You're going to be an amazing queen. You were last time." He looked away from her for a moment. "That said, I deeply regret the way I pushed you, treated you, acted toward you. If

I had been even half as supportive as Larent…" Tolan trailed off. "I should have been better. I should have realized you didn't want this sooner, and maybe we could have picked out someone else. Maybe you wouldn't have to deal with putting the kingdom back together and Larent's loss at the same time."

"I am going to give what I can for at least a decade, and then I might step down," she confessed. "I cannot be this forever, and I refuse to. For now, though, it is my burden."

"It shouldn't be. Not if you don't want it to be," Tolan said, his attitude so very different than before.

Collette gave a laugh and shook her head. "You saw what happened in the streets once I revealed myself. You see how everyone here is looking to me to fix things. I don't really have a choice, Tolan. I've made peace with that. But I am going to be so selfish first. I've made no secret of that." Bringing Larent back was her highest priority.

"I don't consider what you want to do selfish," he said.

"There will be those who do, especially if I end up suffering from any negative side effects."

Tolan shrugged. "Fuck them, and fuck me, too, for thinking you deserved less than what would bring you happiness. You shouldn't have had to pick up this mantle again."

"I shouldn't," she agreed. "For now, I am going to let Arian arrange my husband's transport, Nora and Sara oversee the spell items, and I am going to rest. I suggest you do the same, assuming you have not decided to back out."

Tolan nodded, his dark eyes looking down before his gaze rose to meet her own. Without warning, he leaned in and gently brushed his lips against hers. Collette didn't pull away—she didn't have time, and she didn't kiss him back. All she could do for several beats after he leaned back was blink. She loved Larent. She was going to risk her life to bring him back, but a memory of a discussion she'd had with her husband so long

ago echoed in her mind. *Part of me will always love him,* she had said.

Tolan's eyes were wide with shock, and his lips turned down at the corners. He was upset. "I shouldn't have done that. I am so sorry."

"It's—" she began, uncertain about what to say. She would always love him. It was a love different from what she felt for Larent, but it was there, peeking out to remind her now and again. "Things between us have been complicated," she decided. "We've reached a resolution of sorts. Things happen."

"Still doesn't mean I should have done that," Tolan said. His frown had transformed into a familiar grin, though she read the regret. "You're with Larent, and I'm okay with that now. I just shouldn't have kissed you. I won't again."

Collette nodded. There were definitely barriers between them now, ones she had no remorse in building because they'd been constructed with Larent. Still, a part of Collette's heart would always belong to Tolan. "I still love you, you know. I always will. You were there for me when I had almost no one else. That hasn't been diminished by what I share with Larent, and I think you deserve to hear as much."

"I know," he replied. "And I will carry that with me for the rest of my life." The silent longing in his features remained, and Collette wondered if she would see it every time they met.

"You should go prepare. If everything is set for the ritual, I'd like to get it done tonight."

"The sooner we do this, the better, right?" Tolan asked, a barely there smile on his face. "The ritual will work."

"It will," she agreed. "I will see you in a bit, yes?"

"I'll be ready when it's time."

She nodded again and wordlessly turned to walk back to her suite.

Chapter Forty-Six

Aphros placed Larent's preserved body in the middle of the circle, silently lifting the stasis spell. He could not aid in the attempted resurrection, as he would not be participating in the spell that would bind the lifespans of Larent, Collette, Tolan, and Rion. He would, however, do as he could to supervise the proceedings. Once the spell had been lifted, Aphros exited the sacred space so Collette and Tolan could prepare.

Tolan walked the perimeter of the space, performing the required ritual movements and prayer, a time-consuming process requiring precision and careful adherence to the border. After completing the circle, he had to start over in the opposite direction.

Collette knelt in the middle, making the required preparations to Larent's body. A red-hued oil was used to scrawl ancient runes on his arms, forehead, temples, shoulders, and chest. When she finished, she adjusted Larent's arms so they lay angled away from the body, palms facing toward the sky. Her fingers lingered against his wrist for a moment before she forced herself to keep going.

She stood from the ground when she was done, brushing the dirt from her knees while she repeatedly reassured herself the rituals would work. She glanced at Tolan, who had now completed the second circle, and she crossed the space he had not consecrated.

Tolan joined Collette, the two walking the clearing a final time to make sure they were ready for the first spell. "You're sure about this?" he asked quietly.

She shook her head. "But we're going to do it." She gave him a weak smile. "You can still back out. I don't want anything happening to you."

Tolan shook his head. "I'm helping," he reassured her. "Just like Rion promised."

"Has he not yet returned?"

"I heard him and Whyldon return a few minutes ago. They were successful." He motioned off in the distance, and she spotted the two men near Arian.

Collette smiled, though briefly. "Then we should get them."

Tolan nodded in agreement, and after casting a look toward Larent, the two approached Arian, who stood in conversation with Aphros and the returned Whyldon and Rion.

"Are you certain consuming black spider lily won't instantly kill everyone?" Rion asked as he held up a cloth bag for the elf to observe.

"According to the spell, you'll be protected by amethyst and diamond," Arian said, the words resembling rote memory rather than reassurance. "Those and the recitation should be enough."

"And if not, we have an antidote ready," Aphros said quietly.

"Which we won't need. The binding will go smoothly," Collette said with certainty. "Faron and Sabine walked me through it several times."

"Did they have problems with the spell?" Rion asked, his tone worried and his arms crossed.

"Sabine says no, and Faron said nothing of note," Whyldon replied, his blue eyes cast on the crystals he held. "Which leads me to lean more toward Sabine's account."

"He is protective of his wife," Aphros agreed with a nod. "And I cannot blame him. I was the same with Nerine."

"And I with Adorra," Whyldon added.

Aphros gave him a sad smile. "Come," he said to Tolan and Rion. "Let us get you ready." The men walked back to the circle together, leaving Whyldon and Collette alone.

Whyldon looked over Collette with resolved concern. "I know your mind is made up, and you are fully ready to commit to the implications of both spells," he began.

"I am," Collette confirmed. She didn't look away from Whyldon, but her chest ached, knowing the pain she was causing her father. "I know you understand. You know I cannot go further without him. It's taken everything I have to get this far." She crossed her arms protectively over her middle, her eyes stinging as she shook her head. "I don't know how you made it without my mother."

Whyldon knelt long enough to put aside the ritual crystals. When he rose, he closed the gap between himself and Collette, hugging her gently. "I've had you," he said quietly. "You are so much like her it scares me at times." He sighed wistfully. "I'm thankful you are. She had a kindness and love for others most never experience. You're all the better for taking after her."

Collette let herself lean into her father's embrace, her eyes shut. The physical affection shared now still felt new and strange, but Collette very much appreciated having her father here with her now. "I promise I'll do what I can to remain safe," she said.

"I know," Whyldon replied. "You've been careful and thorough. Let's just get you through the next couple of hours."

He slowly released her, and when she left his arms, Collette rubbed the heel of her palm against her cheeks as Whyldon retrieved the crystals. Together, they walked back to the circle where the others waited.

Aphros was the first to speak. "As you are tethering yourselves together, only Collette, Larent, Rion, and Tolan can be present for the ritual," he reminded the group. "Do you have everything you need?"

Tolan rubbed at the back of his neck, a tanned, muscled bicep showing off the runes he'd painted. Collette would need to do the same. "I think so," he said.

"We will be standing by as closely as the spell permits," Arian informed them. He pointed at Collette with a lecturing wag of his finger. "Do not die."

"You know we'll be careful," Collette assured her chosen brother. She hugged him, only giving the briefest of silent warnings before doing so. She only let the hug linger for a few moments before backing away.

"We'll let you get started," Aphros said. "The spell should not take long, but you will want to be done with both before dawn." He beckoned Arian and Whyldon to follow, and the two men did so without complaint.

Collette looked between her two former lovers and took a deep breath. "I need to paint my runes. Then we can get started."

"I'm going to ask one final time before we do," Rion said. "Are you certain?"

"I am," Collette said without hesitation.

"Then my life is yours," Rion replied. He reached out and squeezed her shoulder reassuringly. "Let's get you ready." He leaned forward and kissed Collette's cheek.

Rion prepared the black spider lily while Tolan helped to paint the runes on Collette's body, his fingers precise though careful. The red oil reminded her of autumn as the spiced fragrance surrounded her. It warmed on her skin, though the sensation wasn't altogether unpleasant. Just unexpected.

She felt Tolan's exhalation against her skin as he worked. His hands were remarkably steady as he continued to paint the runes on her. "This will work," he said, more to himself than her.

"It will," she said quietly, though her certainty remained strong. She put a hand on his arm. "You don't have to help if you don't want to create the connection, you know."

Tolan shook his head. "It's not that. It's more…" He paused, taking a breath before admitting a truth Collette already knew. "I don't like imagining a world without him in it. This needs to work."

"We'll make it happen," Collette promised.

Her runes now complete, she and Tolan joined Rion. "Is the black spider lily ready?"

"Yes," Rion said. "I have it divided up into four piles. The three of us can chew it as needed, but I crushed Larent's portion so we can get it down his throat."

"Good," Collette said. "Where do the crystals go?"

"One on each side of his body. They must be pointing true north, south, east, and west."

"I've got it," Rion said, grabbing the bag Whyldon discarded earlier so he could place the stones.

"What needs to happen next?" Tolan asked.

"We consume the black spider lily," Collette replied in near monotone.

Tolan scowled as his eyes narrowed, but he nodded.

Rion rejoined them, brushing his hands together. "Crystals are placed, and Larent's been out of the stasis for a good ten minutes. We need to get started."

"Right," Collette confirmed. "Get the spider lily, then."

"We should probably give Larent his portion before any of us do," Rion suggested, pointing toward the prepared plants.

"I can do it," Tolan offered.

"Do it quickly," Collette replied.

Tolan nodded and took Larent's portion from where Rion had placed it. He moved quickly to Larent's body. Careful not to touch any of the markings, Tolan gently tilted Larent's head back and slowly poured the mixture into his mouth. His free hand massaged Larent's throat, forcing him to swallow.

Once he was sure Larent had swallowed every drop, he headed back over to Collette and Rion. "Now we take it as well?"

"We do," Collette confirmed warily. She had no plans to change her mind, but the prospect of taking such a potent potion served as a strong deterrent.

"Don't worry, Joss. Arian is within shouting distance with an antidote if it's needed, and I don't think it will be. You've busted your ass making sure you know how to carry this out."

"I hate the risk posed to the two of you, though."

"We're here for you. We wouldn't have volunteered if we weren't. No matter how much Rion has bitched."

"I'm not wrong," Rion replied, though his voice stayed calm and reasonable. "These are dangerous spells."

"You better be glad I understand you," Collette said with a huff of a laugh.

"And you better be glad we understand you," Rion replied. Tolan simply rolled his eyes.

"Are we ready to eat poison?" Rion asked the group.

"I mean, no," Collette replied, shoving him fondly. "But we're going to. Oh!" she said, remembering a last item. She retrieved a red candle from their supplies, placed it in front of her, and lit it. They stood once finished.

Tolan held out a hand for his portion. "This is not the first time I've had to take something that might kill me," he admitted.

"It will be for me, but admittedly, I find ways to nearly get myself killed all the time," Collette quipped once her portion was in hand.

"I've been hunting with you," Rion replied. "The shit you've pulled on this journey is nothing."

"I would like to hear those stories later," Tolan said and then downed his portion. "Oh, Spirits. That's horrible." He gagged but was able to keep the poison down.

Collette took hers as well, closing her eyes for the duration it took to swallow. When she opened them again, she saw Rion had done the same.

"Ritual time?" Rion asked

"We need to stay by you, right?" Tolan asked. "In case there is backlash. Or am I mixing the spells up?"

"Yeah. We need to keep close according to Faron," Collette confirmed.

Tolan moved into place on her left, just slightly behind her, while Rion moved to her right. She felt Tolan move and thought for a moment he might place a hand on her shoulder, but he didn't. "Ready when you are," he said softly.

Collette took a breath and nodded. The three began moving through the ritual, seemingly simple as it was. Collette kept her mind focused, intent on this working. The black spider lily, so far, showed none of the expected effects. She didn't feel lightheaded or dizzy, nor did the associated pain form in her abdomen or limbs.

She heard Tolan take a deep breath, while Rion let out a low, harsh cough. She wanted to turn to check on them, but with the black spider lily consumed, she didn't dare stop the ritual now. Collette let her hand drift down to the pouch on the left side of her belt and took comfort from the feeling of Larent's figure of the Lady inside of it. Closing her eyes, Collette did as the

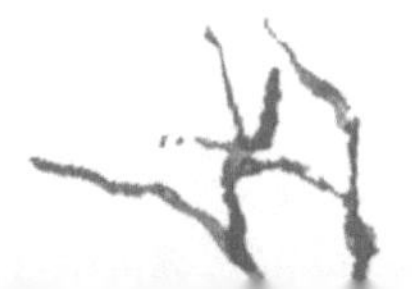

piece of paper instructed and called upon the Lady, since that was the figure Larent had worshipped.

"If your wisdom allowed it, bind my life with Larent's, or Larent's with mine. Bless our love, for it is pure and good. It is what matters most. More than our friends. More than my kingdom. More than my life."

She took a breath and glanced at the two men beside her. "Let these men serve as anchors. They have submitted willingly and voluntarily." She splayed her hands out on either side of her, as though directing some unseeable presence toward them.

Each of the men prayed their request, offering themselves as anchors. Once done, Collette knelt in front of the candle and blew it out, before closing her eyes and waiting.

Barely a minute later, she was surrounded by the sounds of a non-existent forest, the smell of fresh running water, and the scent of lilies in bloom. Peace settled around her, and she thought she might well stay there in her forest. A wolf howled in the distance, and a new feeling engulfed her, leaving her light and happy.

"Wow," Tolan breathed from behind her.

Collette knew what she'd experienced had been shared with Rion and Tolan as well. A tear rolled down her cheek from the sheer hopefulness that now filled her. Collette prepared for the next ritual.

Chapter Forty-Seven

Nana and Pops,

I know I haven't written in a while. A lot has happened, but every time I pick up a quill, I just—I don't know what to write. No, I do, actually.

I almost killed Collette.

That feels like all I should write. Like the beginning and ending of that entire statement and confession could fill pages.

I could tell you that Tolan fucked off in the middle of the night, leaving Collette heartbroken. That I did what I could to help her pick up the pieces, hurting with her the entire time because I understood how she felt. Being abandoned after every-thing that's already happened.

That we kissed, and it was as if my entire life was leading to that one perfect moment, before Arian fucked it up.

I could tell you we found Thomas and how fun watching him and Arian dance around each other has been.

Or that Nawalya and I fucked up and convinced Arian not to tell the others she was having visions of me killing Collette.

That I don't know if she is ever going to forgive me for this, or if Whyldon won't just kill us all on the spot when he finds out.

Because at the end of the day, blood magic or not, my claws tore through her skin. My wolf caused her to almost bleed out in my arms, and the entire time, she tried to comfort me.

No, the only statement of importance here is this: I almost killed the woman I love, and I don't know if I'll ever forgive myself.

Larent

In most cases, following a spell as powerful as a life-linking spell, the participants would cleanse and rest before attempting anything further. It was the wise thing to do. The sort of thing both Sara and Nora had advised upon if possible. "Can you not take a half hour at least?" Nora had asked. Waiting was not possible, though.

With Larent no longer being under the stasis spell, he was dead and his body subject to the associated realities until the resurrection spell was completed.

"Can he not be placed back under stasis?" Sara had asked this time.

"Unfortunately, no," Aphros replied. "Given the nature of the binding spell, we cannot place him back under so soon after. It could disrupt the linking, or worse."

Collette did not know what could be worse than his death, but the brief discussion only solidified Collette's determination to forgo rest and cleansing. It was just as well. She was physically and mentally spent, and stopping now would only render her weaker.

Tolan turned and motioned for the others to rejoin them in the circle so they could aid in cleaning and resetting the space for the next spell. Collette first thought she, Tolan, and Rion could do it on their own, but Arian disagreed.

"You will still wear residue from the first spell. Take the break while we work."

Those with magic—Sara, Nora, Thomas, and Arian—entered the sacred space, carefully picking up the spread of precious stones. Nora wiped away the oiled runes on Larent's skin, her movements careful and reverent, but she did not linger in her work. They had too much to do. When she finished, Sara helped her reposition his body while Arian placed numerous tokens around his body.

When they were finished, everyone but Rion, Tolan, and Collette abandoned the circle, though they did not have to retreat to the tree line this time. Collette met Rion and Tolan's gazes again and took a deep breath. Only then did they begin.

The first part of the resurrection spell required the sacrifice of blood, willingly provided. That part was easy. Collette removed the knife from her belt, the blade glinting in the moonlight, and she considered the best way to proceed. Nora's misgivings about this part, about how it felt too close to blood magic for her taste, gave Collette the briefest of pauses, even though her mother-in-law hadn't discouraged Collette from this path. She'd just warned her about the dangers while also insisting Collette was strong enough to bring Larent back.

Keeping that memory close, as well as the knowledge that soon Larent would be back with her, Collette used the dragger to slice into her arm, enough to draw sufficient sacrifice without causing lasting harm. It would heal sufficiently without her magical touch, and at most, she would have another glorious scar to commemorate the worst year of her life.

She looked between Rion and Tolan, who remained to complete the second spell with her, as she held her arm out so the blood could drip onto the consecrated ground. "I am going to

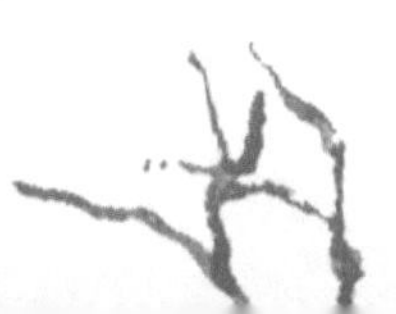

circle the space and return to my position. Then we can start chanting."

Without waiting for responses, Collette began the slow trek around the circle. She held her arm out, letting the steady flow of warm blood leave drops along the grass and dirt.

By the time she reached her original spot, the wound had started to coagulate, and the blood running along her arm grew sludgy and slow. She ignored it. "You two remember the chant?"

"Yes, Joss. You had us study it for hours," Rion called back.

"Of course," Tolan added.

"Good. I will start us off. Tolan can join next, and then you, Rion. Once we are chanting together, the spell will proceed." Collette closed her eyes and took a deep breath. The spell, originally written in an ancient Coralian language, was simple enough to recite, but she felt tired and dizzy, and she doubted she'd feel less so once this was done.

When she opened her eyes, energy temporarily renewed, she loudly began speaking in the old language, each word pronounced with determined, focused strength. As she completed the first chant, Tolan's voice joined her own. His own words sounded just as resolved. When Rion joined, their collective words echoing in the clearing, Collette felt a chill strike through her chest. Was it working?

Together, they stepped closer to Larent's body as they chanted, closing inches between themselves and Larent. The cold flicker in her chest grew outward, but instead of traveling to her limbs as she expected—since her own magic worked that way—it seemed to fill the space between ribs and organs. The longer she chanted, the more the weight of the spell, the abhorrent thing they were attempting, pressed in against Collette. She'd not been expecting it, but the unknown entity and the pressure growing against her lungs told her something was happening.

Chapter Forty-seven

The pressure spread outward from her lungs, and soon, the pressure turned into a tugging sensation. With each word, the unknown thing pulled harder, forcing her to more firmly plant her feet on the ground beneath her.

Collette's lips continued to move rapidly as she glanced across the circle at the others, the first time she'd bothered checking on them. Her eyes met Rion's, and he stood tall in his chanting. She felt her rigid shoulders demonstrating her fight against the pressure of what they were doing, and he raised his eyebrows in concern. She tried to smile, though she could only grimace as she nodded in his direction as the first wave of chanting ended. As one, all three stepped further into the circle.

The closer they drew to the body, the more the spell weighed on them. Collette was the first to go down on a knee, having gone into the spell feeling weaker than she could remember. She pushed through it somehow, the faint burn of the cut on her arm and the itch from dried blood a foothold in consciousness she could hold on to.

As they reached the end of that round of chanting, Collette insisted on starting again, though she could hear the strain in her own voice. Tolan's words also seemed off, though when she looked up, she saw he remained standing. Only Rion looked and sounded as though he did not struggle.

The atmosphere shifted as they continued, a roaring mist filling the space in the circle. Their voices rose, straining against force. Tolan too fell to his knees, but he continued on. The mist thickened around the trio, restricting their senses and their awareness of the rest of their party. Although they'd been prepared for the ritual, for the unknown entity to fight back, they had underestimated its resistance. A fourth person would have been useful, but only they could risk it. *A few minutes more,* she told herself as Rion finally joined the others on his knees.

The mass was solid now, swirling around them in tight, foreboding coils, building some internal pressure slowly choking lungs, depriving them from taking in air. Collette closed her eyes, a final attempt to block the rest of the scene away from her mind, though soon, her loud chants were forced back into forceful whispers. She could not hear Tolan or Rion. She was forced to press her hands against her thighs to stay upright, to continue on.

Sleep. Collette suddenly wanted to sleep more than anything she had ever wanted before.

The quiet returned. Collette opened her eyes, quickly seeking out Tolan, who was now completely seated on the ground, ghostly white but conscious. Rion remained kneeling, though his breathing came out labored and quick. She then drew her gaze to Larent, his body still motionless.

It hadn't worked. He was still dead.

And Collette felt like she couldn't breathe. An abrupt, overwhelming panic she'd kept at bay all these months seemed ready to drown her. How could it not work? How could he have left her? Larent knew better. He knew she needed him. Her gaze fell to the dirt she was kneeling on, unable to look at anyone else. She closed her eyes, unsuccessfully willing away the sharp sting in her eyes brought on by the sorrow ripping through her chest. She wanted to scream, to punch something repeatedly until her knuckles bled.

Furiously, she brushed away the first escaped tears with her forearm as she clenched her jaw in a futile attempt to prevent herself from losing it altogether. Humming filled her ears, loud and chaotic, and she cupped her ears with her hands, hoping to drown out the noise. She took a breath, now even more convinced she couldn't fill her lungs. Had she not already been on her knees, she'd have fallen over. As it was, she sank further into the ground so that she was fully seated and her legs were splayed in front of her.

If the others who stood at a distance intervened, Collette didn't know it. All she knew was this failure and the renewed loss of Larent. How could she get through it? How could she spend another moment in this world. She pressed a hand against her chest, hearing nothing but the humming and feeling nothing but breathlessness.

A flash of light popped in her vision, then she knew no more as the edges of her world grew fuzzy before finally going black.

Chapter Forty-Eight

Freckles,

Tomorrow, we go into battle, and while I know we're going to be fine and you will emerge victorious, I felt the need to put quill to parchment and write something. Just in case.

Which is silly, I know. I'll most likely end up burning this before you ever see it. If, however, you end up finding this letter before I can throw it in the fire—first off, you're obviously snooping through my things, and I will have to do something nefarious to pay you back. I don't know quite what, but I will make sure it is evil. There will be so much committed treason.

Second, know that I love you with every fiber of my being. Everything before you was empty and meaningless, and everything that comes after you will be even more so. I've met people who've spent their entire lives searching for a wonder like you—their other half, their soulmate. That I found you makes me twice blessed by the Lady. You are everything I never knew I wanted, let alone needed, and I will spend the rest of our lives together making sure you know that. I will worship the ground you walk on, kill anyone who even thinks of threatening you, and cheer you *on when you get to that person first. I will always stand by your side and strive to be the person you deserve. All we have to do is get through tomorrow.*

My heart, my soul, my very being belongs solely to you. I love you.

Now if I could just convince you to marry me.

Yours always,
Larent

The air smelled of smoke, thick and pungent enough to sting with each drawn breath. The buzz of surrounding voices did nothing to distract from the acrid air, and the pull of darkness and sleep demanded attention that felt too heavy to fight.

Consciousness faded and returned without warning, though how often remained a mystery. Heavy limbs felt impossible to move, and clinging, unyielding exhaustion refused to be shaken off. Everything felt foggy as consciousness settled in, as though sleep had lingered too long or too much alcohol had been consumed.

Pushing past it continued to feel impossible, as did opening eyes. Using the more reliable senses, like smell and touch, gave little information about location.

Long, sharp claws slowly buried themselves in the ground.

And Larent woke with a gasp.

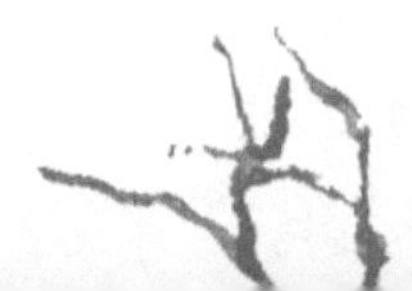

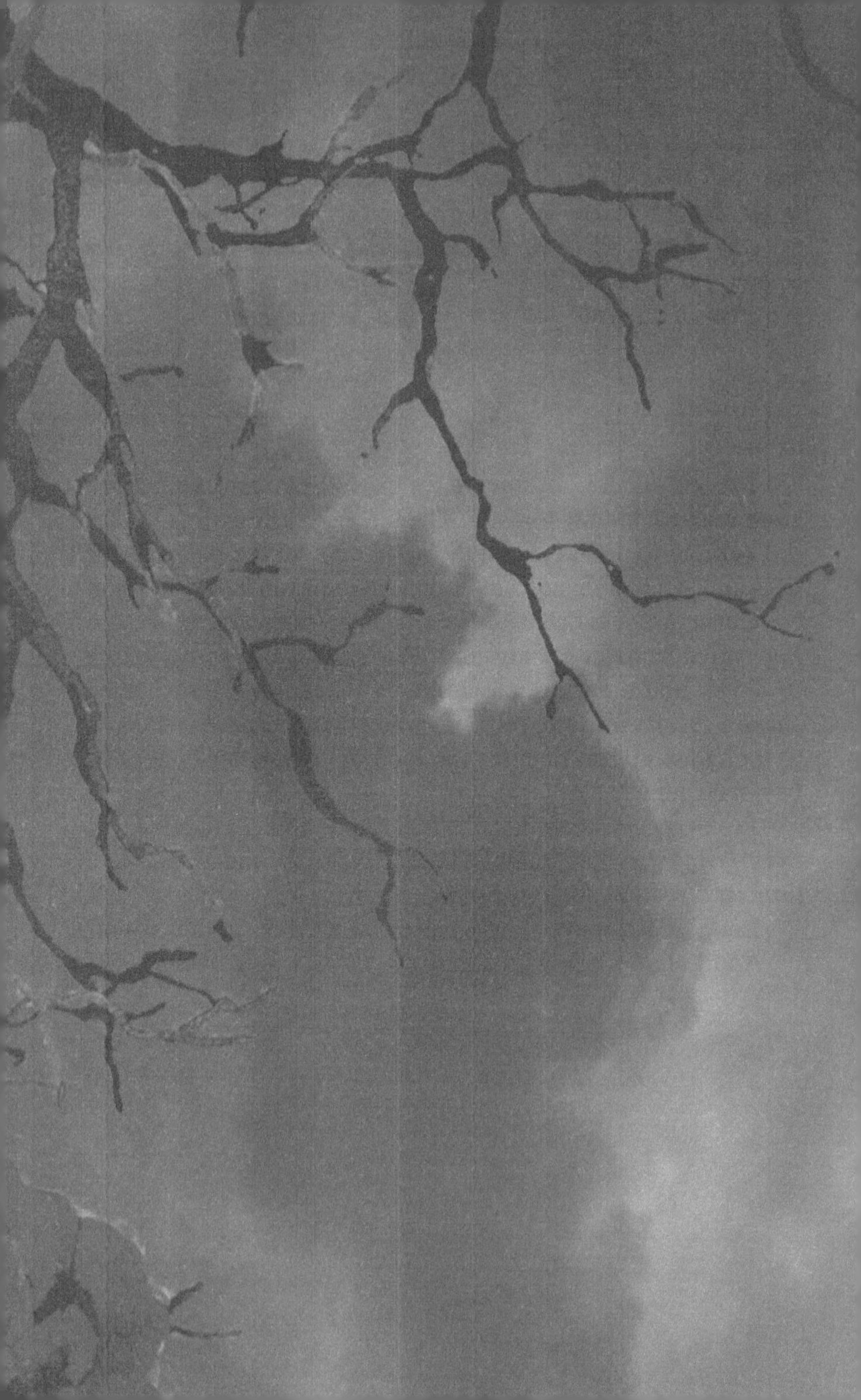

Book Club Questions

1. Do you think there is a path for Collette to forgive Zephraim? Why or why not?

2. Do you feel Barris's actions when it comes to Zephraim count as treason? Why or why not?

3. Should Rhoslyn have been harder on Riken since this is his second failure against Collette? What would you have done?

4. Collette says she's being selfish in wanting to bring Larent back to life, but Tolan disagrees. What are your thoughts?

5. Will Whyldon and Nawalya ever get back together? Should they?

6. Why was Crem not upset when he learned what Collette's true goal was?

7. What do Larent's letters reveal about the shifter?

8. Do you think Collette and Arian were too rash in their decisions to steal the spell and start a rebellion, or was the risk worth it?

9. What should Collette do with Rhoslyn now that she's been captured?

10. Do you think Azmarin is a big enough threat that it needs to be dealt with as soon as possible, or would it be better for Collette to spend more time ensuring her rule is secure?

Author Bios

Kate Jenkins enjoys writing fantasy, sci-fi, and romance as much as she enjoys reading them. She lives in a small town in Idaho with her autistic teen who is her whole world, her parents, and between them, four dogs and six cats. When not hanging with her son, she loves gaming, especially first-person shooters and asymmetrical horror games she can play with friends. She's a K-pop enthusiast and harbors a secret love of K-dramas and anime, much to her mother's displeasure, as she's slowly being sucked into them with her. Her favorite tropes are currently enemies-to-lovers, there-was-only-one-bed, coffee-shops, time-travel-fixes-it, and soulmates/soul-identifying-marks. She is hopeful one day she can talk her co-author into writing these with her.

Morgan Moreau's literary interests span across various genres, showcasing a love for the realms of fantasy, historical fiction, crime, and mystery, as well as contemporary stories. She is an enthusiastic lover of *The Little Mermaid*, as is evident in her vivid red hair, mermaid tattoos, and growing Ariel collection. Morgan also holds a deep affection for pirates, especially those who "wear fine things well," though those in possession of jars of dirt will always hold a place in her heart. She lives in Alabama with her dog, Scarlett, and she looks forward to adopting more puppies in the future. Her current passions include higher education, animal rights, and watching the 1995 *Pride & Prejudice* at least once a month. In addition to her current literary loves, Morgan is a fan of mermaids, vampires, pirates, and superheroes, and she hopes to incorporate this into future works.

Discover more at
4HorsemenPublications.com

10% off using HORSEMEN10

www.ingramcontent.com/pod-product-compliance
Lightning Source LLC
Chambersburg PA
CBHW020240010826
48973CB00006B/1591